COLUMBUS: ASHES
Project Columbus, Book 2

By J.C. Rainier

Columbus: Ashes
Project Columbus, Book 2
Copyright © 2013 by J.C. Rainier
Original Publication: 12 March 2013
Second Edition
Published: 6 August 2013
ISBN: 978-0-9882482-7-4
Publisher: J.C. Rainier

In conjuction with Oakenbrand Press.

Currently Available by J.C. Rainier:

Columbus: Flight

Columbus: Ashes

Coming September 2013:

Columbus: Demeter

Coming Spring 2014:

Columbus: Winter (Kindle Exclusive)

Columbus: Deluge

Please follow J. C. on Facebook or Twitter (@JCRainier), or check http://jcrainier.com periodically for blog updates and sneak previews of the Project Columbus series.

>BEGIN PLAYBACK|

PROJECT COLUMBUS

PER ASPERA AD ASTRA

```
Capt Haruka Kimura
USAF
30 March 2058, over an hour after the crash
Archipelago, Approx. 15 deg N, 112 deg E
1 mile west of ex-Raphael engineering skiff crash site
>|
```

Haruka scanned the floor of the jungle. Tangles of undergrowth dotted the ground beneath many of the larger trees, while patches of brown dirt and rotting leaves carpeted the rest of the ground. The ground sloped gently downward from right to left, and then rose again as she turned. The orb of Alpha Centauri B burned through the thick jungle canopy high above, its heat merciless as it hung high in the sky. Haruka wiped a bead of sweat from her brow with the sleeve of her flight suit, which had nearly dried out from the skiff's water landing.

Lucky we weren't pulverized, burned up, or drowned, she thought with a shudder. *I wonder how many of the passengers survived.*

"What's the bearing of pod eight, Marco?"

"Looks like it's west by north," he replied.

Haruka retrieved a compass from her breast pocket and glanced at it. She turned a few degrees to her right and looked up the slope, about halfway up, at a stand of trees. "Nova," she pointed at the spot. "Check what's up there. See if it's passable."

"Yes ma'am." Nova Weyler bounded her way up the knoll, and then slowed near the target as she navigated through the last few feet of thick brush. She took an awkward step and disappeared from view.

Haruka started to run toward her. "Nova?"

Nova popped out of the brush with a large twig twisted in her blonde hair. "I'm okay," she called back. "Just a bad step."

Haruka came to a stop, panting. She returned the compass to her pocket and leaned her rifle against a tree, then pulled the canteen from her belt. Haruka unscrewed the cap and took a short drink of the tepid water before returning the canteen. Her head throbbed and her vision seemed to tilt and blur for a moment. She rubbed her temples and shook away the vision, then threw her arm up to protect her eyes from the sun.

The days move faster here than on Earth, she thought. *I don't think the sun had peaked by the time we crashed, but we're well past that now.* She rubbed at her wrist, wishing that she owned a watch. Even though she was sure the times would not match on Demeter, she could at least have a relative sense of time.

Mancini sidled up to her. "We're not going to make it to the pod before sundown, you know that, right?"

"Yeah. I didn't think we would." She pointed to a tangled green plant on the ground nearby, a blue hue staining the veins in its leaves, its long thorns curved into a wicked crescent. "We need less of this crap to deal with. Remember when we tried to get away from the lake?"

Mancini shuddered and lifted the torn leg of his flight suit to reveal three long, red scratches on his calf. "I'm not going to forget any time soon. I'm just glad that it cleared up after we got away from the shore. I'd hate to think of where we'd be otherwise."

"Captain," she heard Nova call. Haruka looked over and saw her jogging back.

"Well?"

Nova pointed a finger in the air and doubled over, winded.

"Take your time."

The younger woman's finger pointed to the low spot of the knoll and swept to the left. "Whole valley beyond is full of that stuff. We need to go up a little higher and around. Shouldn't be more than a few hundred feet to the next ridge."

"Alright," Haruka said as she grabbed the rifle. "Move out. Marco, take point."

Mancini picked a course upward that snaked around the mess of ground cover and around the side of the hill. Haruka and Nova followed close behind. When they crested the hill, Haruka saw a depression between ridges that was teeming with green brush and brown snags. A few trees poked out from the strangling shrubbery but a gaping hole in the leaf canopy overhead let a beam of sunlight shine down onto the jungle floor. As they passed through it, Haruka's skin warmed, until she felt that she might catch on fire. Only a gentle breeze gave any respite from the oppressive heat.

They climbed along the ridge of the short hill, then took their bearings and followed just below the ridge line on the other side. Their path took them to a gap between two more hills. Haruka sent Mancini ahead to scout while she and Nova rested.

Nova avoided eye contact with Haruka as she sat with her back to a tree; they drank from their respective canteens in silence. Haruka noticed that her water was getting warmer; the heat of the day had penetrated the container. She breathed deep and listened to the sounds around her. A bird called from somewhere far away. Though its song was sweet and chipper, it grated on Haruka's nerves and made her headache flare up anew. Nova's boot dragged across the dirt as she pushed it back and forth almost mindlessly. Haruka strained and thought she could hear running water. After a minute, Mancini returned.

"Highway's pretty much clear," he said. "Only a few patches of brush, and it looks like we can easily maneuver through them. Looks like a pretty long flat stretch, too."

"Great," Haruka smiled. "Let's go. Nova, your turn up front."

The three survivors moved along the floor between two short rises. Haruka estimated they were no more than 60 feet at their highest. True to Mancini's report, only occasional patches of vegetation were present in the lower elevation, and there were few disruptions to their forward progress. At the end of the valley, a steep hill rose up, taller than its flanking counterparts. The sound of rushing water was clear now.

Always good to find fresh water, she thought.

"My turn to scout," Haruka said. "You two rest a moment."

Haruka slung her rifle over her shoulder and sprinted at the hill. She built up speed before she attacked the slope almost head first. At first it was steeper than she thought, and her fingers clawed into the rich brown soil, grabbing at roots to help pull her body higher. The angle flattened, and she pushed her way to the top of the hill. She glanced back at Nova and Mancini, who sat at the base, sitting separately and looking away from each other like upset children. Haruka shook her head.

Maybe someday these two will play nice without me around.

She turned around and scanned the valley below. It was wider and deeper than those they had been trudging through, and a wide creek roared through rapids below her. Haruka walked down the slope toward the stream. She came upon a thicket of native plants barring her way. Haruka circled in both directions for a minute but was unable to find a way around. She continued around the hill until she reached one of the flanking hills. The creek bent away from view as it rushed to meet whatever lay at its end, far away. A break in the vegetation near the bend caught her eye.

We can probably get through there.

The weight of the pack and rifle made Haruka's shoulder ache, so she sloughed the M4 off and carried it up the smaller ridge, back to her companions. She crested the hill and started down the other side.

Nova and Mancini appeared to be standing and holding a conversation with each other. Haruka smiled for a fleeting second.

Wait, they're not talking. Or facing each other.

Haruka caught a bright glint as Nova drove her bayonet into Mancini's lower back. Haruka tried to scream but nothing came out. Instead she burst into a full run. Nova drew the blade from Mancini and plunged it again into his back. He could not scream; Nova's hand was cupped over his mouth.

"NO!" Haruka's voice pierced the air.

Nova wheeled around to face her as Mancini fell forward into the dirt. The blade glinted red in the sunlight as Nova cast it aside, her face completely devoid of expression. Haruka skidded to a stop. A slight twitch crossed the corner of Nova's mouth, and she turned and ran for the trees.

Haruka dropped to a knee, flipped the safety off of her rifle, and squeezed a short burst from it. A deafening peal made her ears ring as the slugs spilled forth. Clumps of dirt shot like tiny geysers where they hit the earth. Nova screamed and tumbled forward, clutching her leg. Haruka rose up and bolted toward her prone opponent. Nova looked up at her charging commander and clawed at her belt, searching for her pistol. Haruka screamed and brought the butt of her gun up high, then swung it down on Nova's skull just as she freed the Beretta from its holster. Nova crumpled in a heap to the ground.

Haruka stood over the body of the young airman. Anger boiled within her as she let out a primal scream. She dropped to her knees and raised the butt of the rifle again. Deep within, she had the urge to slam it down into Nova's head over and over, but she resisted. Instead, she picked up the pistol and blood-slicked bayonet and moved to Mancini's fallen body.

He coughed and writhed as Haruka knelt before him. She cast aside the weapons and rolled him on his side. Blood poured from the deep punctures in his back and stained his teeth and lips red as he coughed.

"Oh, God. Marco? Marco, stay with me," she pled.

His eyes rolled and met hers. He reached feebly with his blood soaked hand and brushed her cheek. "Haurka," he coughed in a whisper.

Haruka unzipped his pack and pulled out the first aid kit. Her fingers trembled as she tried to open it. The pouch opened and the contents scattered to the ground. She rummaged through them in desperation, trying to find something to staunch his bleeding.

Shit, there's nothing here that will work. Her eyes darted around the horizon. *Why couldn't there have been a full med kit in the skiff?*

Mancini's hand fumbled to the back of her neck. She looked at him again; her eyes watered and vision blurred. "Marco, hang on." She reached down to roll him, but he stopped her.

"No," he croaked. Mancini pressed a small device, barely larger than a cell phone, in to her hand and curled her fingers over it. "Leave me. Go… help…" a spasm wracked his body as he writhed in pain. "Help the others. In the pod."

Haruka opened her fist and saw the radio tracker. A dot on the screen marked the position of the pod. She placed it in her breast pocket with the compass. Her voice wavered as she looked into his bloodshot eyes. "You're coming with me. C'mon, you can make it. Please… Marco…"

"No." His voice was just a hoarse whisper now. "Leave me. Go be… be a hero to someone you can save."

Her lips quivered as she looked at her dying friend through her tears. "Heroes get themselves killed. Didn't anyone ever tell you that?"

Mancini's lips drew wide in a bloody grin. "Nope. Heroes live…. for… ever…"

Mancini drew no breath. His body pulsed for a moment, and he slipped from the mortal world. Haruka drew her fingers down his eyes and closed their lids. She fell back on her heels and dropped her head.

No…

She bit her lip and forced her sorrow down. Her fingers traced down to Mancini's neck, where a glimmer caught her eye. Haruka parted the collar of his flight suit and revealed a set of dog tags around his neck. With one hand she cradled his head, and with the other slipped the chain from his neck. She watched the tags dangle in the breeze as they hung from her finger tips. Haruka balled up the tags and chain and slipped them into her pocket as she rose.

A cough came from her left. She looked over to see Nova struggle in vain to get her feet. Haruka's anger rose again, and she charged at the traitor, kicking her square in the chest. Nova flipped onto her pack and squirmed as breath eluded her.

"What the fuck is wrong with you, Weyler?"

The airman struggled to one knee and managed a crooked smile. Haruka moved behind her and planted her boot on Nova's shoulder, forcing it into the debris covered dirt. She yanked the zipper of Nova's pack open and retrieved the rope from within, then grabbed one of her hands and yanked it roughly behind her back. Nova growled at her captor as her hands were secured.

"Stay there," Haruka commanded and sealed the the pack's zipper. She hurried to Mancini's body and relieved him of his belt and pack. She cinched the belt around her waist and checked the knife and pistol that it contained, then picked up Nova's discarded pistol. After she verified that the safety was secured, she tucked it into the belt and grabbed the pack and carbine.

Nova had climbed to her feet, hands bound behind her back and favoring one leg. Haruka took Mancini's pack and threw the loops around Nova's neck; the young blonde choked and stumbled.

"Oh, shut up and get used to it," Haruka barked. She leveled the barrel of the rifle at Nova's back. "Now *march.*"

Nova looked back and gave Haruka an evil sneer as she hobbled toward the low rise to the side. Haruka followed several steps behind. Only one thought went through her mind as she drove her prisoner up the hill.

Why the fuck did she kill Marco?

. . .

Gabi moaned and sobbed as she picked herself out of the brush. Her arm stung as if a hundred bees had descended upon it and her chest ached with every breath she took. She sat up and looked at the giant metal wall from which she fell, framed by the thick brown trunks of two precariously leaning trees. Thin swirls of smoke wafted over the skin of the pod and into the blue sky above.

She tried to stand up, but something poked her in the foot, and she yanked it to safety. Gabi pulled her leg high in the air so she could check her foot for damage. Her toes wiggled before her eyes, and she realized that she was missing a shoe. Carefully, she rolled onto her stomach and peered into the thick plant. She spotted something pink, just barely within the reach of her hand. Gabi snatched the errant shoe, rolled over, and put it back on.

Gabi stood and brushed herself off. As her hand moved over her arm, the stinging pain renewed, and she cried out. She pulled back the torn sleeve of her shirt and revealed a large, rectangular scrape on her arm. Drops of fresh blood seeped from the wound. Gabi whimpered and clutched her arm as she stood and walked to the metal wall.

Several of the rungs had been torn from the ladder near the ground, so she could not make her way back up. Voices echoed from inside, escaping from the holes in the skin. Gabi listened for the familiar sound of her parents' voices, but she could not make out any specific one in the group. She skirted left under leaning tree trunks and around the wall, and came to the back side of the pod. The entire rear looked like one massive door; one that Gabi had no hope of opening. Thick logs lay under the pod. She scrambled over these and through the brush between them until she reached the far side of the pod, hoping to find a ladder there as well.

A wall of heat sent her back as she rounded the corner. Flames as tall as Gabi licked at the base of the pod, blackening the metal side. Crushed tree trunks crackled and hissed as the fire consumed them. Shivers ran down Gabi's spine despite the heat of the flames; she held still, breathless and motionless.

No! Mama, Papa! Get out of there! She tried to form the words, but her lips quivered, and she began to cry. "Mamaaaaaa! Papaaaaaa!"

Gabi stumbled away from the pod and around to get a better view, and to see if she could find the ladder. She could make out the small dashes of the rungs just next to where the flames licked at the hull. She tried to get to it, but the heat of the fire and the choking smoke drove her back.

Helpless, Gabi sat on a splintered log and buried her head in her hands. She desperately wanted to get inside and find her mother and father, but there was no way in for her. Tears blurred her vision and she wailed. She looked up and watched the fire burn at the lower rungs of the ladder. Someone emerged from the top of the craft and moved to the edge. She could hear them waving and screaming up above, then watched as the person ran back from the edge and out of sight.

A loud explosion rang out through the air, and fresh flames burst forth from near the base of the pod, this time at the rear. Her heart plummeted as she lost all hope of being able to reach her parents. Gabi rose to her feet and climbed her way back to the safe side of the craft. Her feet seemed to move on their own; her mind clawed at the skin of the pod as if it could somehow reach through and pull her parents out. But a deeper, overriding feeling gripped her, and her body started to run as she emerged from the felled timber and into the wilderness.

Get out of here, it seemed to call. *Mama and Papa are dead, and the fire will burn you if you stay. Run.*

Gabi plunged through a tangled bluish green bush. Her knee caught on a branch, and the fabric of her jeans tore open. She paid no attention and picked up speed, leaving the burning metallic wreck behind her. The underbrush cleared out, and was replaced with a forest floor littered with leaves and sticks that covered the dark brown soil.

The trees behind her consumed the landscape, and she could no longer see the pod. The voice inside her kept urging her on. *Keep running. Don't stop.*

Gabi did just that.

· · ·

Capt Haruka Kimura
30 March 2058, 14:00 (est)
About 2.5 miles west of ex-Raphael engineering
skiff crash site
>|

Haruka studied the confluence of the stream and the river from her position on the hill just above. Nova Weyler stood a few feet ahead on her left foot. Blood from her wounds stained the right leg of her flight suit a sickening purple, and a patch of dried blood caked her long blonde hair, hiding the gash from her earlier altercation with Haruka. Nova no longer wore Mancini's pack around her neck; the strain made it too hard for her to breathe, and Haruka had pillaged it for the most valuable supplies before discarding the remnants.

"Thinking of drowning me, I bet," Nova taunted.

Haruka ignored her. She checked to make sure that the ropes were still tight against Nova's wrists. "Stay here."

"Yes, *Captain*," she sneered.

Haruka walked down the gentle slope to the wide bank of the creek. Near where the two bodies of water joined, the tangled vegetation gave way to mud and rock. She looked across the creek at the opposite side, then slung her rifle over her shoulder and picked up a long stick from the muck. She probed the waters with the stick, testing the depth and pull. Cautiously she walked in. The relatively cool, rushing water gave her immediate relief from the oppressive heat of the jungle. Haruka knelt and splashed her face before she resumed charting the bottom of the stream.

It's a little fast, but very shallow, she thought. *We can cross here.* She cast aside her probing stick and went to retrieve her weapon. With almost no warning, her stomach revolted. She was barely able to double over and turn her head before she vomited. She spit and coughed until her innards settled, then slogged up the slope.

"That was really fun to watch, Kimura. Thanks."

"Shut up. Cross right there," she commanded as she nudged Nova with the barrel.

Nova hobbled forward. She tripped on her way down the slope and tumbled down to the bank, stopping just before the water's edge. The prisoner cursed and thrashed, and had to be helped to her feet by Haruka, who grabbed Nova by the collar to steady her as the two forded the shallow stream. Again Nova stumbled on the opposite bank, but kept her footing. A pained grunt escaped her lips.

"March," Haruka ordered, pointing down the bank of the wider river. Her teeth clenched as her captive gave her a twisted smile, and then limped along the shore.

She could at least act like she's just murdered someone. Cold bitch.

The two walked along the river at a glacial pace. Nova's leg prevented any quicker movement. Each footfall of the prisoner's lame leg wore on Haruka, reminding her of her murdered friend. She clenched her teeth and came to a halt, then scanned the way ahead. A steep cut bank ahead would force them into the river, so she ordered Nova to climb a small rise to their right, and they worked their way down the far side, away from the river.

Nova faltered as they came to the bottom of the hill, but struggled to her feet. Haruka leaned the M4 against a short tree and drew the canteen from her belt. She held it to Nova's lips, but she turned her head in refusal.

"Drink," Haruka said in a commanding voice.

"Screw you," Nova shot back.

The rage inside of Haruka boiled over, and she chucked the canteen into Nova's face, sending her reeling and the canteen flying.

"Now we see your true colors, Captain," she mocked.

"Why did you kill him?"

"I don't answer to you."

"What the hell did he do to you that he deserved to die?" Haruka screamed as she pushed her captive's shoulder with each question. "Why the hell did you kill him? What possible reason could you have?"

Nova gave an unnerving chuckle. "He annoyed me."

Haruka's vision narrowed and she felt her anger erode at what little control she still possessed. She took a step forward and kicked as hard as she could into the side of Nova's wounded leg. A howl of pain rose from Nova and she fell to the side.

"He was my friend, you bitch! And now you're acting like he doesn't matter. Who the hell do you think you are?"

"Someone better and more loyal than you, traitor," she spat back.

"I'm not a traitor! I had no idea that any of that... that shit that Shipp was talking about was even going on!"

Nova laughed, although pain was evident in her voice. "We've known what your father and Dr. Benedict were up to for a while. But they changed their timetable, and we couldn't stop them on the ground."

A shiver ran down Haruka's spine. "What are you talking about, Airman?"

"God, you're as dumb as a bag of rocks, Kimura."

"Just answer the damn question."

"Not a chance."

Haruka slammed her foot down on Nova's right leg again. She bellowed and reached her bound hands for the wound, which seeped with fresh blood.

"You *will* answer me," Haruka growled.

"Fine." Nova glared at Haruka as she drew deep breaths through her bared teeth. "I've been watching your father and Dr. Benedict since I arrived at PCRL in Laramie about six months before launch. We knew something was going on, and that they were planning on betraying the government. It was my job to infiltrate, report, and neutralize the threat."

Neutralize the threat. Dad's not a fucking threat, you psycho.

"Benedict's supporters were loyal," she continued. "I couldn't get close enough to any of them to be effective, so I had to change tactics. I'm afraid that Dr. Lang's disappearance shortly before the arrival of the passengers was no mystery, my dear Captain. Unfortunately, he didn't know as much as I had hoped."

Haruka gasped. "You... What did you do to him?"

Nova shrugged. "A little torture, a lot of interrogation. He cracked pretty easily, but again, I didn't realize that he didn't have the information I needed."

"And just what was that?"

"The planned dates for moving the passengers to Laramie and the launch date of the sleepers. A couple days later I got the answer to the first question when the first buses showed up. So I stood by and waited for orders."

"That must have been hard for you," Haruka sneered. "What did you do, walk across the hall to Fox's office?"

"Give it up, Captain. Fox is dead. I didn't work for her anyway."

"Liar!" Haruka kicked her prisoner in the shin, eliciting another scream of pain.

"God damn it, Kimura. I didn't work for that nut bag. She was my scapegoat, not my handler," Nova growled through her teeth.

"Handler?" Haruka paused. "Who the hell are you?"

"Lisa Evans, NSA."

NSA? Oh God. Haruka took a step back. *Then it's true. Dad…*

"So then how was Fox your scapegoat, Evans?"

Evans chuckled sadistically. "It's a good thing the old bat was going insane. It made it really easy to persuade her that she killed Airman Ellsworth."

Haruka's jaw dropped. "What? You mean she didn't?"

For a moment, Haruka saw sorrow in her prisoner's eyes, and her gaze cast downward. "Ellsworth was an unfortunate victim in all of this. He served his country well. His only crime was to accidentally stumble across what I was doing."

Haruka's stomach knotted up as the sinister words of Evans rattled in her mind. "What were you doing that was so terrible he had to die?"

"Exacting revenge." The words knifed Haruka in the gut.

"On who?"

"The conspirators who condemned my family to death. Want me to list them for you?"

Haruka shook her head and closed her eyes. "No. Don't."

"Lieutenant William Shipp," Evans said in a low tone. "Major Daniel Forrest."

"Stop," Haruka interrupted and her eyes snapped open.

"Doctor Jonathan Fairweather," she continued. Her glare felt as if it would burn into Haruka's skin. "Lieutenant Brandon Reid."

"Stop it!"

"Doctor Tadashi Kimura."

Haruka screamed and kicked the prone Evans in the chest, sending her rolling onto her pack, coughing as she struggled for air. "No. You can't go after Dad. I'll kill you right now."

Evans winced as she slowly hobbled to her feet. "I already killed him."

Haruka's heart sank, and she felt faint. "No," she croaked feebly. "No, there's no way." Haruka's stomach betrayed her again, and she threw up.

Evans *tsked* in disapproval. "Silly girl. How do you think I killed Shipp without his sleeper ever going offline?"

"No. His sleeper failed."

"I decalibrated the GDS sensor in his pod." Evans spat a glob of blood onto the soft ground. "Killing the others was just a matter of activating an exploit in the com software that I had rolled back while we were still on Earth."

Haruka was struck with the realization that this blonde menace might have actually found a way to kill anyone she wanted. Her knees buckled and she dropped down on them. "No…"

"Starting to feel how I felt, huh? My father served our country for longer than you have been alive. He was a good soldier and a great public servant." Evans's voice turned cold again. "But your father and Dr. Benedict decided that they didn't want Senator Ryan Evans and his family to come along."

Numbness washed over Haruka. She rose slowly and looked Evans in the eyes again. "If your father tampered with the algorithm to get himself on board, so help me…"

"So what if he did? That's absolutely no different than what *your* father did; using his influence to get his loved ones on board."

Haruka swallowed hard. "So what about Marco? And why not just kill me in my sleep back on *Raphael* like the coward you are?"

"I thought about killing you before. But that damned shit for brains Bartrand screwed up the course of the ship, and you were the only one who could figure out how to fix it. I needed you alive, and knew that I wouldn't have a chance to kill you until we were on the planet." Evans wobbled as she tried to put weight on her lame foot. "I found out the hard way that Mancini was too devoted to you. Everything I tried to break the two of you apart on *Raphael* failed. There would be no way I could kill you with him around and get out alive, so I needed you separated. I thought you had wandered farther away than you had when you scouted. Just a few more seconds and I would have taken care of the little hairy rodent, grabbed the radio tracker, and left you to rot in the jungle."

Haruka rose to her feet and drew the Beretta M9A1 from her belt with a deliberate motion. She flipped the safety off and chambered a round, then raised it level with the head of the NSA agent.

Do it, Haruka, a voice from deep inside called. *Take revenge for Dad.*

"Do it, Kimura," Evans taunted. "Finish the job."

Revenge, she thought. *Revenge would make me no better than her. Killing her won't bring Dad back, or Marco or Brandon.*

"No." She engaged the safety and ejected the round from the slider, then tucked the weapon back in her belt. "No, you're going to have a trial for what you've done."

Evans took a step forward. "You're a traitor *and* a coward, Kimura."

Haruka turned and walked wearily to the tree where the rifle rested. As she reached for it, she heard a rustling and a cracking noise. She snatched the rifle up and wheeled around a split second too late.

With a fierce roar, a tawny brown animal with a long tail, about the size of a large dog, leaped from within a bush and knocked Evans to the ground, screaming. Haruka took a step to the side and aimed the rifle at it, but she was knocked down from behind. The rifle flew from her hands and landed well out of reach. She scrambled to her knees and was confronted by a second animal, which spun around and faced her, its yellow eyes halved by dark slits and its large teeth bared. Twenty feet away, the first animal locked onto Evans' throat and tore it out. Blood spurted as she made a sick gurgling noise.

Haruka reached to her belt and drew the Beretta with lighting reflexes. She managed to ready the weapon just as the beast leaped at her. Two rounds burst forth from the gun, and the creature flailed in mid air. Its claws raked Haruka across the shoulder and the force knocked her on her back. She winced and pushed back on her feet to get away from her attacker, which lay on its side, whining and bleeding.

She clamored to her feet and turned to face the beast that took out Evans. It stood over her limp body and stared at Haruka. If it had been human, Haruka might have taken the look on its face for one of disbelief. Then its eyes narrowed and it bared sharp, bloodied fangs as it crouched. Haruka squeezed one shot from the pistol and the slug found its mark between the eyes of the animal; it fell dead where it stood.

A pained whimper came from her side, and Haruka turned to face the beast that wounded her shoulder. It wheezed and thrashed weakly in the dirt as dark blood trickled from under its side. Haruka took a long look at it. Its body was long and lean, and its claws appeared to retract into its paws.

Predator, she thought. *Looks kind of like a small tiger or a jaguar.*

Haruka took aim and put it out of its misery with one more shot. She scanned the area to make sure no more of their friends were lurking about, and then walked over to the lifeless body of Lisa Evans. Blood pooled behind her opened neck, forming a slow, thick river that rolled away from her. Her jaw was slack and pale, and her lifeless blue eyes had rolled back and were fixated on some point in the jungle canopy above. Haruka spotted the mangled chain of her dog tags lying across her chest. She picked them up and read the name.

WEYLER, NOVA L.

She clenched them in her fist. *No you weren't, you lying sack.* Haruka added the tags to her pocket and rifled through the fallen agent's backpack. She exchanged her partially spent magazine for the pistol for a fresh one, and grabbed an extra meal, stuffing it in her own pack. As she was about to turn from the body, she paused. Evans still had her hands tied behind her back, as if to mock Haruka for letting her die without the ability to defend herself. Haruka knelt down, drew her bayonet, and sliced through the ropes, tossing them aside.

She rose and took her bearings from the tracker and the compass, then retrieved the rifle and jogged off in the direction of pod eight.

• • •

Gabrielle Serrano
30 March 2058, almost sunset
Lost in the jungle
>|

Gabi's feet dragged as she plodded along, plowing tiny streaks of bare dirt in the leaf littered jungle floor. Her pink shoes were caked brown with mud, her long brown hair a tangled mess, and her jeans torn at the knees. She had more than a dozen scratches from her head to her feet, but her skinned arm stung the worst. The only thing that rivaled the burning pain in her arm was a sharp pang that came from her stomach, warning her that she needed food.

She no longer ran. The voice in her mind gave way at last to the idea that she was alone. At this point she could do nothing about it as she was completely lost. An endless sea of trees surrounded her. No human sound reached her ears to guide her, only the chorus of a dozen birds and a thousand insects.

The insects had become a problem as well. As the orange sun dipped to the horizon and shadows lurked ahead, hiding unknown evils, they came out. Most ignored Gabi and went on their way, but there were also bugs similar to mosquitoes. They came from seemingly nowhere and would land on Gabi to feast. When she felt one, she would shriek and slap at it. The bugs were lazy, too; Gabi killed almost every one that landed on her. A few managed to have their fill and fly off, leaving an itchy bump on her skin. In her tired state, Gabi could no longer defend herself from these pests, but she knew she had to press on.

Papa, I'm scared, she thought. *I miss you and Mama.*

She wandered to her right for a minute, continuing her quest for anything familiar. There were no buildings, or roads, or cars. Even the plants around her were strange. On the ground there was a short, tangled bush that had green and blue leaves, and another that seemed to climb the trees and burst with flowers in three brilliant colors. The trees stood taller than a house. Their branches were high above Gabi's head, and bore long limbs bristled with hundreds of long, thin leaves. Birds flittered between the branches above, but their song began to die out.

She heard a loud snap to her left, and she spun around while squeaking. Her eyes met those of a short deer-like creature with a ridge of white, bony knobs that ran down each side of its neck. Its wide eyes blinked once and it slowly chewed on one of the vines that climbed a nearby tree. Its glare felt somehow menacing to Gabi, so she slowly backed away until the animal paid her no mind.

Gabi trudged up a rise several times taller than she was. She stumbled halfway up as she caught her shoe on a rock, but recovered her footing and gained the top of the hill. A new sound greeted her at the top, faint but distinct. Gabi had skipped rocks in enough creeks to know the sound of one. She cocked her head and strained to hear the source of the sound. Once she was confident of where it was, she turned toward it and moved slowly ahead.

The sun had merged with the horizon, and the light dimmed with every moment. She knew that it would be dark very soon. Her stomach growled at her, despite the nerves churning within her.

I'm really really hungry. I want some crackers and cheese and an apple and juice.

She knew none of those things were here, and she couldn't see anything right away that looked tasty. Gabi crossed a low point and over another hill. On the far side, the dying orange glimmer of the sun reflected off of a fast moving creek. She knew she should not cross this without an adult; water was a dangerous thing. Instead, she walked to the shore, cupped her hands together, and drew a drink from the stream. The water helped ease her stomach somewhat, but also reminded her of how thirsty she was.

Gabi sat at the edge and drank until her thirst was quenched, then wandered along the bank of the creek some more. She climbed up on a log and took two steps forward when she stumbled and fell sideways through the canopy of a thick bush. A fresh scratch on her leg welled blood, and she clutched at it as she cried out in pain.

Exhaustion began to set in, so Gabi loosened her grip on her leg and sprawled on her back in the moist dirt. Her stomach gave a sharp reminder of its condition. Gabi grasped her belly in a vain attempt to soothe the pain, and then eventually curled up in a ball. She longed for one of her mother's home cooked meals, especially the enchiladas verdes. She imagined the smell of the cooking tomatillos and peppers as a vision of her mom came to her, gracefully dancing through the kitchen as she cooked.

Gabi could not contain herself. The memory of home and her mother was too much to bear. It was difficult to be in this alien environment far away from home. The fact that her mother was gone sat on her as crushing weight. Gabi cried, this time with the bitter tears of sorrow. She called for her parents, even though she knew they could not hear.

J.C. Rainier

The sun had set, and gloomy darkness descended upon the jungle. The birds were silent, and the insects followed suit soon after. Eerie sounds that she could not identify cut through the silence every few minutes, and her heart raced with fear. She had no protection save for the mass of fallen timber that lay next to her and the shroud of brush above her body.

Gabi ached in body and heart as she closed her eyes and cried herself to sleep.

. . .

Capt Haruka Kimura
30 March 2058, nightfall
About 4 miles west of ex-Raphael engineering
skiff crash site
>|

Haruka ducked down and peered into the gnarled root structure of a large tree. Her flashlight barely pierced the dark, and the shadows it cast under the trunk looked like the cruel talons of some great beast. To her dismay, Haruka found the space under the tree to be too small to shelter her. She heard a snapping noise to her left and wheeled around with the flashlight, bringing her pistol to bear just underneath the light. Nothing showed in the light, save for a patch of brush.

Haruka crept forward with her weapon trained on the brush. She crouched in the hope that she could get a better view, but the leaves of the dense plant barred penetration from her light. She gave a quick nudge to the bush with her toe and then leaped back, but nothing came out of the tangle.

She sighed and lowered the pistol. *Nothing there. Still, this place is creepy as hell.* Her bare left arm tickled as a gentle breeze ran over it. Haruka had sliced the sleeve from her flight suit and used it as a bandage to staunch the bleeding from the predator's wound. *I need to get someplace safe,* she thought. *I can't afford to tangle with any jaguars at night. Or anything else that might be lurking on this planet.*

With a broad sweep of the light, she surveyed her surroundings, then decided to climb over a steep berm and into the swale below. Again she scanned the jungle floor with her light. Her eyes caught another root structure, this time surrounded by thick brush all around. Haruka walked forward to the tree and circled just outside the halo-like shrubbery. The cavity under the tree indeed looked large enough to accommodate her modest height. The underbrush ran all the way to the tree, and in places crept as high as three feet up the trunk.

Haruka stepped cautiously into the bush as she tried to make her way to the root cave with as few scratches as possible. She slipped off her pack and dropped it through a small crack between the trunk and bush, then followed that with the rifle and finally her body. For her troubles, she received a fresh scratch from the shrub, this time on the back of her right hand.

Once inside she found the hole to be much larger than she had first judged. She was able to remove her belt, retrieve items from her pack, and maneuver her light with ease. She taped a small gauze strip to her latest scratch, and then bit her lip and stifled a cry of pain as she peeled off the makeshift bandage from her shoulder wound.

Haruka shined her light on it to get a better view. The dark brown scabs seeped with fresh blood near the edges, and the skin around each of the three cuts was bright red. She reached into the pack and pulled out what was left of the first aid kit, and pulled out two tiny sealed packages that contained antiseptic wipes. She brought the wipes to her wound and gently washed it. Searing pain gripped her; she grunted and panted as she forced herself not to scream. Once she was done with the cleaning, she quickly taped fresh gauze in place and collapsed on her back. Her head spun, and her stomach churned as if she might throw up again.

Not the time to get sick, Haruka. C'mon.

Haruka closed her eyes and forced deep breaths through her lungs. The pain took what felt like an hour to diminish to a tolerable level. Once she could think again, she returned the first aid kit to the pack and retrieved the survival blanket, which she unfurled and began to wrap around her body. After she was sure she could maneuver the rest of the way blindly, she killed the flashlight and curled up. The chilling thought of an ambush from another one of the jaguar-like creatures made Haruka grope along the dirt floor until she found one of the Berettas. She placed it within easy reach, and settled in once more.

The night air was not particularly cool, but after dark the humidity dropped significantly and gave her lungs respite from her muggy trek earlier that day. The ground beneath her was cooler than the air, and she shifted the blanket to compensate.

Haruka listened to the sounds of the night. It seemed that Demeter was not all that much different than Earth from the perspective of an audio track. Staccato squeals in the night air reminded her of fruit bats, and a distant warbling sound could have belonged to either a night scavenger or something similar to an owl. As Haruka thought more about her surroundings, the less alien the concept of the world became. While she couldn't point out any given species on the new planet like she could at a zoo on Earth, she was beginning to understand similar principles between the planets.

The spear-like fronds of the trees under which she had traveled the whole day were quite similar to the tropical palm species on Earth. The bush that served as the barrier to her cave reminded her of a cross between a blackberry bush and ivy, though it was both less prickly and less itchy. It only made sense that there would be other forms of similar life, and it appeared that on Demeter there was a class of predatory cats, just like on Earth.

Her mind flashed back to the moment that one of the creatures tore the life out of Lisa Evans. She replayed the incident in slow motion, like the aerial combat footage in her combat flight training. The height that the jaguar reached when it pounced at her was impressive for a creature its size. Haruka recalled the desperate placement of her shots into the torso of the beast, and the reach of its claws, even as it had been mortally wounded. Then the realization sunk in when she remembered the odd look of surprise on the other animal's face.

A class of predators that isn't afraid of humans. Why should they be? They've never seen us before, and probably haven't seen firearms before.

Haruka knew that any further encounters with these fierce beasts would likely be fought to the death. These creatures might not know the difference between Haruka and dinner, and she had no desire to become the latter. Her hand reached for the pistol, and her fingers brushed against the cold, reassuring steel of the barrel.

Part of her wanted to stay awake and watch for predators. Another part simply wanted to pass out from exhaustion. Yet a third reminded her of everyone she had lost today. A morbid curiosity rose within her, and she repeated names to herself.

Major Nathan Emberley. 2nd Lieutenant Julio Morado. Staff Sergeant Craig Overton. 1st Lieutenant Ignacio Perez. Her mind spoke the next set of names with bitter contempt. *Colonel Marissa Fox. NSA Agent Lisa Evans.* She took a deep breath and put them out of her mind, then continued. *1st Lieutenant Harjit Singh. Captain Zachary Maynard. Airman First Class Nova Weyler.*

Haruka opened her eyes. *No, Nova wasn't real. She was a treacherous plant named Evans.* She closed her eyes, and an image came to her of the first time she met "Nova". Haruka remembered the upset young blonde girl who Haruka cruelly grilled, thinking she was a spy for Fox. For a moment, Haruka truly believed that Nova was a different person than Evans, and that the memory of the vulnerable girl might be able to live separately than that of the calculating assassin.

Haruka's hand fumbled inside her breast pocket and withdrew the broken chain from which Nova Weyler's tags hung. She could not see the tags through the darkness, but she could feel the raised relief of the girl's name stamped in the steel of the tags. She ran her fingers over it several times.

No, she balled her fist over the tags until the rubber edges dug into her palm. *Nova Weyler never existed. Remember who she took from you.* She slipped the chain back into her pocket and rolled onto her side, closing her eyes.

1st Lieutenant Marco Mancini. A lump formed in her throat instantly as she thought of her slain friend. He had been dead only a few hours, and in that time both his companionship and his dorky, arrogant sense of humor had been missed greatly. Haruka felt a tear flow down her cheek as she remembered how he could always find a way to lift her spirits on *Raphael* right when she needed it most. Memories came back about his goofball antics back at the compound in Laramie, where he made officers and enlisted alike roar in laughter. She even recalled with bitter fondness the nights out on the town when Haruka had to save him by beating up a jealous boyfriend and a protective brother.

God, I'm going to miss you. I already do. It's not fair…

She wiped away her tear and took a long, deep breath.

Doctor Tadashi Kimura.

These three words from her mind sliced through her very core like a frozen knife. Tough as she was, there was no way that Haruka could keep from crying like a child at the realization that she would never be able to talk to her sweet, gentle father again. She would never hug him, or tell him about her day; no longer would she be able to surprise him with her cooking, or see his radiant smile. Tears flowed in rivers down her cheek and to the ground.

Haruka felt no spite or anger, as she knew that his assassin was dead; her cold body lay on the jungle floor. A voice of justice cried from within as it lamented the fact that Haruka had not taken the opportunity for revenge. But mostly, she felt sorrow and loneliness. Death had taken her father and her friend. Her only companions on this dark night were her standard issue M4 carbine and M9A1 pistol. As she cried herself to sleep, she knew these to be her only remaining friends.

• • •

Gabrielle Serrano
Planetfall +1 day, mid-morning
Lost in the jungle
>|

Orange light shone through Gabi's eyelids. She groaned and rolled onto her side, and her cheek brushed up against something. Her eyes popped open and for a moment she panicked at her surroundings. Her body rested on hard packed dirt, although thin clumps had loosened and built up around her body as she had tossed and turned during the night. The bleached white trunk of the log was cool and rough to her touch, and the sun pierced the hole in the shrub where she had fallen through.

Gabi stood up and pulled her way out of the hole and onto the fallen tree. She stretched and looked across the swiftly moving creek. Brightly colored flowers pocked the far side in bursts of red, blue, and orange. She scanned the bank on her side of the stream and saw the outline of a large white lizard stretched out on a light gray rock, like a dog might stretch out on a bed.

A sharp pain in her stomach made her double over. Gabi could only faintly remember the last time she ate; in the cafeteria only a short time before she and her parents ran for the rocket ships. Her hands clutched her stomach, and she looked around for something to eat. The trees, mud, and rocks were obviously not going to help her.

Gabi wandered over a short hill along the river. More bushes and trees sprang up from the ground. Flowers dotted some of the taller shrubs. She was about to ignore these plants when something next to a bright yellow flower caught her eye. It looked like a small, round fruit, about the size of a small apple, with a speckled green and orange skin. It grew from one of the flowered shrubs that grew as high on the tree as Gabi was tall. She picked her way carefully through the underbrush and reached for the fruit, then twisted it from the stem.

She turned the fruit over in her hand several times as she inspected it. The skin appeared to be thin, and the soft flesh gave way easily when she squeezed her hand. Gabi sunk her teeth into it and tore a large bite away. Juice from the fruit trickled down her chin, and the flesh had a sweet tang as she chewed. After she swallowed the first bite, her mouth tingled, and there was a slight kick to it like a mild pepper. She attacked the rest of the fruit with zeal, only slowing when she bit into the pit of the fruit, and was forced to pick a dozen tiny seeds from her teeth.

J.C. Rainier

The single piece of fruit helped with her hunger pangs, but did not sate her. She looked around on the same bush but found no more specimens. Gabi trekked to the next bush that she could find, about twenty feet away, and was rewarded with branches that were laden with dozens of pieces. She picked two and carried them back to her hiding spot on the creek bank where she consumed them in under a minute. She discarded the seed pits and then stuck her hands in the creek to wash the juices off. She then ran them over her face. Mud dripped from her cheeks and fingers when she pulled her hands back, so she continued washing until her hands and face were clean. For the first time since she had come to this strange place, Gabi smiled. Her stomach was full, and she had been given a chance to play in a creek.

Her smile was short lived, however. When she stood up, her eyes locked on a large, brown, cat-like creature on the far shore. Its head was down as it lapped at the waters with its broad, pink tongue. Gabi froze for a second, unsure of what to do. Then she saw the cat raise its wide, flat head and lock its yellow eyes on her. Its ears flattened and it bared its long fangs at her. Terror gripped Gabi, and she squeaked and ran away from the creek bank as quickly as her legs would carry her.

The animal let out a deep, throaty scream, and she could hear it splash in the creek. Gabi hopped up on a log and tumbled back through the hole in the top of the bush. From her back, she saw a brown flash as the cat sailed over the hole. She could hear it skid to a halt, and it let out a long, fierce growl. Then she saw it leap over the bush and land on the log. Gabi rolled as far into the shelter as she could. Her eyes met one of the terrible slitted eyes of her stalker. Another terrifying growl echoed into the hole, and was followed a second later by a thick, clawed paw. The cat scratched around in a bid to grab Gabi. She let out a shriek as the paw nearly raked her leg.

"Go away," she screamed at it. The cat ignored her and its paw groped for her again, inching ever closer.

She tried to make herself smaller and recoiled even deeper into the shelter. Something hard poked her in the shoulder. Her hand fell to it, and from the dirt she pulled a rock the size of a cell phone. The cat growled and lunged forth with its paw again, and Gabi flailed out with the rock. By chance she struck the animal in the side of the leg. There was a hiss and a jerk, and the animal retracted its deadly limb from the shelter, causing Gabi to lose her grip on the rock. It clattered to the dirt just below the hole above. Again the sinister eye peered at her.

"Go away," she repeated as her voice became an ear piercing howl.

The animal growled and shoved its paw through the opening once more. Gabi shrieked as the paw edged closer to her. She could clearly see each hooked claw as they dug into the dirt just an inch from her body. Suddenly, Gabi heard two loud booms, like giant firecrackers, and the creature's claws retracted and its leg hung limp.

Gabi whimpered and clutched at her ears as she expected the creature would start clawing at her again at any moment. She stared attentively at the paw in anticipation of a twitch, but instead she saw a trail of blood drip down the long, furry leg and onto the ground. She sniffed and wiped her eyes, and her muscles tensed as she waited for the creature to finish playing its cruel trick and swipe at her again.

Instead, the limp limb withdrew from the hole and there was a thump outside. Gabi looked to the opening in her shelter and saw a flash of blue, followed by a glimpse of dark hair and a pair of brown eyes. Human eyes.

"Anyone in there?" called a woman's soft voice from outside.

Gabi didn't respond. Instead, she lay completely still, staring out of the gap at the woman's tanned arm. She could not believe that there was another person here; she was sure that the fire had killed everyone in the giant metal pod. Gabi drew in a breath and held it.

"It's okay to come out, I killed it," the voice beckoned. Gabi heard a soft *thump* on the wood above, and again saw the woman's eyes looking in at her. "You okay in there?"

"Y-yeah," she stuttered softly.

The woman's face disappeared for a moment, then reappeared right at the edge of the hole. The woman stretched both of her arms into the bush, her hands beckoning to Gabi. Cautiously she crawled closer until the woman's hands crooked under Gabi's armpits and heaved her out of the bush and into the bright daylight. Gabi squinted as her eyes adjusted to the sudden flood of light. Her savior wore blue pants and a white shirt caked in dried blood. Her left shoulder had a bandage taped to it, which was also bloodied. Two straps running down her front told Gabi that she wore a backpack. She smiled at Gabi as the wind teased her straight black hair, partially obscuring her almond shaped eyes.

"You're pretty far out here, sweetie. Are you lost?"

Gabi nodded.

"What's your name, sweetie?"

"I'm Gabrielle," she replied. Gabi saw the woman's smile evaporate for a second. "But if that's too long, you can call me Gabi."

The woman smiled again and said, "Alright, Gabi, short for Gabrielle. My name is Haruka."

Gabi giggled. "That's a funny name. Haruka. Hah ROOOOO Kah!"

Haruka chuckled softly. "Glad you like it. So where are your mom and dad?"

Gabi's lip turned upward and she began to sob. Through her bleary eyes, she could see the woman's smile turn to a frown. Her slender arms reached for Gabi, as if to comfort her. Gabi looked down at the dirt and cried.

"Come here, sweetie."

Gabi felt Haruka pick her up and draw her up in an embrace. Though she didn't know this strange woman apart from her name, the warmth of her arms and the softness of her skin were calming. Gabi wrapped her arms around the woman's neck and cried into her shoulder as she was gently rocked back and forth.

"It's okay. Let it out," she whispered in Gabi's ear. "I'm here for you, sweetie."

Tears flowed from Gabi's eyes and sobs escaped her throat for countless minutes. All the while, her savior held and rocked her, and whispered soothing words into her ear. Finally Gabi calmed down and opened her eyes. Perched on the log behind Haruka was a rifle. It was different than the hunting rifles her father owned; this one was a dull color, and had more angles to it.

Haruka released her embrace of Gabi and looked in her eyes. "Have you been out here overnight?"

Gabi nodded in response.

"Are you hungry?"

She shook her head.

"What about thirsty?"

Gabi thought for a second and nodded. Haruka produced a canteen and offered it to Gabi, and she promptly took three big swigs of water. As she drank, she noticed oddly shaped red blotches on Haruka's arms.

"What are those?" she asked as she pointed.

Haruka looked down at her arms. "I'm not sure. I saw that earlier this morning. It feels kind of like a sunburn." Her gaze met Gabi's. "You sure you're not hungry? When did you last eat?"

"Breakfast," Gabi replied.

"Breakfast, huh?" Haruka looked around. Gabi tried to see what she was looking for, and saw the lifeless body of the giant cat. She shook for a moment before she realized it couldn't hurt her anymore. "Can you show me what you ate for breakfast?"

Gabi looked at her new friend and nodded, then stood up and led her to the fruit bush. She harvested one and offered it to Haruka, who set down her rifle, took the fruit from Gabi, and gave it a thorough examination.

"It was really yummy," she pronounced.

"I'll bet. I'm going to take a couple of these and maybe have them later. I just ate a big breakfast myself." Haruka fished into the folds of clothing around her waist. Gabi caught a glimpse of a pistol tucked into her belt.

"Are you a soldier?" she asked.

"I am, sweetie. Why do you ask?"

"You have lots of guns, and you're wearing blue."

"Yeah, I guess I do." The woman paused as she pulled something out of her clothes that looked like a big cell phone, only with black rubber grips around the edges, and a small compass. Haruka looked at the two items and then turned around. "We need to go this way."

Gabi looked in the direction her friend was pointing and saw nothing but trees divided by the rushing stream. "Why?"

"Oh, there's just some people over there I'd like to say hi to. I've been waiting to hear from them." She looked down at Gabi and smiled. "And I bet they'd want to see a brave little girl like you. Shall we go?"

Gabi was hesitant at first, but then realized that she had nowhere else to go. The jungle was full of scary noises and cats that like to eat kids. She figured that going someplace with a soldier had to be a lot safer, and much less lonely.

"Okay," she said at last.

Haruka's smile widened, and Gabi could see a hint of her teeth. "C'mon, Gabi. Let's go." She offered her hand, which Gabi wrapped her little fingers around. Haruka slung the rifle over her shoulder and the two walked side by side along the creek.

. . .

Capt Haruka Kimura
Planetfall +1 day, late morning
Near ex-Raphael sleeper pod eight crash site
>|

Haruka scrutinized the near river bank, looking for a reasonably easy path to move forward. Snarls of brush and felled trees obstructed the bank ahead, and she knew they would need to soon depart from the river to make way for the pod. Her new companion stayed close by, staring at the local flora. Haruka felt both relief and a twinge of sorrow at the discovery of the battered and disheveled girl whose life she had certainly spared from the jaguar.

Gabrielle. Why did her name have to be Gabrielle? Haruka watched the little girl as she ran ahead to pick another of the strange orange-green fruits from a bush. *Gabrielle. Too close to Gabriel. Dad's ship. Dad… is gone.*

"Gabi?" Haruka asked as her companion returned, sniffing the fruit.

"Yeah?"

"Are you hungry again?"

"Mm hmm," she confirmed with a nod.

"Here, let me get you something to eat." Haruka shed her pack and rummaged through it for a meal pack.

"I want to eat this." Gabi held up the fruit with her arm stretched out so far, Haruka thought she might topple from the weight.

We don't even know if it's really edible, kid.

Haruka tried to put on a sweet smile, hoping that might conceal any hint of concern on her face. "I know. We'll have some later, I promise. I just think you should eat something that will stick with you a little more."

Gabi's nose wrinkled. "I don't want sticky food."

Haruka chuckled. "Then I guess you don't like those fruits, because I bet they're pretty sticky."

Gabi's eyes widened and she drew back the fruit. "But I do!"

"Yeah? You like sweet stuff too, like cake?"

"Yeah!"

Haruka produced a pouch and tore it open. "These have little desserts in them."

Gabi tilted the bag in Haruka's hand and looked inside. "What is it?"

"The dessert? It's for a little girl who eats a good lunch. C'mon, I'll split it with you."

The two sat down and Haruka opened a neatly sealed bag of spaghetti and the utensils package. Gabi licked her lips as Haruka readied the meal. Haruka traded the plastic fork to the little girl for her fruit, and watched as the child attacked the food pouch like she hadn't eaten in days.

Dad said I used to eat like that when I was little. Haruka sighed and bit her lip. Though she had cried the night before, she had no time now to grieve for him. She still had to get to pod eight, a task that would take longer due to her companion's short legs. *At least I've found my first survivor. She's too far away from any of the other pods. Her family has to be at number eight.*

Gabi consumed the whole entrée before Haruka could even get a bite. Her hands and face were stained red with marinara sauce, and Haruka had to break into the wet-nap pouch to clean her up.

"Wow, you ate that fast. You must be a growing girl."

"Yeah."

Haruka opened the dessert pouch and revealed a dry, crumbling piece of preserved chocolate cake. She handed it to Gabi and then started eating the garlic flatbread that the meal's designer intended as a side dish. "How old are you, Gabi?"

She thrust her hand out with her fingers splayed wide. "I'm this many!"

"Wow, five, huh?"

"Yeah."

"What do you like to do? Any games that you like to play?" Haruka knew the conversation was mindless, but she hoped that it might serve to distract both of them for just a little bit.

Gabi hummed a little tune, then looked at Haruka with her sparkling brown eyes and smiled wide.

Haruka paused. "What?"

She hummed again.

"You like music?"

"Yeah."

Perfect. Maybe that will help keep our minds busy.

J.C. Rainier

Haruka stowed their trash in her pack and took her bearings. "Alright. We need to go this way," she said with a jerk of her thumb. "But I really want to hear something while we're walking. What can you sing for me?"

The two started walking, this time away from the river. Gabi took Haruka's hand and her face scrunched up as she tried to think. She cleared her throat and began to sing. Though the song was just a simple children's rhyme, Haruka was taken aback at the clarity and precision of the girl's voice. She smiled and sang the final refrain in chorus with Gabi.

"You're really good at that, Gabi. Can you sing me another one?"

Gabi nodded. She thought for a moment, and then started in on another tune. Haruka didn't recognize the song or the lyrics, as Gabi had started singing in Spanish. The tune was soft and soothing. Haruka closed her eyes as she walked along, imagining her own mother singing it. She could see her mother's smiling face in her mind, and a feeling of warmth washed over her.

Haruka felt a tugging at her arm and realized Gabi had finished singing. "Are you okay, Haruka?"

She opened her eyes and smiled. "Yeah, I was really enjoying your singing. How about one more?"

"No thanks." She pointed to a low ridge ahead. "I want to go pick more fruit for later."

"Alright, but just remember; don't go over the hill where I can't see you."

Gabi smiled and skipped up the hill. Haruka took a moment to examine the bright rashes on her arms. They did not itch like a normal rash, but like sunburn they stung when they were rubbed wrong.

I wonder if I'm allergic to something in the jungle, she thought. She picked at the frayed strands of her shoulder cuffs where she had sliced the sleeves from her uniform. *I had sleeves on yesterday, so it shouldn't be sunburn. It would be the craziest looking sunburn ever if it was.*

Haruka looked up at the ridge and saw Gabi with her back turned. She was not picking fruit, or anything else for that matter. She seemed to be frozen in place, looking off into the distance.

"Gabi?" Haruka called as she ran up the hill. "Are you okay?"

Haruka ran up beside the little girl and instantly saw what Gabi was looking at; just over the next ridge, Haruka could make out the steel form of a sleeper pod between the trees. Haruka let out a sigh of relief and smiled. She turned to say something to Gabi, but she could see her companion's lip trembling and tears streaming from her cheeks.

"What's wrong, Gabi? We're almost there. Just a few more minutes."

"No. We can't go."

"Why not?"

Gabi burst out crying. "They're dead."

Haruka's skin began to crawl and her heart beat faster. "What do you mean, sweetie?"

"There were dead people in there, and then I got out and fell off of it. And then there was a fire."

"Whoa, slow down there. Fire?"

Gabi nodded slowly as the corners of her mouth drew back and her lip stuck out even further. "Mama and Papa were in there."

Haruka looked at the pod and saw a dulled gray exterior. "I don't see any sign of fire from here. Come on, I bet everyone's fine."

"No!" Gabi screamed. "I saw two dead people there! And there was a fire!"

Haruka lost her patience with Gabi. "We need to go there," she said as she grabbed Gabi's hand and started to drag her toward the pod. Gabi shrieked and dug her heels into the ground. Haruka winced as the girl's resistance jarred her torn shoulder. Haruka growled and scooped up Gabi with one arm. "We're going."

Haruka jogged her way around thick masses of underbrush as she picked a course for the pod. Gabi screamed and kicked the whole way, and Haruka felt as if her shoulder might just come apart from all the stress. She gritted her teeth and doubled her efforts.

When they reached the edge of the clearing made by the crashed pod, Haruka saw a patch of blackened metal on the pod about five feet tall and fifteen feet across. Gashes and dents marred the outer hull of the pod from stem to stern. Several people were standing on top of and around the base of the pod, inspecting it. She put Gabi down and pointed at the black mark.

"See? Just a little burn on the outside from where a hydraulic line burst. There's nothing in these things that can make them burn completely through," she said.

Well, unless the chemical thrusters still had enough fuel left to burn up the oxygen canisters, that is.

"And look," she continued. "See all those people there? They're not dead."

Haruka and Gabi looked at the cluster of people standing near the blackened lower rungs of the ladder. Several of them pointed in their direction. One began to run towards them, stumbling over felled logs in a headlong rush. Haruka threw up her hand to shield her eyes. She could make out that it was a woman running for them. A man broke from the group and chased after her.

"Huh, now I wonder what this is all about."

A faint voice carried from the distance fell on their ears. "Gabi?"

"Mama?" she said, almost in a whisper.

"Gabi?"

"Mama!" Gabi jumped up and ran toward the woman as fast as she could. Haruka tried to keep pace with her, hampered by the jumbled piles of felled wood.

The woman stopped, and as soon as Gabi was in reach, scooped her up and held her tight. The man who was following stopped and embraced them as well. Haruka caught up and stopped at their side, out of breath from her scramble.

"Gabi, you're alive," sobbed Gabi's mother.

Haruka's heart swelled as she watched the reunion. Tears streamed down all of their faces, and Gabi was showered with kisses.

"We couldn't find you anywhere," her father croaked, his face buried in Gabi's hair. "We thought you were dead." He looked up at Haruka. Slowly he rose, and stumbled over to Haruka. She flinched as his arms came up and she started to reach for her pistol, but then hesitated. His arms fell across her shoulders and he gave her a hug so tight that her shoulder began to burn again.

"Ow," she protested.

He let go and straightened himself up. "Sorry. I didn't mean to hurt you." His eyes were locked on hers, and she could see his lips tremble. "Thank you for finding her. Thank you for returning our little girl. We thought she was dead. Please, if there is anything I can do for you ever, just name it."

Haruka nodded. "The first thing you can do is watch her closely for the next day or so. Make sure she doesn't get sick."

"W-why?"

Haruka retrieved one of the orange and green speckled fruits from her pack. "Before I found her, she ate three of these."

Gabi's father lost his smile in an instant, and he grew several shades paler. "Are they poisonous?"

"I don't know. They look pretty harmless, and when I cut into one it smelled kind of like a peach. But we know absolutely nothing about the native plants, so we need to be careful. Especially little ones like Gabi who don't know any better."

He nodded. "Trust me, I won't be letting Gabi out of my sight at all for a while. Is there anything else you need me to do for you?"

"Yes. Where are the pod pilots? I need to debrief them."

"I uh…" his voice trailed off as he looked over his shoulder, then back at Haruka. "I don't know who they are. We can ask around, though. Are you part of the ship's crew?"

"Yes, sir. Captain Haruka Kimura, acting commander of the sleeper ship *Raphael*." She extended her hand, which he grasped and shook vigorously.

"Luis Serrano. My wife Maria, and of course Gabi, our daughter. No offense, Captain, but you look like you've been through a lot. Maybe we should get you back to the pod and see if someone there is a doctor. That shoulder looks pretty bad."

"Please, call me Haruka. And thanks. Would you mind carrying this for me?" Haruka slipped her pack off and offered it to Luis, who snatched it from her.

"Of course. Right this way."

The four started for the pod. With the reduced weight load, Haruka could move much more easily. She took notice of the condition of the pod as she moved toward it. *The rear ramp is still closed. It looks fine. Either there's a power failure, or the crew can't open it. There are some bad breaches in the skin, and the hydraulic landing system is shot.*

"So you were all alone out here?" asked Luis.

"No. I crashed in the engineering skiff with two others." Haruka bit her lip. She knew she would have to admit the deaths of Mancini and Evans, but wondered exactly how much she should tell the survivors. "One died in the crash, the other was killed by a native animal," she lied. "The same animal that tried to rip me to pieces."

"I'm sorry to ask, but what did this animal look like?"

"Some sort of predatory cat. The closest thing I can think of on

Earth would be a jaguar, except the fur color is different and it has longer fangs."

She continued her mental assessment. *If the top of this thing is punched through, we might not be able to use it as shelter for long.*

"Anyone here have medical training?" Luis shouted as they approached the base of the pod. The dozen or so people loitering around looked at each other and shook their heads. "Alright, inside we go. Most people are still in there trying to sort stuff out and figure out what to do with ourselves."

Haruka grabbed the ladder and scaled it. Each time her left shoulder pulled her up higher, she felt a twinge of pain. When she gained access to the roof, she walked past another small crowd and climbed down the access hatch into the core of the pod. She looked down the hall and saw the closed door of the ESAARC cockpit. Her heart dropped.

"Has that door been closed the whole time?" she asked as Luis dropped to the deck next to her.

"Yup."

She sighed heavily. "No use trying to find the pilots. I know exactly where they are."

The look of concern that etched his face said that he seemed to know what Haruka meant. He nodded, and then directed her toward a sleeper hallway. "Let's see about that doctor, okay?"

They made their way through the pod to section bravo. Every upper level unit was open, and men, women, and children lay in berths or sat on the ground, engaged in conversation with each other.

"Anyone here have medical training?" Luis asked. A hush fell on the crowd.

"I do." A slender woman with straight, jet black hair maneuvered through the crowd and up to Haruka. "I'm a nurse."

"She's got a wounded shoulder. It's Emilia, right?"

"Yeah. Let me see," said Emilia as she peeled back the tape holding Haruka's makeshift bandage together. Haruka winced as she examined the tender flesh. "Luis, do you remember where the med kits were?"

"Yup. Need one?"

"Yeah."

Luis turned and left. Haruka sucked in a breath of air as the probing continued. "How bad is it?"

"All things considered, not bad. I see you've managed to keep the wound pretty clean, but it has opened several times. We need to find a way to bind it shut and keep it from getting infected." Emilia looked up at the gathered crowd. "Take the kids somewhere else for a minute, please."

The children were shuffled out of the hallway with their respective guardians, and Luis came back with a bulky medical kit from one of the storage lockers. Emilia retrieved some supplies from inside. "This will probably hurt pretty badly. I noticed that there's morphine in this kit. If you're not allergic and you want me to use it, I will."

As much as Haruka wanted to tough it out and continue, she was pleased at the prospect of being relieved of the pain. She nodded at the nurse.

"Luis," she said. "Want to know the next thing you can do for me?"

"Absolutely."

She unslung her rifle and handed it to him, pulled the pistol from her belt and set it on the deck plate, and removed the belt with her second pistol and bayonet. "Keep a watch over everyone for me. No one goes into the jungle until I say so, got it? We have enough supplies here that we don't need to do anything rash."

"You got it."

Haruka turned back to Emilia, who was already preparing a morphine shot. "Patch me up, but don't knock me out."

Emilia tapped Haruka's arm with her fingers, then slipped the needle in and injected the drugs without Haruka feeling so much as a pinch.

"Wow, you're good at that."

Emilia smiled at Haruka. "Twelve years of experience, and I hope to have many more."

Haruka's eyelids drooped as she felt the drugs kick in. She did not try to fight the effects, but instead welcomed the end of her pain in a blurred haze. The light seemed to blend in with the metal as her head slipped to the deck.

"How many people survived?" Haruka asked, barely able to enunciate.

"Shhh. Worry about that later," Emilia soothed.

Haruka tried to lift her head. Emilia's face blurred like a painting in the rain. "You tricked me. I didn't… I said…"

She did not have the strength to battle through both the drugs and fatigue, and she faded out of consciousness.

• • •

2nd Lt Darren Cormack
USAF
Planetfall +1 day, early afternoon
Ex-Raphael sleeper pod seven landing site
>|

Darren climbed down from the top of the pod and into its sweltering belly. There were no trees atop the hill where they had set down, and the sun baked the exposed metal craft all day long. The halls reeked of body odor, and even with the top and rear hatches open, the internal temperature was miserable well into the evening hours. He wiped his brow as his long strides covered the distance from the ladder to the ESAARC cockpit.

He slid the door open and took his place next to Sergeant Daniels. Her face was plain, with an angular nose. She had clipped her wavy brown hair up, and her headset spanned over her folded locks. Her blank expression could have either been that of singular focus or complete disinterest.

"Update please, Daniels."

"No change, sir," she said. "We have had no contact from any unaccounted pods, nor have we heard from Captain Kimura."

Darren sighed. *Captain Kimura should have landed here by now, or at least signaled. She's probably crashed too.*

"Alright, let's go down the list again," he said as he settled his headset. "Status of our pod and passengers."

"Landed safely. Both crew members and all one hundred fifty nine passengers accounted for, no injuries. Pod is fully operational, although our thruster banks are basically out of fuel."

"Pods one and two?"

Daniels looked at a clipboard with some handwritten notes. "Landed safe. All passengers and crew accounted for, no casualties. They are located together about fifty miles east."

Darren nodded and pursed his lips. "Pods three and four?"

"Number three landed hard, twenty miles northeast of here. Sergeant Forsyth reports nine dead and thirty wounded. Pod four crashed on approach to the one-two landing site. Our report came from a civilian. It's not clear just what the extent of casualties is, sir, but it would appear the crew did not survive and there are a lot of civilians dead."

"Hang on a second, Daniels." Darren activated the radio. "This is

Lieutenant Cormack of pod seven, calling pod one or two. Please respond."

There was a crackle and a pause. Darren waited for two full minutes before he repeated his request, and several more seconds passed before a response came through his earpiece.

"Pod two, Lieutenant Marsolek speaking."

"Have you had any contact with pod four today, Lieutenant?"

"No." Darren could hear the sound of paper shuffling through his headset. "From what I see, you've been coordinating communication between pods, so we've been concentrating on getting set up out here instead."

Figures.

"Can you spare a small search party? Pod four is near you. Their crew is dead and there are civilian casualties." Darren snapped his fingers at Daniels and held out his hand.

"I think so. Where are they at?" Marsolek asked.

Daniels handed him a crudely drawn map showing the positions of the pods. "Looks like they're two, maybe three miles northwest of you. Bring them back to your camp if you can."

"Alright, we'll check it out. Anything else, Lieutenant?"

"Not right now. Cormack out." He switched off the radio and looked at Daniels. "Can you believe that? He's dumping coordination duty on us. You'd think he'd at least make an effort to find his neighbors, especially with the manpower they've got over there."

She shrugged. "No offense, sir, but they've got their own problems to deal with. The Operational Guidelines are useless too, since we've lost all of our command officers."

Darren looked out the forward window at the blue sky and cottony white clouds. "Who *is* in command now, Daniels?"

She flipped through a few pages on her clipboard. "Let's see here. Colonel Fox and Captain Bartrand were relieved of duty and are missing. Major Emberley, Captain Maynard, Captain Ford, and Captain Kimura are all missing. So are Lieutenants Mancini, Morado, and Perez. Lieutenants Singh, Kaspar, and Lewis are all dead. It looks like you and Marsolek are the last remaining officers, sir."

"Does Marsolek outrank me?"

"No, you're the same rank. Give me a second to figure this out, sir." Daniels turned on the computer console in front of her.

"Be quick. We need to spare our batteries for the coms."

"I know," she said with an air of impatience. She quickly brought up the crew files and flipped through them. "Marsolek is an engineer, so according to the Ops Guidelines, you're in command." She looked at him and sarcastically said, "Congratulations, sir."

"Gee, thanks, Sergeant. It's everything I've dreamed of."

Darren sighed heavily. *I didn't want a command, ever. I just wanted to put in my tour and go home to open a business. This is about as far from what I wanted as I could get.* He closed his eyes and dreamed of the small café he had always wanted to own; of the cozy tables resting on red tiled floor, taking orders from smiling customers while the smell of fresh baked pastries wafted through the air.

Even though at first his dream appeared to have been dashed by his assignment to Project Columbus, Darren had a glimmer of hope that sometime after a colony was established, he might possibly be able to pursue his goal, even if it was on a different world. That glimmer was buried and his dream crushed when *Raphael* had been destroyed. Instead, his reality was that he was in charge of hundreds of frightened and injured refugees scattered all over an island, far from their intended landing point.

He grimaced and flipped the radio on, then fiddled with the frequency control. "Lieutenant Cormack to any survivor in pod four, please come in."

He repeated his request after two minutes and then once more after four minutes.

"H-hello?" stammered a voice in his earpiece.

"Cormack here, are you from pod four?"

"I.. I think so. How do I tell for sure?"

"Go to the back of the pod, there will be a large number painted on the rear ramp."

"Okay. Let me check." There was a silence for a minute or so. "Yeah, this is pod four."

"Good. What's your name?"

"It's Greg."

"Good. Greg, I need you to do something for me, okay? It's something real simple."

"Oh, okay. What is it?"

"I've got a group headed your way from a nearby pod to rescue you.

We need your people to get ready."

"I-I don't know what to do," Greg responded feebly.

"It's easy, Greg. Just listen to me, okay? There's a ladder that goes to the roof to an escape hatch. Four people go up top and watch for your rescuers, got it?"

"Okay."

"Alright. Next get all your injured people and have them near the rear hatch so they're ready to go."

"Uhm, okay."

"Then get some others to help you gather as many supplies as you can. If you run out of packs, fill up the flight suits and drag them behind you. Food first, then weapons if the keypads on their lockers aren't busted. I'll give you the code in a minute. Grab the med kits, and then as many of the hand tools as you can. Axes, saws, and shovels are the most useful, but anything you can take would be helpful."

"Okay, I think I've got it."

"Good. The access code to the weapons lockers will be zero four two two nine four, followed by pound. Repeat that back to me, Greg."

"Zero four two two nine four pound."

"Good. Just hang tight there and we'll get you out, okay?"

Darren could hear a relieved sigh from Greg. "Thanks."

"Cormack out." He clicked the radio off, rubbed his eyes, and sighed. "Pods five and six?"

Daniels looked back at her clipboard and cleared her throat. "Five is unaccounted for. Casualties assumed to be 100 percent. Six took a hard landing fifteen miles east of us. Sergeant Zhao reports that about a dozen passengers were wounded. His pilot was Kaspar, who was killed on impact."

Lost pod. 100 percent casualties. That's around 160 people. Darren bowed his head. "Pod eight."

There was a slight hesitation before Daniels responded. "Unaccounted for. Casualties assumed to be 100 percent."

"Pods nine and ten."

"Pod nine is confirmed as lost at sea, with 100 percent casualties. Pod ten unaccounted for, casualties assumed to be 100 percent."

It seems like being in a rearward pod may have been a death sentence.

"Pods eleven and twelve."

"We received word from Sergeant Leight from pod eleven that they made an emergency landing on shore, and other than minor injuries, suffered no casualties. He also reported that pod twelve crashed into the surf just off shore. He was unable to get a passenger manifest for their pod, but he said that forty seven survived from pod twelve."

Darren shuddered. He knew from the last report that more had survived the crash, but several were lost in the rescue attempt. He forced aside his growing despair and continued.

"Pods thirteen and fourteen."

"Both unaccounted for, casualties assumed to be 100 percent."

"And the four specialty pods?"

"All unaccounted for. Casualties assumed at two crewmen per pod. Sir, I remember…" her voice trailed off for a second. "I remember Doctor Nelson saying he would take shelter in med pod one. We have to assume he's lost too."

Darren dug his fingernails into the padding of the chair. "Engineering skiff."

"Confirmed as crashed. Other than Captain Kimura, we're unsure who was on board. I've marked down the casualties as four, since that was the capacity of the skiff."

"Escape pods?"

Daniels flipped through her papers. "The records our pod received before the link to *Raphael* was lost indicate no pods were launched."

Damn. Darren closed his eyes and calculated in his head. *We're looking at probably a thousand or more dead. More than half of the ship.*

"Sir? Your orders?"

He slowly opened his eyes and lifted his stare to the horizon. He hushed his voice. "Find all the emergency transponders you can from the cargo pods and see if you can map out their locations."

"Yes, sir," Daniels said as Darren slid out of his seat. She looked up at him and caught his hand with her arm. "Sir, you may be in command of the mission, but don't forget about our own passengers."

Darren nodded and turned away, then walked down the hall to the rear ramp. As he crossed the threshold to the outside air, the stench disappeared and the temperature dropped almost twenty degrees as he was met with a gentle breeze. His boots clanked with every step down the ramp. A group of passengers were gathered at the base of the ramp;

about three dozen by his estimates.

"Anyone here a hunter or hiker?" Darren asked as he reached the bottom. Nearly all of the men, as well as a few women, raised their hands timidly. "Anyone want to do a bit of scouting?" Many of the hands dropped. Darren counted the remaining hands and found ten volunteers. "Alright, all of you come with me, please."

They walked down the gentle slope of the bald hill until they were out of earshot of the other group. Darren looked back and saw the orange globe of Alpha Centauri B burning brightly just above the curved upper hull of the pod.

"We need to know what's in the immediate area around us, folks," he said. "This hill made a great landing spot, but I want to see if it will be suitable for setting up the colony. The other pods are doing the same, and we'll figure out what is best for all. I want to split you up into four groups and send you in different directions, see what's around here."

"Out in the wilderness?" asked a short, wiry young man. Judging by the lack of facial hair and smooth face, Darren could not imagine he was older than sixteen.

"That's right. Two teams of three, two teams of two. Each team gets two rifles and two machetes. The larger teams will also get two sidearms. Also, each of you will be issued a survival pack. We've lost half the day so far, and I want you all back by nightfall. I don't expect you to go very far today, just get a quick lay of the land. Tomorrow you'll go back out and scout a bit deeper."

"What are we looking for?" asked the lone woman in the group.

"General terrain features," he replied. "Water sources. Interesting native plants and animals. Anything that you think could be used as a resource for building a settlement or feeding the survivors."

"What if we find aliens?" chimed a voice from the back of the group.

"There was no alien radio contact on our approach. We didn't see any signs of civilization in the original probe photos. We don't believe there are any aliens on this planet, but if there are, they will be primitive. Don't engage unless you're attacked. Any other questions?" Darren scanned the crowd for a moment, but received no response. "Alright. I want you broken up into four teams. Work that out amongst yourselves, come up with team leaders, and return to the pod in ten minutes so I can issue equipment. Thank you all for volunteering."

Darren turned and strode quickly away to prepare the equipment for his new scouts.

. . .

Gabrielle Serrano
Planetfall +2 days, late morning
Ex-Raphael sleeper pod eight crash site
>|

Gabi rubbed her eyes and looked out of her upper level bed. Muted voices mumbled from outside. She smiled at her mother as she passed by.

"Mama," she called.

Her mother quickly came back to her bed, pulled her out, and set her on the floor. "Good morning, Gabi. Did you sleep tight?"

Gabi stretched. "Yeah. Mama, I'm hungry."

"Okay. I'll get you something in just a sec. I want you to meet someone."

"Who is it?"

Gabi's mom took her by the hand and walked her to the end of the hall, where two other children – a boy and a girl – were huddled in the corner. Gabi stood behind her mom and peeked out around her side. Her eyes met with the girl, who looked bigger and older than Gabi. Her green eyes were surrounded by puffy red circles, and her blonde hair was a mess of ringlets. The boy was about the same size as Gabi, had the same green eyes as the girl, and a thick mop of brown hair.

"Gabi," her mother said. "This is Marya, and her brother Aidan. I was just going to get them something too. Maybe you could sit with them while I get breakfast."

Gabi nodded shyly and sat on the floor across from the two kids as her mother walked away. Aidan put his head down between his knees. Marya sniffed and looked at Gabi.

"Do you know what my mom is making for breakfast?" Gabi asked.

Neither of the children responded to Gabi. She shuffled her feet and looked down at the metal floor. Gabi wondered if she said something wrong to the children, or if they just didn't like her.

"What's wrong?" she asked.

Marya turned her head and rested it on her knees, staring at the wall beside her.

They don't like me. Why don't they like me?

Gabi's mom returned with four brown plastic bags that looked like the kind that Haruka pulled food from when Gabi was in the jungle.

Columbus: Flight

45

"Breakfast is served. Marya, Aidan, you can pick first."

"But Mama, I want to pick first," Gabi protested.

"Manners, Mija. They're our guests, so they get served first."

"But Mama…"

"No buts, Gabi." Her mom sat down and arranged the bags in front of the two other children. Neither looked up. Gabi's mom placed her hand on Marya's cheek. "Marya, come on. You have to eat something."

The blond girl slowly lifted her head and dropped her gaze to the food in front of her. Her arm extended and grabbed the bag closest to her, which she placed next to her feet before resting her head on her knees again. Aidan did the same as his sister, reaching for the closest bag.

Gabi's mom sighed. "Ok, Gabi. Your turn to pick."

Gabi turned the packages so their labels faced her. She took a moment to read the writing on them, and though some of the words were ones she did not know, she recognized the word "pancakes". With a grin, she snatched the open bag and looked inside to see several sealed pouches.

"Mama, can you open these for me?"

"Sure."

Her mother opened the food pouches and handed Gabi a plastic fork. Gabi attacked the food with zeal. She soaked the pancakes in syrup from a small squeeze pouch, and her hands and face quickly became a sticky mess.

As she licked the sweet syrup from her fingers, Gabi noticed that Marya had not moved or touched her food. Aidan picked at it and ate a bite every now and then, but didn't seem to want food. Gabi looked at her mother, who wore a slight frown on her face.

"Mama, what's wrong?"

Her mom leaned over so close that Gabi could feel her breath on her neck. She whispered, "Their mom and dad died in the crash, Mija. They're very very sad."

Gabi glanced at the two children and then back at her mom. She lowered her voice to a loud whisper and replied, "I can give them a hug and make them feel better."

"That's a very nice thing to do, but you need to wait a while. You just met them, and they need some time and space."

"Ok, Mama. Just tell me when and I will."

"I will, Mija." Her mom reached into the food bag and pulled out a wet nap package. "Let's clean your hands and face there."

Gabi giggled quietly as her mom cleaned her hands. She saw her father walk up from behind with a rifle slung over his shoulder.

"Hugs, Gabi," he said with his arms open.

Gabi ran up and threw her arms around his waist. "Where are you going, Papa?"

"Out for a bit. Captain Kimura wants me to go take a look around the jungle."

"No!" Gabi screamed and tightened her grip on her dad.

"I know, Gabi. I missed you," he said as he tussled her hair. "But I need to do this. I'll be back in a few hours."

Gabi fell to the floor, shrieking and crying. "No! You can't go out there. There are big kitties that will try to eat you."

She felt her father's hand on her back, slowly rubbing her. "It's okay. Captain Kimura told me about the kitties and gave me this gun to keep me safe. I'm not going alone, either. One of my new friends is going with me, and he'll also have a gun. We're going to watch out for each other. You know what that means, right?"

Gabi sniffed hard and nodded.

"I'll be back in time for dinner, I promise." Gabi wailed when she heard her father's words. His hand patted her on the back. "Shhh. It's okay. Mama will be here with you the whole time."

"I don't want you to go, Papa."

"Sorry, Gabi. I have to. I love you."

"I love you too," she choked through her tears.

Gabi felt the warm arms of her mother wrap around her, and felt a rocking motion. Her tears streamed for minutes as her mom whispered in her ear.

I don't want Papa to work today. I miss him.

. . .

Capt Haruka Kimura
Planetfall +3 days, midday
Ex-Raphael sleeper pod eight
>|

A stiff breeze flowed through the shattered canopy of the cockpit as Haruka fiddled with the radio controls in front of her. Her knees were drawn almost up to her chest, and her back was starting to ache from being cramped in the chair. She had no foot space to work with; it was occupied by the sprawled out body of James Vandemark. His head and shoulders were stuck inside the partially disassembled computer consoles. An occasional grunt or curse from the open cavity let Haruka know that James hadn't managed to electrocute himself to any severe degree.

"How's that?" James asked. His voice echoed slightly.

"No good. No power."

"Alright, hang on a sec."

Haruka glanced down at her work companion. His white t-shirt was soaked with sweat, and the pockets of his cargo shorts were stuffed with an array of screwdrivers and pliers that he had scrounged from storage. She could see his hand shoot from inside the computer back to a pocket, where he groped for a moment before retrieving a small precision screwdriver.

Sure looks like he knows what he is doing, though. That should help.

She was beginning to appreciate the skill diversity that the survivors had. After forcing the cockpit open and arranging for the dead crew to be buried, Haruka had checked the pod's internal systems for functionality. The worst of the systems damage seemed to be focused on the cockpit; power was available in the body sections, and the rear hatch had opened easily through its main controls. All of the communication and navigation systems for the ESAARC pods were based in the cockpit, however, and Haruka knew that repairs would be needed in order to contact other survivors. When she assembled the survivors and asked if anyone had radio or electronics repair skills, James volunteered without hesitation.

Haruka felt fortunate to have James among the survivors. On Earth, the thirty eight year old man had been a computer repair tech, and worked with HAM radios in his spare time. Even his shorter statue and wiry frame helped in this situation, since there was precious little room to maneuver in the cramped compartment.

J.C. Rainier

As if Haruka was not lucky enough to have James, his wife and three teenage children were already proving to be quite the assets. Their eldest, Will, had joined a scouting party and was out in the jungle nearby, while Jeanette and the daughters helped Emilia with the injured passengers, or ran errands for various other passengers. What seemed to amaze her most was how little the teenagers of the Vandemark family complained about being put to work. Haruka had to wonder if they were normally this helpful, or if their reaction was an acknowledgement of their dire circumstances.

Either way, I'll take it.

Haruka's attention snapped back to the repairs when she heard a metallic bang and a loud curse word.

"Well, *that* wire's live. And it sure as hell was carrying more than twelve volts. Damn."

"You okay in there, James?" she asked.

"Yeah. And quite awake, though if you ask me coffee is an easier way to perk up. Definitely less painful." There was a slight pause. "Ah, crap, I hit my head. Can you toss me a rag from up there?"

Haruka passed the cleanest rag she could find through the opening. "Please tell me you're not bleeding down there."

Again there was a pause. "No?"

"Are you lying to me?"

"Yeah. Don't worry about it, though. It's just a scratch. Give it a try now."

Haruka flicked the power switch for the radio, but its lights stayed dead and she didn't hear any static in her headset. "No, still dead."

"How can that be?" There was an edge to his voice, and Haruka could tell he was getting frustrated. "I know what I just plugged in is hot. I've got a good ground." He growled, which through the opening sounded like a terrier with a can stuck on its head. "I think the power supply on this thing is shot. Fan's not even spinning."

"That's not the radio's power supply. I think you've plugged in the terminals. Let me check." Haruka flipped a switch over her head and fired up the main computer. Lights flickered and an image showed on her screen, distorted by the large spider web crack across its fascia. "Yeah, that's the main computer."

"Son of a…" he cut himself off.

"Don't beat yourself up. I needed that thing on sooner or later.

Give me a second to pull the data that I need."

Haruka tried to access the beacon data from before the crash. Her efforts were hampered by the damage to the panel's touch screen and the limited key controls. It took some doing, but she was able to pull up the records for the last five minutes before the pod hit the ground.

"Yes," she said, doing a little fist pump in the air. "Jackpot."

"What is it?" James asked as he scrambled to his feet. Dried blood caked his forehead from a gash near his hairline.

"Jesus, are you okay?"

He ran his hand along his forehead. Blood flaked off onto his fingers. "Yeah, I'm fine. I'll go see Emilia when we're done here."

"Alright," she said as she turned back to the station. "These are relative beacon positions of the sleeper pods. Now we know where our neighbors are."

"That's good, right?"

Haruka nodded as she jotted them down on a loose piece of paper. "The portable locator I had was almost out of battery by the time I got here. I had no idea it would eat that much juice."

If we had made for Cormack's landing site, its batteries would have died, she thought. *We probably would have walked in circles to our deaths. Well, unless Evans killed us first.*

"Alright," James continued. "What do we do with that information?"

"At some point we're going to need to link up with these people. It doesn't make sense to make a dozen tiny villages when we can pool resources and make one large one."

"You mean... move everyone?"

She sighed and stared at a white dot on the center of the screen that represented their pod. "I know it doesn't sound ideal, but ideal went out the window when we had to do the emergency drop." Her gaze leveled with his. "How much do the pod survivors know?"

"Not a whole lot. Pretty much all of them heard Major Emberley's warning to stay put. We had a rough ride, and the pod rolled when we hit. You're the first crew member we've seen. And we know that's... well, that's because..." his voice trailed off and he swept his arm toward the blood soaked cushioning of the other seat. "What happened up there, anyway?"

"I'm not too sure myself. We were approaching the planet just fine, then something blew and the reactor started to overheat. We knew we couldn't land the whole ship so we evacuated to the pods and ejected. I stayed behind to direct the hull and reactor away from the planet. Me and two other crewmembers who stayed barely escaped. We didn't fare much better than your pod on the way down. We crashed after running out of fuel for the thrusters."

"Forgive me for asking, but what happened to the other two?"

Haruka bit her lip and avoided his stare. The memory of Evans burying her bayonet deep into Mancini's back raced through her brain. It felt as if she cringed with each thrust as it played over and over in her head, almost as if it were her own flesh that the knife pierced. The memory passed as a warm hand gripped her shoulder softly.

"I'm sorry, Captain. I should have known better than to ask. It looks like your crew was pretty tight knit." He paused. "I'm sorry for your loss."

She nodded and adjusted the bandage on her shoulder. "Loss seems to be all we've had so far, but I can't let it affect my duty. Let's see if we can get the radio back up."

"Alright."

James contorted his body as his upper half disappeared back into the console. Haruka rummaged through the trash strewn about the cockpit and found what was left of a notepad, then repositioned her headset. She stowed her makeshift beacon map in the back fold of the notepad, then turned to a clean sheet of paper.

"The good news is that I know where I went wrong in this thing." James's tools rattled and clanked inside the hole, and the power to the main computer went dead. "All I have to do is move the wire over here, and we should be golden. Try it now."

Haruka flicked the switch and the pod's radio lit up. "That's good, James. See if you can button it up so you don't have to fix it again."

"Sure thing."

She made a cursory sweep through the standard frequencies used by the pods but heard nothing. James finished patching the console and took a standing position behind Haruka. As she made her second sweep, she stopped at each frequency for four minutes, giving a standard greeting twice during that time. No responses came through, only the faint crackle of static. She was about to give up the standard channels when a voice responded on the final channel.

"This is Sergeant Seth Leight of pod eleven. Please repeat your ident code, I don't think I heard it right."

Haruka sighed in relief. "This is Captain Haruka Kimura, acting CO of *Raphael*. I'm now at pod eight. What is your status, Sergeant?"

Silence greeted her for several seconds. "Did you say Captain Kimura?"

"Yes, Sergeant, I'm alive. Now what is your status?"

"To be honest, ma'am, we're a little mixed up. I've accounted for all one hundred fifty six of my passengers and both crew, but I've also got forty seven souls from pod twelve that I have to deal with."

"What happened to twelve?"

"Crashed into the surf maybe a few hundred feet from where we ended up. It was a mess, Captain. Don't wanna ever see anything like that again."

Haruka shuddered. Whatever the sergeant saw was likely too much for her to handle at this point, she decided. "Understood. How are you fixed for supplies? Any injuries?"

"A bit strained because of our recent additions. We'll find a way to manage, though. At least we won't have to worry too much about medical stuff. All we've got to deal with are bumps and bruises. From what I heard of the radio traffic on the way down I thought you were in the skiff. What happened?"

Must I relive this every time someone asks?

"Ran out of fuel and crashed trying to find a landing spot, but was able to make my way to pod eight. I'm the only crew member left. My computer's damaged and I don't know if I can pull up a manifest, but we've got just over a hundred survivors. We've got a couple broken bones here, but nothing major, and we've got a pretty good nurse." She looked up at James and smiled. "Even if she is a bit of a tricky devil."

"Do I want to know?" asked Leight.

"I'll just say that if you look like you've been chewed up and spit out, don't ask her for sedation. She'll give you more than you want."

She could hear a chuckle through the radio. "Isn't it just like a doctor to come to some crazy notion that you're overworked or too sick and you need to take it easy."

"Yeah, well this one didn't warn me. I wonder if she got some sort of weird kick out of the whole thing."

"Well, I must have been blessed, because I've got a good doc and two nurses over here."

"So what's the lay of the land, Sergeant? Are your scouts giving you good info?"

"Probably would if I had any, Captain. Most of my people are sorting supplies, gathering wood, or making sure the pod twelve survivors are being cared for. The rest? Well, I have a bunch of sniveling slackers here. I'd go myself if I didn't think that the pod would be on fire and looted by the time I came back. The only scouting party I have is Airman Jenkins and this kinda creepy guy from some tiny speck of a town in Arizona. They've got their hands full."

"I've got a few parties out there," Haruka said. "So far they've reported we're in the middle of nothing. I mean, there's a river nearby, which helps, but we'd have to hack a living out of the jungle here with basically no resources but trees."

"Huh, I wonder if that's the same river that empties into the bay here."

Haruka pulled her beacon map out and unfurled it. "It wouldn't surprise me. I haven't seen any terrain around that would indicate another river. Not of this size, anyway. Hey, you said you were near surf. Do you have beachfront property?"

"Beachfront? No, we're on the beach itself. Our pod crashed into the dunes right off shore, which I guess kept us from being pulverized on impact." Leight paused for a moment. "It's actually really beautiful here, especially as the sun's going down."

Marco's beaches. She clutched at the tags in her pocket.

"Have you heard from any other pods?"

"A few. Lieutenant Cormack from pod seven has been doing some sort of coordination work. You can probably catch him on this frequency tomorrow, but he usually is only on once a day. Last I heard, he figured out what was left of the chain of command, and said that he's in charge. I guess that will change tomorrow, since you're here now. In any case, that guy's a nut for conserving battery power. I bet his radio will work at least until the other ships come."

"Do you know what kind of coordination?"

"Yeah, there's a cluster of pods on the other side of that giant mountain there. It looks like he's gathering everyone together at two different sites."

"Alright, I'll see what's going on with him tomorrow."

"Sounds like a plan. Hey Captain?"

"Yes, Sergeant?"

"Got a plan yet?"

"One step at a time, Sergeant. I don't even know what I'm dealing with here yet."

"I hear you. I've only got an inkling of what to do myself. I call it a good day if no one starves or gets themselves hurt."

"That's a good start. I'll know more about where we stand tomorrow."

"Well, I hope your work won't keep you from enjoying the sunset tonight. The ones on this planet are just…" his voice trailed off.

She nodded, though in her time on Demeter she had not had the chance to see one. "A little stress relief? Alright, maybe I'll take a look at one when I take a beach vacation some day."

"Something tells me with my bunch here, there won't be a shortage of hammocks," Leight said in a mocking tone.

"Great. Save me a mai tai. Kimura out." She killed the power to the radio and looked up at James, who was grinning from ear to ear. "What?"

"I want a beach vacation."

Haruka frowned as she slipped from her seat and through the doorway, shoving the notepad and pen into his arms. "Trust me; it's not going to be a vacation if we go there. Come on, there's more work to be done."

"What's next on the list?" he asked as he followed her down the hall to the ladder.

"Damage assessment. I need to see every hull section up close."

• • •

```
2nd Lt Darren Cormack
Planetfall +4 days, early morning
Ex-Raphael sleeper pod seven
>|
```

"Sir, wake up." A gentle female voice greeted Darren.

"Hrm. Go away." He rolled over and heard himself snort.

Darren tried to go back to sleep, but the human alarm clock persisted, shaking his shoulder firmly. He yawned and flopped on his other side, then opened his eyes.

"What is it, Daniels?"

"You've been asleep for twelve hours, sir. I don't mean Demeter hours either, I mean Earth hours. I was starting to get worried."

Demeter hours, he thought. *It seems that we need a whole new system of time for this new planet, where the days are roughly 20 Earth hours.*

He swung his legs out of the berth and dropped to the deck. With a great stretch and another yawn, he was ready. "Fine, I'm up. Please tell me you have some news that's worth the rude awakening."

"The scouts came back last night after you fell asleep," she replied.

"Why didn't you wake me?" he shot back sharply as he made his way toward the cockpit.

"You were exhausted, sir. I felt it was best to just let you sleep and give you the report in the morning."

"I don't recall my mother being appointed to this mission, Daniels."

He could hear her sigh over their footfalls on the metal deck. "Sorry, sir."

They reached the cockpit and took their seats. Darren shielded his eyes, as the sun was low to the horizon, shining with full intensity through the forward windows. For a moment, the bright light made his head throb, until his eyes could adjust. He glanced over at Sergeant Daniels as she prepared her notes. She did not make eye contact with him once; her head hung and her stare locked the paper in front of her.

"Something bothering you, Daniels?"

"No offense, Lieutenant, but you don't seem to be in a good mood this morning."

Darren scoffed. "Try me again after I've had surf and turf and a night at the Mariott, then I'll be a peach."

She slammed her note pad shut and stood up. "I'm sorry, sir. I'll give you the report later, when you're ready."

"Wait," he blurted. Daniels stopped and looked at him with a scowl. "I'm sorry, I'm taking out my stress on you, and it's not fair. Please sit, I'm ready to hear it."

"It's not good news."

"I know. It's written all over your face. Just sit down. I promise not to make any more smartass remarks."

Daniels slumped back into the chair. She opened the notepad and began to read from her notes. "The pod is sitting on the best ground in the immediate area. That said, we've been unable to locate a source of clean water nearby."

"I thought you said that two of the teams reported seeing water in their initial trips?"

"They did, sir. It was getting late so they couldn't investigate until yesterday. Team Four reports that the large body of water they found to the west is a wide swamp that spans a good chunk of the distance between us and the big mountain on that side. Their team leader didn't exactly have glowing praise for the quality of the water once they were able to take a look at it."

Darren knitted his fingers together. "What did he say, specifically?"

Daniels looked at her notes. "That he's seen cleaner water in a shipyard."

"That doesn't sound promising at all. What about the other team that found water?"

"That was Team Three. They found another swamp directly south, extending to the east. They reported that the area was full of bugs similar to mosquitoes."

Darren sighed. "No help there, either. What did the other two teams report?"

The sergeant flipped to the next page of her notes. "Colorful and obnoxious flora, a species of dangerous fauna, dirt, rocks, big snakes, things like that."

"But no resources of specific note. Damn."

"Well, Team Two did actually find a source of potentially clean water far to the east, but it was so far off that it's not feasible to use for this site. People would have to march all day to grab a bucket and then walk all the way back here."

"So we'll have to strike that as far as an available resource." He paused to collect his thoughts. "What did they report about this so-called dangerous fauna?"

"Team One got attacked by a pair of cat-like creatures with huge fangs. The team was able to neutralize the threat without injuries, but the leader – a guy named Tate – said that they were lucky that they spotted the animals before they were attacked. He said if the team had been ambushed, they probably wouldn't have made it back in one piece."

"Hmm. I'm not thrilled to hear that, but not really surprised either. No signs of intelligent alien life?"

"No, sir." Daniels cleared her throat and tapped her pen nervously. "It gets worse, sir."

Darren picked at the armrest of his chair. "Lay it on me, Sergeant."

"The lack of clean water is what is going to hurt us the most. We haven't even seen so much as a freshwater spring since we got here. If we don't find some water that we can at least treat properly, we'll be out in two days. Three if we're lucky."

So this is what it comes to. After all the crap we've been through and survived, we'll die of thirst if something doesn't change. His hands flexed into fists and then flat again.

"Get everyone together outside the pod, Sergeant."

"Yes sir, I'll get the scouts together."

"No, not just the scouts. I want everyone outside for a meeting in thirty minutes."

Her eyes widened and mouth slacked. "Sir?"

"Just get them together please, and leave your notes here."

"Yes sir." She passed the pad to Darren and left the cockpit.

Darren spent the next thirty minutes eating breakfast, reviewing his sergeant's chicken scratches, and contemplating the potential ramifications of his next move. He was certain that his decision would not be popular, but was just as certain that it was necessary.

He took the long walk to the end of the pod and stopped at the top of the ramp, where Sergeant Daniels waited. All one hundred fifty nine passengers were crowded in a half circle around the base. Parents hushed their children when they saw Darren emerge, and he felt the weight of hundreds of eyes scrutinizing him.

Darren cleared his throat and projected his voice as much as he could without yelling. "We have a supply problem at this landing site that makes it too dangerous to use."

The crowd immediately burst into whispers as neighbors exchanged confused glanced.

He gave them no mind as he continued. "Some of you may already be aware that there is no clean water available at this site. Over the past few days, scouting teams have been sent out to find sources of water that can be purified and used by our camp. Our reports on the nearest water sources indicate that they cannot be safely purified with the resources we have."

The whispers escalated to mumbles, and a few of the passengers pointed at Darren as they spoke amongst themselves. His stomach started to knot, but he pressed on.

"As a result, and in the interest of the safety of everyone here, I am ordering the evacuation of this site."

Whispers gave way to a full on eruption of questions, taunts, and insults. Darren could not pick out any specific conversation from the uproar. He belted out a command of silence. After a few moments, the din faded somewhat.

"Where the hell are we supposed to go?" asked Tate, one of the scouts, over the crowd.

"We're going to join another landing site to the east. They should have…"

"We don't know what else is out there besides the animals your scouts told us about. You expect us to just hike out there? With our *kids?*" another man shouted.

"We're safer traveling as a group," Darren tried to explain. "We will take all of the supplies we can carry, and distribute arms throughout the group for protection."

The crowd exploded in barely intelligible shouts, accusations, and questions. Among them, Darren was able to pick out a few choice phrases.

"Are you trying to kill us?" "Who the hell made you God?" "I should have volunteered; I could have found something better than his blind-ass scouts."

The roar became louder and Darren's repeated commands for silence did nothing to suppress the surging anger. Realizing he couldn't control his passengers with his voice alone, Darren drew his M9A1 and fired a single shot to his right, far clear of any humans. Nearly in unison, the crowd flinched and fell silent, except for the frightened cries of the youngest children. He waited a moment for the throng's attention to turn to him.

"If there was a safe way to stay here, we would be staying," he bellowed. "We are running out of water, people. If we stay here, we die." Darren looked at the faces staring back from the crowd and measured the shock that his words had created. "You know I can't force any of you to go, but staying here is a death sentence. When we leave, we take all the critical supplies with us. That includes the water purification tabs and every drop of water we can carry."

Darren surveyed the crowd and sampled individual reactions; a young girl clutching her mom's leg and sobbing, a somber look on Tate's face, the shocked disbelief of two brothers. Darren's hands trembled as he thought of the damage he had just done to camp morale. Just four days prior, these people's world had been turned upside down, and now Darren was upsetting the frayed nerves of his band all over again.

"Get our scouts and anyone else who volunteers help to pack our supplies," he murmured to Sergeant Daniels. "Water, food, and weapons are our priorities. Next are medical supplies, fire making supplies, and some hand tools. If we have more space, figure it out from there. Have the scouts disseminate instructions to conserve water, since we need to make it last as long as possible when we're out there."

"Yes, sir," she saluted with a slight hesitation.

"We march in one hour," he boomed to the crowd, then spun quickly and walked back to the cockpit.

He took the left hand seat and turned on the main computer and radio, then set the computer to record an automated beacon transmission on the emergency frequency.

"This is Lieutenant Cormack of pod seven, emergency alert to any pod that can hear." His voice wavered as he spoke into the boom. "We are running low on fresh water, and there are no nearby sources from which to replenish our supplies. We are setting out immediately from our site to the shared pod one and two site with one hundred sixty one souls. Hopefully we should arrive in a little under a week." He paused and licked his dry, trembling lips. "If any advance parties can be formed to bring us extra food and water on the way, the assistance would be greatly appreciated."

Darren slumped forward against the console and closed his eyes. He whispered to himself, "Don't put this weight on me." His hands dug into his short hair and tightened. The stretching and dull pain did little to distract him from his troubling thoughts.

I'm barely more than a kid. It's not fair to have this much riding on my shoulders. It's not fair that these people have to rely on me. There were other people better suited for the job, and because they're missing... He sighed heavily and his arm flopped onto the console. *Just get them to the other site, then relinquish command to Marsolek.*

"Are you okay, sir?" Daniels asked.

He looked back at the doorway at the brunette sergeant. Her eyes seemed to have taken on a soft kindness, and her eyebrows were arched.

"This isn't a decision I want to make, but it seems like an impossible situation."

"I get that, the more that I think about it. I don't know if I could do what you just did." She cracked a soft smile. "No offense, but I'm glad I'm not in your shoes."

"I wish I weren't," he muttered under his breath.

"Look," she said as her hand dropped onto his shoulder. "I know that you've got this thing going on where you don't want to get to know people until the colony is set up, but people are going to have a real problem if you don't show up and help us pack. I've heard some grumblings about how people think you're letting other people deal with this mess."

"I *am* dealing with it, Sergeant."

"I know that, but they don't."

Darren's stomach knotted. He didn't want to risk too much socialization; the thought of befriending passengers and then losing them was too much to bear. Darren was keenly aware that no one was safe until a colony had been well established, and research of the local area had been properly conducted. The realization that their landing site was untenable only affirmed his beliefs.

You're in command. You have to be bigger than yourself, Darren.

"Alright. I'm right behind you, Daniels."

She nodded at him and led the way to the crowded staging area, and the waiting mass of refugees.

• • •

J.C. Rainier

```
Capt Haruka Kimura
Planetfall +4 days, early afternoon
Ex-Raphael sleeper pod eight
>|
```

A stiff breeze blew across the top of the wrecked pod, giving Haruka a brief respite from the relentless orange sun. Some of her companions on the gashed metal roof waved makeshift fans to cool themselves; others had managed to scrounge up hats and shorts from the personal belongings stowed in the lockers below. Most sported painful looking sunburns, but Haruka's burn had faded.

"Are you going to tell us why we're up here, Captain Kimura?" asked Troy Bryant. His tanned, leathery skin from years in the sun made him resistant to burning, though his brow looked almost lobster red.

James chimed in, "Yeah, why can't we have this meeting inside where I don't feel like I'm going to burn my eyes out if I look the wrong way?"

Haruka smiled. "I'd like to think that this is my first staff meeting, and I didn't want it to be interrupted by people who shouldn't be privy to the information."

Emilia's eyebrows rose quizzically. "Staff meeting?"

"You're not making any sense, Captain," Luis added. "Why so cryptic?"

"Because I didn't want to get ahead of myself, and I need to be sure that each of you is willing to accept what I ask of you," she replied.

"Alright, now you've got me a little scared," Emilia said in a sheepish voice.

"There shouldn't be any reason for that. What I'm asking is more along the lines of responsibility. As you all know, the military has a chain of command both on unit and service scale. This is something that is common with the private sector, though the lines are blurred a bit. Also, you all know that I am the only crew member currently linked with the survivors of this pod. What you might not be aware of is the fact that I am actually in command of every survivor from *Raphael*."

Haruka watched for a reaction and saw almost everyone exchange confused glances; only James kept his eyes on her. *He hasn't told any of them. Good.*

"Wait, what happened to that major that sent a broadcast before we crashed?" asked Troy.

"Major Emberley was on the bridge when it was exposed to space," she explained. "He and the skeleton bridge crew were all killed before they could even get off the ship. I was his First Officer, so that means I am in command. Now we're all in a sticky situation, and I have no backup for miles. That's where the four of you come in."

More glances were exchanged. Luis spoke first. "Come in how?"

"I can probably manage everyone in this pod as long as people keep focused and morale doesn't completely fall apart, but I don't want to leave anything to chance. I need support staff. I'd like to ask each of you to help me out with various matters, based on what I've seen each of you do." Haruka looked straight at Emilia and smiled. "Like you, Emilia. In fact, I believe you've already helped. Tell me, how is Gabrielle doing?"

"She's fine," Luis interrupted.

"I appreciate that, Luis, but I asked Emilia."

"No, he's right," Emilia said in a matter-of-fact tone. "I've been checking on her for the past couple of days like you asked and she has been the picture of health. That fruit that she ate doesn't seem to be poisonous."

"See? You've already helped me out. James, you helped fix the radio. Luis and Troy, your scouting reports have been very useful as well. What's more important is that all four of you have done what needed to be done without question or complaint."

"I'm confused," Troy chimed in. "Isn't that how you're supposed to act when you're in a tough spot?"

"Should and do are two different things. You four are doers, and that's why I want you to be on my staff. Emilia, how does Chief of Medical sound to you?"

Her jaw slacked and she made a stuttered choking noise. "Are you serious? I'm just a nurse, not a doctor."

"You did a good job patching up my shoulder here." Haruka traced her finger along the edge of the scab, careful not to catch a nail on any of the stitched parts of the wound. "I also heard that you tended to the injured right after the crash. Other than the fact that you went a little overboard on the morphine and knocked me out, you've performed admirably."

Emilia seemed to blush, though through her sunburn it was difficult to tell. "I thought you'd get up and over exert yourself if I didn't do that."

Haruka laughed. "You'd be right about that. You still haven't answered my question."

"Well, I guess it won't be much different from what I'm already doing. I'm in."

"Excellent. James, I'd like to offer you Chief of Ops. You'll be doing a lot more inventory work than you'd like, and you'll probably have to find lackeys when you need them, but your repair skills would also still be put to use."

"You know what?" he replied with a broad grin. "The ship may have crashed, but my family was saved from the War. Between that and the fact that you've managed to get my daughters away from their damn cell phones and texting, I'm on Cloud Nine. I'm your man, Captain."

Haruka nodded and then turned to Troy. "I was a bit conflicted with you, Troy. I know you worked in construction back on Earth, so your skills are unimaginably valuable. But you've also brought me the most detailed reports of the surrounding area. For now, I'd like you to be my Lead Scout."

Troy cocked his head to the side. "For now, Captain?"

"When the time comes I plan to put your other skills to use. If you accept the position, I want you to immediately start grooming one of your scouts to take your place. Trust me, the faith I place in you is great, no matter what the title or skill set I demand."

He nodded. "So you want me to be a scout now and help you build later, then. I can dig it."

"Luis, I understand that Gabi has been having a hard time with you going out on scouting runs," Haruka said. "And that your wife's hands are full with those two orphans. I'm taking you off of scouting assignment effective immediately and keeping you close to your family. I want you as my Chief of Security."

Luis exhaled, his shoulders slumped, and he smiled. "A change would be nice. Thank you, and I accept."

Haruka clapped her hands together. "Perfect. I have a staff now. Let's start this meeting. Since I'm sure none of you were prepared for this, I don't expect much in the way of reports or questions from you this first time around. I know that will change, and please feel free to bring up whatever topics or concerns you have in our meetings." She waited for her staff to nod in agreement. Her smile disappeared and her face hardened. "The issue for this meeting is huge. I don't want any of you to take this lightly because it affects the well being of every survivor in this pod. Simply put, we can't stay here and expect to be picked up, nor can we trust the pod in the long term. We have to move out."

Haruka waited for a surprised reaction or questions about why, but her four companions just looked at her and nodded, stone faced. Shocked, she asked, "Were you expecting this?"

James answered, "We've known it was a good possibility for a couple of days now. The pod has been quickly deteriorating, probably due to the stress of having been rolled during its landing. Take the rear ramp, for instance. It's getting really sticky when opening and closing. We're afraid it won't work at all in a couple more days."

"We held discussions with many of the survivors the night you first got here," Emilia added. "We figured that if you survived out there alone for a night with only a few supplies, that we as a whole group could support each other to move somewhere else. We just never knew where."

Next was Troy's turn. "Also, none of us wanted to give the order. We were kind of hoping you would. We may be forming bonds with people here, but you're a military officer. Your word gets people to move."

I think Sergeant Leight would disagree with that.

"Alright," Haruka said. "Do you think we could get everyone ready to move by first light tomorrow?"

"I think we can manage that if we get to work on it soon," said James.

"Good. Get all the gear in order. I'll give priority lists that you can work through so we maximize the usefulness of what we take. We can use any passenger luggage that has shoulder or arm straps to increase our carrying capacity. Troy, get your four best scouts together; they're going as a separate group on a side mission."

"Pathfinding?" he asked.

"No. I want them to carry as much food and water as you can and make for the area where pod ten went down. There have been no reports from there, but that doesn't mean that the pod is lost. Their radio might be broken like ours was. If you find any survivors, bring them down the coast to the pod eleven site. That's where our main group will head."

"You got it, Captain." He turned to face James. "Mind if I take your boy Will? He's done real good so far."

The color drained from James's face for a moment, but he nodded. "Just take real good care of him, okay?"

Troy laughed, a deep rumble from his belly. "That street goes both ways. You've gotta watch over my daughter Gina while I'm not in camp. Lord help you with three teenage girls around."

James gulped, and his knees looked like they might buckle. "You're a cruel man, Bryant."

Haruka smiled and shook her head. "Luis, I need you to distribute the weapons and make sure that the armed survivors are spaced throughout the party when we move. We should have about a dozen rifles after we're done arming Troy's scouts. If you find that others are willing to carry pistols, you can distribute them as you see fit."

"Will do, Captain," he replied.

"Emilia," she continued. "I want you to show all of the passengers what that fruit that Gabi ate looks like. Let them know that it is edible, and they can eat any they find along the way, but also let them know that we don't know what else may be edible or poisonous, and to avoid consuming any other native plants until we identify and test them."

"Yes, Captain."

Haruka looked at her companions and was struck by the realization that, formalities aside, they reacted to her orders just as a subordinate officer would. *My command,* she thought.

"Let's get to work," she said, and followed them down into the belly of the broken pod.

• • •

Calvin McLaughlin
3 April 2058, 14:37
Michael
>|

He opened his eyes slowly. The stench of body odor permeated the air. When Cal felt along his body, his hands became slick with sweat. His back arched slightly above the sleeper's bed, and his restraints stretched across his chest.

Oh God, not this again.

He reached over and clicked his clock on. 4-3-2058 14:37.

No, no, no, not again.

Cal released his harness and tore the straps loose, then flung his sleeper berth open. His legs shot forth as he aimed for the deck plating, but he ended up slamming back first into the opposing sleepers.

Wait, there's no gravity. It's different this time.

Cal made his way to the ESAARC cockpit and took a quick glance out of the windows. He sighed in relief when he saw the black expanse of space, dotted by hundreds of tiny points of light.

We're not there yet, maybe it's not too late. Maybe this time I'm actually awake.

He snaked his way out of the pod and into the gallery. The lights were about twice as bright as they had been during the journey, though not as bright as when he first boarded. From the forward section of the ship, Cal could just make out a voice. He could not hear the words, but he still knew its owner by the distinctive New England accent: Colonel Dayton. Cal launched down the hall to find the ship's commander.

He has to know. I need to warn him.

As he approached the bridge, he could see the crew arranged just outside the air lock, some holding on to carts, and some floating slowly around like sharks circling in the water. There were also more crew than he had ever seen active; Cal took a guess and figured that the entire crew was awake, not just the skeleton maintenance crew. Dayton was at the air lock, giving orders to the crew.

"Hartley, your team needs to do final maintenance and dump the waste fuel. I want triple inspections on all propulsion systems. Ceretti, your team is to distribute standard emergency supplies to all pods," Dayton barked.

Cal drifted into position just beyond the clustered crew.

"Drisko, your team will begin a full inventory of the cargo pods as soon as Ceretti's team has pulled their supplies from the lower level."

Damn it, this is going to take forever.

Dayton continued, "Gibbins, your nav team is to take control…"

"We need to help them," Cal interrupted in a booming voice.

Silence fell for a moment as the entire crew turned to face Cal.

"Excuse me, Mr. McLaughlin, but this meeting is for the crew only. Please return to your pod until…"

"No, you've got to listen to me. They're going to crash, we need to help them."

A hard scowl scrawled across Dayton's face. "What the hell are you talking about?"

"I saw it! They're going to crash if we don't help them. Please, Colonel. They're all going to die." Cal's voice began to crack as he pled with *Michael's* commanding officer.

"You're not making any sense. What did you see? Who crashed?"

Cal became irritated at the colonel's lack of understanding. He knew that the situation was dire, but no one else seemed to care, even Dayton. "Another ship. I saw it in my nightmares. They crashed on a hill, and there were no survivors. You gave a eulogy and… and.." Cal's eyes raked across the crowd until the fixed on Hunter, whose eyes widened as he realized Cal had singled him out. "You. You kept me from helping them. And then you had your little Honor Guard give them a final salute. We could have helped them, Hunter. You stopped me."

Dayton's scowl relaxed, and his look changed to one of pity. "You're not well, Mr. McLaughlin. Please return to your pod so that Doctor Taylor can look after you."

"Damn it, Colonel, no! Please, get someone on the radio. Warn them. Warn the other ships to be careful. Please, they have to know. We're the only ones that can save them."

"I don't have time for this," Dayton muttered and disappeared around the corner.

Cal swept his eyes across the crowd again. "Damn it, *someone* needs to help them. Hunter, you can make it right. Please… Cameron, you use the radio, right? Just… just call out to the other ships and make sure they know, okay?" The weight of their collective stares weighed on his chest, and he found it difficult to breathe. "What? What are you all staring at? For God's sake *do something* or their blood will be on our hands! I can't take that again. No, not again. Please."

Colonel Dayton emerged from inside the airlock just as Hunter started to speak, "Calvin, do what the colonel says. I'm worried for you, man. Doc will fix you up, I promise."

"This is your last warning, son," Dayton said gruffly. "Go back to your pod right this minute."

Cal studied the expression of every person whose stare fell on him. Some were confused, others seemed to show annoyance. Hunter, Drisko, and Hartley all looked at him with concern. Then Cal's eyes met Lieutenant Josephson. Her impish grin and gleaming eyes gave it all away; she was enjoying watching Cal suffer. Something about her delight struck deep into Cal's soul, and he froze in a moment of fear.

No. No, it can't be. She's making them wait. This is all her fault!

"What are you looking at, Josephson?" Cal asked with a sneer.

She made no response other than to fold her arms and grin wider.

Cal turned back to Dayton. "Colonel, are you just going to let her sit back and manipulate you like that?"

"Enough," Dayton barked.

"You're letting them all die," Cal screamed at the top of his lungs.

Cal felt his arm twist to the side followed by a momentary sharp pain a second later. He craned his neck to see a syringe plunged into a vein. Dr. Taylor pressed the plunger, and its contents flowed into Cal as he looked in her eyes and asked one last word.

"Why?"

His vision blurred quickly, and he blacked out.

• • •

Colonel Eriksen's beard curled into what was probably a smile, or at least as close as the man ever got to one. "That's the last of the duty assignments for arrival, ladies and gentlemen. We're just about home."

Darius sighed in relief. He looked around and saw the same relief wash over the nearly full crew compliment of *Gabriel*. Captain Quinn gave Darius a smile and a curt nod. Darius got the impression that the "nearly full" part was weighing on Quinn more than most.

Lieutenant Reid is still in stasis. They were clearly friends, not just crewmates. Darius felt a measure of sorrow for Quinn. *I hope he understands that Reid knew the risks, just like Dr. Kimura said.*

"One more thing before we start," Eriksen continued. The crew quickly settled down and listened. "I understand that these past forty or so years have been hard on the skeleton crew more than most of you, but my appreciation for the fine job that has been performed by the crew thus far goes out to all of you. Each of you performed your duties admirably from launch, and I have every expectation that you do the same as we bring this ship safely to our new home. There will still be a world of work to do when we arrive, in a very literal sense. Just know that when the time is right, you will all be honored and given extra leave."

Whoops rose from the crowd, and Eriksen laughed for the first time that Darius could remember.

"Now let's bring our angel home. To your assignments, please."

The air was charged with enthusiasm as the crew dispersed to their assigned stations. Darius made his way to his familiar post on the bridge with renewed vigor. As he had done so many times over the many maintenance cycles, he strapped in, carefully settled his headset, and turned on his terminal to check the communications box for ship to ship transmissions.

Another skill that Darius had gained over those cycles was the ability to differentiate between background noise and inter-ship communication by using file size as a reference point. He immediately deleted all the miniscule files that would contain only ticks and statics, and then opened the first of the remaining files.

An intra-ship communication played through his earpiece, and the speaker was a man whose voice he had not heard before.

"This is Sergeant Overton of the sleeper ship *Raphael*. We have arrived two months ahead of your projected landing, so by the time you receive this message, we will be at work on the planet building the beginnings of the new colony. We would like to note that, in keeping with the name of our new planet, the crew has decided to name the inner moon "Arion" and the outer moon "Persephone". We are currently heading for our selected landing site and this radio beacon will be there and broadcasting in case you do not hear this full message. Set your radio beacon trackers and follow the signal in. Should there be a malfunction of the beacon, please land at our pre-selected site: 36.1 degrees north latitude, 126.0 degrees east longitude. On behalf of the crew of *Raphael*, we look forward to seeing you, and welcome home."

Darius scribbled the coordinates on a virtual notepad on his terminal screen, and then opened the next communication file. A different voice spoke this time, and the urgency in his voice and the thunderous background noise filled Darius with dread immediately.

"[static]…Major Nathan Emberley of *Raphael*. We have suffered… [static] …in our propulsion section. We can't land without… [garbled] …going critical. We are maneuvering to emergency drop… [inaudible] …pods will try for the landing site if possible, but… [static] …if we have to. We will need… [screech] …beacons. I repeat, this is… [static] …reactor is going critical. We are launching…"

The final ten seconds of the file contained heavy static, then the transmission cut off abruptly.

Darius's heart sank and his fingers went numb. He stared at the coordinates that sat on the screen in front of them, but the numbers lost all meaning as his mind tried to cope with what he had just heard.

Oh God no…

Darius scrolled through the available files and found more broadcasts that were recorded after the distress call. He opened one up, but it was a repeat of Sergeant Overton's beacon recording. One after another, Darius opened the files in hopes that one contained another transmission or more information. His stomach knotted tighter with each repeat of the beacon recording. He finished with the files in the inbox, but there were no other transmissions, only the distress call and several repeats of the beacon.

His hands trembled as he looked around the bridge to see who else was present. Quinn sat at an engineering station, and he could make out Lieutenant Schneider at nav. Colonel Eriksen slowly made his way to the command chair as he chatted quietly with Dr. Kimura. Darius frowned. He knew that the colonel needed to be made aware of the distress call, but he could not divulge the information in front of Kimura, whose oldest daughter was onboard the stricken ship.

Darius pretended to work, glancing back every minute or so to see if the doctor had left the bridge. He was given no such luck; Dr. Kimura remained at Eriksen's side the whole time. The seconds ticked away and the dire knowledge burned within Darius. He tried to occupy himself and bide his time further, but he could not suppress the need to tell the colonel. He moved up to the command platform and waited for an acknowledgement from his CO.

Eriksen looked at Darius with a piercing gaze. "Can I help you, Mr. Owens?"

"Sir, can I speak with you alone for a moment?"

Eriksen nodded at Darius, and then Dr. Kimura. The doctor bowed slightly and floated gracefully off. As he passed Darius, Dr. Kimura gave him a curious look. Darius swallowed and tried to suppress any visual cues of his discomfort.

"Sir," Darius spoke in a low tone after Kimura disappeared from the bridge. "We received the expected site beacon message from *Raphael*, but there was another message as well. Sir… *Raphael* broadcast an emergency message about their reactor going critical."

"What?" Eriksen rasped under his breath.

"I think it's legit, Colonel. The message had a lot of static and broken sections, but it was clear enough that their reactor had a problem severe enough to warrant an emergency drop."

"You're talking about a worst case scenario, Lieutenant. Have you received any beacon responses from the pods?"

"Negative, sir. I don't know if that means anything yet. The radios on the pods are short range; we probably won't be able to pick them up until we're closer to Demeter."

Eriksen seemed to sink into his chair as the shock registered on his face. "Captain Quinn," he said over his shoulder. "Do you have a copy of the passenger matrix for *Raphael*?"

"Yes Colonel. What do you need?"

"Total passenger count including crew."

"One moment, please." There was a moment of agonizing silence. "Two thousand, two hundred and forty four."

Eriksen closed his eyes and bowed his head. Darius swallowed again but could not shake the lump in his throat. He realized that they would not know whether or not the drop succeeded until they got within the limited range of the pods' emergency beacons.

"Does anyone else know yet?" Eriksen asked.

"No, sir."

"Keep it that way for now. I want you to go through the schematics of the pods' com systems. Figure out how far their signal can go. If we haven't heard by 75% of their maximum range, we will revisit this." The colonel met Darius's gaze. "Under no circumstances do you tell Doctor Kimura, do you understand me? Not even as a friend."

Darius nodded slowly and made his way toward the computer core so he could work undisturbed.

. . .

Capt Haruka Kimura
Planetfall +5 days, early evening
Six miles west of ex-Raphael pod eight crash site
>|

Haruka placed one sweat-soaked boot in front of another as she paced her way toward the rear of the scattered, curling column of passengers. She methodically counted heads as she made her way through the group, slowing down where the crowd was the thickest, so as not miss or double count any passengers. They were all resting for a few minutes, which gave Haruka an easy opportunity to make the count. As she made her way to the end of the line, she beamed.

So far so good, haven't lost anyone in the jungle.

The short days of Demeter, the size of their party, and the presence of a number of small children made their march from the pod very slow. At times, machete wielding survivors had to cluster in front of the party and hack through the denser sections of undergrowth. Haruka wasn't entirely sure how swiftly they could move everyone while keeping the group together, but she was starting to get an idea. The journey that she thought might take two days now looked as if it would take four at the least.

It's a good thing that Gabi's fruit is edible. That will really help stretch our food supplies.

Haruka turned to make her way for the head of the column, where she was accustomed to walking. She made a mental note of how the guards with rifles were distributed, and nodded in silent approval. James strode toward her at a hurried pace. The belt he had been issued fit awkwardly on his slight frame, and the holstered pistol made him look like the world's geekiest cowboy. He waved at Haruka as he approached.

"Well?" she asked.

"We didn't see any other good places to stop for the night. We'll be able to watch over everyone if we stay here; I can't say the same if we try to press on."

"Alright. Have your team distribute any necessary supplies. I'll work on getting this group settled back here. Find Luis and have him do the same up front."

James nodded and jogged off. Haruka cleared her throat to address the weary travelers near her.

"We're going to bed down here for the night," she said in her most commanding voice. "Please take this time to eat your supper, no more than one ration package per person. If you need to, supplement your meal with the fruit that the staff showed you during your briefings. If you are on guard duty assigned to shift two, please try to get some rest right now so that you're fresh later."

Haruka watched as people began to mill about, retrieving food from whatever pack or makeshift sling they had, or looking for a more comfortable patch of ground. An increasing low tone din let her know that the entire camp was engaged in similar activity.

I couldn't have imagined this going more smoothly, she thought.

She slowly walked toward the head of the column, studying the faces of her survivors along the way. She couldn't help but notice the diverse ways in which people interacted; some quietly went about their business as if it were routine, others loudly expressed their safety concerns to anyone who would listen. Children huddled close by their parents, looking at their surroundings with wide eyes as they peeked from under protective arms or over shoulders. Haruka stopped to check on a young mother and her child, making sure that they had all the food and bedding they needed for the night. When she was satisfied with their situation, she pressed on.

A shrill shriek and the angry bark of a woman cut through the noise of the camp. Haruka craned her head in the direction of the noise and doubled her step. Gabi bolted through the camp headlong in Haruka's direction, but did not seem to be paying attention to where she was going. Gabi tripped over a backpack and flailed to a tumbling stop at Haruka's feet. She got to her knees, sobbing, with her eyes locked on the ground.

"What's wrong, Gabi?"

"Mama doesn't love me," she choked through her tears.

Haruka paused as the weight of the little girl's accusation took her voice for a moment. "What? Why would you say something like that?"

"Because it's true. She doesn't love me anymore."

Haruka leaned her rifle against a tree and dropped to her knees next to Gabi. "What happened to make you think that?"

"She yelled at me, and she only pays attention to Aidan now."

"Why do you think she yelled at you?" asked James as he sidled up next to Haruka.

"Because she's mean and she doesn't love me anymore."

"No, honey," he replied. "She might be upset for a moment, but she loves you. I bet she's going to give you a big hug and say sorry in a couple minutes."

Gabi hugged her knees to her chest and a pout stretched across her face. James glanced at Haruka, who returned a stumped shrug.

"Don't worry, I got this. Just keep her here for a minute," he said as he darted off into the thick of the camp.

Great, what the hell do I do now? Haruka shifted her weight as she searched for an answer to the great awkward silence between the two. It was one thing to act as Gabi's protector and try to keep her occupied; this was the premise of her service. Comforting the girl after a family argument was a different level of intensity for which she was not prepared. Haruka couldn't find a way to explain to her why her mother just needed to cool off, at least not in a way she felt that Gabi could understand. The time for her to come up with something meaningful passed too quickly.

"Gabrielle Juanita Serrano!" Maria yelled as she stormed toward her daughter. "You do not run away from me like that, Mija. Get back to our campsite right now and apologize to Aidan."

Gabi's tears flowed anew at the sound of her mother's rebuke. Haruka rose to her feet and stepped between Maria and Gabi, putting her palm out toward Maria. "Take it easy, she's really upset right now."

Maria snorted. "She better be, after what she did."

"What could she have done so wrong that you have to yell at her like that? She's just a kid."

"She hit Aidan in the head with a stick really hard."

Haruka sighed and shook her head. *Oh no, Gabi…* She took a knee and softly asked, "Is this true?" Gabi nodded quickly and wiped away a tear with the back of her hand. "Why?"

"Because Mama loves him more than me now. It's not fair."

Maria's face twisted in shock, and her mouth dropped open. Haruka could see tears form in her eyes, and when she spoke, her voice wavered. "Gabi, I love you more than anything. How could you ever think that?"

"Because it's true. You never hug me anymore and you spend all your time with Aidan and Marya. I was hungry, and you would only feed him and not me." Anger seethed in the girl's voice as she stared down her mother.

Maria moved to her daughter's side, knelt next to her, and rubbed her hand on her back. "Gabi, I've told you this before. Aidan and

Marya's mama and papa are gone, and they're never coming back. They're really, *really* sad right now, and I'm just trying to help them."

"I know, but it still makes me angry."

"Do you remember what it was like when you were alone in the jungle before I found you?" Haruka asked.

"Yeah, I was really scared."

"Did you miss your mom and dad?"

"Yeah."

"And would you miss them if they weren't at the pod when I brought you back?"

"Yeah, a million billion times."

"That's what Aidan and Marya are going through," Maria added. "They miss their mama and papa, and they will never see them again."

Gabi's eyes widened and her jaw slacked as the realization set in. She hung her head sheepishly. "I'm sorry, Mama."

"You need to apologize to Aidan for hitting him."

"I will, I promise."

"Can you promise me something else, Mija?"

"Yeah, Mama."

"Promise to help me with Aidan and Marya. They need you to be their friend."

Impulse drove Haruka, and before she could think, she blurted, "Not their friend. Their sister."

Maria looked at Haruka and smiled. "That's right, they need a sister. Someone to give them hugs, and to play with them, and help them when they need it."

"But I'm not their sister."

"You can be like one," Haruka replied. "I have a sister, and she's one of the most wonderful people I know. We've had some fights now and then, but we've had a lot of really good times. She was on another ship, and I really miss her. Do you know what I miss the most?" Gabi shook her head and looked at her, wide-eyed. "I miss talking with her over dessert about how our days went, and about what our friends did, and about those silly boys. That was my favorite thing when I was a girl."

Gabi giggled. "Silly boys."

"Just remember, there's a silly boy that is hurting and needs a hug. When you go back with your mom, can you do that for me?"

Gabi nodded. James came jogging back with a pack slung over his shoulder, panting hard. On his heels was Luis, who nearly fell on Gabi in his zeal to reach and throw his arms around his distressed daughter. He lifted her off the ground like she weighed nothing and plopped her down in his lap.

Haruka leaned over and whispered in Maria's ear, "Is Aidan okay?"

"Yes. He's got a nasty cut on his head and he's pretty upset, but he's fine. Emilia is with him right now." She paused for a moment. "Good job with her. You made that look easy."

I'm not even sure what I did. I'm terrible with kids. Haruka had to admit to herself that she was on edge about the interaction. She wasn't sure if her words would help or hurt the situation, but they came out without her usual self control. She watched as Luis looked into Gabi's eyes, his hands gently wrapped around her tiny arms.

"Gabi, please don't run off and scare me like that," he said.

"I'm sorry, Papa, I won't."

James unzipped the pack and revealed an assortment of stuffed bears, dogs, and other animals in a dizzying array of colors. "Gabi, is one of these yours?"

She rifled through the animals and her eyes lit up as she grabbed and hugged a fluffy tuxedo-colored cat. Its white spots were smeared with dirt and grime, and its head and face clearly showed a great deal of wear. "Pelusina!" she exclaimed as she squeezed the plush toy tight against her chest.

He smiled and patted her on the head. "You go with your mom and dad back to your camp, okay?"

Gabi nodded and walked next to her father, grasping his hand and clutching her stuffed cat with her other. The three made their way back toward the front of the column. When they were out of earshot, Haruka turned to James with a crooked grin.

"Really? I ask you to pack up critical supplies and leave behind the junk, and you come back with a backpack full of stuffed animals?"

"You've never been a parent," he retorted. "You don't have a clue just how critical these little things are. Look around you, Haruka. How many small children do you see?"

"I don't need to see to know, I have a head count. Eight."

He shook his head. "That's how many there are under the age of eight. You're thinking along the lines of spreadsheets and manifests, not the human element. Almost all of these kids out here are still terrified. Here, a stuffed animal means something to kids as old as fourteen."

"You're joking, right?"

"Not even a little. Kristin, my youngest, started crying when I told her that we were heading out from the pod. I'm talking bawling her head off, screaming like a banshee, wake the dead kind of crying. She hasn't held a stuffed animal in two years, or slept with one in five. I gave her this bear here," he said as he pulled a fluffy panda bear from his sack, "quieted her down in just a couple minutes. To me and Jeanette, sharing the duty of carrying this backpack is more than worth the burden. You've just seen why."

Haruka nodded. "Yes, you showed that quite well. There's something else you just demonstrated as proficiently."

"Oh? What's that?"

"That I chose the best man for the job." She smiled brightly. "Go on; get back to your family. It's dinner time."

"Alright, come along then." Haruka was about to protest, but he hushed her. "I'm not taking no for an answer. You're not spending the night out there alone, so it's either I join you or you join us. And since you've already *commanded* me to go back to my family that means you're coming with me."

Haruka sighed. "Alright, but I'm not sleeping with a teddy bear."

James smirked. "Of course not. You get the stuffed dog."

• • •

A soft light filtered through his eyelids, bringing an end to the darkness and dreams. Cal's head spun and his stomach threatened to turn on him at a moment's notice. A whispering noise slowly filled his ears; at first he thought this was the life support system circulating air, but his core felt a chill when he realized it was something else.

This is on you, the piercing whisper of his own voice cut into his mind. *You failed. Now it's all at an end.*

"No," he croaked through parched lips. His eyes fluttered open to reveal his position. He was strapped into a sleeper berth, and the hatch was wide open. The modest illumination from the hallway bathed him. He tried to bring his hands to his face to wipe away the cold sweat, but they were hampered just above his waist. A glance down his body at a glint of metal told him that someone had cannibalized an empty sleeper for its restraints, and used them to bind him to the berth.

It's only right. You should be treated like a criminal, the hiss in his head criticized sharply. *Two thousand dead, thanks to you.*

Cal felt a quick throb of pain as his lower lip split open when he spoke. "I tried. He wouldn't listen. They wouldn't listen. None of them."

For a moment, Cal thought he saw a fleeting shadow cross in front of the berth. He craned his neck in an effort to catch a glimpse of the source. Unable to spot anything, he strained to hear for any sounds of breath or footsteps that might indicate that he wasn't alone. He pursed his lips and tasted the sharp metallic tang of his blood.

You didn't try. All you did was rant like a lunatic.

"They were against me. Even Hunter." Cal's good hand curled into a tight fist and his nails bit into his palms. "Hunter. He betrayed me. He's supposed to be my friend, to stick up for me. He watched as Doctor Taylor shot me full of… full of…"

A broken, angered curse escaped from Cal's throat like the growl of a cornered animal.

She did more to you than anyone else.

Cal could feel his temper flare. His eyes wandered to a small bandage on his arm that marked the spot where Dr. Taylor had thrust the needle into his flesh. The scene replayed in the recesses of his mind, up until the point where the plunge of the syringe pushed some form of powerful sedative into him, and the blackness overtook all. His blood felt as if it would boil from within. He recounted the hours spent with her, learning to assist her with the passenger checks, working out in *Michael's* gym, even sharing his meals with her. The torrent of rage reduced the sum of all their interactions to a convenient plot to gain his trust.

"She… she betrayed me the worst."

She put an end to your chance to convince Dayton. But she's just an old woman. You are still responsible for letting her get the best of you. You didn't fight; you just sat there and let her ram that needle into you like a pincushion.

"I didn't see her," Cal protested in a hushed voice.

Because you were too busy raving like a lunatic. A distant, haunting laugh sent shivers through his body. *She was right about you. You did go utterly nuts, didn't you? No wonder Colonel Dayton wouldn't listen to you.*

Cal growled again. "Damn it, you're just as bad as the other me. Just show your face, you coward. It's not like I can do anything to you."

The shadow returned along with the clank of long strides on the deck plate. Knowing that there was still no gravity, Cal understood exactly who it was he was about to confront, even before the face came into view through the open berth portal.

"There's a reason for that," his doppelganger said through a smug grin.

"I should have known sooner. After all, I'm utterly nuts, as you've been so kind to point out. It's not a stretch that I'm talking to myself again."

"Ah, but this is a stretch you haven't taken before. Every time you've had the pleasure of my company, you've been asleep. That is, until now."

Cal turned his head and gazed at the ceiling for a moment before closing his eyes. "I'm still asleep."

"So pinch yourself."

"You're kidding, right?"

"Nope."

"You're insane."

"Now there's the pot calling the kettle black," his twin replied dryly.

"Fine," Cal said with a sigh and opened his eyes. His fingers scrabbled at his thigh until he got a good grip, then clenched down as hard as he could. His eyes shot wide and he tried to stifle a yelp of pain.

"Told you."

Cal laughed nervously at first. He tried to comprehend the fact that he was awake, and arguing with a clone of himself that was not bound by the laws of physics. As the realization sunk in, his laughter took on a chilling maniacal tone for almost two minutes, before it broke down into a pathetic sobbing.

"Oh God, it happened. I broke…. I'm *broken*. She's never going to forgive me. She's never going to love me," Cal spluttered through his tears. "No, no… I can't face her like this. I can't…"

"Worry about yourself before you worry about that girl, idiot. She's the reason you've done oh, I'd say about two thirds of the dumb crap you have since you got on board." The patience in the voice of his specter was growing thin.

Cal shook his head hard and tried to bite his tongue, hoping that the pain would somehow make it all go away. His mind raced to the milky white skin of Alexis's cheeks, to her long, unbound hair, and to her soft red lips. Lips that seemed alight to Cal. Irresistible. He felt drawn to them like a moth to a flame. The world began to spin around him as the thought of one more kiss with her consumed him.

"Hey, what are you dreaming about in there?" taunted his twin.

"Her."

"Give it a rest. She's locked up until you reach the planet."

"No, Dayton promised that he'd wake her up during the final approach cycle."

Echoing laughter in his own voice filled his head. "He also promised to let you study for the entire approach cycle. How did that work out, exactly? Let me see here. Oh, that's right. He screamed at you, told you to shut up, and had his medical officer put your sorry ass back to sleep." The hackles on Cal's neck rose as his tormentor leaned in next to his ear and whispered, "A great way to keep a promise, don't you think?"

Cal snarled and lunged with his hands towards the throat of his alter ego, but the restraints held him fast, like a dog at the end of a leash. After a moment of grunting and straining, he gave up, and the restraints went slack.

He's right. Dayton broke his promise to me.

"And there it is. You've finally seen the light."

"God damn it, get out of my head. That's really starting to piss me off."

"I'm sorry, Calvin, what was that?" asked Dr. Taylor from just out of sight.

His specter snickered. "Ooh, company, this could be fun. Let's see how this plays out, huh mush brain?"

Cal let out a long growl of frustration. His fingers locked like talons as anger coursed through him nearly unchecked. Somewhere deep inside of him, a voice of restraint called out, mostly drowned out by his rage.

"I said get out, I don't want you here. Is that too hard to understand?"

Cal's twin spoke at the same time as Dr. Taylor, and the discordant overlapping of their voices made him cringe. He could not understand either of them, but he couldn't wrap his mind around how strong his imaginary assailant's words were against the doctor's voice. Cal growled again, this time both anguished and enraged.

"Please, try to calm down. I don't want to have to sedate you again."

"No," Cal screamed. "No more. That won't help."

"Then you need to calm down. Take a deep breath, Calvin."

As much as he didn't want to talk to Dr. Taylor, Cal did his best to heed her advice. He began to draw in deep breaths of air, and let them out in a regular pattern. His anger started to ebb, and he relaxed his hands.

"Aww, isn't that cute," his specter mocked. "A couple words and you're playing lap dog to Dayton's lap dog."

"Shut up."

"Calvin, I didn't say anything," said Dr. Taylor. She floated into view and to the edge of the sleeper. She edged over, and the right side of her body occupied the same space as that of the left side of Cal's doppelganger. His form morphed at the point where the two came together, distorting his body in a hideous manner. Cal's stomach lurched and he had to fight the urge to throw up. "You look sick, are you sure I can't get you anything?"

Cal shook his head and swallowed hard. "I.. I just need…" he searched for an excuse to get rid of her. "I just need to be alone for a minute, okay?"

"Fine, I can take a hint," said his doppelganger, feigning indignity. Cal blinked and only Dr. Taylor remained when his eyes opened. His stomach settled almost at once.

"Are you sure? You're definitely not yourself, and I don't want you to get hurt," Dr. Taylor said softly.

Cal sighed. "What does it matter? I failed. Two thousand people are going to die because of me, and Colonel Dayton couldn't care less."

"No one is going to die because of you. You've just been acting really strange since you came out of biostasis, and now I'm starting to get the idea that something is truly bothering you. Would you care to explain it to me?"

"You know all about my dreams when I'm in stasis."

Dr. Taylor nodded.

"There was one I had that was disturbingly real. I've had dreams with gravity, or with people I knew, or with the ship, but never in such a combination, or such…" his voice trailed off.

Dr. Taylor stared at him for a moment before breaking the silence. "What? Go on, please."

"Everything was so real: the feel of the grass, the smell of the air, and the voices of the crew. We landed on Demeter, and came on the wreck of a sleeper ship. God, there was so much fire and smoke. I wanted to help, but you and Hunter held me back while the colonel gave a speech. When you guys left, I searched the ship. I didn't find anyone."

"No one was left alive?"

Cal thought for a moment. "No, there just was no one. No bodies, no survivors. Just a burning wreck." He caught her looking over her shoulder as she fidgeted. "What's wrong?"

"Nothing. It's time to start your treatment."

"No," he said sternly. "There's something you're not telling me. I may be nuts, but I still have the right to know."

"Look, you're stressed out and exhausted, to say the least. Let's just…"

"No, God damn it," he yelled. "Tell me what it is."

Dr. Taylor sighed. Even floating in the air in front of him, she looked deflated. Her eyes met his and he could see a deep sorrow within them.

"When we woke from stasis, Sergeant Drisko picked up the automated beacon from *Raphael* giving information on the planet and its moons, as well as the landing site they had chosen. Then we found something else, recorded in the com system. A distress call from *Raphael*."

Cal felt his heart drop into his feet. His nightmare had been realized, yet he knew he needed to hear confirmation, just to be certain.

"We haven't been able to contact *Raphael* since receiving the distress call. From what I know, and I didn't ask too much, they suffered a catastrophic failure. Colonel Dayton is proceeding under the assumption that there are no survivors."

Then that's it. There's truly nothing that can be done.

"How many people were on *Raphael*?"

"Just over twenty two hundred. She was the biggest ship in the fleet."

More than two thousand. Gone like that, and it's on my hands.

"I know you think that this could have been avoided," she continued. "Hunter told me about the rest of your rant. The fact is there was nothing we could have done. He tells me that the incident likely happened about a week ago, before we woke up." She hesitated for a moment. "I'm sorry. Now let's just focus on getting you better."

Cal swallowed and nodded. As Dr. Taylor drifted away from the opening, he again became lost in his thoughts. There was a nagging sense somewhere deep inside that, while he was going to receive treatment for his psychosis, that Colonel Dayton was simply going to shuffle Cal aside until the landing.

He broke his promise to you, he thought. *Your plan to make amends just got crushed. So what now?*

"It's not right," he blurted.

"What's that?" Dr. Taylor called.

"He screwed me."

"What are you talking about?"

"Colonel Dayton. He made a promise, and now he's breaking it. He's got me tied up here so his crew doesn't have to see me."

"He's only making the decisions he feels is best for the crew and the mission. You had a pretty spectacular outburst. Do you even remember it?"

"Most of it."

"So you can appreciate why he had me sedate you, right?"

He thought for a moment and couldn't deny the logic behind it. "Still, I don't appreciate being strapped in here like an animal. It's not right, and it's not fair."

She returned with a large syringe full of a cloudy concoction. There was no needle at the end, he noticed. Dr. Taylor brought it up to his face. "Here, drink this and go back to sleep. I'll see what I can do about your grievances."

He shied away for a moment. "Not more sedatives, right?"

"No, this is an anti psychotic agent. It'll probably taste terrible, but it should help you with the symptoms you're having."

"Like the other me that comes and has a chat with me?"

Dr. Taylor stopped for a moment, seemingly stunned. "Let's hope so. I want to know every time he shows up, okay?"

"Fine," he said, and opened his mouth to accept the medication. It splashed across his tongue and he almost gagged from the bitterness, but managed to choke it down.

"I'll be back later to check on you."

"Thanks, Doc."

She moved out of sight. The lights dimmed slightly, and Cal was left once more, alone and restrained. He waited for what seemed like hours for Dr. Taylor to check on him, or even to come back and talk. His eyelids became heavy and he eventually gave up on the hope of talking to anyone but himself, and shut his eyes.

• • •

This is the task that I have been dreading, Darius thought as he passed the desolate maw of pod one. *I should have done this sooner, Eriksen's orders be damned.*

While Darius understood his commanding officer's reasoning for the delay, he thoroughly believed that Dr. Kimura would have been able to perform his duty despite the heavy news. At the very worst, he might need a day to compose himself and continue on. He could not bear to wait for the pods' radio threshold to be reached, weeks down the line.

The man deserves to know, no matter what. What right do we have to hold news of his daughter from him? It's insubordination, but it's also what's right.

Darius exited the gallery and halted his motion just inside the open airlock to pod four. He sighed and mentally ran through the speech he had prepared. He had no idea why he had bothered to prepare one, other than for a sense of readiness. When the time came to deliver the news of *Raphael's* destruction, he knew that the speech would fall to pieces. Darius shook his head and pushed off of the wall, snaking his way through the corridors to the ESAARC cockpit. He slid the door open and received a warm smile from Dr. Kimura.

"Ah, Darius. I was just finishing lunch," he said as he stowed a thick brown plastic wrapper in one of the storage bins. "To what do I owe the pleasure of your company?"

Darius maneuvered his frame into the seat next to the doctor and loosely pulled the restraints over his shoulders. *I'm about to devastate him,* he thought with a heavy sigh.

The smile faded quickly from the scientist's face, and his brows arched in concern. "Darius, what is wrong?"

"We received a transmission – a distress call – from *Raphael.* They had a reactor malfunction." Goosebumps rose on his skin and he got a sudden chill as Dr. Kimura looked like a deer frozen in the headlights. "We have been unable to make any further contact. I'm sorry, but it looks like there are no survivors."

The doctor's mouth opened as he tried to speak. Nothing came out, nor did Darius expect his friend to be able to respond. Tears welled in

Dr. Kimura's eyes, pooling up until they floated away. His lips trembled and the corners of his mouth twisted in despair.

"H-Haruka?"

"We haven't heard from her. We're still out of range of the ESAARC pods' emergency radio."

Darius could not bear to look him in the eye any longer. The weight pressed on his chest and felt as if it would squeeze the breath out of him.

"I'm so terribly sorry, Doctor."

I can't possibly imagine what you are feeling. When Mama passed my world turned upside down, but I knew the Lord was going to take her. To suddenly have the prospect of losing your daughter, in an accident…

Dr. Tadashi Kimura broke down into a sobbing mess. Darius blindly reached over and clasped him on the shoulder. He felt his own emotions surge within him. Though he meant to comfort his friend, he could do little more than keep his own calm while holding the man's shoulder. Minutes passed as the elder man wept. Darius sat by, waiting for something to break the tension.

"I am losing everything," the doctor coughed between sobs.

"Again, I'm very sorry. I can't imagine what you must be going through, but you've got to keep your head up, for your family."

"My family," he parroted. "They are falling apart. Haruka is dead. Saika is pregnant and I have no idea what the stasis is doing to her. Her husband and I are accused of capital crimes. And neither Sarah nor Saika have the slightest clue as to what is about to hit them."

"We don't know that she's dead, Doc."

"The reactor failed."

"That it did."

"And you have heard nothing from the crew."

"That's right. But like I said, the pods are…"

"I appreciate your consideration, Darius," the doctor snapped, "but we both know that the chances of surviving a reactor breach are almost nonexistent."

Darius gulped and sealed his lips tightly. *Yeah, I know.*

"It might have been more merciful to have left her on Earth to die in the War," Kimura continued as he buried his hands in his gray hair. "She wanted to serve so badly. I was selfish. Selfish to take her from what she wanted to do. To try to keep her close to me, to manipulate the system for my own childish desires."

Darius placed a thick hand on his friend's shoulder. "It's not childish or selfish to want to protect your family, or to want to be with them."

"I did not protect them. I dragged them with me to face death and punishment. I should have come alone into this darkness."

"And they wouldn't have faced death if you left them in the middle of the War? If nothing else, you've given your wife and Saika a fighting chance. They're going to need someone to lean on."

"I am a weak old man. I cannot be leaned upon without falling."

"Then lean on me as you catch your family."

To his surprise, Dr. Kimura pulled together and straightened up. He wiped his eyes and nose and took a deep breath.

"You sound very much like David would have. You're right, just as he always was. Please do me a favor, Darius."

"Anything."

"When we land, I'd like to break all of the news at once to them, but I don't want to make a spectacle. Can you please ask Colonel Eriksen if we may have a private place to do so, after we land?"

"Yes, of course."

"Thank you, my friend. I hate to be such a burden to you."

Darius shrugged and smiled. "I couldn't let you bear that much by yourself."

An awkward silence descended upon the cockpit. Doctor Kimura was lost deep in thought, his gaze fixed on a cluster of stars pulsing overhead.

"I know you need some time," Darius added softly. "I'll forge an entry of your rounds tonight, and you can take tomorrow off as well if you need to.

"That's very kind of you, but I can still perform my duties."

"I thought you'd say that. Just remember, I can disable your terminal access if I have to."

Dr. Kimura forced a weak smile. "Very well then, I surrender in the face of overwhelming forces."

"Good. Don't seal yourself up in here either; I don't think that's healthy."

"And what are you suggesting I do, Darius?"

"I don't know, maybe come to chow tonight."

"Forgive me, but I don't want to be around large groups right now."

"It doesn't have to be a large group. How about just me and Lieutenant Miller?"

Dr. Kimura pursed his lips and considered for a moment. "Very well. Eighteen hundred hours?"

"Nineteen thirty. I'm pulling a long shift tonight stocking pods one and two with emergency supplies, and Captain Quinn enlisted Miller for an extra cooling routine check."

"I understand. I will be waiting outside the pod."

Darius nodded in acknowledgement and left the cockpit. His fingers were numb, and a wave of despair washed over him.

I hope he's wrong about it all falling apart. Raphael was a huge loss. I pray that it wasn't a design flaw that brought her down.

. . .

2nd Lt Darren Cormack
Planetfall +6 days, early morning
Eight miles northeast of sleeper pod seven
site
>|

Darren stretched. He winced as a knot in his back tightened and complained from the movement. Sleeping for the night on the hard ground had taken its toll on Darren. Though they were poorly padded and barely had what one could consider a pillow, the sleeper berths in the now abandoned pod were far more comfortable for slumber. What little luxury they afforded was now just a memory; the party of survivors that he led could only bring with them food, water, clothing, and some weapons and tools. He sighed and reached into his own pack and fished out a sealed ration. A large mosquito-like insect landed on his arm and he swatted it away before opening the meal.

He ate his meal in silence as he watched the bustling camp. It was strewn all over a wide, heavily treed plateau above the nearby marshlands. The camp stretched on for as far as he could see in either direction to the sides. Men, women, and children of all ages were busy eating their breakfast, ducking into the bushes to relieve themselves, or gathering in groups to talk. He was met with occasional glances, but the crowd was devoid of smiles; several people glared at him when their eyes met.

Darren finished his meal and stashed away the packaging, swiping his arm at several more mosquitoes in the process. He zipped up his pack and was about to hoist it over his shoulders when Sergeant Daniels approached with a grim look etched on her face. She snapped to attention and saluted, and he returned one in kind.

"Sir, we may have a problem."

As if we didn't have enough to begin with?

"What's wrong, Sergeant?"

"Sir, I received reports of three sick passengers last night. I mean really sick, vomiting, diarrhea, the whole nine yards. It's some pretty nasty stuff. In any case, I took a note and checked in on them this morning to see if they're any better."

"Let me guess. They're not."

"Correct, sir. None of the three are feeling any better today, and none of them are in any shape to travel. But it's worse than that, sir. There are two new cases this morning."

J.C. Rainier

"Damn it," Darren said as he scrambled to his feet and strapped the pack to his body. "Where are they at?"

Daniels turned on her heels and began to walk toward the rear of the group. "Two of the old cases and one of the new cases are back this way."

"They're not all together?"

"No, sir."

"What about a doctor? Do we have one of those among our passengers?"

"I don't know, sir."

Jesus, Daniels, he screamed in his head. *Either tell me right away when something goes wrong, or figure out how to fix it.* He bit his tongue for a moment to keep from lashing out at his subordinate.

The pair made their way almost to the rear of the column, where Daniels pointed out a young man in his twenties, doubled over and vomiting. His skin was swirled with a muddy sweat, his short blonde hair matted and caked with dried vomit. A blonde woman of his same age knelt at his side, patting his back as he retched uncontrollably. Darren's stomach turned and he had to put his hand over his nose and mouth to mitigate the stench. After a couple seconds of watching the horrific spectacle, he turned around and walked a few paces away, with Daniels on his heels.

"We need a doctor," he muttered to her through his hand.

"Yes, sir."

"Wait here with them."

"Yes, sir," she repeated.

Darren strode toward the front of the column. As he moved, he barked out, "Is there anyone here with medical experience? Are there any doctors among you?" He repeated this every fifteen seconds or so as he made his way almost all the way to the front. As he approached the head of the party, he was intercepted by a rather short Asian fellow.

"I was an ER nurse back in Cleveland, sir," he said.

Darren nodded. "Can you help us out? We have several people who are quite sick."

"I'll do what I can. What medical supplies do we have?"

"A couple first aid kits and a combat medic's kit. It's pretty extensive, but nothing like what you're used to."

"It should do fine. Lead the way."

Darren led the nurse back through the column, stopping briefly to retrieve the medic's kit from one of his scouts, to whom he had entrusted it. With the supplies in hand they returned to where Daniels was guarding the sick passenger. The nurse opened the kit and grabbed a disposable mask and gloves, and then set to examining the patient.

"Hi there, I'm Brett. I hear you're not feeling well today, huh?" he said in an oddly sweet tone. "We'll get you taken care of. I'm just going to take a quick peek at you, okay?"

The patient managed a weak nod. He had, for the moment, stopped vomiting. His companion moved aside to give Brett better access, but her eyes never left him. Darren could tell she was very distressed; her eyes bulged and watered, and she wrung her hands so hard that Darren thought they would snap.

"What's your name?" Brett asked as he began to probe his charge.

"D-Dave," replied the patient, barely able to move his lips.

"Dave, I'm going to ask you a few questions here and then we'll go from there, alright?"

Darren felt a little more at ease about the situation. He leaned in to Brett's ear and whispered, "We'll be just over there when you're done. Let me know what's going on." He received a curt nod from Brett, and paced over to the base of a nearby tree just out of earshot. Daniels followed him and let out a huge breath when they stopped.

"The others are all like that?" Darren asked her.

"Pretty much, sir."

"I want them all close together, and keep them all back here at the end of the camp. I don't think that we can do a full quarantine, but we need to keep the others away from them as much as possible."

"They can't travel, sir."

Darren sighed. "I know that. We're going to have to halt the party here for a day or two and see how it goes. It's going to put a bit of strain on our supplies, but if we're smart about it and make sure people aren't eating or drinking more than they have to, we should be fine. Send the scouts out to collect firewood. While we're here, we need to see if we can extend our water supplies. I know that marsh looks like crap, but we should still be able to at least boil or distill water to help out."

"Right away, sir." She saluted and then darted off into the camp.

Darren turned back to where Brett was tending to his patient. He paced for a moment, but did not have to wait long for the nurse to finish his examination and find Darren.

"What have we got?"

"If you ask me, it looks like food poisoning or the flu. You're right, I don't have all the tools I'd like to have to treat him. He's going to need plenty of fluids and rest, and I don't think that he should travel," Brett replied.

Darren gave him a slow nod. "No, we're not traveling today. Keep an eye on him and the others. I'd like a report before nightfall and another one in the morning."

"The others?"

"There are four more ill. Sergeant Daniels will have them moved together, and I want as little contact as possible between them and the rest of the survivors, just in case."

"I understand."

"Let me know if you need anything else, and I will try to provide it."

"Well," Brett said after a moment's pause, "for now I need as much water as you can give me. Also if you can get some of the sports drink pouches from the meals. That will help a bit."

"I'll see what I can do."

Brett nodded and went back to tend to Dave. Darren leaned against the tree, running his hand over the coarse bark. He picked at it nervously with his fingers, but it wouldn't flake.

He needs more water. I don't have much to spare; that's why we're moving to the other site. Darren dug his fingers into the bark until his fingernails threatened to tear away. *We need to keep moving, but I can't just leave sick people behind. What if those jungle cats attack? No, we need to protect them, no matter the cost.*

. . .

Capt Haruka Kimura
Planetfall +6 days, late afternoon
Eleven miles west of pod eight crash site
>|

Haruka knelt at the edge of the river and splashed its cool water on her face. Her skin tingled and her thoughts began to feel clear again. There was little respite from the heat and humidity of the jungle, so the band of survivors took frequent breaks to soak bandanas in the water, or drink from their supplies. She looked around at the tall palm-like trees extending as far as her eyes could see. A colorful, four-winged bird flittered just above the surface of the river, and then took a sharp angle up into a shorter gnarled tree, where it called out to some unseen companion. Haruka sighed and dunked a makeshift bandana torn from the sleeve of a spare flight suit into the river, then tied it around her forehead.

For Haruka, the rest stops couldn't come often enough. Even the younger children like Marya and Gabi needed fewer breaks than she did. James had gone so far as to stop the column on her behalf; he didn't make it known why, but he had ordered the halt when he thought that Haruka would pass out if she took another step.

"Is that helping at all?" he asked as Haruka splashed her face again.

"It is, thank you."

"The sun's getting to you."

"I'll be fine," she protested.

James smiled and squatted next to her at the river's edge. "You don't need to prove yourself to anyone here. You don't need to rush back and forth to make sure everyone's following; that's what Troy's team and Luis's guards are for. Just walk with the rest of us and enjoy the scenery."

"The scenery is nice, but I'll feel much better once it stops changing."

"We're still pretty far from the other pod, and you know how slowly we're moving out here."

"I blame it on the shorter days."

"Let's not forget how much bushwhacking we have to do just to keep ourselves close to the river. We could probably speed things up if we let the scouts find a path farther away."

Haruka waved him off. "We're less likely to get lost if we just follow the river to the sea. We know that Leight's people are on the actual beach; it won't be hard to find them once we get there. I just don't want to lose any of the kids or run out of food because we're walking in circles."

"We could use the radio tracker you used to find our pod."

"No, we can't. Its battery is dead, so I left it back at the pod. It's just dead weight now."

He scratched at the rough stubble that darkened his chin. "I'd still feel better if we were moving faster."

"Don't worry, James. We have more than enough supplies to get there."

A voice rang out from the top of the river bank, "Captain Kimura!"

She stood and wheeled around to face her top scout, Troy Bryant. Haruka stifled a chuckle when he gave her a sloppy salute. "You don't have to salute me, Troy. What's up?"

Troy scrambled down to the bottom of the bank. He huffed as he worked to catch his breath. "Something you should see. Just a little bit down river, around the next bend. We came up on it on our way back."

"What is it?"

"Looks like wreckage from the ship, maybe a pod. It's a bit banged up and smaller than the one we landed in."

"That sounds like a cargo pod. Show me."

Haruka and James fell in line behind Troy as they went up the steep bank and departed from the main party. They picked their way through the trees and navigated thorny fruit bushes for several minutes. The crash site was obvious as they neared; splintered chunks of wood and leveled trees heralded their approach to the craft, and a massive parachute lay tangled in the jungle canopy overhead. Haruka had no doubt that the object was indeed a cargo pod from *Raphael*. It showed some scarring on the exterior from its rough landing, but overall was intact.

She circled it until she found the door that once was docked to the lower level of the ill fated ship, and then punched an access code into the keypad. The door creaked and slid open two inches, then emitted a harsh metallic shriek and stopped. She grabbed the edge of the door and yanked with all her might. It budged just a mere fraction of an inch. She tried again, but it didn't move. She was out of breath, and her head began to spin. She backed off and sat on a felled tree.

"Troy?"

"I got it," he said as he stepped up to the door frame.

Troy yanked and grunted. He repositioned and pushed as hard as he could. He kicked and swore, and then gave it another try. Inch by inch, he was able to slide the door open just a little bit more. Haruka watched the effort as she caught her breath.

"That's good. I think I can get in there now." She handed James her rifle, took Troy's flashlight, and stepped inside.

The interior of the cargo pod was dark, stale, and muggy. She flicked the light on and scanned the beam through the jumbled, disheveled racks of crates. The contents of the pod did not appear to fare as well as the outer structure. Haruka rummaged through a broken crate near the entry way and found numerous small, sealed packages. She held one up to the light and read the label: "Cherry, Wild." Her heart skipped a beat. She turned the crate over to look at the damaged mechanism on the underside. The smashed control panel and leaking refrigerant tank confirmed her suspicions that she had stumbled upon one of the agricultural pods. She felt around the seal of the plastic heavy pouch and found no tears.

It might not be contaminated.

"Everything okay in there?" James called from the doorway.

"Better than okay. This is one of the most crucial pods."

"Yeah? What's in there?"

"Seeds. Do you have an empty pack?"

"No, should I get one?"

"Yeah. Hey Troy?"

"Yes ma'am?"

"Find a way to mark this area in case we have to come back."

"You got it."

Haruka opened more crates and blindly grabbed handfuls of packages. She tossed each fistful out of the front door, then went back for more. She made sure to plunder some from each crate that she could get to. When she was done and made her retreat out the door, there was a sizeable stack of scattered white packets. Troy walked over to her from the edge of the clearing and looked at the pile.

"So this is what a jackpot looks like, huh? I always thought it would be... well, green."

"I call this winning the lottery. I don't know how many thousands of square miles the wreckage is scattered over, and we could have easily missed this pod. Think about it, Troy." Haruka snatched an envelope of pea seeds and waved it. "We can grow Earth crops. What if Gabi's fruit is the only edible plant on this planet? We need these."

"I guess that just means it's a different kind of green than I imagined," he said with a smile.

Haruka returned a grin. "Here, help me pick these up for when James comes back."

The two worked for about five minutes to clean up the scattered mess and place them in piles on top of the felled trees. James returned with an empty pack and wide eyes.

"Did you clean the stores out there, Haruka?"

"Not even close, but just in case I want to take this stuff with us." Haruka grabbed the sack and shoved pile after pile inside until it was so full that she had to zip it up just to keep the seeds contained. "This is a good day, gentlemen," she said as she tossed the pack to James and picked up her ever present M4.

"I'll take any victory," James chimed in.

"Amen," added Troy.

Haruka looked just over the tree line at the rapidly dropping sun. "We'll be out of light in an hour or two. Let's get back to camp, get some chow, and bed down for the night. Last one there gets trash duty."

Troy stumbled on a log as the three bolted back along the river toward the camp. Haruka laughed for a brief moment until he stormed past her as they left the clearing. She tried to keep up with them, but couldn't. She had to use the din of the busy camp to find her way home.

Damn it… I motivated them too well. Looks like I get the short end of the stick in this race.

• • •

Calvin McLaughlin
5 April 2058, 08:11
Michael
>|

Cal's eyes fluttered open, shaking off the sands of deep slumber. He reflexively brought his hands to his face and rubbed his eyes. Realizing that he was able to do so, he looked at his wrists. He was secured in the berth by the regular harness, but his arms were no longer bound.

I guess they don't feel that I'm a threat any more.

His fingers brushed along the smooth aluminum ceiling. Cal drew in deep breaths as he tried to erase the memories of the nightmare from which he just woken up. He had dreamt of Alexis again. The dream started the same way it always had; Alexis pleaded with Cal to leave her alone. He respected her, and let her go. Then his horror began. As he wandered alone through the mists of the swamp, he came across her lifeless corpse, laid out beneath a brightly lit shade tree in a field of lush, green grass. Peaceful. Serene. But quite dead.

He remembered falling to his knees at her side. He remembered the searing pain, clear even through the dream state. The echoes of his agonized voice ran through his ears as he saw the red blossom of the wound in her belly. The slickness of the blood on his hands as he pulled her limp body to his chest.

No, this can't happen. Not to us... not to her...

Anguish gave way to rage. He vowed to see justice given to her. Off into the mists he ran, trying to track down whoever – or whatever – had taken her life. He lived years of his life in mere seconds of the dream, and while he found his way out of the ever present fog and on to the civilization afforded by *Michael* after its landing, he never was able to garner any further information. Guilt gnawed at him for his lack of effectiveness. Only at the very end, as he was pressing some hapless colonist for information, did he remember that it was a dream, and rouse himself.

He had a moment of claustrophobia as the walls of the sleeper berth seemed to draw closer. Short of breath and panicked, he released the restraints and pulled his wiry frame out of the sleeper berth, and then drew in a huge gasp of the recycled air in the pod. He squinted as the bright hallway lights flooded his face. The chirp of the computer terminal gave away the presence of another of the ship's crew.

"Ah, good. I was wondering when you were going to wake up, Mr. McLaughlin," said Colonel Dayton.

Cal looked around the sleeper section and found that the colonel was the only person besides himself present.

Cal steadied himself on a bank of sleeper berths. "Where's Doctor Taylor?" he slurred.

"I asked her to give us some privacy. I wanted to come see you myself, and to see how you are doing."

"Peachy," Cal muttered.

Dayton regarded him with concern. His downward drawn lips made his thick brown beard vaguely resemble an upset walrus. He pushed from the wall and stopped just a few feet from Cal.

"There's something that's clearly upsetting you. If you tell me what it is, maybe I can help you with it."

That's rich, Cal thought with disgust.

"No disrespect, Colonel, but you're not my therapist."

"You're quite right," Dayton said evenly. "That role belongs to Doctor Taylor, though as she's a medical doctor, psychiatry is a bit of a stretch for her. She's doing the best she can, but you're turning out to be quite a bit more than we bargained for at first."

"Don't talk to me about bargaining, sir," Cal shot back. His mouth felt heavy as the words poured out.

Without skipping a beat, Dayton responded, "And why not?"

Cal was not expecting such a direct tactic from his adversary; he was prepared to dance around the issue with the man until he could corner him. He stuttered for a moment as he searched for his answer, even though it was going to be equally direct. The medication in his system slowed his thoughts, and frustration began to mount as the perfect words eluded him. He continued anyway.

"Because you broke your promise to me."

"How so? How did I break it?"

"You had the doctor sedate me right after we woke up."

"That was for the safety of the ship, Mr. McLaughlin. If I had broken your promise, would I have bothered to wake you up at all?"

No, you wouldn't have.

"Did I revoke your accesses to the ship's systems? To the gym or library?"

"How the hell would I know that? I was put to sleep fifteen minutes after I woke up," he growled.

Dayton swept his arm in the direction of the computer terminal. "You can take my word for it, or you can check the computer. It's your choice."

Cal pushed off of the sleepers and maneuvered around the ship's commander. "You'll pardon me if I trust the computer more than you at this point, sir."

"Of course."

Cal tried to log in to the computer using his credentials. It bleeped at him and spat back an access error. "Trust you, huh?"

"Try it again, Mr. McLaughlin. I assure you I haven't done anything. Maybe you entered the wrong password."

Cal scoffed and assertively re-entered his login. It didn't reject them, and the application selection routine came up immediately. Incredulous, he blinked and pressed on. He checked his accesses to the various systems. None of his permissions had been removed. He even had access to the passenger check and sleeper controls, despite telling Dayton that he would not be involved in the maintenance cycles.

"What the?" he gasped, then collected himself and prepared to continue his battle. "Okay, so I still have access. You could have put that back together at the last second, as a trick. How do I know that you won't just change your mind and put me right back in?"

Dayton sighed and pinched the bridge of his nose. "It's no trick. Check your friend's sleeper berth."

Cal blinked at the Colonel and then brought up the passenger check again. His fingers trembled as he pushed the buttons to call up pod twelve. He could hear Dayton speaking over his shoulder to someone deeper into the recesses of the sleeper pod as he worked, but Cal was focused on one sole task: making sure she was okay.

XCS-02 POD 12 DELTA 14: UNIT OFFLINE

His heart skipped as he read the words from the screen and saw the grayed outline of the human icon. Neither heart rate nor respiration showed anything; they were grayed out as well. Cal couldn't believe his eyes. He exited the program, brought it back up, and confirmed the data.

"Cal?"

It's her. It's really her.

He turned to face her, and put on a brave smile. He was anxious and terrified to his core, but didn't want to let her see it. She would be surprised to be awake and not at the planet, and Cal knew that if he

J.C. Rainier

freaked out again, it would spell the death of any chance he had of redeeming himself in her eyes.

"Hey, how are you feeling?" he asked, tripping over the words.

"Like I want to yack. What's going on here? Why was I woken up? Why was there a crewman waiting on the other side of my door? Why isn't there any gravity?" Her questions were launched at him like rockets, and he couldn't get a word in edgewise. "Who is this guy here? Seriously, what the hell is going on?"

"Explaining will take a while," he said with a nervous laugh. "Let's just say that you're not a play toy, and I'm going to prove it to you if you give me a chance. When we last saw each other, we both know I did something incredibly stupid. I'm going to make it up to you now."

Her eyes darted between him and Colonel Dayton. "And now you've got the crew involved?"

Dayton cleared his throat. "Not the whole crew. Just myself, the ship's doctor, and one of my ops officers. For that matter, I do need to warn you to stay out of the way of the ship's crew as they go about their duties."

"Out of the way of their duties? What is this? Who are you?"

"Forgive me, I didn't introduce myself." He extended his hand toward her. "I'm Colonel Thomas Dayton, in command of the extrasolar colony ship *Michael*." Alexis looked at Dayton's hand but made no effort to reach for it. He retracted it and continued, "We're preparing the ship for landing on the planet Demeter, which will happen in just under two months. As far as what's going on right here and now, I'm fulfilling a promise I made years ago."

Alexis folded her arms against her chest and glared at the two men. "Really?"

Dayton shot a sly grin at Cal and shook his head, then made his way for the exit. "Good luck to you, Mr. McLaughlin," he called as he made his way out of the hallway.

"What's that supposed to mean?"

"I ah… well, he…" Cal tried to think of a way to explain what Dayton meant, but thought better of it as he wasn't ready to lay out all the cards yet. He turned off the computer then waved his hand. "Nothing. Inside joke. Look, we both know I screwed up, but I just want to put this out there. You're not going back into stasis. Any time you sleep, you're going to wake up the next morning, just like if you were in bed back home on Earth."

She turned away from him, grabbing the edge of the hatch frame to stop her spin. "I don't have a home. It was taken from me."

Cal sighed and his head bowed.

Ten minutes. Go ten freaking minutes without antagonizing her, stupid.

"I'm sorry, that's not what I meant."

"Yeah, I get what you meant." Her voice was cold and dead. Cal cringed as the words escaped her lips.

"Alexis, please. Let me make it up to you."

"I don't know how you can. Just leave me alone."

No, not again. I can't take this again.

His heart felt as if it was ripped to shreds as he heard her mutter something under her voice.

"You monster."

Alexis disappeared into the darkness beyond the hatch as Cal was left to float alone, shocked, and numb.

No…

· · ·

J.C. Rainier

1st Lt Darius Owens
6 April 2058, 14:12
Gabriel
>|

    "Sir, I've run the figures over and over again." Captain Tyler Quinn avoided eye contact with his commander as grasped the railing on the command platform. A distinct pinging noise filled the air as he tapped a single finger.

    "It's not good, is it?"

    "No sir."

    "Well, give it to me then, Captain," the colonel said as he rubbed his brow.

    "We're within the extreme range of the pods' emergency transmitters. We should be picking up something. Static. Gibberish. Anything."

    "But we're not, are we?"

    "No sir, not a thing."

    Colonel Charles Eriksen scratched at his beard as he turned his attention to Darius, who clung to the railing opposite Quinn. "Nothing at all, Lieutenant?"

    "No sir, it's like the captain said."

    "And you're sure the pods cleared *Raphael* before the reactor blew?"

    "To be honest sir, no. The distress call was too garbled to tell for sure. We know they planned an emergency drop, we just can't be sure if it happened."

    Eriksen drew his hands to the armrests of his chair and squeezed until his knuckles turned a ghostly shade. Darius could even swear that the man had a fresh patch of gray appear in his beard since the distress call was received from *Raphael*. Eriksen unlocked his chair and turned to face the bow of *Gabriel*. Quinn and Darius in unison turned their heads the same direction, and their sight through the bridge glass fell on the ever growing orange disc of Alpha Centauri B.

    "Are you a religious man, Captain?" the commander asked in a soft voice.

    "No sir, not really."

    "What about you, Mr. Owens?"

    "Yes sir."

"Do you think that God is out here?"

"Sir?"

"Do you think that God has influence out here? Or do you think that it's just on Earth?"

Darius stared off into the nearly dark void as he hesitated. "I can't say that I've thought about that, sir. I'd like to say that he's everywhere. Here too."

"But you're not sure."

No, I'm not. Darius didn't dare speak the words. It was bad enough that he had thought them. He knew that a crisis of faith was one of the last things he needed at this point, and yet he knew from friends back on Earth that such crises always happened at the worst times.

"Sir, what would you like us to do?" he asked, trying to steer the conversation down a different course.

"Open communication with *Michael.* Share the information we have on *Raphael,* see if they have any new information. If there's anything at all that can be done to prevent such a..."

Darius waited for almost a minute for Eriksen to finish his sentence. "A what, sir?"

His right hand rose from the armrest and waved Darius off. "Just get the lines open, Lieutenant."

"Yes sir." He nodded at Captain Quinn before floating his way off the bridge and into the gallery.

As he made his way down the length of the ship, his mind replayed every detail of the distress call from the lost sleeper ship. The echo from the deep recesses sent a numbing chill down his spine.

Thousands lost.

Next was a replay of the harsh rebuke that Colonel Dayton had given Darius during a conversation after he had discovered the com system exploit all those years ago. The daggers in the man's voice and the choice words that he had saved to describe Colonel Eriksen haunted him through untold millions of miles of space.

Even as Darius managed to shove aside Dayton's words, his own commander's tirade about Colonel Dayton rose up. Darius shook his head furiously and clutched at his ears in futility. He knew the memories were in his head and the gesture would make no difference, but it felt somehow natural.

The two colonels have barely spoken to each other this whole time, he thought. *And they've been pissed at each other when they have. Do we really have a chance out here with these two bickering?*

Darius made the transition from the gallery into the support section and into the computer core. He pushed off of the wall and made his way through the parallel racks of equipment to the mainframe interface terminal, then seated himself and strapped in. He turned on the computer and stared at the blinking cursor of the login screen for a moment before proceeding. In a matter of minutes, he had unblocked the com system. Darius retrieved the headset from its position – velcroed to the side of the mainframe's casing – and adjusted it on his head. With a flick of his wrist across the screen, he activated the inter-vessel com.

"Lieutenant Darius Owens to sleeper ship *Michael*, please come in."

Dead air. This was not a surprise to Darius, as the last time he had spoken with anyone live on that ship, there was about a twenty second delay due to the distance separating the ships. Darius waited, but received no response.

"Lieutenant Owens to *Michael*, come in please."

Dead air.

Please answer.

"*Gabriel* to any crew member of *Michael*, respond please."

Dead air. Darius concentrated on breathing deeply as the seconds ticked away. Frustration was beginning to mount for him, but he knew that should he receive a response from another ship, he couldn't afford to direct any anger or sarcasm at the respondent.

What does it matter? Colonel Eriksen didn't want to talk to them anyway. It only took the destruction of another ship for him to change his mind. Why would Dayton want to talk to us?

"Lieutenant Darius Owens to any crew member of *Michael*, please respond. I have a proposal."

Please… please…

A voice crackled through the headset, faint and slightly echoed. "This is Sergeant Drisko of *Michael*. I read you, Lieutenant. Please state your request, and I will relay it to Colonel Dayton."

Darius clasped his hand over the microphone boom to silence the sigh of relief that escaped his lungs. When he breathed in again, he released his hand.

A small miracle.

"I assume you've heard the distress call from *Raphael*. Colonel Eriksen suggests an exchange of information between our crews regarding this matter. He feels it is in the interest of both ships to avert any potential issues we may be facing shortly."

Darius watched the seconds tick by on his console. Seconds turned into minutes. *Come on. Send your response.*

"Yes sir. Colonel Dayton agrees to the exchange. Transmit when you are ready, and we will do the same once we receive your data."

"Thank you, Sergeant." Darius paused for a second. "It's good to hear your voice again."

Darius leaned back in his chair to wait for the response from the other ship.

"You too, sir. Drisko out."

. . .

2nd Lt Darren Cormack
Planetfall +8 days, mid morning
Eight miles northeast of sleeper pod seven
site
>|

Darren paced slowly toward the head of the column, stopping at each cluster of refugees on his way. Discarded meal pouches, torn up undergrowth, and small ash piles served as a reminder that the group had not moved in two days. A few barren patches showed the signs of human use, but their inhabitants were not present; these were the individuals or families that Darren was forced to relocate to the rear of the column, where the thus far ineffective medical quarantine had been set up.

He picked Sergeant Daniels out of the crowd at a distance, and covered the ground with long, swift strides. She saw his approach, snapped to attention, and saluted.

"Do you have the report I asked for?" Darren asked as he returned her salute.

"Yes sir. At the rate we're going through the food, we'll run out in five days."

Darren heaved a great sigh. "Well, that's better than the four days you gave me yesterday. Whatever the hell this bug is at least is keeping people from eating. What about our water?"

"The fresh water we brought with us is almost gone. We don't even have a day's worth for the whole camp."

And there it is. Whatever the hell this bug is has us going through our water too quickly.

"Alright," he said after a moment of thought. "Go get Wu. Tell him I want an update."

"Yes sir." Daniels snapped on her heels and jogged off to the quarantine area.

Darren wandered to his right, to another group of three refugees – a mother and two young boys – clustered beneath a tall palm-like tree. The mother was embracing and comforting the younger of her sons, and she eyed Darren suspiciously as he approached. He knelt in front of them and forced a soft smile. The younger boy coughed hard enough to shake his mother's body, and Darren saw that his face was ghostly white.

"How's he doing?" he asked the woman.

She hesitated for a moment, glancing at her son and then back at Darren. "He's burning up and he can't keep anything down."

"Alright. One of the nurses is coming up this way. I'll have him see to your boy as soon as he can, I promise."

"Thanks."

"Is there anything else I can do for you?"

The woman shook her head vigorously and clutched her son closer. Another coughing fit wracked his body, one hard enough that he seemed to gasp desperately for air. Darren rose quickly and moved away once again toward the front of the column. He had no intention of checking on anyone in particular; he merely wanted to get away from the sick child. He had seen the effects of the illness first hand, and there was no way to get around the fact that they were unpleasant, to say the least. He ducked around a tree and out of sight of the family, then slouched against the trunk, resting his brow on his arm.

Damn it, it's spreading.

Two days prior, there had been five sick passengers. That number had grown to nine just one day later. The young boy would make at least ten, possibly more depending on the report he was about to receive from Brett Wu, one of two nurses among the survivors who volunteered their skills. He kicked nervously at the base of the tree, attempting to push the anxious thoughts from his head, but only succeeded in changing the pattern of dirt streaks on his boots.

I wonder how bad it would be if we just pressed on. He shook is head and banged it against his arm twice. *No, we can't. The sick can't travel, and we have no way to safely carry them.*

Two sharp peals of gunfire made Darren jerk upright, and sent him running in the direction of the noise. He pumped his arms and legs furiously as he ran back down the column. One of his scouts – a scruffy middle-aged man by the name of Hank Adams – stood just to the side of the column, slowly lowering his rifle as he looked off into the woods. Darren pulled up next to him.

"What the hell was that?" he asked.

Hank grunted and pointed at a lifeless brown lump a hundred feet away, tangled in a bushy vine. "One of those damned jungle cats. I thought I saw something coming down that hill over there so I waited until I could see it again. Sure enough, a few minutes later, I see it hunkered over in that bush, looking at me like I'm dinner."

Darren peered into the distance. He drew his Beretta and cautiously walked toward the brown corpse, checking nearby bushes as he passed, searching for other invaders. When he reached the bloody, furry mess of the cat, he prodded it with the muzzle of his weapon. The head flopped limply to the side, revealing a massive exit wound at the back of its skull. Darren holstered the pistol and walked back to Hank. On his way past, he gave the older man a single slap on the shoulder. "Good job. Carry on."

By this time, the noise had attracted a small crowd, including Sergeant Daniels and Brett Wu. Darren motioned for the two of them to follow, and walked to a more private area on a berm overlooking the rear half of the camp. Daniels followed, as did Brett, who at the end of the climb was out of breath.

"There's a young boy near the head of the column who is sick," Darren remarked. "I want you to check on him when we're done."

Brett nodded and panted, but said nothing. Daniels put her hands on her hips and looked at the dirt as she bit her lip.

"It's gotten worse, hasn't it? How many are sick now?"

"Including the boy, nine," Brett replied.

"I thought you said there were nine yesterday. Are you sure about your count?"

"Yes, Lieutenant. Actually, on the bright side, one of the first patients is showing some pretty good signs of recovery. The danger has passed for her, so I no longer consider her an active case."

Darren sighed. "Good. So the boy is the only new case, then?"

Daniels turned away from Darren, and Brett's eyes darted as if he was avoiding his stare.

"What is it?"

"If you include the boy, there are three new cases today. I'm sorry, Lieutenant. We lost two overnight," Brett said in a hushed tone.

"Lost?"

"They're dead, sir," Daniels blurted.

Darren's jaw slacked and he stumbled backwards a step or two before he regained his legs. "Dead. Two dead, one getting better, and nine violently ill. Is that what you're telling me?"

Brett nodded. "But it gets worse."

"How can it be worse than two dead?" growled Darren.

"Whatever this is, it's severe enough to kill healthy adults. One of the victims was a twenty five year old man. From what I can tell, he was in perfect health before this bug got him."

Strong enough to kill anyone in this camp, then.

"Do we even know what it is? How it's spread?"

"I'm still working on that. I have a couple theories, but I'm not sure how strong any of them are. There's no lab out here, and I'm not an epidemiologist."

"So what *do* you know?"

"Well," Brett said as he scratched the stubble that had entrenched itself on his face. "I'm almost certain it's environmental. We're surrounded by a swamp, and all of the patients have what look like insect or mosquito bites."

Darren scoffed as he rolled up one of his sleeves, exposing a dozen large red welts. The pressure of the cuff scraping over them as well as the sudden exposure to the outside air made them itch so badly that Darren wanted to scrape every inch of skin off of his arm with his filthy fingernails. He gritted his teeth again, and through them he muttered, "Like these? I've had these for almost a week now and I'm still as healthy as an ox."

Brett shook his head and sighed. "Like I said, I don't know for sure. It's just a theory."

"Well, you're no good to the sick up here. Thanks for the report. Let me know if anything changes, or if you find out anything more. Now go take a look at the boy."

"Yes, Lieutenant."

Brett retreated down the hill and forward in the column. Daniels turned around to face Darren. She was putting on her poker face, though it had become ineffective rather quickly once Darren figured out that the slight pout on her lips was a tell.

"You want to say something, Daniels?"

"Not my place, sir."

"The hell it isn't. Tell me what's on your mind."

"We can't stay here, sir."

"I know that."

"So what are we waiting for?" She mocked him, before realizing the mistake and evening her tone. "Leave some supplies behind with Wu, two volunteers, and a couple rifles. They'll be fine until they recover or the bug gets them."

"That's very compassionately put, Sergeant," he retorted sarcastically.

"Sorry, sir. Just thought I'd play at your level."

Ouch. Is that what she really thinks of me? That I'm some callous bastard?

"Look, we're not splitting up and leaving the sick behind. We'll just have to figure something else out."

"With all due respect, sir, but what?" Her gaze locked with his. "We're just about out of water. The crap they've dredged out of the swamp takes forever to boil or distill. Whatever this is keeps taking new victims, and it's scary as hell."

Darren arched his brows. "Are you scared?"

"To be frank, yes sir. I don't know about you, but death by diarrhea isn't on my top ten list of ways to go."

"Mine either."

"So let's move the camp out."

Darren thought about how the civilians might react if they left behind a group of the sick and made for their destination. An image of leaving behind a terrified, sick child came to his mind. He imagined how much of a fight his mother would put up if he dared to separate the two.

"No, I can't. But you're not staying."

A puzzled look spread across her face. "Sir?"

"Take three people with you. I don't care who, as long as it's not Wu or anyone who is sick. Head for pod one and have Marsolek send help to meet up with us and bring us home. If you have to, order him to on my behalf."

She thought for a moment and nodded. "Alright sir. We'll get out there on the double."

"I appreciate it, Daniels. The quicker the better, given the shape we're in."

Daniels snapped to attention and gave a smart salute before she wheeled away and stormed down the rise.

Darren heaved another great sigh as he looked around the camp below.

You're right, Daniels. I definitely don't want to die here, or like this.

• • •

Capt Haruka Kimura
Planetfall +8 days, late afternoon
Sleeper pod eleven site
>|

Haruka smiled as she drew in a deep breath of air. The salty tang was very clear now, and she knew that her ragged band of survivors was close to where pod eleven had landed. The tree canopy was thinner ahead, and bright blue sky filled the gaps where there was no green. Fluffy white clouds seemed to dance from treetop to treetop.

She was weary, and her legs felt like they were dragging lead weights. Her rifle and pack had been shed miles ago, carried now by James somewhere near the head of the column. He had insisted that she sit and take a break, but she ignored him and left him to pick up the weight she left behind.

Maybe I should have stopped for a few minutes.

James had gone ahead as Haruka lagged ever slower. Luis had come to keep her company, and had given her the same plea that James had. She had shrugged him off, determined to make the final push to the beach with the refugees.

There was a buzz in the air that leaped among the refugees. Rumor had always spread quickly, but this was different. Everyone seemed invigorated by the smell of the sea and the knowledge that they were almost to their destination. Even the younger children like Gabi were complaining less about the long walk. Haruka also felt as if she had just a little more spring in her step, but she still was unable to keep up with the group. With a sigh, she sat down in the shade of a palm tree. Luis sat down next to her and loosened his pack.

"Finally taking my advice, huh?"

Haruka opened her canteen and lifted it to her lips, taking a deep swig of the warm water. "If I don't, I'll fall over."

"You're still taking on too much yourself. You've got to let yourself rest. Let James and me do the work for you," he said emphatically.

"I have been, Luis. All I've been doing for the past couple days is following the group around, and making a morning check of the camp and an evening check."

Luis looked at her for a second, and then brought his hand up to her brow. He nodded and withdrew it. "Are you sure you're feeling okay?"

"I'm fine, quit your worrying."

"Have you talked to Emilia?"

"I said I'm fine," she protested. "Just give me a day without a march and I'll be fine."

"Have you been eating and drinking enough?"

"Seriously. Am I sitting next to Luis Serrano, or are you really just Maria in disguise?"

Luis chuckled. "Hardly. You wouldn't stand a chance against her."

A whoop and a cheer rose up from ahead of them. Haruka smiled and rose to her feet, securing her canteen to her belt. Luis strapped his pack back on and stood.

"Something tells me we're here," she said. "C'mon."

Haruka jogged along the river bank as she paralleled the winding human column. Ahead she could see the mouth of the river, surrounded by bright white sands, and a brilliant green-blue sea. Her pace quickened and she almost plunged headlong off the bank into the river in her excitement. She reached the edge of the tree line and shot forth onto the gleaming white beach, where she collapsed to her knees and grabbed two fists full of sand. She let out a noise that was half laughter and half crying as the bleached grains slipped from her fingers. A pair of white, four-winged birds flew over the shore, dipping and rising, calling and dancing. The clear water showed a sandy bottom for several hundred feet out from the shoreline, before fading into the dark blue of deeper water.

Here's your beach, Marco. It's beautiful. I wish you could have seen it.

"Are you alright?" Luis asked as he knelt in front of her and put his hand on her shoulder.

She looked up at him, and the breeze tickled and cooled the tears streaming down her face. She wiped them away with her hand and nodded. "Sorry. I was just thinking of someone who should have been here to see this."

Luis nodded and stood up, offering his hand. "Come on. I see the pod a little farther down the beach."

Haruka took his hand and hobbled down the beach toward the dark gray mass of the sleeper pod as her aching legs tried to buckle under her. The sleeper's rear end faced them and the ramp was lowered, exposing the inner hallways. The stream of refugees from pod eight were beginning to congregate outside of it. The children broke off from the group of the adults and ran up and down the beach, giggling and squealing. Beyond pod eleven, another pod lay broken and half sunk in the water about a hundred yards off shore. She shuddered as an incoming wave slammed into the body of the pod, sending a wash of spray over its roof.

No wonder so many from that pod were killed.

Five minutes later, Haruka and Luis squirmed their way through the wall of bodies and to the base of the ramp, where James was waiting with a broad-shouldered man with sandy blonde hair and a scraggly attempt at a goatee. He was barely an inch taller than James, but he carried himself in a way that made him look twice as big. Their eyes locked on Haruka as she and Luis approached. The stranger snapped to attention and saluted, and Haruka caught the outline of dog tags through his sweat stained t-shirt and wings tattooed on his bicep.

"Staff Sergeant Seth Leight, *Raphael*, ma'am!" he barked.

She returned his salute. "Captain Haruka Kimura, *Raphael*. At ease, Sergeant."

His arms dropped to his side. "You win a fight against something out there, Captain?"

"I'm sorry, what?" she responded, confused.

"The bruises on your arm there. Looks like it got a little rough for you there."

"Probably just bug bites. They itched like hell at first," Haruka said as she looked at the blotched purple and red skin of her forearm, and then quickly tugged the sleeve of her flight suit down to cover them. Luis gave her a concerned look, and James craned his neck to try to sneak a peek.

"I see. Well, it's good to see you made it in one piece anyway, Captain."

"Thanks. What's your sitrep?"

"We're hanging on. Jenkins is overwhelmed with scouting the area, and I've got my hands full trying to get these slackers around camp to do anything but mope and whine. We've got plenty of clean water thanks to the river. Holding out for now on food."

"Have you been able to forage at all?"

"Not much. There's some pretty good eats here from the fish and crabs we've found, that's about it."

"I can help a little more with that," she said and motioned Luis to turn around. She unzipped his pack and grabbed one of Gabi's fruit from inside, then lobbed it at Leight, who snatched it out of the air. "We found that these are edible. Whole jungle's full of them."

He sniffed it and then took a deep bite, causing juice to burst all over his hand and facial hair. Leight nodded and spoke as he chewed, "That's pretty good."

"Glad you approve. We need rack time, and maybe a meal or two. Where do you want my people?"

"Just beyond the tree line would be safest," Leight replied without skipping a beat.

Haruka exchanged confused glances with James and Luis. "No, seriously, Sergeant. What berth assignments can you give us?"

"No disrespect, Captain, but we're full up," he explained. "I've only got one pod full of sleepers and more than a pod's worth of people. We've got people sharing berths or sleeping on the decks already. You guys have already spent days in the woods, so you should be fine holing up in the trees. There's plenty of room out there for all of you, and it'll keep our people out of each others' hair."

"You've got to be kidding me. We've got children out here," she protested, her voice rising in pitch and volume.

"Yeah, we've got kids in here too."

"Fine," she spat back. "We'll set up in the tree line. Just get us some damn chow."

Leight sighed and his shoulders slumped. "I can't do that either. Maybe you weren't listening; I've got too many mouths to feed. We're just keeping our head above water out here as it is."

"That's an order, Sergeant."

"So haul me up on charges then. I'm still not giving you any of my supplies." Haruka clenched her jaw and drew her pistol, which made Leight laugh. "What, are you going to shoot me here in front of everyone? That won't help with your food problem, Captain." He turned and stormed up the ramp.

"Get back here, Sergeant," she bellowed.

"Good night," he responded and disappeared into the pod.

Haruka gripped the gun tighter and made a move toward the ramp, but James blocked her path. He shook his head and placed his hand on hers, pointing the barrel down into the sand. "Let him go. We've got a couple more meals left in our supplies. We can deal with him in the morning."

She sighed and holstered the weapon. "Fine. Luis?"

"Yeah?"

"Get everyone together up there. Use the pod as a windbreak and set everyone up just beyond the first trees. James, I want a full inventory of our tools by morning."

"Yes, Captain. But can I have a minute?"

"Of course. Luis?"

Her Chief of Security nodded his head, turned to the gathered crowd, let out a loud whistle, and pointed to the bank. There was some muttering and grumbling, but the survivors of pod eight picked up their packs and made the climb up to the line of tall palm trees that edged the sandy beach. As James and Haruka walked back up the beach and away from the pod, Luis set to herding the children and the stragglers.

"What's your plan, Captain?" James asked as they padded through the white sands.

"He said to haul him up on charges. That's what I'm going to do."

"May I make a suggestion?"

"Of course."

"Confronting him directly might spark an incident. Have you thought about a softer touch?"

Haruka looked at him as if another head had sprouted on his shoulder. "Now *you're* kidding me, right? You want me to beg him for help?"

"Not at all. I think we should work with him. Gain his trust and respect."

"Ugh, James. You know he's my subordinate and he's supposed to take my orders without question. What he did back there…"

"Is in the best interest for the people he is protecting," he interrupted. "Or at least in his opinion. Frankly, I don't blame him at all for stonewalling you. We're also just a tad far away from any sort of command structure, or even law for that matter. I don't think he's trying to spite you, I think he's just trying to keep his people alive."

"So am I."

"Yes, and doing a great job of it so far. We're not as bad off as it may seem. I've seen a couple things that we can take advantage of since we've been here."

"Like what?"

"Food. Leight said that there's fish and crabs here, so we set people to work fishing for our group.   If we fend for ourselves, it will show him we're not trying to leech off of his resources."

Haruka mulled the thought over in silence for a moment. "Good point. What's the other thing you think we can take advantage of?"

"I noticed he has a thorn in his side," he continued. "He's mentioned twice now that people around his camp aren't motivated to work, and that this Jenkins guy is overworked. If we have Troy and his teams take over scouting duties that would probably be a good gesture. I'd also like to try getting the troublemakers on his side off their butts and working."

"He can have Troy's teams," she replied. "I just can't afford to have you spending all your time organizing Leight's people when our people need direction too."

James smiled wide and a winked. "Don't worry about it. I'll brief Luis on what needs to be done. You don't need me to watch the flock, Captain. They can do it by themselves."

Haruka returned his smile. "Sometimes I wonder who is really in charge here, you or me. Alright, let's do it."

Don't make me regret it.

. . .

Calvin McLaughlin
7 April 2058, 07:12
Michael
>|

Chemical formulas danced across the back of Calvin's eyelids as he closed his eyes for a moment. The concepts that he was learning were taking some time to get used to, and the boy that he was back on Earth would have given up and found something else to do by now. The sink or swim impetus provided by a new life on Demeter made him study the otherwise mind numbing science behind biodiesel with an unprecedented fervor.

All the same, hours in the cramped ESAARC cockpit learning about reactions, titration, and catalysts took their toll on him. His progress was further slowed by the medication that Dr. Taylor administered for his psychosis. He needed to stop frequently and re-read individual sentences that were twisted or blurred by the haze in his mind.

Cal glanced at the clock on the console and found that it was early morning, though he had not slept for hours. His ordeal with sedation had also served to throw off his schedule, and he was often asleep while the crew was awake. This made his existence quite lonely. Cal could have easily corrected this issue with Dr. Taylor's help, but he chose not to; he knew that Alexis would need some time and space to digest the idea of being revived from stasis early, and being in her sight would make him a target for any negative emotions she had on the matter.

Cal put his lips to the valve of a drink pouch and took a swig of the stale, bitter coffee that it contained, then flipped the page in his chemistry book. Words jumbled on the page, and after three attempts to read the first paragraph, Cal gave up and closed it.

Time for a break.

He stretched, released the shoulder straps, and opened the door leading out of the cockpit. His heart stuttered and he was given a start, as Alexis was braced on the other side of the door, burning holes into him with her intense stare.

"Alexis?"

"What right did you have to do it? To wake me up?" she seethed.

"None. Look, I'm sorry..." he replied, but was cut off.

"Why did you do it? You had no right to do it, so what made you think it was alright?"

"The first time, it's because I wanted to show you something that only a couple people besides the crew will ever see."

"Why *me*? If you were lonely, why didn't you pick someone else? The guy in the berth below yours, or next to yours? Why not just hang out with the crew?"

Cal could see tears welling in her eyes, and her lips contorted as she tried to keep up her stern front. Her body wobbled a bit as her arms shook, and her knuckles where as white as snow as she dug them in to the door frame with all her might.

"It could only be you. It would have been meaningless if it was anyone else."

"For who?"

"For me." *I wish you could say the same. I thought we had a connection.*

Alexis regarded him with her green eyes, almost aflame with intensity. Her grip on the door frame relaxed somewhat, and she nodded. "At least you're honest about it. Now."

"I've never been anything but honest with you. Stupid, yes, but honest."

She brushed past him and grabbed the back of one of the seats, then craned her neck to view the stars through the dorsal windows.

"So you woke me up the second time to try to prove to me that I'm not your play thing?"

Cal sighed. "When you put it that way, it makes me sound like a douchebag."

"A very self-aware one, it looks like."

Okay, you deserved that one, Cal.

"Look, I know I'm probably one of the last people you want to see right now. I'll stay out of your way if you really want, but I just have to know something first." He waited until her gaze again leveled at him before continuing. "You kiss me, then you curse me. You say you don't want to see me, and call me hurtful things, but then you come and find me when I leave you alone."

"Wait," she interrupted. "What have I called you that has you all hurt?"

Cal's eyes drifted slowly closed, and he uttered a single word, barely above his breath: "Monster." The image of Alexis, curled up, bleeding, and crying in his dreams lingered for a moment. When the image passed and his eyes opened again, her look had changed entirely. Her hand was over her mouth, and her stare seemed to have the softness of the girl he first met back on Earth.

"Anyway," he added. "You've got me confused. You say that I mean nothing to you and you don't want to see me, but you act like there's something there. A connection. So which is it?"

There was a hesitation before her response. It wasn't much, but it was enough that Cal wondered if she was thinking of a lie.

"No connection. If you had gotten to know me a bit more first, you'd know that I'm kind of a flirt, so I guess that's why you're confused."

I don't believe you. Cal smiled innocently and reached his hand out, placing it on top of hers. A tingling sensation ran through his hand, and a moment later, he was wracked with pangs of guilt. *No, I believe you. Every time I touch you, it's... it's all me.* He shied away and pushed his way out of the cockpit without a word or backward glance. His guilt quickly abated, and the void was filled with a terrible emptiness.

Cal hoped that Alexis might call after him or try to stop him, but her silence spoke volumes. He exited pod twelve and floated aimlessly toward the bow of the ship. He had to go sort out his feelings, and he knew that he needed to do it quickly and in solitude; anger and sorrow roiled within him, and he thought that he might explode if he came across a crew member. It occurred to him that at this time of the morning, the crew would all be at their posts, so he decided to make way for the gym at the forward section of the lower gallery.

After the long journey, he locked himself in the room and began a furious exercise routine. Each repetition of the machines made him work harder, and the pace at which he attacked the routine ramped up until even the exercise could not drown out his emotion. With a scream, his workout routine ended, and he buried his face in a towel. He wiped his face repeatedly, muttering curses to himself.

I'm such an idiot. I really thought she was interested in me too.

Another part of his psyche spoke out, and he began to argue with himself mentally.

She's just giving you an excuse, telling you what you want to hear to let her go. You gave her the opportunity and she took it.

She's called you a monster and turned her back to you. It wasn't an excuse, she's telling you how she feels. Of course she sought you out to hash it out face to face. She's trying to keep you from putting her in another uncomfortable situation. Try it one more time and she'll probably punch your lights out.

J.C. Rainier

She's not the kind of girl that would do that. Did you see that front she was putting on? She's trying to let you down. Stop letting her do it. Make sure you don't leave any doubt for her. Sweep her off her feet.

Cal laughed audibly for a moment as his mental debate continued. *I hope that wasn't a gravity joke. How are you supposed to top showing her the stars? Commandeer the ship from Dayton and declare yourself the pirate king? Hey, it might just work. I hear girls always like a bad boy.*

If that's the case, then I think it's time I go ask the doctor if I can raid her alcohol stash again. Underage drinking in outer space. Yeah, Cal. You're a real badass. Maybe ask Hunter to join your little space gang?

Ah, Cal. You're damned if you do, and you're damned if you don't. So just do it. At least that way you can say that you've tried.

Aren't you forgetting something?

What?

You're nuts, remember?

Cal nodded slowly. *Yeah, I suppose talking to myself is kind of proof of that. Doc's treating me, though.*

I see how well that's working.

Cal growled and repeatedly snapped the towel into the seat of the apparatus, and then threw it at the wall, where it seemed to splatter like liquid before it began to float around the compartment.

"God damn it, shut up. Shut up, shut up, shut the hell up!"

Screaming at yourself won't make you any more sane.

• • •

The voice in his earpiece, thick with a New England accent, cut through the silence of the computer core, startling Darius. His hand jerked and almost made him cut out a good section of code from the com system software that he had painstakingly worked to repair.

"Colonel Dayton to *Gabriel,* come in please."

The colonel himself is calling? This must be important.

"This is Lieutenant Owens of *Gabriel*, Colonel. What can I do for you, sir?" As Darius spoke, he heard Dayton's voice again through the headset. Darius almost stuttered from the distraction, but pushed through.

Damned delay.

He adjusted his shoulder harness and ran his hands along the arm rests as he waited for a response from the other ship. His nerves began to tingle in anticipation, and he was unsure of what to expect.

"I have a couple orders of business, Lieutenant. Are you ready?"

"Yes sir."

Static crackled in his earpiece as he waited a little over a minute for the response.

"First, I agree to Colonel Eriksen's proposal about information sharing. The thought of a reactor breach scares the tar out of me, and if there's anything we can do to avoid it, I'm all for it."

"Thank you, sir. I will inform him."

"Second, I want to propose that both ships land at the beacon site, the one *Raphael* picked out for all three ships to land at. It was big enough for the whole of Project Columbus, and I don't think we have time to pore over the maps of the surface to find another spot." There was a brief pause, and Darius opened his mouth to respond, but he heard Dayton continue. "I looked over the reports we have here and I don't think it was anything in the approach or atmosphere that made *Raphael* have its issue. Best not to complicate things, right?"

Sensible. I can go to Eriksen with that.

"Understood, sir. I'll run it by Colonel Eriksen and send his answer."

"Good. Drisko will be transmitting our report of the disaster, and we await yours."

"I'm sending it right away, sir. You'll have it before I get to the bridge."

Darius waited for nearly two minutes for Dayton to reply. As Darius was about to give up and leave, the colonel's voice came through one final time. "Understood. Thank you, Lieutenant. Dayton out."

True to his word, Darius commanded the mainframe to send their version of the incident report to *Michael*, and then left the core for the bridge. The trip forward was no longer as eerie now that the entire crew was awake. Whereas during a maintenance cycle he could make the entire trip and never see any of the other nine crew members that were awake, there were now forty. The upper gallery, while not bustling, was now filled with the echoing noises of carts being opened and closed and equipment being repositioned for landing. As he approached pod two, he came across Lieutenant Miller and a sergeant moving a load of hand tools from the lower level, bound for the emergency supply lockers of one of the sleeper pods. Darius nodded an acknowledgement to the men and proceeded past them to his final destination at the front of the sleeper ship.

As he approached, Darius could hear Colonel Eriksen having a conversation with Captain Quinn about the propulsion systems.

"You're sure that running the braking drive at full power isn't going to burn out the reactor?"

"Absolutely certain, sir. The braking drive isn't as big as the main drive, so we don't even have to run the reactor at full output. Between that and other ship systems, we could run the reactor at maybe seventy five percent, and we'd still have plenty of power left over for an emergency."

Darius crested the stairs and pulled his way onto the command platform just as Eriksen nodded at the engineer. "Do it."

Darius sidled up to Eriksen and used the railing to pull his body upright. He saluted, and received a return salute. "Sir, I just spoke with Colonel Dayton."

The colonel's brows rose quizzically. "Oh? Dayton himself?"

"Yes sir."

"What did he have to say?"

"He accepts the unconditional exchange of information regarding the loss of *Raphael*. He also wanted to relay another proposal, sir."

Darius could see Eriksen clench his jaw as he nodded. "What is it?"

"That both ships land at the beacon that *Raphael* dropped on the planet."

There was a pause of several moments before Eriksen responded. "Did he say why?"

"Yes sir. He said that the site is big enough for all three ships, that they haven't seen anything on the approach to the planet that would explain the reactor breach, and that it might take too long to go over the probe maps to find another suitable site."

"Good reasoning," Eriksen said as he tapped at the small console attached to his left armrest. "Which map was it again, Mr. Owens?"

Darius moved to look over Eriksen's shoulder. His finger hovered over a screen that was tiled in thumbnails. After a moment of examining them, he tapped on one, and an aerial view of the selected site filled the screen. Green grass spread for thousands of meters from the banks of a wide, gently meandering river. A pair of large islands split the river at one point, making it flare out like a tennis ball in a sock. At the periphery of the image, to the west and north, clumps of dark green trees dotted the lighter grass. Darius made circling motions over the ground just to the north of the river.

"From the images, it looked like this would be the best place to land. More than enough room for both ships and it looks like this side's got easier access to wood resources up here." Darius crooked his finger at the north edge of the image.

He could see Colonel Eriksen bob his head up and down. "Alright. This is the site, then. Let Dayton know, and tell him north side of the river."

"Yes sir." Darius tried to hold back his grin.

Finally, we're getting somewhere.

"Oh, and one more thing, Mr. Owens."

"Yes sir?"

"Don't disobey my orders again," Eriksen said in an eerily soft voice. "I found out that you told Kimura about *Raphael*."

"Sir, he needed to know," Darius protested.

Eriksen's glare hardened. "An order is an order, Lieutenant. I did not want him informed until after his final passenger checks."

J.C. Rainier

Darius's first impulse was to argue the point further, but he knew that to be a futile exercise. He nodded and took his leave to inform Colonel Dayton of the new plan.

. . .

2nd Lt Darren Cormack
Planetfall +10 days, late morning
Eight miles northeast of sleeper pod seven
site
>|

Darren winced as the stabbing pain tore at his innards. He gasped for air and prayed that he didn't suck any of his vomit back into his mouth as his stomach turned out the last of its contents. The dirt on which he curled up – shaded by a gnarled vine tree – was cool against his burning, flushed skin. The stench of his various bodily discharges burned his nostrils and throat as he sucked in air.

Not now, not like this.

His body was wracked with another massive spasm, and his empty stomach heaved. The motions were that of throwing up, but he had nothing left to eject from his body but bile, which stung his throat and left a terrible acrid taste in his mouth. The shredding pain in his abdomen made him start to wish that he was, in fact, dead. Darren could no longer keep track of time, and it had felt as if he had been sick for days. His mind wandered to a morbid estimation of how much longer he believed he could survive against the disease that was ravaging his body.

A day, maybe two. I'd rather they just shoot me.

Drawing in deep breaths, he managed to quell the spasms that churned his bowels. Darren rolled onto his back and flopped an arm across his eyes to shield them from the light. His ears picked up the sound of footfalls drawing near. They came very close to him and stopped, and he could feel the weight of someone's stare upon his chest.

"Go away," he croaked, the stench of his own breath nearly making him gag again.

"Not likely," retorted Brett. Darren felt the nurse's fingers on his wrist as his pulse was checked, then the back of a cool hand across his burning forehead. "You still have a fever."

"Thanks for the update. I would never have figured that out on my own."

"I see your sarcasm hasn't been dulled one bit."

Darren sighed. "How long have I been out?"

"Just overnight."

A loud burst of gunfire erupted from nearby, and Darren sat bolt upright. He looked around, but only saw a blur of brown, green, and blue. He tried to concentrate on something to his side, and could guess that it was a tree, but his eyes could not make out any detail besides a rough shape or color.

"What the hell was that?" he asked. "Ah, shit. I can't see. Why can't I see?"

A blob of blue in front of him moved, and he felt a hand on his shoulder, gently pushing him back to the ground. "Take it easy. You need to rest, and not to worry. Here, drink up."

Darren felt the hard rim of a canteen against his lips. He drew a deep swig of the warm water, and nearly threw it up right away; he coughed and sputtered, but managed to keep the liquid down. There was a slight metallic aftertaste to the water, and he had to concentrate again on breathing. Once his body had calmed down, he asked again, "What were the shots for?"

He heard an almost imperceptible sigh from Brett. "Probably another jungle cat. We're seeing them more often now."

This is nuts. They just won't go away.

Darren struggled to a sitting position, shaking off his caretaker's attempts to get him to lie down. He blinked furiously in a bid to clear up the fog in his vision, though in vain.

"Get Hank. I need an update."

"Just lie down, Lieutenant," Brett replied with a hint of nervousness.

"God damn it, no. Get Hank right now," Darren squawked.

This time the sigh from Brett was not quite so imperceptible, but rather like a sweeping gust. "Hank's sick."

The words kicked Darren in his gut, and he almost threw up again. He dug his fingertips into the hard soil and scraped them until he felt as if his fingernails would tear off. He clenched his teeth and tried to recall which of his remaining scouts would be the most trustworthy.

"Fine. Get me Laura." Darren blinked at the blurred mass of the nurse in front of him. The silence he received in return, and the lack of movement, spoke volumes. "Laura's sick too?"

"Worse."

Worse?

"What the hell do you mean, worse?" There was another pause. It seemed to Darren that the whole jungle hushed just a bit as he sat in anticipation of the negative news.

"Laura's gone."

"What?" Darren exclaimed and tried to scramble to his feet. He couldn't gain his balance, wobbled, and toppled onto his hip. "She was just here yesterday."

"I know. She was gone this morning. Sixteen others, too."

"Sixteen? Jesus, why didn't you tell me this bug is so bad?"

"Huh? Oh, no, no. They're not dead. They took a bunch of supplies and left the camp, as far as we can tell."

It took a minute for the implications to sink in. Darren was not only suffering the single most painful and humiliating illness in his life, and in danger of dying, but the injury had just had the insult of losing control of his camp heaped on top. He could feel his rage boil within him, but that quickly gave way to nausea. He rolled over and gave another agonizing heave as his stomach again emptied what little was left in it. When he regained control and the spasms left his body, he was given another drink of vile, tepid water.

Seventeen people just up and left. Do they even know where the hell they are going? Did Laura take... crap.

"What about the arms?" Darren asked, anxious to know if his supposedly trustworthy scout had raided the precious supply of weapons that protected the survivors.

"Hmm?"

"Did she take any arms? Rifles? Sidearms?"

"I... I'm sorry, I don't know. If Hank were better, he could count what's left."

"I need you to do it, then."

"I can't. I've spent too much time on you as it is. I need to tend to the rest of the patients."

Darren muttered a curse under his breath. "I'm sure you can get what's-her-name to do it for a bit. What was it, Mindy?"

His question must have struck a chord with Brett, because he fell silent again. Darren sat up just in time to see the blue bulk of his blur squat even lower, into what he presumed was a sitting position.

"She's dead."

Darren hung his head low, until his vision was a uniform wash of fuzzy brown. His heart sank and thoughts of despair settled in his mind. Mindy didn't deserve to die, he thought, as the possibility of his own death crept in. Like Brett, she was a nurse who had volunteered to help with the ever growing legion of the ill. Darren hadn't even been aware that she had been ill.

She must have gotten sick just after I did. Damn, this thing can kill fast…

He closed his eyes and lay back down on the ground. "What's the count today?" Silence greeted him as he waited for a response. "How many, please, Brett?"

"Including Mindy, four dead. Including you, there are now eighteen ill. Five have fully recovered."

Six dead total now.

"How about food and water?"

"Well, we're doing okay on the water for now. We're able to purify it a little quicker than we're using it. Food is another matter. I'm afraid that Laura and her group took quite a bit of what was left."

God damn it. Darren sighed heavily as he saw a fleeting image in the back of his eyelids of a phantom Laura grabbing a pack and running away. *How the hell did I not see that she'd do this?*

"Understood. Thanks. I've kept you too long."

"Please, Lieutenant, just get some rest."

He could hear Brett's strides fading as he jogged off into the camp. The shifting sun had begun to cast its burning rays through the tree canopy, and the stench of his surroundings was unbearable. Darren got to his knees and crawled into the shade of another nearby tree, and lay down as close to the base as he could. He closed his eyes and listened to the sounds of the encampment. A general murmur of activity was occasionally accentuated with the haunting groans or labored retching of the ill.

Not now. Not like this.

. . .

Gabrielle Serrano
Planetfall +10 days, midday
Sleeper pod eleven site
>|

The warm white sands tickled the soles of Gabi's feet as she ran, giggling gleefully, away from a leggy seven year old boy. She darted to her right, nearly running headlong into the surf. The boy tagged her gently on the back as she tried to duck under his arm. She shrieked and dropped onto her shins.

"You're it," he exclaimed with a wide grin. "No tag backs!"

She gained her feet and felt the gentle waves lap at her feet. She paused for a moment as she thought she heard a rumbling noise. The green and blue sea sparkled almost endlessly as she looked over its expanse, but in the distance, just above the horizon, a band of inky black clouds shrouded the sky. She took a quick look above, and then back toward the massive gray metal dome that her mother and father called a "sleeper pod". She could make out her mom, at work near the edge of the trees where they had spent the night before. She waved at Gabi, and Gabi flapped her arm, returning an exaggerated gesture.

A much older girl, with flowing brown hair, darted across Gabi's field of vision, and she launched herself at her new target. She had nearly caught up with the girl when she laughed and outran Gabi quite easily. Gabi persisted, once again catching up, but the older girl sped up again and veered to the left and into the surf where Gabi dared not follow.

"No fair, you cheat!" she screamed.

The girl just laughed, bounded deeper into the water, and dunked her body in the surf. Gabi ran into the waves until she was waist deep, at which point a wave knocked her over and sent her tumbling back to shore. She sat on the sand for a minute and pouted, then heard taunts of other children from over her shoulder. Gabi giggled again and sprang up, locking her focus on Aidan.

He's smaller; I can run faster than him.

She pumped her legs and flailed her arms as she chased him down. He ran toward where the river joined the sea, and looked over his shoulder. His eyes got wide as Gabi closed within reach. Aidan jerked to the left to try to dodge her tag, but was unable to get out of her way. Gabi's fingers touched his shoulder just as he slipped, and as he went down, her knee ran into his head, and Gabi tumbled head over heels into the sand. She landed awkwardly, and scraped her hand on a small, jagged rock obscured by the sand. Pain shot through her hand and she immediately clutched it and began to whimper, but the noise was drowned out by a sudden, loud scream from Aidan.

Gabi turned and plopped her rear on the beach, and while nursing her scrape, she looked at Aidan. Tears streamed down his face, and a large red bump rose from his forehead. His eyes were closed and his mouth was wide open, with a deafening wail coming from within.

"Shhh, it's okay, Aidan," she said as she crept forward.

"Get away from him!" she heard Marya yell. Gabi looked up and saw Aidan's sister running in their direction. "Leave my brother alone!"

Gabi was barely able to get the words "I'm sorry" from her lips before Marya closed the gap, lunged at her, and knocked her back into the sand. She was in utter shock, unable to understand why Marya would do such a thing. Before she could react, Marya began pounding her fists on Gabi's chest. Gabi screamed and tried to wiggle away from the larger girl, but her efforts were only rewarded by a fist bashing into her cheek. She flailed desperately, and managed to loosen her arms from underneath Marya. Gabi brought her hands up to her face to protect it. Blows rained on her arms, occasionally slipping by and hitting her sides or head. Gabi shrieked a long, loud, blood curdling scream.

"Ow, stop it! Stop it!" she sobbed.

"Stay. Away. From. My. Brother!" Marya drove each word home with a punch.

"You're hurting me," Gabi protested.

A moment later, the hits stopped. She could hear the yells of adults in the distance, but her body and head throbbed and stung, so she curled her body into a ball. Quickly she shot a glance around, and saw Marya standing above her, and a long flash of brown. Gabi barely had time to throw up an arm before the driftwood crashed down on it with a sickening crunch. Her arm fell limp at her side, and suddenly it felt as if her arm were on fire and being cut, all at the same time. Gabi's scream intensified, and she could hear nothing else until at last she ran out of breath and stopped.

Marya hefted the chunk of wood over her head again. Gabi rolled over and closed her eyes, waiting to be hit again. The blow never came; there was a shuffling sound next to her, Aidan crying, and a jumble of voices. Then Marya bellowed, "Let me go! She hurt Aidan!"

"Gabi? Gabi, are you okay?" her mother's voice cut through the ruckus.

Gabi cried again, her arm still in tremendous pain. She shook her head and curled up again. She felt arms around her, and the sensation of being lifted out of the sand. Her eyes fluttered open and she saw her mom's face framed by the pale blue sky. Her body was jostled, and she took a quick look around. Her mother was carrying her from the beach, and behind her, her father had a screaming and struggling Marya tucked underneath his arm. The older girl whom Gabi had chased earlier had Aidan in her arms, walking alongside her father. A throng of adults and children followed behind.

"Mama, it hurts so bad."

"I know, Gabi. Hang on, Mija. We're going to see a doctor. He'll make you feel better."

Gabi was jostled again as her mom bounded onto the ramp to the pod. She squealed as renewed pain shot through her arm. She could barely make out the walls of the hallways as they came in from the sun. Her mom lay her down on the metal floor. She curled her chest to her knees and cried. Gabi could tell her mom was talking to someone, but she could only pay attention to the agony that was throbbing, pulsing, and shooting through her arm.

Why did she do that to me? Gabi's attention drifted to a chubby man with a sunburned face kneeling next to her. He had been talking to her, but she hadn't been listening. He smiled as she made eye contact with her.

"What's your name?" he asked.

"G-Gabi," she sniffed.

"Hi Gabi. I'm Doctor Petrovsky. Your mom tells me you've got a pretty big owie. Can I look at it?"

She shied away for a second. "It really, really hurts!"

"I know it does, sweetie. I want to look at it so I can make it feel better, okay?" Gabi nodded and offered her injured arm. The doctor took it gingerly in his fingers. He started examining from her fingers up. "Let me know when it hurts," he said. His fingers probed farther up her arm. The pain intensified a little, and then he reached a point that he touched and the flood gates opened. Gabi screamed and tried to pull her arm back, but he kept her from doing so.

"It hurts!"

"Okay, that helps me tell how to fix it. Does this hurt?" He poked and probed again, and she could feel his fingers, but the pain remained in the last spot he checked.

"No, it only hurts here," she said as she gently placed her finger next to where her arm was throbbing.

Dr. Petrovsky nodded. "You've got a broken bone in your arm, Gabi. I need to fix this up. I'm going to talk to your mom and be right back with you, okay?"

Gabi nodded and curled up again. She whimpered, and as she waited for the doctor to return, she overheard part of the conversation with her mom.

"…Do you just want me to give her something for the pain?" he asked.

"Yes, please." Her mom's voice was quivering, and Gabi knew she was very upset. "Just fix up my baby."

"Alright. Does she have any medical allergies?"

"No, just bees."

"Okay. I'll sedate her. You're going to need to watch her for the rest of the day."

"I will," her mom promised.

Gabi could hear rustling noises near her as the doctor slipped on a pair of disposable gloves and laid out some medical tools next to him. Her mother knelt behind her and held her across her chest. The embrace of her mom helped dull the pain, until the doctor returned with a syringe, placing it on a tray next to him. Panic started to grip Gabi as she stared at the shiny tip of the needle. She recoiled, but could go nowhere as her mother held her fast.

"I'm going to give you a shot that will make you feel a lot better. It will sting for a minute, and then you'll sleep for a little bit. When you wake up, your arm will be in a cast, and you won't be able to move it for a while. We need to do this so your arm can heal, okay?"

Gabi looked up at her mom, who gave her a nervous smile and nodded. Gabi looked back at Doctor Petrovsky, pursed her lips, and nodded. He swiped a cleaning wipe across her other arm, retrieved the syringe, and pierced her arm with the needle. She barely felt anything as it went into her skin. She watched as the clear medicine was pushed into her, and the needle was pulled back.

"That didn't hurt at all," she said bravely. A moment later, her head began to swim. The pain in her arm quickly faded. She looked up at her mom. "I feel funny, Mama," and then slipped into sleep.

• • •

Capt Haruka Kimura
Planetfall +10 days, early afternoon
Sleeper pod eleven site
>|

"There's been an incident."

The look on James's face told Haruka quite a bit. She had learned that he had a tell when something was eating at him. His eyebrows would furrow so deeply that they would weave together, and he would scratch his cheek. As he stood in front of a stand of wiry palm trees just off the beach, he went through this routine. Haruka sighed as she lifted herself to her feet. She wobbled once and he made a move to help her, but she waved him off.

"You still feeling a bit off?" he asked.

Haruka nodded and steadied herself on the trunk of another tree. She had thought that a day of rest would be enough to get her back on her feet after the ordeal she had endured since *Raphael's* reactor went critical and the pods crashed, but she was just as tired this day as the day that pod eight's survivors had arrived at the beach.

"I'm fine," she insisted. "This incident, what happened?"

James eyed her for a second and scratched his cheek again. "It took a while for me to get the whole story, but I guess a bunch of kids were playing on the beach, and Aidan got hurt. One of the kids that saw it says that Gabi accidentally knocked him over and he hit his head, but his sister attacked Gabi."

Haruka's heart sank. She was very fond of Gabi and her family, and it made her anxious to know that another child had intentionally at-tacked her.

"Is she alright?"

"She's got a broken arm, but she's seen the doctor from pod eleven," James said with a measured bob of his head. "It could have been much worse. Luis says that Marya clubbed her pretty good with a piece of driftwood, and was about to hit her again before he, Maria, and Kristin broke up the fight."

"That's pretty severe for a little kid to be doing that. Have you talk-ed to Marya?"

"I have."

"And what did she have to say?"

"Well, she was upset, but I'm pretty sure she thought that Gabi hurt her brother on purpose."

Haruka cast her gaze down at the packed dirt and let loose a sigh. "Those two have been a bit of trouble since I returned Gabi from the jungle, haven't they?"

"Yeah."

"And now this."

"Yeah."

Haruka thought the situation through. She knew that the orphaned children would be struggling for some time with the loss of their parents, and that the Serranos had shown great kindness by taking them in as their own, but Gabi and Marya together at times were like a powder keg waiting to explode. Gabi didn't understand the grief that Marya or her brother were dealing with, and Marya was so emotional that she was prone to irrationality.

And now violence.

"Get Luis for me please, James. I also want to speak with the doctor, if you don't mind."

"Understood. What about your meeting with Leight?"

I hadn't forgotten, James. But thank you.

"A little demonstration for him, I'm thinking. If you could, bring all three of them here," she replied.

His eyebrows perked up and his eyes widened. "What are you planning?"

"You said he believes we're a burden, right? I'm just going to show him that we can handle ourselves."

James gave her an incredulous look before he nodded and headed off toward the sleeper pod. A distant clap of thunder rolled through, nearly drowned out by the rustling of the breeze through the canopy of palm leaves above her head. Haruka paced parallel to the beach, emerging from behind the pod's shadow. As she looked across the sparkling sea, she saw storm clouds on the horizon, closing in.

Great, just what we need.

A tiny yellow streak amongst the clouds, and a white flash silhouette of another cloud confirmed the presence of lightning, and almost a minute later, the faint rumble again taunted Haruka's ears. She looked back at the camp where the survivors from pod eight had set up. Other than the trees and a few makeshift tents woven from fallen palm fronds and wood debris, they had absolutely no protection from a storm.

This is a tropical area, too. Haruka's eyes swept back to the dark, roiling mass on the horizon. *If this storm is anything like those on Earth, we're in danger.*

She paced back to the patch of dirt that she called "home" for the moment. She took a seat, rolled up her sleeves, and examined the dark purple and red blotches on her arms. She ran her hands across the surface of her skin, scratching a couple itchy bumps on each one where she had been bitten by native insects.

And another problem we have to deal with. Aggressive cats, toxic insects, storms... this planet has been real fun so far. I suppose it was only time before something happened between the survivors, too.

She glanced up and saw four men approach from the beach; James and Luis were easy for her to distinguish, as was Sergeant Leight. With his facial hair growing and becoming increasingly shaggy, Leight's goatee threatened to be lost within a blossoming beard. The fourth man was a portly middle-aged man in a soiled button-down shirt. His sleeves were rolled up, and his rotund cheeks and broad nose were brightly colored by sunburn. Haruka stood to receive them, exchanging salutes with Sergeant Leight.

James introduced the stranger to Haruka. "Captain Kimura, this is Doctor Ken Petrovsky."

"Pleased to meet you, Doctor," Haruka said as she extended her hand. He gripped it firmly and shook, and she caught him glancing down at her arm for a moment before they broke contact.

"Likewise, Captain," he replied. "I understand you have had quite the adventure over the past week or so. You were on the ship when the reactor breached?"

"Not on the ship. We escaped before the reactor went critical, just after one of the generators blew. Besides, I think everyone has had a rough time. We're just trying to make the best out of a bad situation. Speaking of, how is our little patient?"

"Resting. The medical supplies available to us aren't very extensive or advanced." Dr. Petrovsky's shoulders slumped as he sighed. "I was able to make a splint for her, but I have no idea how I'm supposed to make a hard cast later when she needs it. She's going to have a long and hard road ahead of her. She's also going to be sore all over for the next few days. When I was working on her I noticed several bruises forming all over her face and body."

Haruka glanced over at Luis to see his reaction. She could see him repeatedly square and clench his jaw, and he wrung a small palm front in his hand. She thought he might try to tear it, which would be no small feat, as the survivors had found just after arrival that the leaves were tremendously tough and fibrous.

"You have my thanks, Doctor," she continued. "I don't know if James has told you this, but we have an experienced nurse in our group; a woman named Emilia Reiber. If you need her for anything, she is at your disposal."

At this, both James and Leight raised their brows. *Good, that got his attention.*

"I appreciate that, Captain. I hope I won't need to take you up on that offer."

"I'm sure at some point you will. As much as I'd like to think that everything will go perfectly from here on out, luck hasn't been on our side. Again, thank you. You may go."

Petrovsky reached his hand out again, and when Haruka shook it, he leaned in and whispered in her ear, "Do they know yet?"

A moment of confusion made Haruka's response slow. "Know what?"

"How ill you are."

A chill ran down her spine and a lump rose in her throat. "What? No. No, I'm not…"

He recoiled and let go of her hand. A frown marred his face, and he looked at her with great concern. "You… you don't know?" She just looked at him, completely aghast, numb inside. "Come find me after your meeting. I will explain it to you."

She nodded curtly, and Dr. Petrovsky waddled away. She watched as he went, and saw him plop down in the sand just outside of earshot.

What the hell is he talking about?

"Haruka?" James interrupted her thoughts.

"Hmm?"

"Are you okay?"

"Sorry, lost in thought. Luis."

"Yes, ma'am?"

"I don't want you to take this as slight. I think the world of you and Maria, and what you've done for Aidan and Marya." She watched as he reversed his grip on the palm frond and wrung it the opposite direction. "Marya and Gabi can't be together, for their safety. I'm going to have James find another suitable couple to take custody of Marya and

Aidan."

Luis said nothing. He simply nodded and concentrated his frustration on the leaf in his hands. Haruka knew he was upset, and he wanted to say something. The fact that he didn't was unsettling. He turned and walked away with a single backward glance.

The sooner this day is over, the better.

"Sergeant Leight," she said in a firm tone.

"Yes, Captain?"

"I'm sorry for the burden we've placed on your doctor today. We've been trying to stay out of your hair. This is just an unfortunate circumstance. So, it would seem, is that," Haruka said, leveling her arm and pointing at the billowing black clouds in the distance. "As much as I don't want to, I need to ask you for help."

Leight nodded. "Tell me what you're looking for, and I'll consider it."

"Shelter for the children, for the duration of the storm."

"I can't take another hundred people in the pod," Leight replied, a frown twisting his shaggy beard downward.

"I'm not asking for a hundred. Just twenty or so for the children and the parents of the younger ones."

"What about the rest of your people?"

"We've managed to make some tents out of these palms." Haruka dropped to a knee and drew a diagram of the beach, a large rectangle representing the pod, and several smaller squares right next to it. "If we move them to butt up against the leeward side of the pod, it should give them a good amount of shelter. We can lash the tents to rocks as well as a few hard points on the side of the pod."

"What?" James exclaimed. "That's nuts! You're going to have us outside? What if that thing is a hurricane?"

Perfect, she thought. *Sow the seed of doubt in Sergeant Leight.* Haruka's plan was spontaneous, and she hoped that her gambit would work. She had no intention of letting her survivors actually spend the night outside during the storm, but Leight had already shot down the idea. It was time for a new angle, and unorthodox seemed to be the best way to go about it.

"We'll be fine," she replied coolly.

"You don't even know what's out there," he complained. "Seriously, Haruka. Think about it; what if this is a hurricane? I mean, this place reminds me of the Caribbean. Know what happens in the Caribbean? Hurricanes."

She could see Leight deep in thought, his fingers scratching the fur on his chin. *It's working.*

"That's enough, Mr. Vandemark," she growled.

Shock registered on his face, and his slacked mouth looked as if it might catch flies. "What?"

"That's enough. I've made my decision."

"You can't be serious."

"I am. You are dismissed."

He stammered, trying to find a response. His face turned bright red, and stormed off.

Haruka turned back to Leight, who was still lost in his thought. "I'm sorry about that. Can we count on you to protect the children?"

His head snapped up and his eyes met hers. "I'm sorry, what?"

"The children. Can they stay in the pod?"

Leight sighed, and she saw his stony façade melt away. "You know, your man Vandemark there isn't wrong. It'll be cramped, but it's better than putting your folks in danger. All of your people are welcome to stay in the pod for the duration of the storm."

Haruka pushed her elation deep down and feigned surprise. "All of them? Are you sure?"

"Jesus, Captain. Do you really think I like the idea of someone dying out there because I shut them out? Just make sure everyone brings food and bedding. You might want to bury your tools and other supplies next to the pod, where you wanted to put your tents."

Beautiful.

"Thank you, Sergeant. We'll be out of your hair when it's done."

Leight nodded. "You've kept your word so far, so I don't doubt you'll do the same this time. Have your people onboard by nightfall. We're going to seal up then and ride this out."

With a salute, the sergeant took his leave, passing Dr. Petrovsky on the beach. Haruka's nerves began to jitter anew as she walked toward him. She was at the same time curious to hear what reasoning the doctor had for his conclusion, as well as anxious as to what he had in mind.

"You wanted to see me, Doctor?" she asked as she reached his spot on the beach, overlooking a tiny reef in the water.

"Yes. I'm sorry for the way that I approached your situation there. I thought you knew."

"There's nothing to know. I'm not sick."

"May I?" Petrovsky pointed at her sleeves. She nodded, and he rolled them up, exposing the patchy discolorations. "This is a condition called purpura. Basically, you're bleeding under your skin."

"Like a bruise? I've had my fair share of scrapes getting here," she scoffed.

"Bruises are predictable. See how uneven and blotchy these are? It's something else. Tell me, have you been unusually tired?"

Her stomach began to churn. She answered only with a nod.

"And I bet your first day or two on the planet you were ill?"

She nodded again. A feeling of dread blanketed her and her fingers began to tingle.

"How much radiation were you exposed to while you were on the ship?"

"Enough to trigger the alarms in the engineering compartment."

"I see," Petrovsky said as he looked into her pupils. "How much is that?"

"I… I don't know. I'm a pilot, not a nuke tech."

"I see. I need to find out, but I don't think I'll like the answer when I do."

Haruka swallowed hard and her hand trembled. "Why?"

"You're exhibiting the symptoms of acute radiation syndrome."

Haruka lowered herself to her knees, then sat on her ankles, fearing that she would collapse if she didn't get off her feet. The diagnosis was devastating, but it also made sense; the generator could have damaged the reactor, or the steam that powered the generators could have become contaminated.

"Am I dying?"

"I don't know," he replied. "Even if I find out what level of radiation triggers the alarms, you could have been exposed to a lot more. Best case scenario, you get some ugly skin discoloration and a heightened risk of cancer. Worst case…"

"I die." The words rolled off her lips, cold and dead.

"I'm sorry. It's a distinct possibility. Without proper supplies, even two or three grays of radiation…"

She cut him off. "I don't need to know any more."

"Other than just now, I haven't had a chance to examine you," he added. "I want you to come see me once a day for the next week. We'll go from there."

Haruka slowly stood up. "Thank you again, Doctor. I have more work to do."

He nodded, and Haruka left the man sitting on the beach. She stumbled numbly back up the bank to the survivors who she watched over. Their lives suddenly seemed so different than hers. They would live to face whatever hardships and rewards Demeter had in store for them, but now Haruka's fate was uncertain. *Raphael* had given her one final stab from its orbital grave.

"Captain!" she heard James shout. She spun to her side and saw him marching purposefully toward her. "Captain, please tell me you're not serious about riding out the storm behind a bunch of leaves."

She took a deep breath and shoved her emotions into a deep recess. "Of course not, James. It was a ruse to get Leight to help."

He stopped mid stride, his brow furrowed, and he scratched his cheek. "What? You mean that whole bit…"

"That's right. It worked too." She slapped him on the shoulder as she walked past him. "Come on, we've got to get everyone packed up."

He caught up with her in a few strides. "Next time, a heads up would be nice."

You don't need to know everything, James.

• • •

Calvin McLaughlin
9 April 2058, 11:50
Michael
>|

Two meal pouches drifted lazily across the top shelf of the locker. Below, each of the four remaining shelves was stuffed to capacity with neatly banded stacks of meals, two deep and a dozen across. Cal considered unbinding a new bundle of meals to have a better selection, but instead opted to take the two from the top shelf.

I can refill the shelf later, anyway.

With his plunder tucked under his arm, he maneuvered out of the inner pod hallway and into sleeper hallway delta. He arrived at Alexis's berth – which had its hatch open – and gently rapped on its metal.

"Go away," Alexis's voice replied from within, her harsh tone denoting irritation.

Two days, and she's still pissed at me.

"Look, hiding in there is going to be pretty boring. Besides, I've got something to show you."

"Yeah, I've fallen for that one before."

Touché.

"Doesn't mean that you should be a hermit," he shot back. "C'mon. Let's go up to the bridge for lunch."

After a brief pause, Cal heard the unmistakable rasp of metal on metal as a restraint was released, and Alexis popped her head out from inside her perfectly sculpted cave.

"The bridge? You know I'm not supposed to get in the way of the crew."

Cal grinned, hoping she might display a hint of emotion other than annoyance. "I have my ways. We'll be out of their way."

He did get a reaction, though not one that he hoped for; she rolled her eyes at him. "Buying more favors from the captain?"

"Colonel. And no. They'll be having chow by the time we get up there, so there should only be one guy up there."

"One guy can still tattle."

"Not when he's your friend, or when his CO doesn't care. C'mon, let's go."

Her eyes narrowed as she slinked weightlessly out of the berth.

Alexis had donned a flight suit, courtesy of the crew. She still made his heart flutter despite the one piece, utilitarian threads she wore. All the same, her scrutinizing stare bored into his chest, and it almost felt as if it pushed him back. The seconds marched on into minutes, and the longer she kept her eyes locked on him, the smaller he felt. He wanted to disappear, but he was committed to the moment, and he felt that running away might be the nail in the coffin of his attempt to reconcile with her.

"I suppose you won't take no for an answer," she said at last.

Cal sighed. "Look, I'm not trying to be a pain in the ass here. You've made your point. Please, just let me do this for you."

Her response came after a short pause, though far quicker than he expected. "Fine. Let's go."

She pulled past him and through the hatch without making eye contact. He followed her, watching her flowing hair snake and whip about as she hastily made her way out of the pod. She turned left after exiting the connecting hallway and entering the gallery.

"Um, Alexis?" She rolled onto her back midair and looked at him as she floated toward the rear of the ship. "Other way. That's the engine room."

She glanced at the airlock to the rear, and then floated back first into the wall, before shoving off toward the front. "Oh, right. I knew that." Cal pursed his lips and stifled a chuckle. "Don't even think about it."

"Mm hmm," he mumbled and shot off of a structural brace, straight for the bridge.

The half kilometer journey to the front of the ship was made in near dead silence. Cal knew the lack of activity and sound meant that the crew was eating; most would be in the crew pod below the bridge. While Cameron Drisko and Colonel Dayton would not mind him bringing Alexis to the bridge, he did have a concern that some of the other crew members might have an issue if they lingered too long. Lieutenant Traci Josephson might even cause an altercation; he would need Cameron to keep him informed of her assignment and, if possible, movements. Cal felt a slight tingle of excitement at the thought of an almost covert operation to spend time with Alexis, though he knew in the end that Colonel Dayton would do nothing more than sanction him.

The pair passed through the airlock leading to the bridge and crew pod, and Cal guided Alexis up the staircase to the bridge. The vast canopy of glass gave a full view of the stars in nearly all directions, but Alexis's attention was firmly planted on one singular star; Alpha Centauri B, a small orange orb barely the size of an pencil eraser, which lay dead ahead.

"This is what I wanted to show you," he said, trying to suppress any hint of pride. "In just under two months, we'll be landing on the planet, and this will be our new sun."

Alexis grasped the railing and locked her silent stare on the star, occasionally adjusting her body when it had drifted too far up or down. Sergeant Cameron Drisko glanced up from his operations station just to the right of the command chair, nodding at Cal. Cal smiled and nodded back. He left her to visit with his friend briefly.

"Is everything set?" Cal asked.

"Just like you asked," Drisko replied. "The nav stations are locked so you can't accidentally change course."

"What about Josephson?"

"She's on inventory duty back in cargo pods seventeen and eighteen. It's perfect, dude. I told you it would be." Drisko clapped Cal on his shoulder, and his grin was wide enough that Cal nearly mistook him for the Cheshire Cat.

"Thanks, I owe you one." He gave Drisko a fist bump before he coasted back to Alexis on the command platform.

"It's not a joke, is it?" she asked, eyes wide as balloons.

"Not a joke. Not this, not what I've done, and not what I will be saying."

Her eyes snapped up to meet his. "That sounds ominous."

Cal let go of the railing and gestured toward the forward nav stations. "Like you said, it's not a joke. I don't want to freak you out or anything, but I do think we need to talk about it. Have a seat."

"Wait, talk about what?"

"Life once we get there."

She gave him a wary look, but pulled her way to the rightmost nav seat and secured herself. He selected the center seat, making sure that he would be next to her for the upcoming conversation. He retrieved the meals from under his arm and handed her one, which she accepted. He waited for her to open her pouch, and the almost inevitable scattering of the contents that happened when one was not used to the lack of gravity. He helped her retrieve her food, and then opened his own pouch with a deft swipe.

"So what about life on the new planet do you think we need to talk about?" she asked, and then took a bite from the sandwich that she had unwrapped.

Here goes everything.

"Why do you think you're here?"

The question made her stop mid bite. She thought for a second, and slowly started to chew again. When she swallowed her bite, she gave her response. "I don't know. Maybe it's because I was a refugee. Maybe it's because of my age."

Cal nodded. "There were other refugees. Other nineteen year olds."

"Hey, how did you know how old I am?" she asked.

A very slight smile crossed his lips. "I overheard some of your details when Colonel Dayton was grilling me just after I woke up. I came out of stasis under really odd circumstances. There was a point at which he thought we were part of some weird conspiracy."

Her eyes narrowed and locked on him. "Are you serious?"

"I swear. This crap is too weird for me to make up. In any case, those were two of the reasons, but not all of them."

"Okay, smarty pants. Were there other reasons?"

"Well, from what I remember Cameron saying, your love of camping and your ability to cook were also on that list."

"Those are weird reasons."

"Maybe, maybe not," Cal continued. "I never really asked anyone about it, but I did give a lot of thought to it in my spare time. Other than the ship, we're not going to have any shelter until we build stuff, right?" Alexis paused and then nodded. "So we might have to camp outside the ship, depending on what goes on. Also, pretty much everyone here has a specialty, and for a reason. You were a line cook, so you can help feed everyone here, right?"

"Uh, I guess that makes sense."

"Right. Cameron's shown me a sample of the kinds of people we have aboard. There are doctors, nurses, carpenters, and loggers. Teachers and preachers. Architects, geologists, and farmers. Almost everyone has a place."

"That's the second time you've said almost. Who doesn't have a place?"

Cal sighed heavily and looked through the glass in front of him at the star. "Me."

"You? What kind of crap talk is that? If I'm here for a reason, you're here for a reason too. C'mon, tell me what it is you're good at."

Screwing things up.

"Nothing. I haven't really succeeded in anything at life. I don't really have any useful skills. I'm not supposed to be here."

Alexis let out an exasperated sigh. "Quit being so difficult. They must have chosen you for a reason."

"They didn't." Cal looked into her brilliant green eyes. She wore a smile on her face, as if she was on the trail of some great mystery, and solving it would bring her satisfaction. It made Cal feel all the more guilty that he was about to shatter the mystique. "Dad somehow pulled some strings and got me on board. I was never chosen to be up here. There *was* a conspiracy, but it was my dad who was part of it, not me. I only got the benefit of whatever it was that he did."

The smile on her face was quickly erased, and a blank look of disbelief replaced it. "You're joking."

"I already said that none of this is a joke."

Alexis blinked at him twice in slow succession, then turned to face the sun, and continued eating. He likewise turned and consumed his meal, near complete silence forming an almost impenetrable barrier between them.

At least she knows the whole truth now.

Cal and Alexis finished eating almost at the same time, and Cal collected the waste into one pouch. Alexis broke the silence.

"So what are you going to do when we get there?"

"At first? Odd jobs. Whatever I can do to make myself useful. I'm sure that Dayton can find something for me to do. After that…" his voice trailed off as he considered the wisdom of what his mind conceived so many years ago, shortly after his revival from stasis the first time.

"Tell me."

"Well, it'll take a little while to get going, but I think it will be useful in the end. I'm going to make biodiesel. Maybe also do something with the waste products."

"Biodiesel? Are we even carrying any cars in this ship?"

Cal laughed nervously. "Not quite. There's some diesel generators and pumps, and a few diesel pickups and bulldozers. I think they even said they had a couple specialized power tools that run on diesel. Anyway, I figure this might be useful just in case they run out of fuel before they can find and drill more. I might not be able to run them all, but every bit counts, right?"

Alexis nodded and gave him a wry grin. "Well, if that's your plan, then I guess there's no doubt that you're from Texas."

"Huh? Why?"

"Come on. Texas? Oil? Diesel? This has got to be the punch line of the joke, right?" she laughed.

Cal laughed as he thought about it. There was an undeniable yet odd poetry to the idea of it all, and yet he hadn't considered the point before Alexis brought it up. He let himself drift in the moment. His mind captured an image of her lips parted to reveal her white teeth as she cackled at her own joke. A memory caught up to him of her soft lips when she pressed them against his in the ESAARC pod. For a brief moment, he thought that all was right again, but then he turned away, a voice inside nagging that it was already too late.

He composed himself and asked, "So what about you?"

"Hmm?"

"What are you going to do? I mean, once things have settled down a bit and you're not needed for a soup line, that is."

"I… I don't know," she admitted. "I haven't had as much time to think about it as you have, I guess."

Cal nodded and managed another nervous smile. "Well, you've got about two months to figure it out before everyone's lives are turned upside down again."

"Cal," she blurted. Her mouth was slightly agape, and she seemed to be catching her breath, as if his name wasn't meant to come out.

"Yes?" he replied casually.

"I was wondering," she said with a hesitation. "Do you want to start working out together again? I mean, it gets kind of lonely down in the gym. I understand if you don't want to, but you know..." She turned and muttered under her breath, "Damn."

Butterflies formed at once in his stomach, and he had to remind himself not to freeze up. "Yeah, I'd like that."

"Okay." She paused again, and her eyes met his again, sending a nervous tingle down his spine. "Tonight, before dinner?"

"You got it."

"Thanks for lunch, and for the view."

Despite the voice in the back of his mind protesting, Cal impulsively lurched forward with his plan to reconcile with Alexis. "I'll give you a better view when we're closer. This planet has two moons, you know."

"It does, huh?"

"Yeah. Want to see them from space? You know, before we land?"

Cal's first reaction was to ball up his fist and shove it in his mouth for blabbing like a spellbound schoolboy, but he resisted. He also resisted his second reaction, which was to throw up from the stress.

"I'd like that," she said, looking away for a brief moment as she answered.

He did not, however, keep himself from grinning like a fool as he saw her out of her seat and off the bridge. "I'll make arrangements."

• • •

```
Capt Haruka Kimura
Planetfall +12 days, mid morning
Sleeper pod eleven site
>|
```

It wasn't a hurricane. I think we can be thankful for that.

Haruka surveyed the bank above pod eleven, where her group of refugees had slept until the storm forced them to seek refuge. Felled trees scattered the ground, their trunks snapped in half over rocks or other fallen timbers. Other spots on the camp ground were untouched by anything but rain. She grimaced as she scrambled up the bank and calculated how much time would be needed to clean up and make a suitable campsite again.

A mess. We would have been hammered out here if we had been forced to stay.

James walked ahead of her and pushed on a felled log, which only moved the slightest bit. "Well, this sucks."

"One step forward, two steps back," Luis commented from just behind her.

"I hope it's not three," she added.

"What do you mean?" asked James.

"Have we heard from Will and his group yet?"

James dug his fingernails into the bark of the tree and sighed. "Not since they left the march party to find that other pod."

Haruka had found James to always have a calm demeanor and a very even keel. Even though he had allowed his son Will to lead a scout party to pod ten in a search for survivors, he had dealt with the separation well. James had told Haruka along the journey about how proud he was of his boy, and how resourceful and disciplined he was as well. But for the past two days, James had been a ball of nerves. He could barely sit still inside the pod as the storm lashed at it. Somewhere in the jungle was his oldest child, possibly caught out in the open during the tempest.

He won't be right until Will is home. I hope they found shelter.

Haruka put on a brave smile. "He'll be fine, James. Just give him a little more time."

"I can't just sit here any longer. I've got to do something."

"So put yourself to work. Keep your hands busy, and the time will pass before you know it."

James grunted, turned around, and leaned on the fallen trunk. "This camp site is almost hopeless. It's stable for now, but it will take a ton of work to clear out. It would almost make more sense to find some place new to set up shop."

Haruka nodded. *I was starting to think that myself.*

"Luis, go get Troy for me."

"Sure thing." He quickly took his leave and made off for the side of the pod, where Haruka could see Troy digging for the tools they had buried.

"Can I go now?" James asked.

Haruka shook her head with vigor. "Not if you're going to do what I think you are."

"I need to find my son," he growled.

"Alone? Over my dead body, because I don't want it to be over *yours*," she snapped back.

"You really think that will stop me?"

"Probably not," she said as she saw Luis return with Troy, and waved them over. "But I can probably change your mind."

"Yeah, Captain?" Troy said with a broad smile as he bounded up.

"Form all of your remaining scouts into two teams. You lead one, James leads the other."

James's mouth twitched as he tried to suppress a grin. "You're giving me a team to look for Will?"

She shot him a glare. "Don't be stupid. Troy's going to look for Will. You're staying close by with the rest of the scouts."

"What? Why?"

"Because I need you to organize and analyze, which you do better than anyone else here," Haruka explained. "I want you to scout around the immediate area and find out which of these little hills here would be most suited to a permanent settlement."

"Permanent?" all three men asked in chorus.

"Permanent. That is, unless you know of a reason why we shouldn't just stay here."

"Don't you think that Leight might have something to say about that?" asked James.

"He might, but we'll be out of his hair. I think that was his bigger issue. He just didn't want a bunch of leeches taxing his supplies.

Besides, we've got to do it sooner or later. Why not here? It's warm, there's this beautiful beach for the kids, and there seem to be some pretty useful resources here." Glances were exchanged around the circle. Each man fidgeted and scratched his hair or beard, but they didn't come up with any objections. "That's settled. James, you're scouting for a place to set us up. Troy, you take your group and try to find Will and his group. See if you can help speed them home."

Troy clapped James on the shoulder, and with a grin said, "Don't worry, bud. Your boy will be home soon."

"Thanks, Troy," he said, relaxing his shoulders slightly.

"Get to it, you two."

"Yes ma'am," they said in an eerie reminder of her former crew-mates. For a moment, she flashed back to an image of the bridge of *Raphael*, and of Colonel Fox demanding obedience of her crew. A shiver went down Haruka's spine, and she had to keep herself from shuddering in disgust.

No, I could never be like her.

She watched her Chief of Ops and Lead Scout move off to the rear of the pod and up the ramp before she turned to Luis.

"How is Gabi doing?"

"Scared. In pain. Really upset. She doesn't understand why Marya hurt her."

Haruka nodded. "Gabi didn't deserve that. I don't believe for a second that she meant to hurt Aidan."

"Neither do I."

"How are you and Maria?"

Luis shrugged. "I can't say that we feel good about what happened, or your decision. I'm upset with Marya for hurting my baby. I don't know, maybe after everything settles I'll understand it all better. I'd avoid Maria for a bit though. I think she's taking this a bit personally, and she thinks she could have worked it all out."

"You two didn't fail. I want you to know that, Luis. This is unfortunate for sure, but it could have happened even if the orphans were being cared for by someone else. All I'm trying to do is give them a little space from Gabi and maybe keep something like this from happening again."

"I know. I just need some time to get used to it."

"Right. We have more work to do, though. Can you go help dig up those tools? We're going to need them."

"Yeah, sure. What's on your plate?"

"I need to talk to Leight again. He sent word a little bit ago that he has information for me."

Luis nodded. "Good luck with that."

"Thanks, I might need it."

Haruka strolled down the bank and walked across the soggy sands toward the pod. Every step seemed to take an increasing amount of strength, and by the time she reached the ramp, her calves were tight and sore.

I have to remember to make time for Dr. Petrovsky today.

She trudged up the ramp and down the long central hallway to the ESAARC cockpit, where she found Sergeant Leight waiting for her. He beckoned for her to take a seat, which she did. Haruka noticed that the com system was turned on.

"What's this?" she asked.

"We've known about a couple other groups of survivors since shortly after we landed. A few days ago we lost contact with one of them, but I thought you might want to talk to the other group. Pods one and two, if you're interested."

More survivors. Best news of the day.

Haruka put on the headset and took a few seconds to adjust it before taking the system off of standby.

"Captain Kimura at pod eleven site. Come in, please."

Almost immediately, she was rewarded with a response. "Lieutenant Marsolek, pod two here. Good to hear from you, Captain."

"Likewise. Sitrep, please."

"Screwed up, Captain. Have you heard from Lieutenant Cormack lately?"

"Not since before I crashed," she replied.

"Huh. Well, we haven't heard from him in over a week. It's like his pod just disappeared off the face of the planet. We were just about to call them MIA, when his second in command showed up out of the blue today with a couple civilian scouts, and updated us on their status."

"Go on, Lieutenant."

There was a noticeable hesitation before Marsolek continued.

"There was something wrong with the water supply at their landing site, from what I gather. They packed up and tried to head out for our position, but got stopped well before they got here when a bunch of their people started to get sick. His sergeant asked us for help, but then she started throwing up and passed out."

Why can't it be just plain good news for once?

"Are you going to send help?" Haruka asked.

"I have to think about it. The report I got was pretty scary. Whatever this bug is that they've got has killed people. Healthy adults, too. And it spreads like wildfire."

So, like Leight, Marsolek is cautious, and will protect his people.

"How many refugees at your camp, Lieutenant?"

"Just under five hundred. There are about a dozen or so I'm not sure will survive, though. We picked them out of pod four, which was a horrible wreck."

Haruka closed her eyes and forced down the welling disgust within. She was about to give an order that she never thought that she'd give, that was against what she believed in, but it was for the good of Marsolek's survivors.

"Make the call, Lieutenant. If you haven't done it already, quarantine the sergeant. Protect your camp and your people. Do you have fresh water nearby?"

"Yes ma'am."

"Good. Hole up there for now. Scout around a bit and see if there's a good place to make a permanent settlement. If not, get to the coast and follow it around to the west. You'll eventually get to us. We're building here."

"Yes ma'am. Marsolek out."

Haruka shut down the com system and tidied up the station. When she looked up, Leight's eyebrows were raised so far they threatened to jump off of his forehead.

"We're building here?"

"That's right, Sergeant," she beamed. "We're moving out and setting up shop."

"Great. I'll notify the beach bums that they can get back to their sunbathing," he moaned.

Haruka snickered. "They won't have enough time when James is done with them."

"I'll believe it when I see it."

"I hope you've got a good lawn chair and a nice view then, Sergeant." With a smile, she left the cockpit and went to find Dr. Petrovsky for her daily checkup.

. . .

2nd Lt Darren Cormack
Planetfall +12 days, late morning
Eight miles northeast of sleeper pod seven site
>|

The stench of rotting flesh assailed Darren's nostrils as he staggered along the row of bodies, hidden out of sight far away from the encampment. His feet dug minute trenches as they dragged through the dirt, and as he drew near, he had to pause for a moment to keep his stomach in check. He made a mental count as he passed each cairn that served as a headstone, making sure that what he had heard from Brett was accurate. At the end of the row sat an open grave with two bodies, resting at the feet of two grim looking, sweaty men with shovels.

Thirteen total. Damn.

Almost one in ten of the survivors from pod seven now lay dead at his feet, their bodies ravaged and finally broken by the illness that ran rampant through their ranks. He knew well the suffering they had encountered before their deaths; Darren himself had been gripped by the disease, and at times, felt as if he was only inches away from death's door. But the fever had broken yesterday, and while he was not as strong as before the ordeal, he was out of danger and recovering physically.

Darren's emotions were a different matter, however. The walk he took put a human face on the issue that he had tried so desperately to reduce to a calculation. He could not ignore the devastation that he knew weighed on the families of the victims. He also understood in a very real way that these thirteen dead colonists were his responsibility, and that his actions since planetfall had ended in the death of each one. He turned away after his eyes fell across faces staring lifelessly back from the grave. They were those of a young mother and one of her two sons – the very same that he had met days earlier under the shade of a palm.

He was only four. His brother has lost everyone he knows.

He'd seen enough; it was time to go back to camp and check in with Brett and his patients. "Close it up," he said as he began to walk away. Darren's skin crawled as he hurried away from the eerie rhapsody of burial made by the dirt and rocks as they rasped on the heads of the shovels. He mounted the knoll and made his way over the series of bumps and troughs that covered the quarter mile or so between the grave and the quarantine at the rear of the encampment.

The quarantine area had grown to cover nearly a third of the total encampment. The ill were strewn about the ground like logs, haphazard and almost random. They would be placed in the shade when brought back for care, but would invariably crawl or be dragged from one spot to another as the shade marched along the ground, or when their patch of earth had become too toxic from vomit and feces. The smells of the quarantine area had also become far viler. The stench of bodily functions, in their current concentration, would carry with someone for almost an hour after leaving the area.

The only mercy of this horror was that the local jungle cats finally seemed to stop trying to make meals out of the colonists. Whether this was because the stench was just too great or because so many cats had been shot in defense, Darren could not possibly know. Like all blessings that came on this planet, however, there was a downside; a species of rodents had showed up and begun scavenging the camp with near reckless abandon. The creatures were about the size of rats, though nearly completely devoid of fur. Their tails were twice as long as their cousins from Earth, and they had no fear of humans whatsoever. Darren had to resort to stockpiling their dwindling rations in one pile, and setting two people to guard them.

He shook his head at the sorry state of their refuge, and then sought out Brett. He found the nurse tending to a sick passenger; the patient was a once portly man who was a ghost of his former self after fighting with the disease for two days. He didn't quite look emaciated, but he had certainly lost a great deal of weight through his ordeal. Darren waited for Brett to finish, and then beckoned him over.

"How are you feeling?" Brett asked as he joined Darren.

"Functional," he replied. *Alone, broken, guilty,* he thought.

"Hmph. I guess that's as straight an answer as I can expect."

Darren ignored the jab. "What's our status today?"

"Well, you'll be glad to know that Hank is finally better. I've let him and a few others go from quarantine. We've also got only one new case today, which is pretty good."

"Agreed. What about our food…"

"Lieutenant Cormack!" a harsh voice yelled from his right. Darren and Brett spun around to find the source of the disturbance, which was from none other than his lead scout, Hank Adams, and a group of a dozen angry looking survivors.

Shit, this can't be good.

"Hank? What the hell is this?" he asked, putting a scowl on his face.

"It's time for us to pack up and go." The crowd gathered behind Hank muttered and shouted in agreement.

"We can't go." Darren pointed emphatically at a group of ill lying on the ground just a few feet away, their loved ones kneeling at their sides. "We can't move the sick."

"Leave them," yelled a voice from the disgruntled throng. "We don't want to sit here and die waiting for them to do the same."

"What the hell is wrong with you?" A short, middle-aged woman with mud caked skin and tangled brown curls screamed as she stormed over from the group of patients. "My husband is dying and you want to run off? You fucking chicken."

The target of her ire pushed his way to the front of the crowd. He wore the tattered remnants of the shirt he was wearing when the pod landed, and his jeans were torn and stained brown from the dirt. He glared at the woman with intense brown eyes. "Give it up. He's as good as dead. I don't want to join him just because you and the lieutenant can't see what's going on here."

By this time, the argument had attracted the attention of much of the camp. Two groups formed in arcs on either side of Darren and Brett; one seemed to be comprised of the loved ones of the sick, the other mostly by those who had not been affected or who had already recovered.

A man from the group defending the ill retorted, "You've got to be kidding me. We stayed here while Hank was sick. Same for Lorenzo and Nina. You can't just decide you want to leave now."

That group erupted in cheers and affirmations, while the other hurled back insults and taunts. Soon there gestures exchanged between both sides, and the noise escalated. Only a few voices could be heard over the din.

"No one else should be forced to stay and get sick!"

"What makes you think you have the right to decide for the rest of us?"

"Let it go. Save yourself."

"Heartless jerk!"

"Quiet!" Darren bellowed at the top of his lungs. Almost instantly, both sides fell silent, and their heads swept to him in a wave. "We can't be at each others' throats like this."

He knew at once that he would be forced to make a decision. The way that both sides looked at him, pleading with their eyes, told him that, and either way it wouldn't be pretty. He began to collect his thoughts, but the pressure of their collective stare made it hard for him to concentrate.

Hank broke the silence. "At least give us the guns and let us go on our own."

"Are you nuts? We need them to protect our families," the brunette lady opposing him shrieked.

"From what, the rats?"

"The cats, moron."

"The last time we saw one of them anywhere near camp was two days ago," Hank snarled back. His cheeks grew rosier and it seemed as if he was panting. Darrin knew that the scout was becoming very agitated, and the insult would do nothing to help.

"Please, let's all calm down for just a second."

"Calm down my ass," yelled Lorenzo from near the back of the pack. "Let's go, Hank. Leave these idiots here to get sick and die. I've wasted enough time with them. Just grab the guns and food and let's go."

Shit, they're serious.

"Wait," Darren blurted. Silence fell as all attention was on him once more. Almost before he could think it through, the words came out. "Anyone who wants to go should go. Anyone who wants to stay can. But we leave two rifles and half of the food behind."

"We?" asked Brett. "You're leaving us behind?"

"I am," he admitted. The shame of abandoning the helpless began to gnaw away at his insides. "We haven't heard from Sergeant Daniels or anyone from the other pods. At this point, I think I need to go on and try to get help from Lieutenant Marsolek."

"But we need you here," he protested.

"No, I can't do anything to help you here. You're needed here, not me."

"Just give me another day."

"You can have as many as you want if you choose to stay behind."

Brett's eyes opened wide and his jaw slacked. "What? Are you serious?"

"I am. You have the option. I'm pretty sure I know what you're going to do, though."

Brett nodded and turned away, back to his patients.

Darren looked around at the two crowds. Those who championed leaving were congratulating each other, sharing laughs, and patting each other on the backs. The display sickened Darren, and he shook his head. The other crowd merely turned their backs, glared, and muttered to each other as they returned to their ill family members. Darren's guilt stabbed him in the gut, and he second guessed his decision.

Maybe I should stay with them, he thought. *It's cruel enough having the others abandon them, but me?* He shook off the thought. *No, I'm more useful going to Marsolek to get help.*

Darren dragged his feet as he wandered away from the camp and back to the graves. His conscience screamed at him, beating him from within. His chest tightened and his breathing became shallow. The grave diggers nodded at him in passing on their way back, but he did not acknowledge them, only listening to his own guilt tearing at him. Darren stopped at the top of the berm just above the grave and looked down at the two fresh cairns, lined up with the previous eleven.

What the hell have I done? I tried so hard to keep everyone safe, and these people died. Now I'm throwing away the lives of others? Darren drew his hands through his hair, closing them around his mane and pulling until it hurt. *I'm supposed to protect people. That's my job.*

"Rough day?" Hank asked, startling Darren. He wheeled around to face the scout.

"You," he spat.

Hank put his arms out to his side, palms up, as if to offer peace. "Take it easy. I don't like what I did either, and I'm sorry that played out the way it did."

"You could have stopped it. Instead you led it."

The scout let out a scoffing laugh. "You have no idea that I just saved your life, do you?"

Darren paused as he absorbed the question. "What the hell are you talking about?"

"Those guys actually wanted to take you out. I convinced them to let you have your choice. Either way, they were walking away with food and guns. Some of them are just plain nuts, man. They've seen too much death, and they're scared. I can't blame their fears, but I think Lorenzo is about to snap. If we don't get him out of here soon he might just execute all the patients."

A chill ran down Darren's spine. "Are you serious?"

"Look, it doesn't matter what you think about what I've done. I'm with you, man. We need to keep these people safe. I'm a bit worried that you're not seeing the whole picture here. Just let me help you, okay?"

"And what about those we're leaving behind? How are we helping them?"

"By giving them a chance, thanks to you," Hank smiled. "Food and rifles. I talked to Brett real quickly after you wandered off. He thinks that in a day, pretty much everyone who is sick will be recovering."

"Or dead," Darren interrupted.

Hank ignored him and continued. "Brett says they'll be walking wounded at that point, but they should be able to follow us. All he wants is for us to leave an obvious trail. If that's all it takes, I'll do it myself."

Darren began the trek back to camp, and Hank fell in at his side. "It's not like I have a choice any more. Make sure you've got whatever tools you need to mark the path for the others."

"Don't worry about a thing. I've got it covered."

Easier said than done.

. . .

```
Capt Haruka Kimura
Planetfall +14 days, midday
Camp Eight
>|
```

She heard the distant cracking noise, followed a second later by the crash.

Another one down, she thought. From where Haruka sat – in the shade of the trees just behind the sleeper pod – she could not see the work progressing on the short hill just south of the river and east of the crashed pod. Short was a relative term, as well. It was actually one of the tallest hills for miles around, but as most other hills were less than fifty feet tall, the lofty hundred and fifty feet that this peak reached would have been short compared to most hills on Earth.

Dr. Petrovsky placed his fingers on her wrist, bringing her attention back to the daily checkup. The past two days had been better for her; her energy was returning, and the doctor had expressed cautious optimism about her condition. Still, having to take the time out of her day to be checked seemed to be a waste. There were dozens of other things that came to mind that she could be doing instead.

"When do you get to stop fussing over me?" she asked.

His chubby face stretched into a cheeky smile. "When I feel that I've tortured you enough. When will you command types ever learn that you don't get to duck away from the doctor, eh?"

Haruka chucked. "You sound just like Emilia."

"No doubt. We're all trained the same way: to annoy you. You should have figured that out by now. Show me your arms, please." Haruka sighed and slid the sleeves of her flight suit up as far as they would go. Dr. Petrovsky gently took her left arm by the elbow and squinted as he examined it more closely. "I want you to take it easy today. This arm's looking a little worse for wear today."

Her smile quickly disappeared and she growled in irritation. She then turned her lower lip out in a pout and used her brown eyes to try to sway the doctor.

"Nuh uh. That's not going to work on me, Captain."

Haruka sighed. "I need to go up to the work site and do an inspection," she protested.

"Oh, you can do that. But so help me, if I hear about you picking up a saw again, I'll have Leight lash you to a bunk for two days."

"Oh? Who tattled on me?"

"I'm not naming my sources," the doctor replied with a wry grin.

Damn it. Being treated like an invalid was starting to wear on her nerves, but having someone in camp spying on her and reporting to the doctor was a little added salt in the wound. Haruka needed to be useful, and she wasn't getting that just by walking around from place to place.

She was just about to try to extract the information from Dr. Petrovsky again when a chorus of cheers rose up from the beach. She turned her head, but the trees obstructed her view, so she jumped to her feet and scrambled down the embankment onto the beach. A large group of pod eleven survivors were running up the beach and collecting in a circle a few hundred feet away. Haruka jogged through the sand with Petrovsky on her heels, calling out to her to slow down.

"Doctor," she yelled back as the crowd began to depart. Through the wall of bodies she could see another mass of bodies, headed by Troy Bryant and Will Vandemark. The younger man had numerous cuts on his face and hands, and walked with a stiff limp. He no longer carried his rifle; the fact that Troy had two led her to believe that somewhere along the way he had lightened Will's load.

"My God," Petrovsky exclaimed as they reached the pack and saw almost a hundred bedraggled survivors stumbling and dragging their bodies down the beach toward the pod.

"Troy," Haruka called out. "Go get Emilia!"

He nodded and bolted for the pod. The crowd on the beach parted, allowing the new arrivals a wide berth. Haruka grabbed Will's hand when he tripped as he walked past her.

"I'm okay," he muttered breathlessly as Haruka helped him to his feet. Her eyes met Will's sister, Kelly. Her hands were cupped over her mouth, and a tear formed in the corner of her eye.

"Kelly, go get your dad, quickly!" she barked. Kelly shot off for the hill as quickly as her awkward teenage legs would carry her. Haruka helped Will to the bottom of the pod's ramp and eased him down slowly into the sand. "What happened?"

It took a minute for him to settle down enough to speak, though his hands still trembled. "There was a storm."

Damn. They got caught out in it.

Emilia charged down the ramp with a medical kit and knelt beside Will. She started to check him over, but he pulled back his arm and waved her off. "I'm fine. Go take care of the others."

"Will, you're hurt. Let her take a look."

"Really, I'm fine. There are others who are hurt worse."

Like his father. Others before self. Haruka nodded to Emilia, who began to check others in the group that quickly filled the beach near the pod. Troy took only a second to replace Emilia at the side of Will.

"We caught up with them last night, across the river and a couple miles up the beach," Troy said. "Looked like hell when we found them. Out of food too, so we gave them all of ours."

Haruka nodded. "Good work, Troy. Do you have a head count?"

"Yeah, Captain. We lost one of our own from Will's group. It was Eckert. Damn shame."

Eckert. The team leader, married with a little girl, and a skilled carpenter. Fuck.

"A huge loss," Haruka replied solemnly.

"As for the folks from pod ten that our people rescued," Troy continued, "two dead in the storm. Ninety one made it back here."

That means about sixty or so killed in the crash.

"What about crew from *Raphael*?"

"Both dead, Captain," Troy replied as he snapped a twig in his hands.

Haruka nodded. She had expected as much when the pod couldn't be raised on the radio, but the confirmation gave closure to the issue. She could now count on two hands the number of crewmen left from *Raphael* that she knew to be alive. That list was by no means stable, either, knowing that Sergeant Daniels of pod seven had collapsed of illness as she reached Lieutenant Marsolek's encampment.

Will's lips quivered and his voice trembled. "We tried to save them, me and Eckert… we tried so hard to get them anywhere they'd have some protection."

"It's okay, Will," soothed Troy. "You did good. They're all safe now."

"Not all of them. Eckert, and that mom and girl that he ran out into the storm to try to save… I tried to stop him. There was no way he could get to them, and I tried to stop him, but he wouldn't listen," he bawled, burying his head in his hands.

Troy leaned over to Haruka and whispered in her ear, "Eckert probably thought of his own wife and kid before he ran out there. How terrified they'd be if they were caught in the open like that. Damn heroic if you ask me."

Haruka shook her head and sighed. "Heroes get themselves killed. Didn't anyone ever tell you that?"

"You're still alive," he retorted.

That's because I'm not a hero. All I've done since I've gotten here is struggle to stay alive.

"Will!" James shouted as he ran full tilt across the beach with Jeanette, Kelly, and Kristin charging up behind him. He skidded on his knees and nearly tackled Will, and Jeanette came up from behind and threw her arms around them. "Will, you're alive!"

"Mom, Dad," he choked as his sisters fell at his feet, joining in the family embrace.

Haruka and Troy took the cue and left the Vandemarks to their reunion. Haruka motioned for Troy to follow, and they walked off the beach toward the hill that overlooked the beach. She caught Luis running from the embankment and stopped him.

"Luis, I need you to take control here."

"Of course, Haruka."

She sighed and looked him square in the eye, her hand on his solid shoulder. "First I need you to find Mrs. Eckert. Her husband didn't make it back."

Luis's face registered his shock. He stammered for a moment, then nodded. "I understand. I'll take care of her."

"Thank you."

"Hell of a week, Captain," Troy remarked as they continued along.

"No argument there, my friend."

"I take it by the fact that I see fewer trees up there that James found a good place to set up shop while I was gone?" Troy asked as he pointed to the peak.

"I think so. Close enough to the river to get water, high enough to keep from getting flooded. Not too steep. Pretty decent all around, I think. I wanted to get your professional opinion, though."

Troy nodded. "Well, from down here it looks pretty good. Let's see what it looks like from up top."

"Good, because your new duty starts now."

He stopped and his brows shot up quizzically. "Captain?"

She smiled. "Troy Bryant, I hereby relieve you of the duty of Lead

Scout. I am appointing you to a new position. You are now the Chief Civil Engineer of Camp Eight."

"Camp Eight?" He burst into a jog to catch up to Haruka. "I'm sorry, but do you mind filling me in? I think I've missed a bit in the past two days."

"It's the nickname that our people have given to the settlement we're building," she explained. "I know it sounds a bit cheesy, but that's what they're calling it. At times I think that it still hasn't sunk in with some people that we're really staying here."

"Are you having a hard time adjusting?"

"No, I get it. Actually, I'm pretty excited that it's here. A little sad, too."

"Because of your friend? What was his name, Mancini?"

Haruka closed her eyes for a second and caught a glimpse of him in her mind, telling a joke at mess. She smiled warmly and opened her eyes. "Yeah. He would have loved this place."

Troy nodded. They walked a few feet in silence before he spoke. "I talked with Gina about it for a little bit when I was saying good bye a couple days ago. You know, it's funny. Back on Earth I was busting my butt off trying to keep food on the table and a roof over our heads, but we used to dream about living in paradise some day. After her mother left us, it was the one thing we could talk about no matter how hard our days were, and no matter how dark the news of the War got."

Haruka grew quiet for a moment. She was aware that Gina's mother was not in the picture, but never dared to broach the subject. "I'm sorry about her mother," she said timidly.

He shrugged, and one corner of his mouth turned down slightly. "Don't be. Our life before was nothing to be proud of. Her mom and I were both addicted to drugs. The state had taken Gina from us a bunch of times. Every time it happened, it felt like I died a little inside. I'd bury myself in drugs and alcohol, then get sober for a few days and they'd bring her back. It took me the longest time to put two and two together. I decided to get sober for good so my little girl wouldn't get taken away. It was hard as hell, but I did it, got myself clean. It's just too bad that Sharri couldn't kick the habit. The pull of the drugs was too much for her. I gave her the choice: us or the drugs. Well, you probably know which she picked."

"I had no idea, Troy. I'm sorry."

"I'm not. It hurt like hell for a while, but both Gina and I realized that she could have easily dragged us both down with her. Instead, we carved our own way. Now that's going to take on a whole new meaning."

"Oh? How so?" she asked as they finished the climb to the summit.

Troy turned around and swept his arm across the panoramic view over the beach. Clear blue sky met green and blue sea. The gray mass of the pod starkly contrasted the white sand around it, and the beach bustled with the activity of triage. Just over the horizon, the bright globe of Persephone began a breathtaking daytime rise.

"We're not just going to live in paradise. We're going to build it with our own hands."

. . .

2nd Lt Darren Cormack
Planetfall +14 days, midday
Twenty miles east-northeast of sleeper pod
seven site
>|

Nina stretched out at the base of a tree, a flight suit wadded behind her head as a makeshift pillow, and her jacket folded several times over and draped across her eyes to shut out the sun. Her military-issue pistol rested in a holster just beyond her fingertips. Darren stood above her and considered the wisdom of disarming her. He was still haunted by Hank's revelation that he was a target for murder, and though the scout also told Darren that his cooperation had saved his life and pacified the would-be assassins, he still didn't feel entirely safe with them still armed. At his feet was one of the three main conspirators; the others were Lorenzo and a man by the name of Josh Denning. The latter was a name unfamiliar to Darren until two days earlier. His great success in keeping himself isolated from the passengers worked too well, as Hank had pointed out. Darren had no clue what was going on in his own camp, and he nearly paid the ultimate price for it.

"I know you're standing there," she mumbled without moving a muscle. "What do you want?"

So she's still awake, he thought. *Maybe later.*

"Get up," Darren said as he prodded her leg with his toe. "We need to keep moving."

"Nope."

"You wanted to get going back there, so get your ass moving."

Her hand reached to her head and whipped the jacket off. Her hair was a matted, sweaty black mess, and her face was sunburned so thoroughly that no patch of skin was spared. The snarl on her lips revealed her crooked teeth, stained dark yellow from years of smoking.

"Bite me. I need a few minutes."

"You've already had a half hour. We're ready to go."

"That's nice," she said, throwing her arm over her eyes.

"You know, for someone who was so eager to leave camp and move on, you sure are taking your sweet time," he snapped back. "We're not here to pick the flowers. Get up, *now!*"

Nina bolted to her feet and stared him down, just two inches from his nose. "For someone who wanted to sit there and die, you're in a big fucking hurry now aren't you?"

Darren stood fast at the challenge. He returned a steel gaze as he watched her nostrils flare and her eyes burn wild with hate. He flexed his fingers, ready to snap them to the sidearm on his belt should she decide to go for her own. The game lasted just under a minute before he scoffed and broke the silence.

"Get packing and fall in."

Her eyes narrowed for a second. She wheeled around and snatched her meager belongings from beneath the tree. Darren's heart beat in double time as she reached for the gun belt, but when her hand fell on the leather instead of the weapon's grip, he allowed himself to relax for a moment.

Definitely have to get that from her.

With her packing complete, she stormed up the berm with Darren a few feet behind. His long strides allowed him to easily keep pace with her as she joined the nearly four dozen members in the march party. Darren halted for a moment and signaled for the group to move out, which they did with little fanfare and without a smile among them. He listened to the thump of their boots and clank of various items ranging from canteens to hatchets as they kicked up a thick cloud of dust. When he was sure that they were on the move again, Darren unstrapped a hatchet from his pack, and chopped a six inch swath of bark from a nearby tree, then notched the remaining bark in the direction of the party. He nodded, then replaced the axe and jogged off to catch up with the party.

As he approached from behind, he was regarded with a few cold glances over shoulders. He took his position in the rear and followed behind, and in short order overheard a caustic mutter from someone just ahead.

Josh Denning. Another troublemaker.

Darren cleared his voice and projected it over the crowd. "Care to repeat that, Mr. Denning?"

The arrogant nineteen year old didn't even bother to turn around and face Darren, instead raising his voice in kind. "I was just saying how nice it was for you to wait around for Hank before we left."

Darren rolled his eyes. Hank had gone scouting ahead of his own will earlier in the day. The mark that Darren had cut in the tree just minutes earlier, along with dozens of others he had made over the past two days, were all trail indicators, designed so both Hank and any stragglers venturing out on their own from the quarantine camp could find their way.

"He's fine, kid. Just keep moving."

"Your concern for him is touching," he replied sarcastically.

Lorenzo chimed in next. "Hey guys, I was wondering. With how easily he left the sick folks behind, and how he's left Hank behind now, who wants to bet who the next person he leaves behind will be?"

"I've got five bucks on you, Lorenzo," Josh chuckled.

"Bullshit. You ain't got five bucks," added Nina.

"Knock it off, guys. How can you even say shit like that at a time like this?" The voice of his defense came from far up front, from a woman by the name of Denise.

"Oh, come on, we're just having a little fun. It's boring out here," Lorenzo protested.

"Well shut up about Hank," Denise retorted, "because I see him up ahead, coming this way."

Darren went to jog around the column, but everyone broke out of formation and swarmed forward to intercept the group's scout.

"Lieutenant Cormack," he yelled as he approached. "You've got to come see this."

Darren shoved his way through the crowd and ran after Hank as he darted back into the trees and over a short hill. He caught a glimpse of something white waving in the wind as he crested the hill.

Is that a… parachute?

He charged down the hill and almost plunged into a thick sticker bush. The rest of the group followed behind as he mounted the second hill and skidded to a stop. Ahead of him, flattened trees were strewn along the jungle floor, and there was the unmistakable glare of the sun off of the metal pod surface. There was no doubt that this had come from *Raphael*. The smaller cargo pod had suffered significant damage during the crash and the door had popped out, resting halfway up the hill.

"Please tell me there's something useful inside, Hank," he panted as he walked down the hill.

The scout nodded and grinned broadly. "It's the mother lode."

Darren stepped inside the pod and was immersed for a moment while his eyes adjusted to the filtered light. At his feet lay an over-turned crate, its contents of food packets spilling forth. He let out a yelp of joy and began laughing.

"What is it?" asked Lorenzo.

Darren bundled up as many packages as he could carry and lobbed them gently through the door. "It's a provisions pod. One of these things carries enough meals for three hundred people for a year."

A cheer rose up from the crowd and people scrambled like hungry dogs to snatch up the packages that Darren had thrown onto the ground. They broke off into small groups after picking their prizes, and immediately set to devouring the rations.

"Give me a hand in here, Hank," Darren said.

The scout stepped over the threshold into the pod. "What's up?"

"Somewhere in the back of this thing are crates of iodine tabs and water filters. Help me find them."

Hank almost knocked Darren over in his zeal to help. The ragtag band barely had any fresh water left, and only a couple meals. The contents of the cargo pod meant the difference between life and death, and Hank was not about to waste any time in distributing them. The two men made quick work of finding supplies, and carried them out of the pod. Hank prepared the equipment, and Darren personally handed them to each individual in the party. He noted the reactions that he received as he went around. Several people, including Denise and a family with teenage children, all smiled graciously when they received their supplies. It was no surprise that Lorenzo, Nina, and Josh eyed him with suspicion. He continued on, giving them little mind.

After distributing the supplies, Darren stashed a filter pump and a bottle of iodine in his own pack, and then retreated to the edge of the felled trees with a ration. He tore it open and wolfed it down, sating his gnawing hunger. Darren then took a moment to relax and take in the scenery for a moment. The green jungle canopy had a gaping blue hole torn in it when the pod took down more than a dozen trees, and the pod's parachute dangled and waved in the wind. It reminded him of a white flag, as if *Raphael* was signaling its defeat from beyond its stellar grave.

And then, on the crest of the hill, a movement caught his eye. His head snapped to attention, and he caught the forms of two people staggered over the hill. Slowly he rose to his feet, and his jaw dropped in disbelief. Three more souls dragged their way up to the top of the hill.

It can't be. So soon?

His suspicions were confirmed when he saw others stream over the hill, some carrying children on their backs, others lending their bodies as support for their families. Bringing up the rear of the group, and supporting a sick woman on his shoulder, was Brett Wu. Darren glanced across the way at the troublemaking trio from his own group, and was rewarded by catching the incredulous and shocked looks on their faces.

Darren maneuvered over the splintered logs to the open pod. He met the incoming survivors at the door and handed out meals and purification supplies. As he had done earlier with the advance group, he studied the faces of those who had caught up. To his dismay, most of the group gave him little more than a glance. When they did look in his eyes, he got a cold stare in return. His heart fell into his feet.

They think I abandoned them.

At last, Brett came face to face with Darren, who dropped his head low.

"I'm sorry," he said.

The nurse curled the corner of his lip. "I told you to give me a day."

"We were all running out of time. I couldn't wait for Sergeant Daniels to come back with news."

"So you left behind more than half of your people, possibly to die?"

"No," he protested. "I was going for help."

Brett shook his head. "Doesn't look that way to those you left behind. Are you prepared to deal with the consequences?"

He closed his eyes and sighed. "Tell me."

"Eight more dead. Although by no small miracle, no new cases in the past two days."

Twenty one dead now. Let's hope that's all.

"I understand. Would it help to have all the fresh food and water you need?"

"It would. Thank you for that, at least," Brett said, though Darren could hear the grudging undertone in his voice.

"We can rest here for the rest of the day too, if that helps."

"It would help if we could stay a couple more days, and if you could mark the trail a little more. We had to leave a few behind just to catch up with you."

Darren nodded. "I believe we can do that."

Brett nodded as he grabbed a meal pouch from Darren's hands, then turned off to find a place to consume it.

Damned if I do, and damned if I don't. Darren sighed and retreated to the dark of the pod to prepare for the inevitable calls for supplies. *The sooner we get to Marsolek, the better.*

. . .

Capt Haruka Kimura
Planetfall +16 days, late morning
Camp Eight
>|

The early morning sun filtered through the thousands of thin blades of the palm trees lining the shore. Haruka sat in the shade, watching a group of children building a sand castle, while a few adults waded out to a shallow rock outcropping in search of a fresh catch. Around her, a few of Leight's more stubborn passengers lounged around. Most of their compatriots had finally given in to the pressure that James and Troy put on them, and were making themselves useful. This last group of five holdouts seemed to have no interest whatsoever in the improvement of their own conditions. Haruka felt a greasy knot of disgust inside when she looked at the lazy outcasts that surrounded her.

Inexcusable. They should be doing something. She curled her lip into a sneer as she caught the eye of one, a seventeen year old blonde girl who appeared to be working on her tan. Haruka received an eye roll in return, and the girl flipped over onto her stomach. *I can't stand this. If I have to be off my feet, the least that Leight can do is keep me away from these leeches.*

She was not the least bit happy when Dr. Petrovsky had ordered her to rest for the day. He had strictly forbidden her from doing anything pertaining to the colony, including oversight of personnel. She would be allowed only to take short walks, and then only to stretch her legs or to take her meals.

Haruka decided that it would be best for her mental state if she didn't spend her time with the particular company that had gathered near her. She slowly stood up and steadied herself against the trunk of a tree, swiping the sweat from her brow. Her head spun for a moment, so she waited until the sensation had passed before making her way along the tree line toward the river.

As she wandered, Haruka could hear the sounds of progress from the hill above her. Troy and James had assembled every able bodied person from pods eight and ten and put them to work. Some fished, while others were set to the task of foraging for edible plants or tough palm fronds. The bulk of the workforce was on top of the hill, however, clearing selected trees and stumps, and building the beginnings of shelters. Haruka didn't think it looked like much the last time she had seen it, but Troy assured her that given a little time, there would be houses. She had a difficult time picturing them, as her concept of a house had been drawn up long ago by her experiences on a heavily populated Earth. Possibilities of what Troy had in store filled her imagination.

Haruka came to the estuary where beach, river, and trees met. This was one of her favorite places to come and think. Wild birds skimmed the beach in search of food, and the river flowed past with a soothing babble. Yet unlike the beach near the pod, it had far less traffic; only once had she visited when there were others around. More often, she was greeted by various small creatures that lived in the jungle, such as a small herbivore species with protective bony knobs on its neck, or a variety of hairless rodent that moved with incredible speed.

The walk did little to quell the swimming feeling in her head, so she went down to the sand and dipped her feet in the river. The water rushed over her feet, melting away the sand from the soles of her feet in a tiny white-and-brown cloud. The contrast in temperature felt good against her skin, but the spinning sensation would not go away, so she lay down in the sand to rest. As she rested her arm over her eyes, her body felt as if she was floating and twisting in the air, without the ability to control herself. Haruka concentrated on the sounds of the river and her breathing. Seconds passed into minutes, and she was vaguely aware as the rolling passed that she was drifting off to sleep.

Her rest was fitful, dancing between images of home, family, and the sleeper ship disaster. Her father's wrinkled face smiled back at her over a meal out at a restaurant, and they walked under starry skies to the first home she remembered – in Laramie, but not on the compound grounds – where they watched the skies for shooting stars. Yet when she stood up, she was on the bridge of *Raphael*, being stared down by a snarling Colonel Fox. She shook off the image and brought back a memory of trying on a dress her mother had sewn for her. As she looked at herself in the mirror, she remembered the occasion: Saika's wedding. Yet moments later she relived the last seconds of flight before the engineering skiff crashed in the jungle. She escaped the horror and the sensation of drowning, and found herself in a room with Saika, talking about life. When she was comfortable again, they got up and walked through a door, and Haruka found herself in the propulsion control room of *Raphael*, with the stare of Captain Maynard's bloodied corpse boring into her.

Haruka felt as if her chest was being squeezed and she gasped for air. She turned for the escape hatch, but it was closed. Her fingers clawed in futility at the latch, but it would not budge. She turned about and hunched in the corner, drawing her knees to her shoulder. Maynard's stare was fixed firmly on her, and even in death seemed to judge her. She closed her eyes, brought her hands to her ears, and screamed.

She felt hands clamp down on her shoulders and pin her to the hard metal. She kicked her legs, but more hands fell upon her ankles and immobilized them. She could hear shouts from around her as a dark feeling of dread blanketed her, threatening to smother her all over again.

"Captain Kimura, stop kicking!"

The voice was familiar, but it was not Maynard's. She forced her panic aside and waited for the voice, though her muscles tensed against the hands that restrained her.

"Relax, Captain. Everything is going to be alright," the man's voice soothed.

Her eyes shot open and she sucked in a big gulp of air. The round face of Dr. Petrovsky looked down on her, framed by the plated metal ceiling of the sleeper pod. She glanced down, where Luis held her ankles fast, and then up into the worried face of James, who had a firm grasp on her shoulders. Realizing she was awake and indoors, she relaxed, letting her fingers brush against the metal floor. She was soaked in sweat, and a terrible thirst lingered in her mouth. She did not rest quite flush against the surface; something was wadded up underneath her back.

"What the hell happened?" she asked.

"Gave us all a scare, that's what," James replied.

Dr. Petrovsky placed his hand on Haruka's propped-up shoulder, and his expression became grimmer. "James brought you back to us, burning up and barely breathing."

"What?" she shot up to a sitting position. "But I was just asleep!"

Her three companions exchanged looks of concern.

"You got this wound in the jungle, correct?"

Haruka looked at the doctor, then placed her hand on the shoulder that had been slashed by the jaguar weeks ago. She winced as pain shot through it, and her temperature rose. "Yeah. I was attacked by one of the local jaguars."

"Well, it looks like it's become infected," Petrovsky continued.

"What? How? It's been two weeks!"

He leaned in to her ear and whispered, "I could tell you in private if you wish, or we can do this in front of your men. Sooner or later you need to tell them."

That means the radiation has something to do with this. She cast her gaze down and, biting her lip, nodded in solemn approval.

Dr. Petrovsky straightened up and cleared his throat. "Somewhere, at some point, your wound came in contact with infected material. Could have been something as simple as a scratch, or maybe there's a local bacteria that we haven't encountered yet. In any case, your condition exacerbated it, and it's run rampant."

"Her condition?" asked James. His dark brown eyebrows arched high toward the roof.

"Gentlemen, the captain has allowed me to discuss her condition with you. I urge you not to repeat it without her permission, as it is still a sensitive matter." Petrovsky paused for a few seconds, glancing up as if to make sure his audience was captivated. "Captain Kimura was exposed to significant radiation during the disaster on the sleeper ship. She is suffering from what a layman would call radiation sickness. Her immune system is compromised, and at the very least, she is very prone to the various cancers."

Haruka examined her Operations and Security chiefs carefully as the news sank in. Both were shocked, their mouths agape, unable to respond. Luis was barely able to make eye contact, shying away when she caught his gaze.

"It's okay," she said. "I've known for a little bit now. Dr. Petrovsky knows and can take care of me. Right, Doc?"

The doctor pursed his lips and paused uncomfortably.

"Doc? Everything's fine, right?"

"I've done a little digging," he finally added. "The alarms on *Raphael* were set to go off when potentially dangerous doses of radiation were detected. Sergeant Leight allowed me access to the radio to have a conversation with Lieutenant Marsolek, who knows much more about the ship's reactor than anyone else that we're aware of. It's his opinion..." his voice trailed off.

A veil of silence fell in the hallway. Haruka's nerves were on edge and her hands shook, waiting for the doctor to finish his sentence. The deliberate way he avoided an answer made her suspect the worst.

"She's dying, isn't she?" asked Luis, almost under his breath.

"It's a distinct possibility."

Haruka closed her eyes and gulped. "How distinct?"

Dr. Petrovsky released a deep sigh. "It's hard to tell. Given the medical equipment I have access to..."

J.C. Rainier

"How distinct?"

"Fifty-fifty, give or take."

Haruka laid back down slowly. Her hands tingled, and her core grew numb. *Fifty percent chance of dying. Fuck. After surviving the crash and the trip out here, the God damned ship will end up killing me after all.*

Luis and James both rested their hands on her. "Is there anything we can do to help, Doctor?" queried James.

"Not unless you can find me better medical supplies. Leight tells me there were a couple cargo pods full of supplies onboard the ship. Maybe one of them crashed near here."

"No," Haruka blurted. She could feel the weight of their stares fall upon her, but she fixed her gaze at the ceiling. "No, those pods were both in the front of the ship. We only ran across one pod, which was probably number fourteen. Medical supplies were in pods three and four. If they're out there, they're hundreds of miles away, lost in the jungle."

"We can find them," Luis replied hastily.

"No. Marsolek has a better chance of finding them."

James hesitated for a moment as he formed his question. "So what are you saying, Captain?'

Haruka bit her lip and forced back a lump from her throat. A single tear streamed down her cheek.

"All three of you are witness to this, so listen carefully. Military command structure dies with me."

"You're not dying," James insisted.

"Please, just listen to me, just in case. There aren't enough crew members left to justify rank; make sure that Sergeant Leight understands that. We're a colony now, and he doesn't take command just based on his uniform. James Vandemark will take over my responsibilities at Camp Eight. Continue to build and secure the population through any means available. Form a government. Make sure that laws and expectations are clear, do you understand me? Make sure the people live."

Her eyes opened, and she received the response she had anticipated: the nods of all three men.

"One more thing, just for James."

"Anything, Captain."

A second tear rolled down her face, but she held her voice steady. "If we ever manage to make radio contact with the other ships, tell them… tell Saika that her sister sends her deepest love. Tell Sarah Kimura that I don't believe a word of what they say about Dad."

Tell them that I will see him in Heaven, she thought as James clasped her hand and nodded, swallowing hard and doing his best to hide his emotions.

. . .

2nd Lt Darren Cormack
Planetfall +16 days, midday
Twenty miles east-northeast of sleeper pod
seven site
>|

Darren rubbed at his throbbing lower back with one hand as the other shaded his eyes from the high noon sun. He licked his parched lips and took a moment to catch his breath. The rows of crates he had pulled from the cargo pod wreckage lay canted between two fallen palm trees jutting out from under the pod. His work of pulling the crates from the pod was nearly complete, and he would be able to move on to the task of distributing the food to the survivors. The plan was to mark the pod for later supply retrieval, while replenishing from its stores before marching out at first light the next morning.

He stepped just inside the door of the pod and hoisted one of the three last crates that he had staged for removal. His fatigued muscled strained against the weight, and he grunted with every step he took. He walked to the end of the row and dropped the crate in place. As he again waited for his breath to calm, Darren caught a foot resting on the tree out of the corner of his eye. He looked up and found Brett Wu standing with his arms crossed and a grim look on his face.

"Something tells me this isn't a social visit."

Brett shook his head. "It's not over. There are five new cases today."

"Five? But I thought you said that there weren't any new cases since we left the last camp!"

"There weren't until today." Brett took a seat on the log and ran his hand over the back of his head. "None of the previous patients should have been contagious. It's got to be something in the environment."

Darren nodded. "Any idea what? I mean, that's kind of vague."

"I'm not even completely sure what kind of illness we're dealing with here. It doesn't look like the insects spread it, as not everyone who has fallen ill has had bites. I don't think it's fungal, and it runs its course too quickly to be parasitic."

"So what does that leave?"

"Viral or bacterial," Brett replied. "I'm leaning more towards bacterial, though."

"Alright. Why?"

"Well, we're in a jungle here. This place is probably the perfect breeding ground for bacteria. And since we have almost no antibiotics, we're at the mercy of our immune systems to cope with a completely alien bug."

Darren took a seat on the log next to Brett as he absorbed the information that the nurse had laid out.

If he's right, we're defenseless unless we can find the medical cargo pods.

"But you can't tell me what's causing it, right?"

"For sure? No."

"Any ideas on what to do?"

"Keep moving," Brett responded with a heavy sigh. "I hate to admit it, but Hank and Lorenzo were right to move on. While we're on the move, we seem to be a step ahead of this. As soon as we stop to rest and regroup, it catches up."

Darren furrowed his brow. "That's insane. I'm still not sure that leaving was the right decision, and now you're telling me *this*? I mean, I've never heard of a sickness that gets better when you keep moving. All I've ever heard from doctors whenever I'm sick is to rest and drink fluids."

"I've heard of a disease that acted this way in groups of people," Brett retorted. "And like what we're experiencing now, it had a high mortality rate and kept people on the move. Although that was more from fear than any scientific or medical need."

"Why do I get the feeling I'm about to get a history lesson?"

"I'll keep it short, Lieutenant. Back during the days of westward expansion in the United States, one of the diseases that emigrants feared the most was cholera. Many of them moved on when party members were stricken, fearing that if they stayed they would also contract the disease. At the time it seemed to work, although we now know that cholera is a bacterial infection, most commonly contracted through contaminated food or water."

"Water," Darren repeated as he leaned his back against the top edge of a rations crate. "Could it be in the water here? Could it have survived purification?"

"It's possible. For instance, those iodine tablets you distributed won't kill cryptosporidium"

"I know that. Those are for an emergency in case the filters don't work or aren't available."

Brett shrugged. "Those pump style filters were designed for water-borne threats on Earth. It's possible that something here can slip past them. The disease slowed down, but didn't stop, when we started boiling the water."

"So it's probably water borne then."

"Could be food borne too. There are scavengers and vermin all over this planet, just like Earth."

"But the rats didn't show up until we had been at the camp for several days," Darren pointed out.

"All it would have taken is one back at the pod to infect our food supplies and get the ball rolling. I can't rule it out. All I know is that we can't stay here, or more people will die."

"Two days ago you were spitting venom at me for leaving the sick behind, and now you *want* me to do it?"

Brett nodded solemnly. "As much as I hate to say it, we have to. We can't afford to wait for them to get better."

Darren could barely believe that Brett was advocating for abandonment, but this disease had ravaged the survivors, leaving twenty one dead and the group divided. Brett had a wild, almost fearful look on his face as he waited for Darren to deliberate.

"Alright. I'll move all the healthy survivors out again. Do you need anything else to care for the ill?"

"I'm coming with you," Brett replied without hesitation.

"What?"

"I'm not staying behind to get sick. Not this time."

"You're abandoning them too? But they need your help."

"I don't want to die," the nurse blurted.

He really is scared. I can't blame him.

"I'm not taking you with us."

"Then I'll go on my own."

"Brett, please…"

"No. I'm not staying."

Darren gave an aggravated growl. "Fine. I can see I'm not going to convince you otherwise. Help me get everyone together. We meet here in fifteen minutes."

He strode off into the thick of the group, spreading the word of the meeting to all he encountered. After informing a few groups of survivors, he found Hank and enlisted the scout's help. The work of notification went much faster with the help, and after only ten minutes, Darren was back in front of the pod, looking at the faces of every single person in camp as they waited eagerly for him to begin.

"I'm not going to mince words," he said. "If you're not already aware, the disease has struck camp again. On advice from our medical staff, we are leaving as soon as we can pack up our supplies. We'll put as many miles as we can from this place tonight, and continue on to our destination."

At once, grumbling and protests rose up from the gathered crowd. Survivors talked amongst themselves and made gestures of general disapproval. Hank shook his head and walked away, and the trio of Lorenzo, Nina, and Josh wore matched smug grins.

"Lieutenant Cormack," called Denise from within the throng. "Can you help me find someone to carry my husband?"

A knot rose in his throat, which he cleared loudly. "We are leaving the sick behind, for the protection of the rest of the group."

"What?" she shrieked. The rest of her sentence was drowned out by shouts from the crowd.

He put up his hand and tried to shout over the din. "Please, we need to get moving."

Shouts and taunts came at him from all directions. There was no division in the crowd this time; their ire was squarely aimed at him. He scanned the crowd for Hank, but he had already gone. Brett had made himself scarce as well. Panic started to rise within, as he looked for Lorenzo. As his eyes picked him out of the crowd, his jaw dropped. The troublemaking trio had been set upon by the raging pack of survivors, and they were being beaten with fists and sticks. Their weapons were quickly stripped, and Darren saw the glint of a pistol in the hands of Denise.

His hand shot to his waist and drew the Beretta from the holster on his hip. He flicked off the safety and chambered a round as Denise pointed her commandeered weapon at him.

"Drop it," he yelled.

She hesitated for a moment and the barrel dipped. He kept his own pistol trained on her, waiting for her to comply. Then pain shot through the back of his head and he stumbled forward, dropping his gun. Darren rolled to his back and saw Hank standing above him, with his rifle's stock pointed in Darren's direction. Darren drew his hand to the back of his head and felt a slick, warm liquid. His hand came back in front of his face, and the red blood that tinted his fingers gained his full attention."

"Hank?" he asked in a weak voice.

The last thing Darren saw before his world went dark was the butt of the scout's rifle crashing into his skull.

• • •

"Are you ready?" Dr. Petrovsky asked as Haruka leaned forward. The salty air made the old wound sting slightly, but it would be nothing compared to having it lanced and drained.

She balled up a torn and soiled flight suit, then buried her head in it and nodded. She flinched slightly as the scalpel sank through the skin on her shoulder. Haruka grunted in pain, though it was muffled by the cloth. An odd pinching sensation followed, and the air was filled with a putrid stench.

"Almost done," the doctor soothed.

She let the cloth fall from her face and brushed it off of her lap. "It doesn't hurt as much as last time."

"It shouldn't. I don't have to drain as much this time around, and the wound looks much better."

"So can I go back to work now?"

Dr. Petrovsky chuckled, which irritated her. "Not yet. I'll draw an imaginary box around you that you're not allowed to leave, if I have to."

Haruka groaned. "Fine, can you at least tell James where you're tying me up?"

"Gladly. Of course, with orders that he's not allowed to untie you," he grinned.

"Of course."

"Are you ready for the next part?"

Haruka nodded and retrieved the scream rag. Liquid ran down her shoulder, cold at first, then turning to a searing sensation as the peroxide invaded the wound. She took a deep breath and held it, pushing through the mounting pain. She exhaled and drew in another breath, repeating the process until the doctor washed and dressed the wound.

"That part never gets any easier," she remarked after he finished.

"Well, hopefully you'll only have to endure it a couple more times. You've made a lot of progress in the past few days. We'll see what it looks like tomorrow, okay?"

"Thanks, Doctor."

He stood up and brushed the dirt from his knees. As his eyes met the horizon, he smiled. "Looks like I won't have to tell James where I've stashed you away. He's on his way over here."

Haruka slipped her shoulder and arm back into her suit and quickly zipped it up before getting to her feet. James approached from the beach, escorted by Sergeant Leight. Her relief to see James waned quickly when he got close enough for her to read his face. His lips were downturned slightly, and he repeatedly went through his nervous tell. Leight's usual stone demeanor was missing, and he approached with a grim look.

"What's wrong, James?" she asked as came up.

James's jaw dropped as if to speak, but no words came out. Instead, he sat down, and cast his gaze into the dirt.

"You might want to sit back down, Captain," Leight said in a soft voice.

What the hell happened this time?

She complied with Leight, setting herself down across from James. Dr. Petrovsky sat as well, offering his hand to Haruka. She took it and squeezed it nervously.

"There has been an incident involving your security chief, Luis Serrano." Leight paused for a moment. "I'm sorry, Captain. He's dead."

"What?" she gasped.

"He was murdered, Haruka," James muttered through gritted teeth.

Haruka stuttered, and then began to hyperventilate. Her head began to spin as the news began to sink in. Dr. Petrovsky leaned in and talked her through taking deep breaths. She calmed down after a few minutes, though her hands shook, and her body was numb.

"How?" she asked feebly. "Who would do such a thing?"

"You don't want to know," James replied.

"Just tell me, James."

Leight interjected with the details. "He was beaten to death. We're still trying to figure out who. We got a good description from a witness, I'm just trying to confirm my suspicion."

"Good. When you find out for sure who it is, tell me. I want to make this bastard pay."

"That might be a little hard right now, ma'am."

"Why?" she shot back. "It should be easy to find one person in our little community."

"Of course. But he's fled into the jungle, according to the witness. Frankly, he'd have to be a complete idiot to just waltz back in."

Haruka nodded. The idea of Luis's murderer returning to camp and submitting voluntarily to punishment was laughable at best. The settlement they intended to build was just in its infancy, and no prison existed. Even if he were to return, Haruka would have no place to hold him. On the other hand, she considered that the problem might solve itself; if the killer was not an experienced survivalist, the aggressive predators in the jungle could easily finish him off.

"Alright, once we find out for sure who killed Luis, we can keep an eye out for him. If we bring him back alive, we could probably put him through a quick trial."

"We don't have any judges, and only one lawyer," James pointed out.

She thought for a moment about a potential solution. "Have the lawyer give two people brief training, one as a prosecutor, one as a defender, and have him act as the judge. Would that work?"

Leight nodded and broke off eye contact. James scratched at the bristles on his cheek.

"What, is there something wrong with that plan?"

"No, it sounds fine," James replied. "It's just that... just..."

"What is it?" she probed. She had never seen James at a complete loss for words before.

"I don't even know how to tell you this." The words escaped his lips as little more than a whisper.

"Tell me what?"

James shook his head but remained mute. Leight cleared his throat when his companion failed to speak. "This is going to be difficult for you. Please try not to let it affect your handling of the situation any."

"Go on," she said after a moment's hesitation.

"The witness who gave the description of Luis's murderer was Maria Serrano. Gabrielle was with her. They both stumbled across the attack when they went to go have lunch with Luis down by the river."

Oh fuck.

"The attacker turned on them, Captain."

"Shit. Are they alright?" Leight shook his head slowly. "What happened, Sergeant?"

"They tried to run. He caught up with them and threw Maria to the ground." Leight raised his head suddenly and stared at Haruka. The pain in his eyes was evident. "He raped her in front of her child."

Oh shit. Gabi... Maria...

"Gabrielle screamed. Will and Jenkins were coming back from a mission and heard it. The guy was gone by the time they got there. He probably got scared off."

"Fuck," she blurted as fury built inside of her.

"It's real bad, Haruka," James finally chimed in. "He probably has Luis's rifle. Jenkins couldn't find it when he searched the area. This ass-hole is armed, and he knows that if any of us see him, he's toast."

"Then he's going to force a fight if we catch him. We can't afford to lose anyone else. Take him down if you find him, James."

"We can't just execute him," Leight protested. "Even if he is armed, due process says that we're supposed to try to capture him so that he can be tried fairly."

"Due process?" she scoffed. "Look around you. Where are we going to process him? And how? This guy is a threat."

"Do what you want, Captain," he said as he lifted his muscled body from the ground. "If I find him, I'm going to treat him the same way we would back on Earth. If he draws on me or my life is threatened, yeah, I'll take him out. But not before."

"Suit yourself, Sergeant. But I'm not going to let this maniac kill anyone else on my watch."

"He's right, Captain," Dr. Petrovsky added. "We may be in the middle of nowhere, but we're all from the same place. We all grew up with the same expectations of law and treatment."

"I hate to admit it, but I agree," grumbled James.

Her shoulder throbbed as she stood up too quickly. She stifled a wince of pain and steadied herself as the ground beneath her seemed to sway. "I am not letting him harm anyone else. That is final."

She checked the magazine on her M9 and re-holstered it, then walked away to find some solitude.

• • •

2nd Lt Darren Cormack
Planetfall +22 days, late morning
Just outside pod one and two combined landing site
>|

"We're almost to the other site now. You're not going to cause any problems if we cut you loose, are you?" Denise asked.

"No ma'am," Darren replied without hesitation.

"Good."

She nodded to a teenager with dirt and mud caked over the acne pocks on his face. He flicked out a small knife and sawed through the thin cords around Darren's wrists. They snapped and fell at his feet, and Darren wrung his hands over the raw, red ligature marks on each wrist. He grudgingly thanked his captors for the courtesy.

"One more push should do it," the boy remarked, folding the knife up and shoving it in the front pocket if his jeans. He retrieved a rifle that was leaning next to a tree. "We ready to move out?"

Hank stood up and slung his rifle over his shoulder. "Yeah, let's go. Oh, one more thing." He reached into his pack and produced a belt with a holstered pistol, handing it to Darren.

"What's this," he asked, giving an incredulous look.

"It's for show. We can't have you walking up looking beat up and disarmed."

"Are you kidding?" Denise protested.

"Don't worry, it's not loaded. I'm not that big of an idiot. Let's move. Should be about a mile that way," he said, jerking his thumb to the east. "I saw the top of one of the pods earlier when I went ahead."

With little fanfare, the remaining one hundred and eleven survivors packed up their meager possessions and set to march. Darren took a position near the front of the column, marching next to Hank, and behind Denise. The pace at which they took off was easy for him to keep without his hands bound; earlier he had been prone to stumbling or falling behind as his bindings threw his balance off. However, after just a few minutes, the band slowed down again as the sick stragglers had to catch up.

Progress had been very slow for days. The insistence of his captors in keeping the group together had prevented them from reaching the site of Marsolek's pod. With every step, Darren calculated just how much earlier they would have arrived if they had left the ill to fend for themselves.

One day, he thought. *A full day. Maybe two if it had just been a few people moving ahead, like me and Hank.*

As they waited for the dozen or so patients to catch up, Darren scanned the crowd, looking for Brett Wu. He spotted the nurse, and was relieved to find him in the middle of the march party, also relieved of his bondage. Darren also picked out the troublesome Lorenzo, Nina, and Josh. They stuck out like sore thumbs; Denise had apparently convinced the rest of the captors to keep those three bound at the wrists like criminals.

She must have thought they're too much trouble. If she doesn't want me walking in bound and unarmed, I guess it speaks volumes about her opinion of Lorenzo and his cronies.

So close to the pod site that they had sought for nearly a month, Darren doubted that anyone would cause trouble. Even Josh, who Darren took to be quite hot-headed, carried himself forward with long strides and a muted smile, rather than the bowed head and dragging feet that he would have expected of a prisoner.

Anyone would want to see the end of the hell we've dragged ourselves through, I guess.

The stragglers caught up, and the leaders adjusted their pace to accommodate those at the rear. Time dragged on, but after the second hill, Darren caught a glimpse through the treetops of a sleeper pod, not more than a mile away.

"There's our destination," Hank remarked.

"Well what are we waiting for?" asked the boy. "Let's just hurry up and get there."

Denise stepped across his path. "Hang on there, kid. We all go in together, remember?"

"Are you serious? It's right there. It's not like they're going to get lost or miss it."

"We stay together," she repeated. "We're not leaving anyone behind."

"No, we're not," Hank added. "Have a little patience, Logan."

The youth sighed and adjusted the load on his shoulders. "Fine."

Darren did not address anyone in the group; while he was relieved to see the top of the gray steel cylinder, he reflected on the loss of so many of his survivors. He imagined for a moment the terror of living through the landing, unable to see anything from within the dark coffins of the sleeper berths. If that wasn't bad enough, so many had fallen ill with the terrifying sickness that struck without mercy. He had lived through half of that himself, as the disease tore up his body and left him wanting to die. He counted himself lucky that at least he was able to see on the way down from his seat in the ESAARC cockpit.

I've done everything I possibly could to isolate myself from them as well. It's no wonder they hate me. He let out a heavy sigh. *Marsolek will probably do a better job with this command. At least we're almost there.*

Again the band pressed on through the jungle. As the minutes passed and the hill on which the pod was situated drew near, the crowd began to mutter thanks and converse excitedly with each other. Darren did not pay any heed, focusing his attention on the thinning clumps of trees just ahead. The layout of the land seemed eerily familiar, as if it was almost a mirror image of the pod they had left three weeks prior.

He shook off a sudden dark thought that gripped him. *No, if they're still here, they have to have fresh water somewhere.*

The jungle stopped abruptly just before the base of the hill in a tangled mess of brush. Hank, Denise, Logan, and Darren stopped at the edge and looked at the thick brambles and vines.

"Guess we could just cut through," Hank remarked as he and Logan drew machetes.

They were joined by a few others from the group, and after a few minutes managed to cut a thin path through the vegetation. Darren looked up the hill at the dome just peeking over, and noticed five figures walking over the hill, cradling rifles as they slowly marched down the slope.

Something's not right. Goosebumps spread across his arms.

Hank ripped through the last few vines in their path and stepped to the far side, followed by the men that had hacked through the brush.

"Go on," Denise prodded.

"Wait," he replied.

"What?"

"There's something wrong. Wait a minute."

"Just get your ass through there," Logan said, shoving him forward.

Behind him, Darren could hear Hank yelling up the hill at the welcoming party. "What the hell do you mean?" the scout shouted.

"Move it, old man," repeated Logan.

Darren backed up further into the cut. "Wait just a second. You've got to listen to me."

The teenager rolled his eyes and darted under Darren's arm and through the opening on the far side. Darren spun around and thrust his hand out to catch Logan, but missed, instead brushing his fingertips along the hot, sun-baked steel of the M4's barrel.

The next minute or so seemed to play out in slow motion for Darren. One of the men who approached their group trained his own carbine on Hank.

"God damn it, I said you need to stay in the jungle until you have no more ill."

Then Logan's M4 dropped from his shoulder. Apparently unaware of what was unfolding in front of him, the young man hoisted it in one hand. Two men on the hill saw the movement and spun to face Logan, bringing their weapons to bear. Darren felt Denise try to push her way past him.

"Look out!" one of the pickets shouted, crouching to attack.

"NO!" he screamed, elbowing Denise in the chest and throwing his arms as wide as he could across the cut. She crashed to the ground behind him, and just in time.

Loud booms rang out in staccato bursts from all over the hill. Darren felt a searing pain tear through his left shoulder. He winced and stumbled back a step. More shots rang out and Logan collapsed in a heap before his eyes. An instinct took over, and Darren reached with both arms and grabbed thorny vines, which dug into his flesh. Behind him, Denise coughed as she struggled to her knees.

More gunfire erupted, and Darren watched as every man on the far side of the brush was cut down by the welcome party. Hank was the last man standing, and he managed to get off a couple defensive rounds before falling himself. Then the five gunmen turned on the wall of brush, and began firing wildly. Two more slugs hit Darren; one ripped through his knee, causing him to pitch forward, and the other caught him in the gut. His hand released from the vines, and with the last strength of his good leg, he threw his body on top of Denise.

Only a few more seconds of shots rang out, and their echoes were quickly drowned out by the rising screams of panic from the pod seven survivors. His face was now turned into the jungle, and he watched men and women fleeing in all directions into the woods. Lifeless bodies lay scattered amongst the groaning wounded, who clawed at the dirt in a bid to escape.

"Why are they shooting us?" Denise shrieked.

"Shhh," Darren clamped his bloody hand over her mouth. "Stay down."

He lay on top of his former captor as the minutes ticked by, keeping her from making any noise, for fear that their assailants would reload and finish them off. He heard the men approach, checking on the status of each man on the far side of the brush.

"Yup, kid's dead," one of them remarked callously. "Why the hell did he go for his gun? Stupid, stupid kid."

"They thought that Logan was going to fire," Darren whispered, coughing up a glob of blood. "What the hell is wrong with them? He just dropped his rifle, he wasn't going to shoot."

"What the hell is this?" a woman's voice barked from on the hill.

"They went for their guns, Sergeant," one of the men responded.

"Are you kidding me? Give me that rifle, Sinclair. And get your ass back to camp right this second." Darren knew the owner of voice. Although his head was swimming from the pain, he could recognize the woman that he had served with for a long time.

"C'mon, Daniels, we were just enforcing the lieutenant's quarantine orders. This kid went for his rifle."

"Enough," Sergeant Daniels roared. "All of you back to camp right this second or I'll have you shot."

The men did not talk back to her; instead he could hear them shuffling off, grumbling. He continued to play dead as long as he could, but couldn't hold back another cough. Darren heard the approach of several pairs of legs. Hands grabbed at his arms, and he was rolled onto his back, into the freshly cut vines. He looked up and saw the familiar face of Daniels, as well as two airmen. When she assessed his condition, she bit her lip, and a look of grave concern grew on her face.

"Sir, you've been shot."

"Thanks for the update," he coughed. "My people... how bad?"

Daniels nodded to the airmen, who continued on through the brush and into the jungle. "Not sure yet, sir. At least four dead, including the boy, and Hank. Just hang on. We'll get the doctor to take care of you."

Darren became aware of soft sobbing next to him. He looked over and saw Denise, with her knees to her chest, crying. "Why the hell are they shooting?"

"It's over. Daniels is here."

"Logan... they killed Logan. Oh God..."

He heard more footsteps, and saw shadows blur past as he began to lose focus. More hands grabbed him, and he was lifted onto a stretcher. His body rocked and jostled as he was carried up the hill.

"Daniels?"

"Yes sir?"

"Do you have..." a coughing fit wracked his body, interrupting his query. The jerking of the coughs renewed the pain from his wounds, and he moaned in agony.

"Take it easy, sir. Just stay with us until we can get you to the doctor."

"I need... need to know."

"It can wait, sir."

"Marsolek." The rising pain as his adrenaline wore off made his breathing labored, and he could barely utter the words. "Need to talk..."

The swaying stopped and he felt his back against the ground again. There was an almost imperceptible pinch in Darren's arm, and seconds later he felt as if he would float away. The pain subsided quickly, but his thoughts became clouded and jumbled.

"Marsolek," he whispered.

"Shhh. Let the doctor take care of you."

· · ·

Haruka sunk her teeth into the speckled orange flesh of the fruit. "Pepperine" was the name that camp dwellers had given the edible fruit that Gabi had inadvertently discovered. It was suitable, as it had qualities of both a nectarine and a pepper. Haruka found the tiny seeds to be more like dozens of grape seeds, but otherwise she felt the description to be accurate. All comparisons aside, it was one of her favorite foods of the new planet; the sweet fruitiness blended well with the slight spicy kick. By comparison, the edible leaves and roots they had found were either bland or tough and fibrous.

She finished the fruit and tossed the core upstream into the river, then watched as it passed by her; several fish had come to investigate and taste the bobbing treat.

The animals on this planet sure aren't shy, for better or worse.

The moment of solitude took the edge off of the feelings of guilt and uselessness that had plagued her since Dr. Petrovsky had ordered her not to work. Her shoulder bothered her only a little now, though the cuts from lancing the wound would take time to heal. Haruka splashed her feet in the refreshing waters of the river as she sat in the sands at its mouth. The tang of the sea was particularly pungent in the air this morning, and both Arion and Persephone hung well over the horizon. The former was a barely distinguishable shape, though it had moved in the last hour to a position in front of the brighter Persephone, causing a partial eclipse of the moon.

Damn. That's a hell of a sight, she thought as a grin crept across her face. *That couldn't happen on Earth.*

Her eyes were glued to the skies as she watched Arion dip toward the horizon, outrunning its orbital partner. Once the show concluded she wandered down the beach in the direction of the sleeper pod. The tide was in, and the usual gentle rollers that washed on shore were replaced by small, foaming breakers. Haruka looked up at the clear blue skies, noting barely a cloud in sight. A slight breeze cooled her skin as she padded along the white sands. A couple of the older children were braving the waters, but the younger ones were not on the beach. Notably absent were Gabi and her mother, who had been fixtures on or near the beach up until the death of Luis. Haruka's lip curled upward and her fists clenched at the thought of his murder.

She silently cursed the name of the murderer, Lon Carney. After Leight and James had accounted for the colonists on the day of the crime, only two were missing from the ranks: Luis, who was the victim of the heinous act, and Carney. Sergeant Leight confirmed the identity of the murderer; his description was a dead match for the young man.

Haruka still could not wrap her mind around why Luis would be a target for murder. She knew of no altercations between her Chief of Security and any refugees. He was well liked and respected, and his devotion to the cause of carving out a new home from the wilderness was second to none.

She shook the thought from her head and focused on the task at hand; she had not had her daily visit with Dr. Petrovsky, and she wanted to get it out of the way and move on with her day. She mounted the ramp to the pod, pausing at the top to note the waves lapping even farther up the beach than just minutes ago.

Wow, really high tide today.

Haruka poked her head around the corner and down a sleeper hallway, looking for the doctor, but it was deserted. She looked down the other hallway and came across Sergeant Leight performing his daily internal inspection of the pod.

"Hey, have you seen Dr. Petrovsky?"

He shook his head without as much as a glance in her direction. "Not for a while. He left after chow this morning."

"Any idea where he went?"

"I think he went to check on Gabi Serrano and a couple of the injured from pod ten. I expect he'll be back soon. Actually, I'm a bit surprised he isn't already. You're welcome to wait if you want."

"Well, he *is* a doctor," she said dryly. "If he's taking a vacation day, he's either golfing or fishing. I wouldn't be surprised if he was casting his line from the top of the pod right now."

Leight closed the berth he was inspecting and gave her a confused look. "What would he catch? Sandrunners?"

"Huh? No, fish."

"Hope he's got a hell of an arm then. I don't think I could cast and hit the water from here with the tide out."

"The tide's not out, Sergeant. It's all the way in, and higher than I've ever seen it."

"What?"

He spun around and squeezed past Haruka. The two walked to the top of the ramp and at the waves. Haruka gasped as she realized that in just a few minutes, another twenty feet of beach had become submerged, and the sea was not much more than another twenty feet from the pod.

"Damn it." Leight turned and yelled down the hall at the cockpit. "Jenkins! Get out here, now!"

The cockpit door at the far end swung wide open, and Airman Jenkins came running out at full steam. His curly brown locks flopped in his face in rhythm with his strides, and his shaggy beard was quite out of place on his youthful face. Jenkins came to a stop at the top of the ramp and saluted.

"No time for that," Leight snapped. "We need to get this tin can unloaded this second. Food, medical supplies, and tools first. Anything that's not nailed down after that."

"Yes sir!" he replied and darted back inside the pod as Haruka ran down the ramp.

"Captain, where are you going?"

"Getting help," she called back without hesitation.

Haruka made a beeline for the bank and scrambled up. Her legs tired quickly; her strength was still sapped by the effects of the radiation poisoning. Among the trees she found only the children and a couple of the mothers who took their turns watching the group. She raced parallel to the shore and came across Dr. Petrovsky, James, Maria, and Gabi. The doctor was admiring Gabi's splint and tying up the sling when Haruka approached.

"James, you need to help Leight at the pod right away," she huffed, doubling over.

He sidled up next to her and placed a gentle hand on her shoulder. "Easy, catch your breath. What's wrong?"

"No time. Get over there now. Need to evacuate the pod."

"Evacuate?" His eyes grew wide with shock.

"Come on," Dr. Petrovsky said as he tugged the knot on Gabi's sling tight. "Gabi's doing great, let's go help Seth."

Haruka turned to follow the men, but they easily outpaced her in their full sprint across the beach. Even the older doctor – who had lost a fair amount of weight in the three weeks on Demeter – left her in the dust. She panted and heaved, and then gave up the pursuit, dropping down to have a seat under a palm. Her heart felt as if it had sunk into the ground.

I'm useless. I can't even keep up with these guys for a hundred meters.

She growled at her failure and flung a handful of sandy dirt at the pod looming on the beach. James and Dr. Petrovsky darted up and down the ramp with supplies handed to them by someone within the pod; she presumed them to be Jenkins and Leight. Several of the teenage children seemed to see what was going on, and rushed from the bank to help the men carry, push, and drag the supplies off of the beach. Haruka took a deep breath, relieved to see that there were others willing to spring into action.

She recovered just as Maria and Gabi caught up. Maria started to speak, but Haruka stopped her with a raised hand, and continued her jog to the rear or of the sleeper pod. Heavy rollers slammed into the side of the pod, and the base of the ramp was submerged. A line of refugees stretched from the top of the ramp down into the water and onto the shore, and they passed crates, packs, tools, and weapons down the line in an effort to salvage the pod before the encroaching waves could invade it. Beyond the shore, pod twelve had slipped below the water. No trace of it could be found, despite Haruka's best efforts to locate it.

Leight wandered around the top of the ramp barking orders to Airman Jenkins as to what he wanted pulled from the pod next. Leight grabbed an ammunition box and passed it down to James just as a large wave slammed into the side of the pod, sending a wash over the ramp. James was knocked to his knees, but regained his footing. Kelly Vandemark, the older of James's daughters, was swept off her feet and was dragged out toward the sea by the undercurrent. Haruka gasped as she saw the teenager struggle against the powerful ebb. Doctor Petrovsky was able to lunge out just in time to catch her and keep the sea from swallowing her.

Haruka shouted from the shore, "Leight! Get out of there! It's too dangerous!"

He continued his work on the ship as another wave knocked the doctor off balance. Petrovsky yelled something at Leight, but she could not hear what, as the breakers drowned out the sound. The doctor and the teenagers abandoned the pod and trudged to the shore, leaving James, Airman Jenkins, and Sergeant Leight aboard the pod. James tugged at the sergeant's arm, but Leight shook him off like he was a ragdoll, and disappeared into the pod. Another wave crashed into the back of the men, and Airman Jenkins had to steady his older companion, whose step faltered just moments before they reached safety. Once under the canopy of the palms, the soaked men looked back.

"Leight!" Haruka called out.

The surging surf slammed into the bank, spraying the considerable sized crowd that had gathered around, as well as the crates and supplies that lay scattered under the trees.

"Get those supplies up the hill," she barked.

The survivors descended on the pile of goods and began to clear them out. There was little order; some supplies were dropped as two people would grab for the same item, and others looked at the jumble with confusion as to what they needed to do. In the shuffle, Haruka saw a half dozen of the encampment's youngest children huddled near-by with no supervision. She scanned the crowd and locked her focus on Maria Serrano.

"Maria," she commanded sharply. "Get these kids out of here."

"W-where…"

"To the hill. Get them up there and keep an eye on them."

Haruka quickly turned her attention to the rabble on the beach. She looked for signs of Sergeant Leight, but he was nowhere in the crowd. Water began to flood over the lip of the embankment, and she could see that the main hallway of the pod was submerged in about a foot of water.

"Leight! Get your ass out of that pod, now!"

She waited, but still the sergeant did not emerge from within the pod. She repeated her calls to him every few seconds until her voice became a hoarse rasp.

Damn it, Leight! Get out of there!

A large roller washed completely over the bank, and water flowed past Haruka's boots and the small piles of clothing, food, and tools that the colonists could not carry in the first wave. Water surged down the hallway in the pod. Then, as the wave ebbed, the ramp of the pod was visible again for a moment, and then the whole pod lurched to the right a few degrees, startling her. Haruka's heart raced as she wondered whether Sergeant Leight had been injured by the sudden shift.

"Leight!" she bellowed again.

Sergeant Leight appeared from inside the dark hollow of the pod empty handed. His legs pushed the shin-high waters out of his way as he made for the ramp, then his legs disappeared a few inches at a time until the swirling, rushing waters consumed them. He waded in to his chest, where the bottom of the ramp had been minutes earlier, then turned for shore. His progress was very slow, and the sergeant seemed to labor as he struggled to walk against the current as it pulled away from shore. His teeth were clenched, and his brow was red.

"Come on, Sergeant!" she beckoned as she walked to the bank's precipice.

He reached for her, but was knocked down from behind as he stretched. The spray made Haruka turn her head, and when she turned back, Leight had rolled over on his back, and the sea was dragging him out into the surf.

"No!" she screamed.

She was about to lunge forward when someone caught her arm and pulled her back. Dr. Petrovsky yanked her into her arms and squeezed with a bear's grip. From the corner of her eye, as she turned back, she saw Troy Bryant run headlong into the surf. Leight was rolled over and smothered by an incoming wave, but Troy was on him in an instant, grabbing the stout sergeant by his flight suit, and dragging him back to shore. Petrovsky released his iron grasp, and Haruka knelt next to pod ten's commander. He coughed and gagged as his lungs expelled the salty water.

"Damn it, Leight. You could have been killed."

"I had to try, Captain," he coughed.

"Try what?" she retorted. "What was so damned important?"

"Trying to seal up and shut down the pod so the computer doesn't fry."

Haruka nodded and bit her lip. The loss of the pod's computer paled in comparison to the prospect of losing Sergeant Leight. She fought back the urge to ream him for his stupidity.

"That was a hell of a ride, though," he added. "I thought the whole damn thing was going to roll over there. Thought that might be the end for me."

I don't want your end to be something so foolish, damn it. I don't want your end to come at all.

. . .

2nd Lt Darren Cormack
Planetfall +23 days, midday
Pod one and two combined landing site
>|

The orange globe of the sun shone through the thick canvas of the tent, its size grossly distorted by diffusion of the light through the fabric. Darren's head swam as he looked up from under the extra flight suit that was draped over his body. Between his wounds and the morphine, he could barely lift his hand to shield his face from the sun. He licked at his parched lips and relaxed again, waiting for the return of the nurse who tended to him.

He had spent most of the day drifting in and out of consciousness. He knew that he had been borne back to the camp for pods one and two, and that he had been tended to by a doctor, who had sedated him heavily after a quick examination. Afterwards, his sleep came in fits, and every time he woke up in a cold sweat. Sometime during the night he became fully conscious, and the excruciating pain of the wounds kept him in agony for what seemed like hours. His restlessness must have caught someone's attention, as a nurse had entered the tent in the darkness and, with a flashlight as a guide, put him under sedation again.

It wasn't until the sun came up in the morning that he could see the dressings on his wounds. Blood seeped from the bandage on his abdomen, and there was a rancid smell. There was little doubt in his mind that the situation was dire. Information was something he was in short supply of, so Darren resolved to ask for more details about his condition and that of his group of survivors as soon as the nurse returned.

Darren grunted as a shooting pain in his gut brought him back to the moment. The haze of the drugs was beginning to wear off; the seam of the tent came into sharp focus when he concentrated, and he could hear the lapping of water from somewhere nearby.

Water. I knew it.

He heard approaching footsteps outside the tent, and several shadows quickly flashed across the side of the tent, moving toward the front. The zipper pulled open with a long groan. Darren lifted his head slightly to see who had entered. The face that poked through the flap was one he had not expected to see.

"Denise?" he mouthed.

His former captor entered the tent. Her civilian clothes had been abandoned in favor of a clean flight suit. Her right hand was wrapped tightly with gauze, and she bore a listless expression. Her brown eyes blinked, but he had difficulty reading her emotion.

"Lieutenant," she acknowledged in an equally flat tone.

"What are you doing here?"

Her eyes scanned him from head to toe and back again, and she shook her head. "I'm sorry. I… I'm not sure what I was expecting."

"What do you mean?"

"They told me that the doctor had a lot to do to put you back together. I know I should be waiting to tell you this, but I couldn't. Not now."

Darren tried to lift himself up on his elbows, but both his shoulder and abdomen responded with a searing rebuke. He winced and dropped back to the floor.

"What do you mean? What's going on?"

"For what it's worth," she said, averting her eyes and wiping away a single tear, "I wanted to thank you for saving my life. You threw yourself in front of me when the shots started flying, and then on top of me when hell broke loose."

"You're welcome," Darren replied. He hadn't planned to use his body as a shield, but in the heat of the moment he had simply reacted without thought.

"I was wrong about you. I thought you were just some callous prick with a gun herding us around. You made it feel like we were all beneath you, and that you weren't approachable. Like some sort of God just because you had stripes and a weapon. But yesterday I learned that, despite my view of you, and how I treated you over the past few days, you're actually a hero. You sacrificed yourself for me."

Sacrificed. His throat began to tighten and his heart sunk. *I'm dying.*

"I know the way I handled things was wrong. I was just doing the best I could with what we had and what I knew. I couldn't handle it."

Denise frowned slightly. "You could have asked for help."

"I should have. I'm sorry."

"You don't have to apologize to me. Not after what you've done for me. I just wanted you to know that even if no one else appreciates you, I do."

"Thank you," he said with a nod.

She turned and exited through the flap, and seconds later was replaced in the tent by Sergeant Daniels, who wore a grim look.

"You don't have to tell me, Sergeant. I know I'm done for."

"I'm so sorry, sir."

"No need to apologize. You're not the one that shot me."

"Don't worry, sir. I'm dealing with him."

"Dealing with who?"

"Sinclair. The one who opened fire on your group when they came up. The others who were with him started firing because they thought they were under attack. Turns out the only one of your group that even got a shot off was Hank. He fired twice and missed."

"Take it easy on him, Daniels. It might have been a misunderstanding. I heard him yell when Logan grabbed for his rifle." Darren sighed and closed his eyes, recalling the moment. "The damn thing slipped off the kid's shoulder. Logan was just trying to pick it up. It was really tense, so I guess that's why he might have misunderstood Logan's movement."

"Sir, it's going to be hard for me to take it easy on someone who wounded eight and killed nine."

Ten. I'm as good as dead, he thought. *At least my failure is at an end and the survivors have made it.*

"Don't take revenge on my part. I deserve this."

"No you don't, sir," she said, furrowing her brow at him.

"I do," he retorted. "I know that we wouldn't have lost so many along the way if I hadn't tried to keep control over everything. I didn't want to get tangled up in their lives because I thought it would keep me from making emotional decisions. It just kept me in the dark and all alone."

"It kept you strong."

"It kept me arrogant. Blind." He stared into the sergeant's eyes and saw his own stone demeanor reflected within. "Don't make the same mistake that I did. I was an idiot. I never would have made it on this world anyway, acting the way I did. You need to make it. These people need you, Daniels."

"I'm here for them, sir."

"No, you're not. Sergeant Daniels is here. Karen Daniels is not. Do you know the difference?"

She paused and bit her lip in thought. Her head bobbed in acknowledgement, and a chink in her emotional armor showed through as her shoulders slumped and her gaze lowered.

"Good."

"Lieutenant Marsolek is here to see you," she added softly. "When you're ready."

"I'm ready now."

Daniels reached for his hand and squeezed it as she gave Darren a somber smile. As she left the tent, he caught a glimpse of her snapping to attention and giving a salute to someone outside the tent, presumably Marsolek. A moment later, a tall thin man with an immaculately shaven face entered the tent. His ice blue eyes peered at him from behind floppy locks of sandy blonde hair. Lieutenant Marsolek's flight suit was almost as clean as his face, and it struck Darren as being odd that, in the midst of a camp with very few amenities, there would be a man who was able to keep himself so meticulously groomed. Darren waited for Marsolek to salute – which the lieutenant did with utter crispness – before Darren returned his own weak gesture that more closely resembled wiping his forehead.

"I'm sorry that we had to meet under these conditions, Lieutenant," Marsolek began. "I bear a measure of blame for what happened to you and your people. I had instructed my pickets to turn back any group that had signs of the disease until we could verify they weren't a threat to our camp. Something went horribly wrong, and Sinclair and his men opened fire. Trust me that I will investigate and…"

"Shut up, Marsolek," Darren coughed. "I don't care what you promise to investigate. I only care about one thing."

Marsolek spluttered and let slip an indignant huff, then closed his eyes and drew in a deep breath. "I'm sorry. That was rude of me. Please, go on."

"I want to make sure that my people are taken in to your camp and taken care of accordingly. They'll be an asset to you out here."

"I'm sorry, but there were a number of your march party that showed signs of the disease. Your scout, Sergeant Daniels, showed up here over a week ago and almost died at my feet while giving her report. We took her in and gave her care, but two of my people got sick and almost died themselves. We got lucky, until your second group showed up, all twelve of them."

"Twelve? There were seventeen when they left our camp." Darren felt it best to omit the fact that they had stolen supplies from the camp when they left.

"Hmm, that might explain why they were in such a hurry to have the two sick ones in their group taken care of. So we took them in and cared for them, but both of their ill died, and one of my own people. That's when I knew I had to set up the pickets and keep out anyone else who is sick," the lieutenant explained. "That's why I can't take your people in until we're sure this is over."

"You lost one person?" Darren growled.

"Yes. It was a damn shame, too. She was a nurse. All she wanted to do was see them through until they recovered."

"Then take Brett Wu and we'll be even. He's a nurse, and he's got a lot of experience with fighting this bug."

Marsolek shook his head and crossed his pencil-like arms across his chest. "I'm not going to risk another one of my people."

"Listen to yourself," Darren spat. "*My* people. *My* people. You're like a kid with an ice cream cone. They're *people*, you son of a bitch. All of them. It doesn't matter if they're from pod one, two, or seven. Shit, where the hell are you even keeping them if you're so damned insistent that they not be around *your* precious people?"

Marsolek shifted his body slightly and he avoided eye contact with Darren. "Those that we could find are at a camp a mile away from here."

Darren sat upright, pushing through the intense stabbing in his gut. "Do I even want to know if you left them with any supplies? Weapons?"

"Of course they have food, water, shelter, and tools. What kind of a monster do you think I am? We just took away any firearms. I mean, after what happened, did you really think we'd just let them walk right in here at night and kill us all?"

Darren could barely believe the admission. "An idiotic monster, that's what you are. No one was going to storm your precious sleeper pod. We all know you're as well armed as we were, possibly even more so. But you're having them sleep out in the jungle with no protection? God damn it, Lieutenant, do you even know what's out there?"

"Uh, trees? Birds? Bugs?"

"And an aggressive predatory cat with no fear of humans, you moron." Darren grunted as he clutched his stomach. He felt something wet, and he drew back his hand, covered in blood.

Damn.

"Daniels," he shouted at the top of his lungs. "Get in here."

In a matter of seconds, Sergeant Daniels had returned to the tent.

"What's this about?" Marsolek asked.

"Fixing your mistake. Daniels, go to the camp where the pod seven survivors are quarantined and bring them back here."

Marsolek blurted, "But they can't come here if there are any sick."

"Damn it, Lieutenant, they're out there scared out of their minds and defenseless against everything. You've had one person die, right?" Darren waited for the shocked lieutenant to nod. "I've watched almost thirty people die, some from the disease, some from your so-called pickets' paranoia. If you really think that you share a measure of responsibility for what's happened, then you need to do just that. Take responsibility. Give them a tomorrow to build. Don't condemn these people to death because you're afraid of it yourself."

Marsolek hung his head in shame. Darren knew that his message had finally sunk in. "Alright. They're all welcome in, no matter what."

"One last request," Darren said with a cough.

"Yes?"

"Take me outside. I want to die with the sun on my face."

Marsolek and Daniels both paused for a full minute. Darren could see a little more of the emotional armor erode from his former second in command every second. Marsolek simply tried to pick up a façade of dignity after having his guilt flaunted in his face. They nodded in silent agreement, and in short order carried him to a secluded spot on the shore of a small lake, where they lay him underneath a tall, willowy palm. Lieutenant Marsolek left shortly after, but Daniels stayed by his side. She did her best to hold back her tears as she recalled stories of better times: times before the destruction of *Raphael*.

After a few minutes, Darren began to cough violently, and his lungs gasped for air. The three wounds burned with pain for a moment, and then they were numb, and a feeling of euphoria began to wash over him. He looked to his side at Daniels, who capped an empty syringe of morphine and tucked it into her pocket.

"It's time, sir."

"Darren."

"Darren," she repeated with a tearful smile.

"I'm not ready," he mumbled, his lips becoming heavy.

"I wasn't ready either," she replied.

He closed his eyes and dreamed for a moment of the life that could have been, of the café he had planned. Of sandwiches made on fresh crusty bread, and pastries being eaten by children.

Darren passed from the world.

. . .

Capt Haruka Kimura
Planetfall +25 days, early evening
Camp Eight
>|

The reflection of Alpha Centauri B glinted off of the blue sea, its form stretched in a long orange oval running from the shore to near the horizon. It was interrupted only by the dark hulk of pod twelve, over a hundred feet off shore and partially submerged. From her vantage point on top of pod eleven's roof, Haruka could see the entire beach, from well past the river mouth at the north, to where a spit of land jutted into the ocean to the south.

Squeals of joy drowned out the calls of four-winged native gulls as children played games in the waning sun, their duties for the day complete. The last few stubborn fishermen waded from shallow shoals with their latest catch of surf crabs, mottled sharks, and a form of anemone that, if stewed, was both incredibly delicious and mildly intoxicating. Several adults could be seen in the tree line near the river taking down the laundry that had been hung out to dry earlier in the day. The sounds of construction from nearby Camp Eight had ceased for the day, and Haruka knew that hundreds of crash survivors would soon gather on or below the hill to share a meal and stories of the day.

It's almost like it never happened.

Haruka sighed and sat cross legged on the domed metal roof of the sleeper pod; she had selected a point just to the port of the centerline, which was now the level point thanks to the list that the pod developed courtesy of the extreme tide a few days prior. A fresh breeze kicked up and swirled her jet black hair into her eyes. The activity of their newfound settlement was a disheartening paradox to her. On one hand, she was relieved to see that the survivors from all four pods were integrating well, in no small part due to the efforts of James to keep every person occupied with a task. Even Sergeant Leight's problematic beach slackers had given in to his orders without much of a fight. The other part of Haruka was bitterly conflicted, knowing that the Serranos were struggling to cope with a heinous act committed against them, and Maria had withdrawn from Haruka. No matter what she tried, the woman that she called "friend" would not let her help, or even provide company and conversation.

Only I could make hell out of paradise, she thought as she closed her eyes and gave a long sigh. *I wish you were here, Marco. Not for the view, or the beaches. I need you.*

The rhythmic clank of rubber on metal to her left gave away the approach of a visitor. She opened her eyes and glanced over, watching as Sergeant Leight emerged from the pod below. He nodded and crossed the roof in a stooped walk, then sat down next to her without a word. His stare locked on the horizon, beyond the beach, where Haruka's had been just minutes before. She resumed her hawk-like observation of the beach below, and an uncomfortable silence settled in the void between them.

After a few minutes, it became more than she could bear. "It's bad, isn't it?" she blurted.

"We'll live."

"Do we know what the hell it even was? That tide thing?"

Leight nodded. "We do. At least I think I understood the explanation that I got."

"So someone has an idea what that mess was all about a couple days ago?"

"Either that, or there's someone down there that can bullshit me well enough to make me believe it. Science teacher. She thinks that it had something to do with the fact that both moons passed over during the daytime, and the pull from both of them plus the sun made a 'supertide', as she called it."

"That's a little disturbing."

"You're telling me. As soon as she said it, I had this image of some apocalyptic tidal wave sweeping away our whole camp," he said, gesticulating in a dramatic motion to illustrate the point. "She said we shouldn't worry too much, though. She doesn't think that it will regularly, if ever, get past where the bank is there at the tree line. She said that if it did, all those trees would be dead and buried in sand."

Haruka grimaced. "That's comforting. I think."

"That doesn't mean that it hasn't screwed up our little slice of heaven, though, Captain."

"It did something to the pod, didn't it?" she asked.

Leight chewed on his lip and nodded.

"Well, first off, knowing that there is this tide thing going on, I don't think we can allow anyone to sleep in the pod any more. We don't know how often this happens, and if it happens over and over, the salt will rust out the bottom of the can anyway."

She nodded. It was a little early to set her plan in motion, but it had been something she had considered ever since James had explained why Leight was apprehensive of helping them. "That's ok. There's tons of room outside, and we've already got an established camp. Things might be a bit cozy for a while, but everyone is welcome in Camp Eight."

She could hear a sigh of relief escape his lips. "Thank you, Captain. I was hoping you wouldn't hold a grudge."

"It's not about us, it's about them. We band together, everything goes smoother. Agreed?"

"Agreed." He gave a fleeting smile, and then turned back to the setting sun.

"Something else is wrong, isn't it?"

The corner of his mouth stretched downward in a solemn grimace and he nodded. "I'm sorry. There's no other way to put this, but we're completely alone now. Sea water got into the battery compartments and shorted everything out down there, despite my efforts to seal it up."

No power. She shook her head. "Any hope of repair?"

He shook his head again. "Even if I could dry out the batteries, which would probably take weeks, it's all going to be corroded to hell once it dries up. These cells were never meant to be taken apart. I don't think we can do much to clean them up." He placed a firm, calloused hand on her shoulder. "I'm sorry, Captain. Without juice we can't run the radio. We have no way to call your father. Or the other ships."

She slowly lay down on the top of the pod and looked straight into the darkening blue sky. A numbness began to spread within her. "It's okay, Seth. It's not your fault. It's no one's fault."

He paused a moment before replying, "Captain?"

"Call me Haruka. Let's just drop the rank. It's just you, me, and Jenkins left."

"If you insist." He fell silent and watched her, apparently waiting for some form of response. "Are you okay?"

"No. Why should I be?" She waited for him to answer, but only the shouts of adults summoning their children to dinner greeted her ears. "Being here has only brought hardship and heartache for most of us. Some have been extremely fortunate to only experience a little, like the Bryants and the Reibers. For some of us, well," she laughed nervously, "I wonder how we make it day to day. Aidan and Marya. The Serranos. The Eckerts."

"The Kimuras," Leight added.

"This isn't about me or Dad," she shot back.

"Then you're lying to yourself."

Haruka rolled to her side and propped her head on her elbow. Sergeant Leight had his eyes locked on her, and behind them she saw a softness she had never seen before.

Crap, she thought. *Now he's going to give me a speech about how it's okay to take a moment for myself or some other psychological bull.*

"Don't you even," she warned.

He laughed and glanced at the sky for a split second before returning his attention to her. "No, Captain. I've seen your type too many times. Officers who are driven to achieve their own insanely high standards of perfection and performance. I know better than to try to convince you to join reality. Reality will do that to you soon enough."

"Then what?"

"I was just trying to get your attention when I said that."

She scowled at him and was taken aback for a moment at his admission, but then nodded and prepared to listen. "Alright, it worked. You have my attention."

"Perfection and performance to you is measured by the success and happiness of those around you. You love to see people flourish. I've seen how you smile after you've talked to the Bryants, Reibers, or Vandemarks. But when something goes wrong for anyone that you know, and sometimes those you don't really know, I see it eat at you. Those two orphan kids…"

Haruka sighed. "I can't even begin to tell you how terrible that is. To be in a strange place is hard enough on a kid, but to be there without your parents must be a nightmare."

"See? There you go, you're doing it."

Haruka began to get irritated with the sergeant. "So what? It's the truth."

"You passed them off from couple to couple," he noted coolly.

"Because Marya beat the living shit out of Gabi," she retorted. Her hand clenched, but she barely noticed.

"Speaking of, how are she and Maria doing?"

"I couldn't really tell you. Maria will maybe say four words to me on a good day. And Gabi's changed. I rarely see her anymore, and when I do…" Haruka shook her head and bit her lip.

"Kid's going to have a hard life, that's for sure. More so than anyone else in the village."

The village.

It was a simple term, but used more frequently by the band of survivors. Every day it seemed as if the concept of Camp Eight being their permanent home had taken hold just a little more firmly. Conversation about survival on the planet had changed over the weeks since the destruction of the sleeper ship. The question of where the colonists would go had disappeared and been replaced with debates about where to build farms, or how to design fishing boats with the minimal tools available.

"Where are you at, Captain?" Leight asked, stirring her from her thought.

"The village," she replied. "And I already told you to drop the rank."

"Fine, Haruka, whatever." He paused. "What about it?"

"Just thinking about how everything is progressing."

"Is there something wrong? Should I get James or Troy?"

"No," she replied, waving her hand dismissively. "Everything's actually going quite well. Other than when the planet throws an interesting new problem at us, like these 'supertides', or whatever they're called. There is something you can do for me, though. I didn't want to bring it up until now because of the fresh wound."

"What's that?" Leight asked, cocking his eyebrow.

"My staff is short one person right now. With Luis gone, I have no Chief of Security. I'd like to offer you the position."

Leight shook his head and grimaced. "There's no need for that. The village is secure. What would I even do with a title like that?"

"See if you can find out what happened to Lon Carney. If he's still alive, take him out. But until we know where he is, the village isn't safe."

"I already told you I'm going to bring him in alive if I find him, Cap… I mean, Haruka."

"As long as whatever you do ends with Camp Eight being safe from that prick, I don't care."

"Fine, I'll take the job. I see you're still planning every last detail that you can think of."

"Just making sure that all of the pieces are in place, Seth."

"In place for what?"

"When I die," she replied, holding back the bitterness.

Leight's mouth opened and he let loose a torrent of unintelligible stammering. He composed himself, then growled, "You're not dying."

"Doc says if I'm not, I'm still probably going to be horribly sick. You think I'll be in any condition to run the colony if I can't even get out of bed?"

The sergeant climbed to his feet and crossed his arms. The reflection of the sun off of the water behind him looked like a brilliant orange fire, and the dark silhouette of Arion hung just over his left shoulder.

"Just take it one day at a time. You have no idea what you mean to these people. They look up to you. What do you think they'll do if they find you've just gone and given up?"

"I can afford to now that you've accepted the position and we're all finally one colony. And they'll do fine without me. They'll have to."

"You're a real piece of work, you know that?" Leight muttered. He continued to grumble under his breath as he traversed back to the hatch and climbed back into the shell of the dead pod.

. . .

"This is unbelievable," Troy beamed as he wiped a finger over the thin, white crust that had formed on the trunk of the tree. He brought it to his mouth and sucked the tip of the finger.

"Now you're licking trees?" she looked at him, incredulous.

"Just try it," he grinned.

Haruka shrugged and ran her index finger along the trunk of the giant palm. Tiny white crystals sloughed from the bark and stuck to her finger. She dabbed it on the tip of her tongue. The tang of salt burst forth in her mouth, almost as if the air itself had somehow concentrated on her tongue. She did not believe what she had tasted at first, and repeated the ritual a second time for her affirmation.

"Salt?" she asked.

"You bet. And this tree hardly has any on it, because we've already harvested it. You should see some of the ones farther down the beach," he replied. His eyes twinkled and his grin stretched his wrinkled, burned skin even wider.

Haruka leaned to her left and looked through the dense row of trees that ran alongside the dead sleeper pod.

"And you're telling me it just grows on trees?" The words seemed ludicrous to Haruka, even as they escaped her mouth.

"In a way, I guess."

"Salt. Growing on the bark of a tree. On what planet does that make sense, Troy?"

"Demeter," he replied without a pause.

"I guess I walked into that, didn't I?" she groaned.

"Want to know how?"

If that smile of his gets any bigger, his head's going to explode.

"Alright, go for it," she replied.

Troy rubbed his hands together and he cleared his throat, though his face remained contorted by his proud grin. "I was wondering how these trees along the shore stay alive if they get flooded from time to time by those supertides that we saw. I mean, that kind of salt getting in the ground back on Earth would do serious damage to plants, but these things here are huge." He jerked his thumb skyward. "Every day I'd come say hello to these buggers and just look at their leaves. Green as the day before. And the day before. Well, then one day as I'm leaning on one of them, these little crystals flake off onto my hand. I'm probably the world's biggest idiot for sticking something in my mouth without thinking about it, but I tasted them. Tasted like salt."

"You're not the only one who's done something like that since we got here," she interrupted, recalling that Gabi had eaten pepperines before anyone had identified them as edible.

"I know," he continued. "Anyway, I gathered some up and took them to Charlotte to see what she had to say about them."

"I'm sorry, Charlotte the science teacher?"

"The very same. Anyway, she came down to look at the trees and we talked a bit about them, and she says that it's salt. Just plain, simple salt."

"That grows on trees," Haruka added.

"Right. Charlotte says that the trees absorb the sea water when it floods, and then over time they sweat the stuff out. I'm guessing since there aren't any huge mounds under them that it probably builds up at their bases and then most of it gets washed out to sea when it rains hard enough."

"How much salt are we talking here, Troy?"

He leaned against a palm and folded his arms. His posture and smug grin reminded her for a brief moment of Marco Mancini. "Enough for the colony. Enough to season our food. Probably enough to preserve fish and meat, so we can keep a steady source of protein if there are any lean times."

If this planet's going to eat our pods, I suppose this is the least it can do to pay us back.

"Great work, Troy. Let's get someone out here to collect it."

She heard someone clear their throat, and Troy looked up and behind her. Haruka glanced over her shoulder to find James Vandemark lurking by another nearby tree. He scratched at the beard on his cheek as he beckoned to her. She took four steps and reached his side.

James leaned close in to her ear. "We have a problem. Come with me."

Haruka sighed and nodded, then pardoned herself from Troy. James turned from the beach and took the boot-worn trail up the hill to Camp Eight, with Haruka only a few steps behind. They emerged from the jungle into a clearing on the shoulder of the hill, occupied only by dozens of stumps, the beginnings of a few log huts, and a timber longhouse that had yet to receive a roof. James led her through an empty door frame and around a short partition wall, into the main room of the building.

"What are we looking at here, James?" Haruka asked as she surveyed three overturned storage crates in a haphazard heap on the floor.

Crates of supplies were stacked against the rough-hewn log wall, serving as rests for dozens of axes, saws, and other hand tools. Thinner arches made from a smaller species of tree spanned overhead between the walls, forming the skeleton of the longhouse's roof. The structure ended at the arches, as suitable roofing material had yet to be stretched over the rafters.

He shuffled his feet and scratched at his right cheek. "Theft."

"What's missing?"

"Looks like food, mostly. But it could be anything: clothing, tools, ammunition. We keep everything here, and I won't know for sure until I run another inventory." James shook his head and rubbed his chin pensively. "This is not how I wanted to spend my day today."

"It needs to be done. You know that every last scrap that we scavenge from the jungle has to be accounted for."

"Yeah, I know."

"I don't suppose you saw who did it?" she asked in the vain hope that the thief was as careless as they were bold.

"I didn't see it. Doctor Petrovsky heard the commotion and came to check it out. He saw the guy running like a bat out of hell when he got here." James scratched his cheek again.

Haruka grimaced and her stomach knotted. James's nervous tell spoke volumes about the situation. She glanced at the mess and back to her Chief of Operations.

"What is it?" she prodded.

James seemed to shrink and deflate as he sighed. His shoulders slumped and he avoided eye contact with Haruka. "The doctor said that whoever did this was armed."

"Armed," she parroted.

"With a rifle. He saw it clearly as the guy ran away."

Lon Carney, she thought immediately.

"Shit, then Ken's lucky to be alive."

"Maybe, maybe not. Doctor Petrovsky couldn't have caught Carney if he had tried, so why would he gun him down in the middle of town? Why attract Leight and the security staff? Or one of the scouts?"

"Why did he gun down Luis?" she spat back with a snarl.

James simply shrugged and replied, "Maybe you should ask him next time he gets hungry and strolls in here for a snack."

Haruka growled and kicked an empty crate, sending it hurtling through the air, almost to the far end of the longhouse. It clattered to the floor with a racket and kicked up a cloud of dirt as it slid to a stop.

"This cockroach has killed one of my friends and survived alone in the jungle for how long now, two weeks?" She waited for James to nod in acknowledgement. "Believe me, if I knew when he'd be coming back, I'd be waiting for him."

"I know, Haruka. I know."

"Get Seth. I need to talk to him right away."

James bowed slightly and left the incomplete building in search of Seth Leight.

. . .

Cameron's a smart guy. I need to thank him for this idea later.

"Seriously, this is taking forever," Alexis complained. "Now I'm being a good sport about this, but if you don't take this damn blindfold off soon I'm going to start thinking that you're doing something really creepy."

Alexis remained in the position that Cal had prepped her in; her arms were folded across her chest, her legs shot straight out and her ankles were crossed so as to keep her straight as a board, which made her look as if she was doing a back float in a pool. An unused cleaning rag had been fashioned into a blindfold that wrapped around her head. Cal carefully maneuvered her by the elbow up and over the forward railing on the bridge's command platform. It took all of his control to keep her moving in the direction that he had wanted.

"I know," he replied. "I'm almost done. I just didn't want to ruin the surprise, and this is a little trickier than I first thought."

"What exactly are you doing, anyway?"

"You know how we were just below the bridge when I put the blindfold on, right?"

"Yeah."

"Well, you're on the bridge now. Just trying to get you seated before I take the blindfold off."

"Yeah, I figured that out already. But what are you *doing*?" she asked again.

"Keeping a promise that I gave you," he replied with a smile, even though he knew that she couldn't see it.

"What do you mean?"

"You'll see."

She sighed, and her lip curled into a mocking pout. "Fine."

"Bend your knees like you're sitting."

Alexis untangled her ankles and brought her knees up. Cal rotated her with one hand, and then flipped her forward. He fine-tuned her position over the seat of the nav console, and when he was satisfied with her alignment, he pushed her slowly down. Alexis landed in the seat almost perfectly, and Cal slipped one strap of the harness over a shoulder.

Tetris with humans, he mused silently before taking a seat next to her. Once he was secure, he reached over and untied the blindfold, which drifted away. Alexis rubbed her eyes and looked out of the front of the canopy. Her eyes popped wide open, her jaw slacked, and she gasped audibly.

With a smug grin, Cal turned and took in the scene that had Alexis at a loss for words. On the left side, near where the canopy glass curved and stopped at the engineering stations, Alpha Centauri B could be seen. The globe was much larger than before, now nearly the size of a grape. She had seen the star before, and Cal knew that her focus had been drawn to a small green and blue semicircle just to the left of the center glass. It looked similar to a picture of Earth that Cal had once seen as taken from the Moon, only smaller, and the land masses were unrecognizable. Any doubt that this was the planet Demeter would have been erased by the two dark dots creeping at a snail's pace across its equator.

Cal pointed at a tiny dot about the size of a pencil lead. "That closer moon is Arion. I've seen the pictures that the probe sent back. It's really dark colored, so we think that it will barely be visible at night, even on a full moon."

"Oh my goodness," she finally squeaked. "It's real. And it's here. We're actually going to land there?"

"Not on Arion," he grinned.

Alexis gave him a playful slap on his shoulder. "I know that, you dork. I meant the planet."

"That's the plan."

Alexis drew her hands to her mouth, almost as if she was praying. Her eyes locked on the planet millions of miles away. Cal had seen it several times before; instead he kept his attention on the girl by his side.

"Tell me what you're thinking."

"I... I don't know," she admitted. "Excited. Scared."

"Why scared?"

Her gaze broke from the window as she me his. "Oh, come on now. A strange place that no one here has been to, full of who knows what, and all we've got to survive is what's on this ship. We're explorers and pioneers now. But we've got no backup if something goes wrong. Yeah, we could build a brand new home on this planet, but we could die just as easily."

"I should have died years ago. In the War, I mean."

"You never fought in the War."

"Thanks to Dad. If it wasn't for him somehow getting me on this ship, I'm sure I would have been drafted. Then someone would have slapped a stripe on my shoulder, given me a gun, and sent me off to be slaughtered with all the other kids."

"You say that like it means nothing," she said in a cold voice, turning away.

"It would have meant nothing. We were losing, Alexis. More than half of the people on Earth were dead, our military was almost broken, and we had lost the West Coast. You think that me and my friends fighting on the front line would have made a damn bit of difference?"

"Shut up."

Cal bit his lip and closed his eyes, his head bowing slightly. *Her brother,* he remembered, too late. *Damn the meds. Damn… no, it's my fault.*

"Look, I…"

"Just shut up."

Cal put his foot on the console and brought his thumb to his lips. Nervously, he chewed at the nail on his finger as he looked out of the canopy at the blazing star in the distance. He silently debated with himself as to what he would say, or whether he would even say anything at all. Then he would flex and inspect his hand, which he had not yet become accustomed to using after the splint had been removed from his mended finger two days prior. At times he would be on the verge of speaking, but thought better of it, and the process would start all over again. After a few minutes, he could no longer hold back.

He brought his hand to the bridge of his nose and pinched. "I don't know how many times I can say sorry for it, Alexis."

She swung her head around and glared up at him, her mouth tightened until he thought it would simply disappear. "For what?"

"Being completely unable to express myself to you."

"You talk a lot. I don't think that's your problem," she retorted.

"It's exactly my problem. When I'm around you, I need to either shut up or think harder before I speak. And being on the meds makes it even worse."

"Oh, so now you're putting this on me?"

"What? No! There, it just happened again."

"What did?"

"Somehow I made what I wanted to say to you sound horrible. It's not about you. I just… God, I shouldn't say it."

"Oh, but you're on such a roll," she retorted.

"Please don't."

"I insist."

Cal grinned nervously and shook his head. "Fine, don't say I didn't warn you."

"Oh, I'm all ears."

He swallowed hard and forced his pride aside, knowing that it wouldn't serve him while she was upset. "I can have normal conversations all day long with Doctor Taylor or Cameron or Hunter. Hell, even Colonel Dayton doesn't even make me blink any more. But when I talk to you, I get all tongue tied and goofy. Care to guess why?"

"No. Enlighten me."

"It's because every time I see you, I get butterflies." He waited for her to react, and saw the expression on her face soften. Her brows arched and her eyes widened, but she seemed at a loss for words. "That's right. I like you. After all the stupid things I've done, and all the things you've said to push me away, I like you. It might be simpler for both of us if I didn't. If I could just let you push me away. Don't get me wrong, some of the things you've said hurt like hell. But when you're not mad at me, the way you smile, the way you give everything your best…"

"Don't do this, Cal," she interrupted. He could hear a slight crack in her voice as she spoke.

"The way you act when you're around my friends, too. They love hanging out with you, Alexis."

"I told you already, I'm a big flirt."

"No you're not," he responded. "I've seen you with the boys on this ship. You don't flirt with them. Hell, you barely treat Cameron different than Doctor Taylor. So unless you're saying that sixty one year old women do it for you, I'm not buying it."

"Please, stop it," she begged.

"So what is it? What exactly are you afraid of? Is it that I'm a 'monster'?"

Alexis's mouth dropped wide open, and sorrow flashed in her eyes.

"How did… what… where did you hear that?"

He ignored her and pressed on. "I know I screwed up, and I admitted it. What was it that I did that makes you think that way about me?"

"It… it wasn't you."

Cal felt a sudden shock at the revelation. He just stared at her, slack jawed, with his arms dangling weightlessly at his side; he lacked the presence of mind to keep them under control.

Alexis bowed her head and folded her hands in her lap. "It was about me. I hate myself for how I've been treating you basically since when you put me back to sleep. I was pissed at you for that, but after a couple days I understood why you had to do it. But when I realized that you still wanted to spend time with me, I freaked out. I mean, I've kind of had a thing for you since before we left Earth, and you did this really romantic thing for me, but then I spat in your face, and you kept coming after me anyway. I was afraid, and that's why I pushed you away."

Cal reached for her hands and took them in his own. A surge of emotions hit him at once; relief, regret, nervousness, and love overwhelmed him, and he had to force himself to breathe. Then panic set in as he remembered the symptoms of the psychosis that Dr. Taylor had been treating him for.

Damn it. Don't lose your shit right now, Cal. He took a deep breath and concentrated on the moment, and when he came back, he was keenly aware of Alexis's stare on him.

"Are you okay?" she asked.

"Yeah, sorry."

"Are you sure? You look a little pale."

"I'll be fine. Just an old thing I need to talk to the doctor about."

"You gave me a scare for a second there."

"I guess I've been doing that lately. I'm sorry. I didn't mean to."

Alexis wrinkled her nose. "It's not the same. This was a 'hey, I hope he's not dying' scare, not a 'hey, I hope he's not stalking me' scare."

"I wasn't, you know. Stalking you, that is. Or dying."

"I know. It took me a while to figure out. And to be honest, I did a little asking around about you."

"Oh?" he asked. The butterflies in his stomach began to flutter again.

"Just the doctor. I wanted her opinion as a woman."

"About?"

"You," she replied, squeezing her fingers gently around the palms of his hands. "She told me all she could about you as a friend, and then told me a story about one of her old co-workers and how he was too shy and almost lost the girl."

"Doctor Taylor has quite a few stories. What was the moral of this one?"

Alexis smiled and leaned in toward his ear. "Don't let him lose the girl," she whispered.

Cal's heart skipped a beat. *Does she mean what I think?*

"Is that so? Was it the right story?"

"It was."

He leaned slightly toward her. "I won't lose the girl. I promise."

Their lips were just about to meet when someone cleared their throat, and Cal startled.

"Get a room, you two," Drisko said as he gagged mockingly.

"Damn it, Cameron. Go away," Cal growled.

Drisko moved swiftly to his ops station and buckled in. "Would if I could, but it's time to get back to duty. You should clear out; Dayton's on his way to the bridge right now."

Cal sighed and looked at Alexis. "Rain check?"

She nodded. "I'll be cashing it in, trust me."

• • •

```
1st Lt Darius Owens
27 May 2058, 15:15
Gabriel
>|
```

"Are you ready to present your calculations, Lieutenant?" Eriksen asked with a booming voice.

Darius glanced over his shoulder and watched as the eyes of all nine other crew members on the bridge peered over the command platform at him. He nodded at the commanding officer and turned to his console.

No pressure, right? He thought. *You're just dictating how time is going to be measured, that's all.*

"Lieutenant Miller, begin ship wide broadcast. Tie the feed into the extracom and broadcast it to *Michael* as well," Eriksen added.

Roger Miller – sitting next to Darius at another ops station – immediately complied with Colonel Eriksen's order. He nodded to Darius, indicating that everything was ready. Darius took a deep breath, held it, and pushed it out, along with much of his nervousness.

"Good afternoon to both crews. I am Lieutenant Darius Owens. At the request of both Colonel Dayton and Colonel Eriksen, I have taken the data about the planet Demeter as well as the planetary system, and calculated how long the days are on the planet, as well as how many such days are in a year down there. From this information I have created a calendar and clocking system that should easily be understandable both to crew and civilians. It will take some getting used to, but I believe it is very workable.

"First, the basic calculations. The planet has a diurnal period of almost exactly twenty Earth hours. The variance from this mark is so negligible that we're only going to need to adjust our clocks about two seconds every year. Demeter makes a full orbit around the star Alpha Centauri B, or 'Bravo', every three hundred forty seven Demeter days.

"Second, the adjustments we will need to make. With the Demeter day being twenty hours long, this is pretty simple. We just reprogram our clocks so that ten is the top of the clock, not twelve. That is to say, that 10:00 is noon, and 19:59 rolls into zero-hundred hour. The calendar of days may take a little adjustment, but keeping the existing twelve month system, with their original names, should help. Each month has twenty nine days, with the exception of February, which will retain its original number of twenty eight. From my calculations, it doesn't appear that a leap day will be needed."

Darius tapped at the screen a few times and attached a pair of files to the broadcast, sending them to all terminals on the ship. After his conversations with Sergeant Drisko, he was sure that *Michael* would be able to retrieve and compile the files for their own viewing.

"I'm sending a picture of an adjusted analog clock," he continued. "Digital clocks will be easy to refit and display time correctly, but removing two hour marks from an analog clock, it's going to look a bit strange. You'll notice that every hour mark is now at an interval of six minutes instead of five. I've added a double hash mark at every old five minute mark as a visual cue to help with time estimation. This should do until we figure out a better way to make them. The second picture is a quick draw up of the new calendar. It's pretty straight forward.

"At this time I'd like to open up the channel of discussion. Because this broadcast will be delayed for *Michael*, I would ask that you com flash my terminal on the bridge if you have any questions. I will capture them and send responses in a list for later viewing. Thank you for your attention."

It took only a few seconds for the first flash to reach his screen; he was barely ready to capture the questions.

XCS-02 ENG GARZA: What if someone's birthday falls on the 30th or 31st of a month? How do we know when it actually falls on the new calendar?

Good question, Doug.

RESPONSE: The individual would choose either the 29th of their birth month or the 1st of the following month as their official birthday on Demeter.

XCS-02 NAV SCHNEIDER: With twenty hours in the day, are we going to have enough time to get a good night's rest?

RESPONSE: Please direct your question to the medical staff. I cannot answer that for you.

XCS-02 CO ERIKSEN: You mention 20 hours per day, and 347 Demeter days per year. Doesn't that make the year short by Earth standards? How will that affect our life expectancy?

Darius stopped for a moment. "Roger, can you run some math through your calculator real quick?"

"Yeah," his partner nodded.

"Can you figure out how long a Demeter year is compared to an Earth year?"

"Yeah, give me a second."

Darius split his attention between his screen and his partner's. Roger's fingers danced across the touchscreen of the terminal as he ran the calculations.

"Seventy nine point two two percent."

"Thanks."

RESPONSE: You are correct, the year is a little over seventy nine percent as long as an Earth year. If we assume that our life expectancy doesn't change based on any factors of the planet, our life expectancy in Demeter years will be much longer. The average might be somewhere around ninety five years. A little shorter for those of us who were born on Earth and have already lived a number of years.

XCS-01 MISC MCLAUGHLIN: That's a pretty short year. Can we grow anything from Earth in that amount of time?

Miscellaneous code? What the hell? Who is this guy?

"Captain Quinn," Darius belted. "Can you find out who this Mc-Laughlin guy on *Michael* is and what he does?"

RESPONSE: There are crops that grow on Earth that are able to grow to maturity and harvest well within a normal season.

Darius felt a prickling sensation on the back of his neck. He turned back to find Eriksen and Quinn staring at him.

"Did you say McLaughlin?" asked Eriksen slowly.

"Yes sir. Is there something wrong?"

"Maybe. Quinn, get on it."

"Yes sir."

"Carry on in the meantime, Mr. Owens."

"Yes sir," Darius replied and turned back to his screen.

What the hell is that all about?

XCS-01 CO DAYTON: Have you calculated what the date and time will be when we arrive, given our current trajectories and deceleration?

RESPONSE: Yes, Colonel. We may want to get our agricultural passengers ready as soon as we land. It's going to be the calendar equivalent of March 24th. They're going to need to break ground quickly to plant crops for harvest this year. It's hard to pin down the exact time we're going to land, but I'd estimate about 14:00 Demeter time.

Darius waited for more questions to come through, but Dayton's was the last he saw after several minutes of waiting. He closed the file and sent it off to all recipients. He stretched, unbuckled, and made his way across the command platform to the engineering stations. Colonel Eriksen clutched the railing just over Quinn's shoulder, looking over it with burning intensity.

"I have the profile of that McLaughlin guy, Lieutenant," Quinn chirped.

"I want to hear this too," added Eriksen.

"You're never going to believe this, sir."

"Just tell us, Captain."

"Calvin McLaughlin. Born in 1997 in Dallas, Texas. His father is..."

"General Andrew McLaughlin," Eriksen finished. "I'll be damned. What's he doing on that ship? And awake?"

Quinn tapped at his screen, scrolling through pages of data on a young blonde-haired boy. "I don't know for sure, but they've given him access to parts of the ship. It doesn't look like a hack, either. He was in stasis at the start of the trip, but somewhere along the way he was woken up, and Dayton has given him a login."

"Has that chowderhead lost his mind?" Eriksen fumed. "You don't just wake up a civilian and set them loose on the ship. Everyone has a place, and that *boy's* place is in stasis."

"Should I send a request to Dayton?" Darius asked.

"Requesting what, Lieutenant? If he's let McLaughlin go this far, he's not going to stick him back in a berth for three days." The commander sighed and scratched his whitening beard. "He's not my problem. As you were, gentlemen. Let's just concentrate on our final approach."

"Yes sir," came the synchronized reply.

. . .

Capt Haruka Kimura
Planetfall +70 days, dawn
Camp Eight
>|

Haruka lay on the top of the abandoned sleeper pod, casting her gaze at the puffed white clouds above as she picked at a rusted scar in the dull steel. The air smelled of the sea and damp earth; there had been a rainstorm the night before. She could not sleep with the rest of the colonists in the few ramshackle huts, the medical clinic, and single longhouse that had been constructed on the shoulder of the hill. Anxiety gnawed at her, so she had taken a walk in the darkness and rain. Solitude from the masses was what she had craved, and she found it in the listing ruin of pod eleven. The droning of the torrent on the craft's skin had finally soothed her nerves to where she could rest through the night.

It was certain that her absence had been noticed by now, but she didn't care. The muttering voices of fishermen from below drifted up to her ears, yet she ignored the words that she could understand. It was perfectly clear what they were talking about. Everyone in the colony was sure to broach the same subject at some point, and it was the source of her restlessness.

Lon Carney.

The fugitive was the subject of many rumors since he murdered Luis Serrano and terrorized his family nearly two months earlier. Some among the village whispered of the failure of Project Columbus to weed out criminal elements from the passenger lists. A few dared to accuse the research staff of loading prisoners onto the colony ships to provide brute labor for the colony, a suggestion that made Haruka scoff whenever she heard it. But mostly, talk of Lon Carney was of speculated sightings in the jungle surrounding the village. Only one confirmed sighting had been made; Doctor Petrovsky had seen Carney flee the colony after a brazen daylight raid of the village supplies. His gamble had paid off, and the renegade's take included food, ammunition, and a pair of hatchets.

Haruka sat upright and folded her legs. Her eyes wandered to the hill, where she could make out villagers winding their way up the hill to Camp Eight like ants returning to their home. Near the top of that hill was the longhouse that the villagers had dubbed the "Palm Palace". Two guards took shifts patrolling the Palace and village perimeter as a deterrent to Lon Carney. She grimaced when she thought of all the labor that those two colonists would have contributed to building the settlement if Seth Leight hadn't been forced to assign them to their current detail.

He's just as likely to surprise the guard as he is to get caught.

She reached into her pocket and retrieved the tags that had belonged to Mancini and Evans. Her fingers traced the edges of the flat metal tabs. Seeing Mancini's name brought back memories of her murdered friend.

Haruka closed her eyes and called to mind a particular memory of the mess hall at the Laramie complex, weeks before the launch of the sleeper ships. Mancini had fashioned a chunk of bread into a crude facsimile of Colonel Dayton's facial hair, and was standing on his chair, barking ridiculous orders at anyone passing by as he mimicked the officer's thick accent. Haruka remembered the laughter that he got from their table companions, as well as the confused or shocked looks from certain officers who just "didn't get it", as Marco would later say.

She opened her eyes and glanced at the other tag bearing the fake moniker that Agent Evans had adopted. The smile waned quickly from her face, and anger welled within her. She clenched the tag in her fist until it bit into her flesh.

Marco never got the chance for justice, she thought. *I denied him that when I didn't pull the trigger. Now the best I can do is hope that someone has the blind luck to stumble across Carney and bring him in somehow.*

She began to doubt her ability to serve justice at all. As the leader of Camp Eight, she was ultimately responsible for dealing with Lon Carney, and through her shared failure with Leight, Carney had managed to strike a new wave of fear and speculation in the colony.

Why couldn't he have just gotten himself eaten by a jaguar?

Haruka clamored to her feet and raised her arm to throw the tag in frustration. Something kept her from following through. She stopped and thought for a moment about what she was doing, and she had a realization as to why she wanted so passionately to see Carney dead.

It's because Marco never got justice. She sank to her knees and brushed her fingertips over the letters in his name. *He's been dead for more than two months. Evans, too. There's nothing I can do about any of that. Evans was never held accountable for what she did. How can I even think to lead these people if I can't give the Serranos the justice they deserve?*

Haruka shook her head and placed the dog tags back in her pocket, then made her way down the side ladder to the sands. She walked

J.C. Rainier

toward the hill, passing a group of fishermen on the way. They looked at her and whispered amongst themselves as she passed. She could feel their eyes judging her. Their whispers made goose bumps rise on her blotchy, discolored arms. Ignoring them, she marched over the last dune and along the freshly worn path leading up to Camp Eight.

As the trail wound its way around the base of a shorter hill, Haruka encountered few other colonists going about their duties. Mostly she saw children and the teenagers that had been assigned to look after them. The path picked up around the side of the hill, on which Camp Eight was built, and then started to climb more sharply. Haruka had to stop and rest for a few minutes, as her legs didn't have the stamina to make it all the way up without a break.

At last she came to the longhouse. The gaps in the salt palm logs had been sealed with brown clay. The roof of woven palm fronds, while proven to stay dry in the rain, had a tendency to rustle in a gentle breeze such as the one that blew as Haruka approached the open maw of the doorway; the double woven frond curtain that could be stretched and anchored across the threshold had been tied back. Several male voices echoed from inside the hall, overpowering the sound of the roof and nearby trees.

Haruka took a deep breath, and stepped inside. She was knocked back as the smell of body odor assaulted her nostrils. To her right, along one wall, a few young children gathered in a circle around Charlotte. The young science teacher was clad in dingy jeans and frayed t-shirt. Her curled brown hair bobbed as she gesticulated and spoke to the children as she delivered her lesson. Haruka nodded as she stepped past, receiving a short nod from the teacher. At the far end of the longhouse, Troy met with Airman Jenkins and Will Vandemark. As she approached, she could hear their discussion about the recent find of a wrecked pod in the jungle.

"So if you really think you need to go back, then you need to think carefully about what you haul back to the village," Troy snorted at Will. "I mean, the soaps are probably useful. The scissors too. I can't see much else from there being too useful. At least not right now."

Will smoothed out the peach fuzz that adorned his upper lip, a gesture that made Haruka stifle a laugh. "As sweet as this 'stache looks, it's really itchy. I'm sure I'm not the only guy here who would like to shave. And poor Jenkins here can't grow a beard right. He looks like someone attacked him with duct tape."

"Hey!" Jenkins protested.

"Alright, boys," Haruka said sweetly as she stepped between them.

"What's this all about?"

Troy shook his head and shrugged. "Will found a pod out in the jungle full of grooming and cleaning supplies. I'd love a good wash, Captain, and our clothes need to be scrubbed out good, but some of the stuff in there just isn't worth our time."

"Come on, you I can carry back a couple cans of shaving cream and a few razors along with everything else," Will cut in. "Just give me a chance."

"No way. I'd rather you drag back a little more detergent or a few more pairs of scissors."

"Where was the pod found?" Haruka asked, almost interrupting her top civil engineer.

"Five miles north and a mile inland," Troy grumbled.

North. The direction that Lon Carney ran off, according to the doctor.

"How much does a bath mean to you, Troy?"

"It'd be nice, but I can live without it."

"Good to hear," she nodded, "because you're not going back out there at all, Will."

"What?" he groaned. "Why not? I can leave at first light tomorrow and be back for supper."

"Because I want you to concentrate your efforts to the south," she replied.

And because I don't want Carney to find you and get the jump on you just because you can't stand an itchy lip.

"Last I checked, Troy made me Lead Scout," Will retorted as he folded his arms across his chest. "So I can go out whichever way I want. I just thought I'd give old man Bryant here a shot at letting me know what he wanted from the pod first before I went out."

Haruka turned to face Will directly. She did not hesitate to look him in the eyes and glare, though he was a couple inches taller than her. "And the last time I checked, Lead Scout was still a staff position and reported to me. Go south, young man, unless you want to spend the next month splitting logs for Troy."

Will growled and stormed out of the Palm Palace without a word, though the grumbling did startle the children and disrupt Charlotte's lesson. Charlotte rolled her eyes and shook her head before resuming her classroom duty.

"Skip your breakfast this morning?" Troy grinned.

"Nope. Just making an executive decision."

"And applying your charismatic personal touch at the same time."

Haruka checked to make sure that Airman Jenkins had not wandered away. Impishly, she grinned, and barely loud enough for the two men to hear said, "No, if it was personal touch I'd tell you to stop gawking already and ask Charlotte on a date. It's allowed, you know, since you're both single and attracted to each other."

She lingered just long enough to watch his jaw slack and a single unintelligible syllable to escape his mouth. She turned away, and a little louder added, "Don't try to deny it, either."

· · ·

Cal placed the palm of his hand on the cold aluminum door of a closed sleeper berth. Though gravity pulled his feet to the ground for the first time since Earth, its grasp was not very strong, and he found that he had trouble walking without tripping over his own feet. Alexis was faring better, although not by much. The grace that she seemed to exude all the time disappeared in the slowly increasing gravity. *Michael* shuddered hard, and Alexis lost her balance. She pitched forward into Cal's arms, and both of them fell slowly to the deck. His arms fell around her waist, and he did not hesitate to use the opportunity for a light hug. She craned her neck up to look at him.

"Gee, it's almost like you planned that there, mister."

"I take what I can get."

He staggered to his feet and helped her up. A vibration began to build in the deck plates of the pod, and a low hum echoed in the hallway.

"We don't have much time left," he said, glancing at the two open sleeper berths on opposite walls.

Her bright green eyes flashed at him vibrantly, and she smiled at him. "Did you get to ask Colonel Dayton?"

"I did."

"And?" she asked, her voice full of hope. Cal pursed his lips and shook his head. The smile disappeared as quickly as it had come. "Why not?"

He sighed and took her hand. "He says that he needs the bridge stations for his crew. There aren't any spares up there, and he wants us strapped in just in case something goes south."

Like it did on Raphael.

"Can we at least sit in the pod's cockpit thing?"

"I asked that too. Same story. I'm sorry, but we need to be strapped into our berths for landing."

Her head dropped as she avoided his gaze. Her lower lip curled into a pout. "I understand, I guess."

"Hey, it wasn't for nothing," he said as he stroked her soft hand.

"Dayton's giving us a little treat when we land."

"Yeah? What's that?"

"He's letting us be the first civilians to walk off of the ship. Right behind him, in fact."

She snapped her head up in an instant, and the disappointment had washed from her face. Her emerald eyes sparkled as she smiled again. "Really?"

"Really. He's promised. And he did it in front of Hunter, so we've got someone who will hold back the masses for us if we need it."

Alexis giggled joyfully and threw her arms around his neck, causing them to tumble back onto the deck plating. She then grabbed the front of his flight suit, catching him by surprise, and drew him into a kiss. When she let go, his head fell back onto the floor with a thud.

"Wow. Excited much?"

She bit her lower lip and nodded. "I think we've been cooped up in here too long. Don't you?"

"Forty four years? Nah. I could do a few more in this bucket."

"Liar. You know that you'd knock down Dayton in a heartbeat to be the first one off the ship."

Cal chuckled. "Yeah, you're probably right."

You're completely right. After all the nightmares and suffering, there's nothing more that I want than to get off this ship. Well, almost nothing more.

The low rumble began to crescendo, and Cal could feel the rattling through every bone in his body. Over the din, he heard Colonel Dayton's voice over the general address system.

"This is Colonel Dayton to all passengers. We're entering the planet's atmosphere. For your own safety, remain in your berths with your restraints on until you are cleared by a member of the crew. All crew to ESAARC position one. Com flash when ready."

"It's time," he said, staring deep into her eyes. She pushed off of the deck, but he drew her close and held her tight. "Just a few more minutes, and then we'll be out of there and walking off this ship. Together."

"Not if you squeeze me to death first," she gasped.

"Sorry."

He let her go, and she gave him a quick peck on the cheek before clamoring into her berth and strapping in. He followed suit and glanced back at her. She wore a warm, gentle smile as she looked across the hallway at him. He lingered as long as he could before shutting the door, waiting until he could no longer see her face.

His thoughts drifted to his friends on the bridge. Cal knew they would have their hands full keeping the half-kilometer-plus long ship under control for its descent. Everything was at stake, and Cal was thankful that none of it rested on his shoulders. He couldn't imagine the pressure that Cameron, Vince, or Hunter were under at that very moment.

Keep us safe, guys. Bring us home.

. . .

1st Lt Darius Owens
30 May 2058 (Earth calendar)
24 March, Year of Landing, 13:32 (Demeter calendar)
Gabriel
>|

Tight straps across his chest kept Darius firmly planted in front of the console as the vibrations in his seat grew. His screen streamed with information about the network systems on board *Gabriel*. He kept his eyes glued to one router in particular that was located between the upper and lower galleries just outside of pod nine. Chatter from the crew filled the earpiece of his headset as the roar of entry drowned out the voices on the bridge.

Good. Looks like the backup router kicked in. Darius puffed out a short sigh and let himself relax ever so slightly, turning his attention to the conversation being held over the ship's com system.

"Doctor Kimura, final status of the passengers, please," Eriksen barked.

"The biostasis system is offline. All passengers are accounted for and awake, Colonel."

"Understood. Report to Sergeant Marks in the crew pod right away."

"Yes sir."

And there it is. He just says yes, and goes to face his arrest. The sleeper ship was still aloft, so there would be no place for Doctor Kimura to hide. Yet Darius did not know if, faced with similar circumstances, he could accept his fate with such composure. He shook his head and tried not to think about it.

"How are we holding up, Captain Quinn?" asked Eriksen.

"Hull's heating up, but we're still looking good. The reactor readings have barely budged."

Gabriel shuddered and rocked, and Darius had the sudden sensation of free fall. Despite the roar of atmospheric entry, he could have sworn he heard a collective yelp of surprise from the bridge crew. His breathing became shallow and his mind started to race. A few moments later, the ship felt as if it was floating again, and the panic subsided with a few deep breaths. His heart continued to pound in his chest like a hammer, and his fingers tingled. Darius carefully tapped commands into his terminal, running another diagnostic on the network.

Keep focused. Keep focused.

"Sorry Colonel, I wasn't expecting that," Lieutenant Schneider explained.

"Just keep us in the air."

The inky black of space gave way quickly to a deep blue shimmer and the curvature of the planet Demeter. The seconds ticked past, and the dark blue in turn abdicated in favor of ever lighter shades of blue sky.

"Three minutes to landing, sir."

"Have you made the adjustments I asked for, Schneider?"

"Yes sir. South side of the river, like you asked."

"South side, sir?" Darius blurted.

"That's right, Lieutenant."

"But sir, we had agreed to meet Colonel Dayton on the north side."

"I'm aware of that."

What the hell?

Darius pressed on. "So why are we landing to the south?"

"Mind your station, Mr. Owens."

"Sir, has something happened?"

"I said mind your station," the commander snapped back. "That's an order."

A message popped onto the diagnostic screen in front of Darius.

XCS-02 ENG QUINN: Just wait until we're on the ground.

No, I need to know. What's so important to him that he has to break his promise?

"Sir, I need to know why we are going off mission. Is there something we need to be aware of?"

Shivers ran down his spine, and he had the sensation he was the target of someone's stare. Darius looked over his shoulder at the command chair. Eriksen had turned it to face Darius, and he leaned over as far as his harness would allow. His streaked red hair and beard seemed to glow like fire, and his eyes could burn holes through Darius. His jaw clenched, ground, and unclenched several times.

"Clear this channel or I'll have you relieved, Owens. Final warning."

Darius stared incredulously as Colonel Eriksen turned his chair and went back to barking orders through the com. Something was amiss, but he couldn't risk drawing further ire from his CO.

Is there something wrong with the landing site?

He turned back to his terminal and abandoned the network diagnostics. He quickly called up images of the landing site, as well as 3D projections of the terrain that had been made by a probe from *Michael*. Darius pored over every detail he could think of as to why it would be necessary to have a different landing site. The terrain on both sides of the river was similar, and there was plenty of space to land both ships on either side.

The river averaged five hundred meters wide at the landing site, and toward the eastern edge it flared out and several small islands broke its flow into channels only a hundred or so feet wide. Trees lined both banks, but otherwise there was little hazardous vegetation on either side of the site.

I can't see an advantage to doing this. We're better off pooling our resources with the other crew.

Doubt crept into his mind. The more he thought about it, the less he thought this was a move of safety and the more he thought that it was meant to snub Colonel Dayton. Darius sent a com flash to Captain Quinn.

XCS-02 OPS OWENS: Did you know about this?

XCS-02 ENG QUINN: Don't worry about it. Colonel's got a plan.

XCS-02 OPS OWENS: Did he tell you about Colonel Dayton?

Darius waited for a response to show up, but as the time passed, he realized that there would be no answer. The fact that Captain Quinn had sent him a flash to begin with indicated that he knew more than he was giving Darius. The sky was a light overcast gray. Darius felt his weight being pressed deeper into the seat as the thrusters worked to slow the massive ship.

"Thirty seconds to landing, sir," Schneider reported.

The schematic of the coms lit up from stem to stern on Darius's terminal as Eriksen activated the shipwide address system.

"This is Colonel Eriksen. We will be landing in a few seconds. You may feel a bump or a jolt. Don't worry, this is expected. Remain in your berth until directed by a member of the crew."

Darius noted the terseness with which Eriksen spoke, even addressing the passengers.

Something's got to be eating at him.

"Ten seconds."

Darius drew in a deep breath and wrapped a hand around each of the vertical straps and counted down the seconds in his head. He reached zero, but nothing happened. Then as he turned his head to look at Lieutenant Miller, there was a sudden, sharp jerk and an echoing metallic boom that left his ears ringing. He clutched his head and tried in vain to squeeze the noise from within. Nothing worked, so he just sat until his hearing returned to normal.

As he was about ready to remove his restraints and shut down his station, he felt a hand on his shoulder from behind. He craned his neck to find Colonel Eriksen, kneeling at the railing behind him, reaching down to him. Behind the CO stood a grim-faced Captain Quinn, arms folded across his chest.

"You're coming with me. We need to talk."

• • •

J.C. Rainier

Calvin McLaughlin
23 March, Year of Landing, 14:10
Michael
>|

An ear-splitting squeal pierced the air in the ship's lower gallery. Cal winced at the noise made by the heavy rear ramp as it lowered into position. The closed airlock only dampened the noise; Cal wondered if the noise would have been too much to handle had it not been there. He glanced to his left at Alexis. She held her hands up to her ears, and had an expression on her face that was half a squint combined with the puckered cheeks of someone who had just bitten a lemon. She mouthed something to him, but the words were drowned out by the metallic screech.

After nearly two minutes of nerve-grating sound, there was a loud clunk. After the echo faded away, a silence settled in the broad, modestly lit hallway. Cal watched as Colonel Dayton, who stood before him with his back turned, tightened the grip on his M4 carbine rifle. Glancing over his shoulder, he caught a glimpse of Hunter, similarly armed. Even Dr. Taylor and Alexis wore pistols at their hips, though Alexis had only done so at the insistence of Colonel Dayton. Cal looked down at the holster on his own belt, and brushed his trembling fingers against the grip of the Beretta that it held.

In just a few more moments the airlock would open, and they would take their first steps on the alien world that was to become their new home. Cal's breaths quickened, and goose bumps rose on his skin. He felt a warm hand wrap around his, and looked to see Alexis entwine her fingers with his. She smiled, but he could tell that she was just as apprehensive as Cal.

"We're here," she whispered.

"I know. "

The thought ran through his head every moment. He had dreams of Demeter, or at least what his subconscious had made Demeter out to be. He hoped to see vast green fields and rolling hills, but at the same time, was terrified that he might hike over a hill and find the remnants of *Raphael* littering a valley floor.

Colonel Dayton turned his rotund frame to face them. For a moment, Cal thought he recognized fear and concern in the commander's eyes. As the man squared his shoulders, the illusion disappeared, and his normal controlled demeanor was apparent.

"History," he said. There was a slight pause. "Does it really feel like history to you? It's odd. I know we're about to make history the moment we step off that ramp. I just didn't think that making history would feel like this."

"Like what?" Cal asked.

Dayton shrugged. "Like life. Like Christmas morning as a kid. Or like meeting a pretty girl. Or breathing in the ocean air as you blast down a coastal highway. I don't know, I just thought it would be more... grand."

"Those are no small moments," Dr. Taylor said with a smile. "I can understand the notion. It's kind of the same thing. I've got more than a few butterflies myself."

"I'm a little excited and a little scared," Alexis added.

"And I'm hungry," Hunter chimed in. All eyes turned to him. "What? I thought we were sharing a moment here."

Dayton chortled and shook his head, then turned back to the airlock. "Open it, Lieutenant."

Cal tightened his grip on Alexis's hand as the airlock door slid open with a groan. Light and color filtered in from the gaping maw at the end of the ship. Dayton began to march forward, and the rest followed suit right behind him. They walked down the ramp and emerged under the overcast sky of Demeter. Despite the clouds, Cal still had to squint and adjust to the light.

It's like coming out of a theater. He smiled and nervously laughed to himself. *Except I can't find my car.*

The sound of footsteps clanking on the ramp gave way to the soft rustle of green grass against their boots. The smell of damp earth permeated the air. Tall trees marked the banks of the river, stabbing their green and brown spears deep into the gray skies.

Alexis gasped audibly and clutched at him. With her free hand she pointed to a pair of birds in the sky, diving and dancing in the wind. Cal blinked in disbelief as he counted four wings on each of the large, black birds. Then a brown blur out of the corner of his eye caught his attention, and he craned his neck just in time to see a large animal loping away over a hill. Its arched back and bounding movements reminded him of a giant slinky with fur.

"Wow. Did you see that one?" he whispered to Alexis.

"Where? What?"

"Damn. You missed it."

"What was it?"

Cal hesitated. "I'm not sure. It was pretty weird looking though."

A cold drop of water splashed on Cal's forehead. He wiped it off, and two more dripped on his arms.

"Come on, up this hill," Dayton ordered.

The group made their way up a short hill just a few hundred yards from the stern of their ship. As they walked, the rain slowly increased in intensity. The crisp patter of raindrops on the ground filled Cal's ears. He shivered as a gust of wind blew across the face of the hill. Alexis laughed.

"What?" he asked, slightly annoyed.

"You know, for someone who has spent so much time in that ice bucket back there, you're really a weather wuss," she replied with a playful smile.

"I'm cold," he growled. "Isn't that what happens when it rains?"

Alexis giggled and ran ahead of him. She twirled in the rain with her arms flung out wide. She threw her head back and seemed to drink in the rain as she spun. Cal shook his head and laughed, and Dr. Taylor joined in with him.

"You're nuts," he said.

Alexis ran down to him and grabbed his arms, then dragged him up the hill with her. "Come on. A little rain won't kill you."

"It's freaking cold," he protested.

"Did you forget your jacket on the ship?" she teased.

"Son of a bitch!" Colonel Dayton roared at the top of his lungs.

Hunter bolted past Cal and Alexis. Confused and concerned, Cal sprinted after him, mounting the hill in just seconds. Dayton paced at the top, occasionally looking across the river and letting an expletive escape his lips.

Hunter reached him first. "What is it, sir?"

The disturbed commander shot his arm out, finger straight as an arrow, pointing across the river. On the far side, barely visible above the tree line, was a massive gray shadow. At first Cal took it for a mountain, but after inspecting it again it was definitely not natural.

"You've got to be kidding me," Hunter said, incredulous.

"Is that… the other ship?" asked Cal.

"It is," Hunter replied. "What the hell are they doing over there?"

"I knew it," fumed Dayton. "I knew I shouldn't have trusted that pompous bastard. What the hell was I thinking?" His voice took on a mocking tone. "Let's land on the north side of the river together, Colonel. We'll pool our resources and live in the lands of fairies and rainbows."

"Sir, calm down."

"Fuck that, Lieutenant. Shut down the extracom when we get back."

Hunter sighed. "Yes sir."

"No contact with the other crew at all, do you hear me?

"Yes sir."

"Wait, why no contact, sir?" Cal asked.

"He's made a statement today, Mr. McLaughlin."

"What do you mean? What statement?"

"That we're not worth his time. That he thinks he's better off without us. If that's what he wants, by God I'll give it to him."

"Sir, please don't do anything rash."

"I'm not, he is."

"Colonel," Dr. Taylor interrupted. "Calvin's right. Just radio them when we get back. I'm sure there's a good explanation for it. Maybe there was a reason they couldn't land on this side of the river."

"Thank you all for your advice," he sneered, "but I've made up my mind." He looked up at the clouds and the rain that still increased in intensity. "Everyone sleeps inside tonight. I'm not setting up camp outdoors in the rain until we know that we won't be flooded out. I also want to make sure the local fauna won't think we're breakfast. We'll begin unloading in the morning. Hunter, I want three scouting parties made up. Each team gets a crawler, two rifles, and appropriate supplies for three days."

"Yes sir," Hunter repeated.

"That is all. Let's head back."

Cal followed Hunter and Dayton down the hill toward the ship. He tried to think of a good reason as to why either commander would react the way they had. He could only think of the animosity that existed between them that Cameron Drisko had mentioned during the voyage.

Whatever this is, it's not over a sandwich, Cam.

• • •

Colonel Eriksen sat hunched in the command chair, scratching at his beard. Rain streaked the canopy, and the trees beyond loomed like dark sentinels in the dying light. Darius knew that Colonel Eriksen was displeased, and the way he twisted both his face and body made him look like a gargoyle clutching to its perch. To the colonel's right stood Captain Quinn. His stare was almost dead, as if he was looking through Darius.

What does he want now? He already chewed me out for questioning him about the landing site.

Eriksen had made his disdain for the incident clear. He was not going to give Darius a reason for landing on the south side of the river, counter to his agreement with Colonel Dayton. What shocked Darius was that afterwards, Quinn stonewalled him when he pressed for more knowledge. In the air, the engineer had assured Darius that there was an explanation, and that he would get it when the ship landed. Quinn had never lied to Darius before. He got the distinct feeling that the colonel was behind this sequestering.

And what is he waiting for, anyway? I'm right here. Why doesn't he just get it over with?

The commander drummed his fingers on the armrest of his chair. Quinn shifted his weight from one foot to another and back again. Uncomfortable silence weighed on Darius as their stares bore into him. He was about to speak when the com system chirped.

"Lieutenant Miller to Colonel Eriksen. We're ready."

"Bring them up."

Bring up who?

"It's time to get this over with, Lieutenant."

Footsteps clanked on the metal stairway to the bridge, and Darius turned around. His confusion melted away and was replaced with a grim solemnity as Saika Reid and Sarah Kimura walked onto the bridge with Lieutenant Miller at their heels. Darius knew what this was about, and yet his recent lecture had pushed it out of his mind. He felt foolish and unprepared for what he was expected to do next.

Damn it, sir, he mentally cursed. *Couldn't you have given me some warning? I mean, Doc wanted me to tell them, but I thought I'd have a little more time. Not just surprise them the second they woke up.*

The women glanced at each other and whispered as they approached. Darius couldn't help but notice the look of worry on Sarah's face; her wrinkles were more pronounced than usual, and the corners of her mouth were turned down. Her companion, Saika, seemed more interested in gazing at the scenery beyond the windows. She barely made eye contact with the elder Kimura as they came to a stop in front of Darius.

His hands began to tremble as he recalled that Saika was pregnant. He was the bearer of what was sure to be devastating news. Their eyes met his, and his nerves almost erupted. He had to close his eyes and take a deep breath.

"Darius? What's wrong?" asked Sarah, her voice barely audible over the wash of rain.

Yank the bandage off. Do it quickly.

"I'm sorry to have to give you this news, but Doctor Kimura and Lieutenant Reid are under arrest," he said. "They're accused of conspiring to commit treason."

"What?" shrieked Saika. "No, that can't be."

"I'm so sorry. I know this is a shock…"

"No. You're wrong. Brandon would never do anything like that."

"I understand this is hard to hear."

"Understand?" she laughed nervously as her voice cracked. "You don't understand at all. Where is he? I need to see him."

"There has to be some sort of mistake, Darius," added Sarah.

"I wish it was," he sighed. "Your husband turned himself in over forty years ago. I was the one who took custody of him."

The women stared at Darius in shock. For a moment, only the rain could be heard. Then Saika uttered a pitiful wailing sound, and fell into the arms of her mother. Sarah cradled her daughter's head in her hands and whispered into her ear as she stroked her hair.

Darius felt a sharp stab of guilt in his gut. He knew that the news had to be broken at some point, and no matter how or when it was done, it would be a cruel blow. As he watched Sarah try to comfort Saika, barely able to keep her own emotions in check, Darius shook his head and turned to Colonel Eriksen. The man's face was a stone wall as he surveyed the scene, but a crack soon appeared. Darius could tell that his teeth were clenched, and he took two hard swallows. Darius took his chances and approached the commander, bowing slightly to whisper in his ear.

"Sir, at least let them see their husbands. Just for a couple minutes."

Eriksen's hand shot up, as if to silence Darius. But then he closed his eyes, nodded, and activated his com. "Marks, bring them up."

In less than a minute, Dr. Kimura and Lieutenant Reid were ushered to the bridge by a slick-haired, grizzled sergeant. The approach of the accused showed a very different demeanor between the two. While Dr. Kimura shuffled his feet and bowed his head, Lieutenant Reid marched in step, holding his head high. If he was bothered by the accusations against him he did not show it, whereas his father-in-law seemed crushed under the weight of his sins.

Saika looked up from her mother's arms and caught a glimpse of her husband. She jumped out of the protective arms that held her and ran headlong into the chest of Lieutenant Reid. He wrapped his arms around her and kissed the top of her head. Sarah Kimura plodded slowly toward her husband, giving him a much more somber embrace. The couples spent many minutes hugging, talking, kissing, and crying. As much as he tried, Darius could not keep his eyes off of Saika and Lieutenant Reid. The more he spoke with her, the more upset she seemed to get.

Is he admitting his role to her?

"Sergeant Marks," Eriksen said in a low voice. "Take them back down."

"Give them a few more minutes, Colonel," Darius protested.

Colonel Eriksen shot a burning glare back at him. "Damn it, Owens, did our little discussion earlier not sink in?"

"Sir, they're not going anywhere," he insisted. "Let them have a little more time. Miss Reid and Missus Kimura are going to be punished enough by their husbands' imprisonment and trials. Don't tear them away so soon."

"Give me one good reason why I shouldn't have you hauled up on charges of insubordination, Lieutenant," Eriksen growled.

"I can't think of one, *sir*, and I'm proud of that. But I can think of a great reason why you should at least let Miss Reid have a few more minutes with the lieutenant."

"Try me."

Darius leaned in to his CO's ear once more and whispered, "Because she's pregnant, and Doctor Kimura thinks that the stasis might have been screwing with her body. You tear her away right now and you might just be killing their unborn child." He paused a second as Eriksen turned his scraggly bearded face to meet his own gaze. In the man's brown eyes, Darius could see utter shock. He raised his voice to just above a whisper. "Do you want that on your conscience?"

Eriksen paused a moment, and then his eyes dropped away and he shook his head vigorously. "Disregard my last order, Sergeant."

"Yes sir."

He rose and motioned with his hand to the rear of the bridge. "Gentlemen, let's give them an hour. They have a hard road ahead of them."

He walked around the couples and off of the bridge with Quinn, Miller, and Marks on his heels. Darius brought up the rear, and the quintet exited the bridge section and into the gallery. Lighting had been brought up from the minimal levels, and the eerie shadows that once dominated the desolate expanse were no more. In their place, Darius could see every inch of the dull, steel inner structure of the massive sleeper ship. He had never before realized just how industrial looking the interior of *Gabriel* was. It shouldn't have been a surprise, but the time he had spent awake was more focused on duty rather than aesthetics.

"Lieutenant Owens, a moment please," called Eriksen as he beckoned from beyond the group. Darius walked over as Eriksen moved out of earshot of the other three men. "I want to make it explicitly clear that I will not tolerate any more incidents of you questioning my orders in front of others. Do you read me?"

He paused for a moment. His initial inclination was to nod, but an idea swelled within him, filling him with an almost arrogant confidence. Instead of the nod, a wry grin crossed his face.

"I read you, but I don't care. My enlistment expired decades ago, Colonel. I'm only as bound to you as a civilian, and that gives me the right to speak my mind whether or not you like it."

He turned on his heels and stormed off toward the rear of the ship. He expected Eriksen to yell at him or send Captain Quinn after him, but all he heard as he moved off was incoherent stammering.

• • •

Cal stared into the soft glow of the lantern in the center of the circle of sleeping bags. Its small propane canister assured a steady flow of fuel that produced a stable light when burned, though Cal could swear that the light danced and played tricks in sync with the softly plucked guitar. One of his legs started to cramp up, so he uncrossed them, stretched, and crossed them again the other way. He swiveled his back each way, releasing the pressure with a satisfying series of pops.

"You okay?" Alexis asked as she rubbed his leg.

"Yeah, just getting a bit tired."

Cameron Drisko, directly across the circle from Cal, paused for a moment to tweak the tuning of his acoustic guitar. "Well, we've had a hell of a day today. I can't say that I'm not a bit worn out myself."

Cal looked around the ring at the faces of his friends. Alexis sat to his right, alternating her gaze between Cal and Cameron. To his left lay Hunter Ceretti. The lieutenant had already crawled into his sleeping bag and had his hands folded behind his head. Vince Hartley, the acting chief engineer, was between Hunter and Cameron. His attention was fixed on the lantern; it seemed that he had been in his own world for the last fifteen minutes. One spot in the circle remained empty, between Cameron and Alexis. Cal had originally thought that Dr. Taylor might be joining them, but Hunter had reminded him that she wanted to spend the first night on the planet with her family, in the sleeper pods above them.

Her son and his wife. Her grandson. Asleep the whole way.

Hunter had let the group decide as a whole how to spend night, and they chose to pass the evening in the lower gallery near the rear airlock. Almost two thousand people occupied the upper gallery and sleeper pods, and a measure of solitude was too much for Cal to resist. Alexis was quick to join in when she caught wind of the excursion to the lower floor.

Cameron plucked at a couple strings, testing their tone. Apparently satisfied with the results, he resumed playing. Cal could not help but notice the precision with which his friend could pick individual notes. Cal had tried to learn to play the guitar when he was a teenager, but could never get past strumming a chord that sounded like a strangled cat.

Cameron's really good, he thought. Cal stretched again and leaned back, planting his hands on the floor to keep him upright. Alexis found his hand, and soon his fingers were locked with hers. A smile bubbled up, and despite the lack of heating in the lower gallery, Cal felt warm. A dim light in the distance bobbed and swayed. Cal watched it as it grew larger and larger.

"Hey, I think someone's coming, guys."

Hunter looked up, and Cameron craned his neck around to see. Out of the darkness emerged one of the crew, holding a lantern in one hand and cradling another object in the crook of his other arm. The light made it difficult for Cal to make out what the item was. By contrast, the man's inky skin and shining white smile gave his identity away immediately.

Hunter rose up and gave a sweeping, flourished salute. "Captain Gibbins, sir. How fine it is to see you."

Captain Donnell Gibbins smiled and snapped his own salute in return. "Lieutenant Ceretti. It's my pleasure."

"If you please," Hunter said, gesturing to the unclaimed sleeping bag as he took a seat on his own.

"Of course. First things first, though." The man's coal black eyes met Cal's. "I presume you're the Calvin that everyone's been talking about?"

Cal could feel himself blush. "I guess that's me."

"Doctor Taylor wanted me to give this to you. She said you'd know what to do with it."

He stretched out his arm and handed Cal the item that he had tucked under his arm. Cal looked at the leather bag with the valve at one end, and his fingers tightened, causing the liquid within to give way and distort the shape of the leather.

"What is it?" Alexis asked, leaning over to get a peek.

Cal twisted the valve open and took a sniff. The vapors of alcohol made his nose burn ever so slightly as he inhaled. "I don't believe it."

"What?" Alexis prodded.

"Captain, did she say why?"

"She said it was a present to celebrate the landing."

"C'mon, Cal," Alexis begged.

"It's alcohol," he said, a little shocked. "From her private stash."

Hunter laughed. "Well don't just sit there, have a drink!"

"I'm underage, Hunter!"

"So? We just finished traveling over four light years and touched down on an alien planet with this bucket. Live a little," his friend smiled. "And if you don't, I'm going to live a little for you."

Cal looked at the skin of alcohol. The brown leather reminded him of the belt he wore when he walked off the ship earlier in the day. Memories rushed back of the grasses, shrubs, trees, and strange birds he had seen earlier. The significance of the day's events thrust themselves into the forefront of his mind. He smiled, and started to draw the skin up to his lips, but then paused.

"Wait, this isn't right," he said.

"Of course it is. I'm not saying you should drink every night, but this is definitely an occasion where bending the rules is a no-brainer."

"That's not what I mean. It's not right that I should go first." Cal climbed to his feet. "Captain Gibbins, sir."

"Please, call me Donnell."

"Maybe later," Cal said with a grin. "Captain, I know you were at nav through the whole landing process. Without your skilled hands and quick wits, we'd be in a million pieces or so. Sir, it would be my honor if you took the first drink."

Donnell nodded and took the pouch from Cal. He drew a deep sip of its contents, then wiped his mouth as he handed it back to Cal.

"Whoo, boy. Doc's got some good taste," he said as he laughed.

Huh? She said the selection on Earth wasn't very good.

"Captain Vince Hartley. Thank you very much for making sure that all of the ship's systems were kept in working form, so that we were able to get here."

"Cheers," Vince said as he took a drink from the skin. "Yeah, that's the stuff."

"To Sergeant Cameron Drisko. You were our eyes and ears for the voyage. Not only that, but you have provided so much for our ears to listen to. I look forward to hearing much more from that six-string of yours once the colony is set up."

"Thanks, buddy. I appreciate it." Cameron shook Cal's hand before taking the drink. As he swallowed, he exhaled audibly. "Wow. The doctor must really like you to give you that as a present."

Cal looked around at the others, puzzled. "Ok, that's just weird. The last time Doc and I sat down for a drink, she apologized for giving me the cheap stuff. What gives?"

Donnell, Vince, and Cameron exchanged glances. "Maybe you should try some. That tastes like well-aged scotch to me. I'm talking single malt, probably at least eighteen years," Vince said.

"It's probably more than fifty years by now," retorted Donnell, eliciting a laugh from the men.

Doc, you sneaky little…

"Wow. I… I don't know what to say about that." He paused, then shook his head and hoisted the skin toward Hunter. "Lieutenant Hunter Ceretti, my friend. Thank you for teaching me so much along the voyage, not to mention saving my bacon a time or two."

Hunter nodded and took his sip. Cal looked down at Alexis, and extended his hand to her. She looked at it, and then up at his eyes. She took his hand, and he gently helped her to her feet. He spoke no words, but simply offered up a drink. She took the skin from his hand and put it to her lips, drawing in a long swig. She winced as she swallowed, and tried unsuccessfully to stifle a cough. Cal smiled at her.

She's not used to drinking.

"Alexis," he whispered. "Thank you for being there for me. You always were, even when I was asleep. I hope you always will be."

She returned a gentle smile that threatened to turn Cal into a puddle. "I will. Thank you for showing me the stars. Thank you for finding a way to show me the world before anyone else."

She leaned in slightly, and Cal brushed the hair away from her ear with the back of his hand. "I love you, Alexis."

Her eyes widened as they drew into a kiss. At first she was a little tense, but her hesitation melted away after a fraction of a moment. Cal could taste a hint of alcohol on her breath as the passion intensified. Then, from behind them, a chorus of whistles rose up from their companions.

"Way to go, Cal," Hunter cheered.

He broke away from Alexis and turned his head. "Shut it, Hunter. You're not helping."

Hunter laughed from deep within his belly, and Cameron smiled broadly as he began to pluck at his guitar strings. Cal felt the warm hand of Alexis brush along his cheek, turning him to face her again. Her eyes twinkled in the dim light with an unusual brilliance.

"I love you too," she whispered, and drew him in for another kiss.

She grabbed the skin of scotch from his hand and took a step back. She cleared her throat and said, "To Calvin McLaughlin. Sweet, brave, and determined Calvin."

"To Calvin," the men toasted in chorus.

Cal put the valve to his lips and drew a long sip from the skin. The scotch tickled his throat, which gave way to a slight burning as it went down. There was no doubt that Doctor Taylor had gifted a high quality drink; there was a night and day difference in smoothness from the last drink she had given him. He sat down. Alexis joined him, tucking her arm under his and stroking his leg.

"A toast to *Michael* and *Gabriel* for safely transporting us all to our new home," he said.

Cal took another drink and passed the skin around, starting with Alexis. A silence fell in the great hallway as each person had their share of the toast. Even the guitar fell silent. When Hunter's turn came, he raised the pouch with his head bowed slightly and his eyes cast down at the light.

"To the lives lost on *Raphael*. May they find eternal peace."

"Amen," Cal and Donnell muttered.

The skin was passed around in silence for the solemn toast to those lost in the tragedy. When it came back into his possession, Cal found that little remained. He swallowed the last of the scotch and set the skin aside. Cameron's guitar came back to life, but his earlier upbeat music was replaced by a strummed dirge. Alexis repositioned herself to lay with her head on Cal's lap.

"So what happens now?" Cal asked after a few minutes of silence, stroking Alexis's hair.

Hunter cleared his throat. "So now we build."

"Right, but how? I mean, what do I do?"

Only music answered him. His friends appeared lost in the pale glow of the lantern on the floor. Hunter chewed on his lip, while Vince lay down and pulled his sleeping bag over his body.

"No one knows what I'm supposed to do, do they?" he asked, releasing a long sigh.

"I'm sure we'll have jobs for you to do," Hunter replied. "There's going to be all kinds of work that needs to be done. Maybe you could help set up and maintain the power equipment, or join an exploration team."

"I'm sure there will be something available in construction," Donnell added.

A great chasm of doubt began to slowly open within him. He truly did not know what he could do to be of immediate help. He had been studying how to make biodiesel, but knew that would require the colony to be at least somewhat set up for him to start. Cal needed something to do in the meantime, but his lack of skills left him with great apprehension.

"Whatever the case is, you're needed now more than ever," said Vince. "With Colonel Eriksen deciding not to join with us, we're probably going to have lots of holes in our workforce. I'm sure you will be plenty busy."

"What the hell is up with that, anyway?" asked Cameron.

"I don't know. I've been racking my brain on it all day. Has anyone managed to talk to any of their crew since landing?"

"I talked to one of their ops guys a while back," Cameron said. "But nothing since we entered atmo. Colonel Dayton had all the coms shut down after we landed, so I don't think I'll get to talk to him again."

"Damn. I'd love to know just what is going on inside that ship."

"Just let them be. We'll be fine."

"I know. We're equipped to be fully self sufficient. Still doesn't mean that we couldn't use the help."

Cameron smirked. "So let it be known that this is where the angels fell. This is where we rose as men."

The conversation stalled out as each person seemed to get lost in their thoughts. Alexis yawned and fidgeted. Cal looked down and watched as her eyelids began to droop in fatigue. He closed his eyes and put himself back in his dream where *Raphael* lay broken and scattered on a hillside. The eulogy that Dayton presented ran through his mind over and over.

"Concordia," he said as he opened his eyes. The gaze of all present lifted in unison from the light to his face. Cameron's fingers stopped and he squelched the guitar by placing his hand across the strings. "Concordia. That's the name of this place in my dreams."

"What are you talking about?" Hunter asked.

"In my stasis dreams. I kept dreaming over and over of *Michael* landing, and of a crashed sleeper ship just beyond. Every time, Dayton gives a speech to the citizens of Concordia, who marched off of our ship. It was always a remembrance of *Raphael*."

"*Raphael* burned up or exploded, Cal. There's no wreckage here."

"But the plants and the hills… I remember them so vividly. I know *Raphael* isn't here, but the message was clear. A ship was destroyed, and we made a place for ourselves here. We called it Concordia."

Hunter nodded and stared off again. Alexis looked up and said, "That's a beautiful name. What does it mean?"

"Place of agreement," Hunter replied. "Kind of an ironic name, don't you think?"

Cal sighed and nodded at Alexis, who slipped from his lap and curled up in her bag. He wrapped his own bag around his body and sighed. "I don't know. I guess. That's just the way it was in my dreams."

"Well, dreams take work. Tomorrow, work is our reality." Hunter leaned across and shut off the fuel valve on the lantern, and the circle became dark.

. . .

>END PLAYBACK|

Credits and Acknowledgements
7 February 2013
The real Earth, somewhere in Washington State
>|

This marks the end of another cycle of writing, editing, and publication in the Project Columbus series. The past six months have taught me many lessons about the whole process of independent publication. As with *Flight*, there have been ups and downs in the course of this book. The support of you, the readers, has been possibly the single most important highlight of writing this installment of the series. It has been very fulfilling to read the feedback that has been given and the comments made. I look forward to more in the future.

I would like to take a moment to recognize the memory of Neil Armstrong, who passed from the Earth just after I had completed *Flight*, and as I was outlining this book. He was a courageous pioneer in the field of space exploration, and I hope that his legacy inspires future generations to reach heights that others have not dared to.

Thanks go out to all of my test readers, including Rob, Karie, and Sarah. Their insight has kept me focused on the story path and kept me once again from falling into the pit of such space-time foibles as putting characters on the wrong ship. I'd like to thank Mathew Reuther for his continued wisdom in navigating the waters of publication, and Bridgette Reuther for the second wonderful cover thus far in the series.

My friends also have my gratitude, for pushing me now and then when the will to edit had started to flag. In no small part to them, this book will be available by my originally intended release date. Finally, my wife Megan (who again is rattling my cage for more to read) and my boys deserve my eternal thanks for the unconditional support they give.

To the readers who picked me up for *Flight*, I am honored, and welcome you back. To those who are new to my works, welcome!

I will see you all in a few months for the next installment of Project Columbus.

. . .

About the Author:

J.C. Rainier is product of the Pacific Northwest, born in the Seattle area in 1978, and living in the Puget Sound area his whole life. He is the younger of two children in his family, and his older brother proved to be a giant pest up through his teenage years (as siblings tend to be).

J.C.'s parents were both educators working at the middle school level, and he married into another family of educators. In his family, counting in-laws, there are now two retired principals, two retired teachers, a retired school counselor, and an active science teacher.

In his youth, J.C. read quite a lot. The Call of the Wild was one of his early favorites, and into middle school he began to devour other books such as Anne McCaffrey's Dragonriders of Pern series. Unfortunately, J.C. developed a form of dylexia that made reading from the page of a book difficult. It was later discovered that the curvature of the page itself caused the issue, and the advent of the eReader (with its perfectly flat screen) has allowed him to once again enjoy reading as he used to.

He enjoys both indoor and outdoor pursuits including computers, cars, and camping. J.C. and his wife enjoy hockey, and set aside time several times each season to watch the local WHL franchise.

J.C. and his wife are raising three boys, including a set of twins. If his blog ever fails to make sense, he's probably had a very long night just prior to writing it. If said writing is just a random set of characters similar to "adsk,wr3.1", then one of the children has managed a surprise attack on his laptop.

. . .

www.ingramcontent.com/pod-product-compliance
Lightning Source LLC
Chambersburg PA
CBHW071140170626
46809CB00002B/703